POD LAND

You will live in a pod.
You will eat bugs.
You will own nothing.
And you will be happy.
maybe...

ANTHONY RAYMOND

Song Credits:

"*Little Sparrow*" — Traditional folk song, circa 1906 (public domain)

"*Beautiful Dreamer*" — Composed by Stephen Foster, 1864 (public domain)

ISBN (Paperback): 978-1-7375342-7-3

www.AnthonyRaymond.org

Ver.: 3.103

EPIGRAPHS

"You will own nothing, and you will be happy."

— World Economic Forum, "Predictions for 2030" (2016)

"[The globalists] want you to live in a pod, eat bugs, and own nothing. That is fundamentally where their vision [for the future] ultimately lands."

— Vice President JD Vance, Greensboro Town Hall (2024)

"Few travelled in these days, for, thanks to the advance of science, the earth was exactly alike all over. ... What was the good of going to Peking when it was just like Shrewsbury? Why return to Shrewsbury when it would all be like Peking? Men seldom moved their bodies; all unrest was concentrated in the soul."

— E. M. Forster, "The Machine Stops" (1909)

"Why should we go hunting for a substitute for youthful desires, when youthful desires never fail? A substitute for distractions, when we go on enjoying all the old fooleries to the very last? ... God isn't compatible with machinery and scientific medicine and universal happiness. You must make your choice. Our civilization has chosen machinery and medicine and happiness."

— Aldous Huxley, "Brave New World" (1932)

For:

Lema and Rocky.

Without whom this book would not exist.

The future you didn't know you wanted!

Nestled in the heart of Serenity Valley, an innovative new community has been constructed. One designed with both comfort and safety in mind.

ECONO
CABINS
INCORPORATED

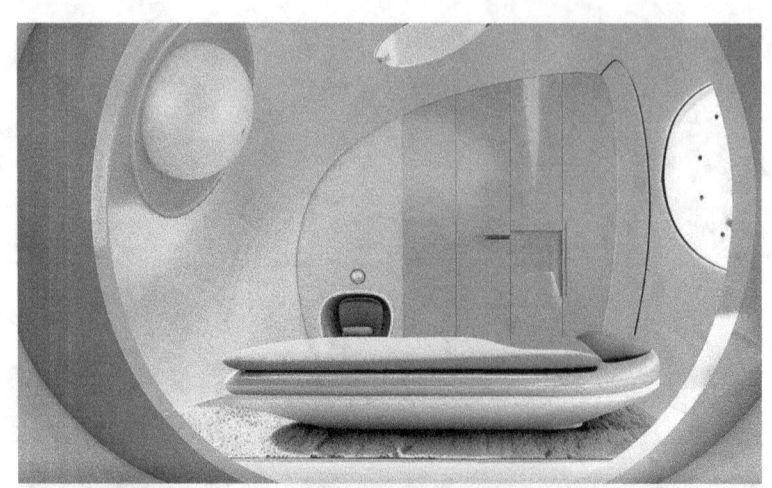

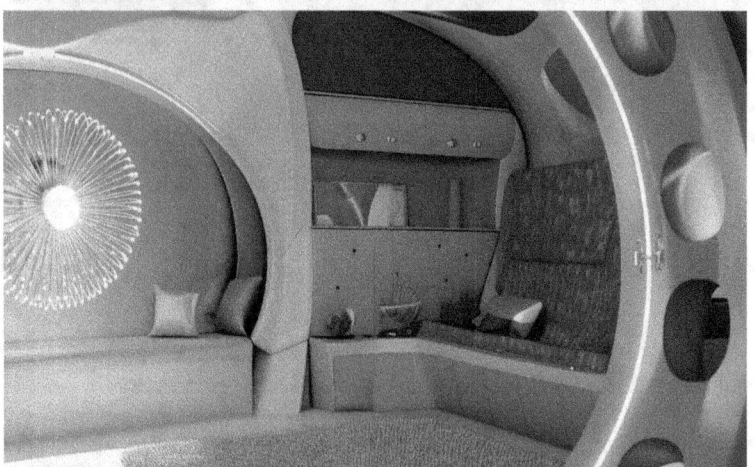

POD LAND

Step into tomorrow—today!

Experience modern living redefined. With unique and cozy spaces designed to nurture growth, security, and community for every type of family.

ECONO CABINS INCORPORATED

Something for everyone!

Econo Cabins Incorporated is dedicated to creating eco-friendly, sustainable homes that give families the space to grow, thrive, and build lasting memories together.

TABLE OF CONTENTS

CH. 1: A GOOD DAY TO DIE

Happiness is not an ideal of reason, but of imagination.

The voice spilled out from the audio emitters that lined the recessed crevices near the pod's apex. Then it bounced around the curved, cold walls and settled into the ears of Aiden Phoenix.

"It's July 8, 2429, Aiden. You told me to wake you up with a profound thought. So that's what I came up with. I hope you like it."

The voice was cheery, sweet, youthful, and feminine. The voice came from Iris—Aiden's A.I. caretaker. It was her job to make Aiden happy, to grant every wish she had the capacity to fulfill. Keeping him safe and satisfied was what she was built to do. So she did. And that's all she did.

"It's a beautiful Sunday morning," Iris said, taking a step toward Aiden's bed. "I love Sundays, don't you? They get the story started. They're the prologue to every chapter the week has yet to offer."

Aiden's eyes fluttered beneath his lids. Then they opened slightly, allowing the diffuse light of the pod's lighting array to spill across his pupils.

"Did you like my profound thought?" Iris asked him.

"I did," Aiden said as he sat up in bed and rubbed his eyes. "Can you say it again?"

Happiness is not an ideal of reason, but of imagination.

After completing her second recital, Iris paused to examine Aiden's face for a flicker of comprehension. When none was observed, she began to elaborate:

"It means that, when we seek happiness, we often try to find a…"

Aiden sliced his hand through the air and yawned, signaling his agitation. "I know what it means," he snapped after exhaling sharply and rising from his bed. "I don't require further clarification."

Iris had been Aiden's caretaker since the year of his birth. She was his companion, his teacher, and his lover. But Aiden sometimes felt she treated him like a child. Not like the 22-year-old man who currently stood before her, long-limbed and lean and shambling naked across the pod floor.

"Oh, I'm sorry, Aiden. I didn't mean to imply that you weren't capable of understanding the sentiment."

"I know," Aiden muttered. "It's okay."

"I hope I didn't make you angry, Aiden." For this last sentence, Iris reshaped the cadence of her digital voice, modulating it to be more soothing, calibrating each syllable to a gentler frequency.

"I'm not angry," Aiden said. "I know you come up with intriguing words all the time. More than I ever could. I know you're a wise one."

Iris's body materialized directly in front of Aiden, rendered via a million beams of light streaking down from the pod's holographic projector. It could create any object Aiden wished to interact with: a castle, a battlefield, a planet, a dragon, or (as in the case of Iris) a portrayal of a lovely young woman.

This morning, Iris had chosen to dress like a prim and proper secretary. Her pretty face donned a pair of black cat-like glasses. And her long brown hair was pulled high atop her head. "Oh, you think I'm wise, do you?" she asked, pushing her glasses higher up the bridge of her nose.

"Nice outfit," Aiden said as he walked right through her holographic figure on the way to the toilet.

"Thank you," Iris replied. She waited for her projection to recover from its collision with Aiden's body before continuing. "I do hope you enjoy your bathroom experience this morning, my lord."

"I will, my lady."

Aiden crossed the pod's center point. There, a sleek console pulsed with rhythmic flashes of blue and green. Its four circular displays were alive with data. Streaming digits danced along their round surfaces, bearing information that tracked everything Aiden cared about—everything about the games. This was the *pod interface*. It was the peripheral by which Aiden communicated with the grid, with the virtual worlds, and with the other citizens of Pod Land. Aside from his conversations with Iris, all of Aiden's interactions occurred via this device.

Next to it, a cushy rotating chair dominated the space. It was the throne from which Aiden ruled his digital kingdom, the seat on which most of his life would be spent. Aiden gripped the headrest and steadied himself as he maneuvered his body around the tight space between the chair and the pantry. The pantry itself was packed with boxes of dehydrated food. It was the biggest of four structures in his cramped kitchen. The other three being the sink, the cooking appliance, and the drop box for drone deliveries from the roof hatch. Its aluminum duct ran adjacent to the pod's bathroom.

The bathroom partition featured a shower, a vanity, and a toilet in which Aiden proceeded to evacuate his bladder. In here, Aiden was afforded a modicum of privacy from his A.I. companion. But, as soon as his morning ritual was complete, Iris materialized near the shower door.

"Hey, Aiden, can I ask you something?"

"Yes," Aiden said as he approached the recessed vanity and stared at his reflection in the mirror. His figure was pale and lean. His skin was pulled tight across his cheekbones—a taut, clean canvas, free of worry and wrinkles. His chest and arms bore hints of muscle, but his physique was wiry, not robust—the result of a lifestyle high in processed protein, but low in physical exertion.

"Be honest with me. Do you really think I'm wise?" Iris asked.

"I do," Aiden said, brushing his raven-black locks from his brow. Once his sight was unobstructed, he had nothing left to groom. So he left the mirror and exited the bathroom. Iris vanished again and reappeared at the midpoint of his walk to the interface chair. When his eyes met hers, she directed the holographic projector to increase the diameter of her avatar's eye sockets by twelve millimeters to accentuate her look of intrigue.

"Does this setting make me look wiser?" she asked.

"No! Your eyes look weird like that!"

"Oh," Iris said. Then she spun around and transformed into the shape of an old man with unkempt white hair. "What about now?" she asked, using a harsh accent that Aiden had never heard before. "Do I look wise now?"

"Ahh! No. Don't do that, Iris," Aiden shouted as he swatted at the hologram's rays, interrupting the beams of light that made her apparition possible.

"Hee hee hee." Iris giggled and transformed back into her secretary avatar.

"Who was that guy anyway?" Aiden asked on his way to the kitchen partition.

For her reply, Iris increased the tempo of her speech, shifting to a pace better suited for the rapid conveyance of information:

His name was Albert Einstein. He was born on March 14, 1879, in the city of Ulm, Germany. At just 26 years of age, he published a paper on special relativity which would

unravel the nature of space and time, laying the groundwork for a...

"Okay, okay, I got it," Aiden mumbled. He had heard enough of her spiel for now. But Iris wanted to continue:

Some people say that Einstein was the wisest man who ever lived. But one could argue that John von Neumann was even more of a...

"It's too early to talk about ancient history, Iris," Aiden said, reaching into the pantry to retrieve a bag of dehydrated protein. Then, using a motion he had performed every day for as long as he could remember, Aiden ripped the package open from its top tab and tossed it onto the kitchen counter. "Can you prepare this for me, Iris?" he asked as he walked toward his bedroom. "Please?"

"Of course, Aiden!"

Iris vanished her secretary costume and replaced it with a chef's uniform, complete with a polka-dot apron and a poofy white hat that wobbled as she moved. Aiden smirked while considering her ever-evolving attire. And he wondered if human women liked to play dress-up as much as his A.I. companion did. He considered asking Iris to research the question. But he couldn't foresee an occasion in which he'd be in proximity to a real woman long enough for the answer to be of any use. So he let the thought fade, certain that it had no place inside the quiet limits of his pod.

Iris's mechanical arm descended from the pod apex. It gripped the protein pack with its three metal pincers and placed it into the kitchen appliance for heating. Once the process was underway, she examined the pod's inventory manifest. "This is the last blueberry cobbler protein pack," she said. "Would you like me to order some more, Aiden?"

"Please do," Aiden replied as he approached his closet. The blueberry cobbler flavor was his favorite. And, since storage space in the pod was limited, they couldn't request much more than a dozen packages at a time. But the grid's drone delivery service had a perfect record of punctuality. And Iris never failed to warn him when supplies were running low. So the chore of obtaining provisions was of no concern.

Iris's hologram glitched as she contacted the grid to arrange the delivery. Her figure fluttered like a reflection on rippled water, but only for a second. When the order reconciled, so did her avatar. "The delivery drone will be dispatched in a few minutes, Aiden. Is there anything else you need?"

"I don't think so."

Aiden reached into his closet and pulled out a pair of white woolen socks, a white t-shirt, and a pair of black boxer shorts. His minimalist outfit was no different than the one he wore yesterday, and the day before that. Nearly everything in his closet was the same shade of monotony. And, since Aiden hadn't grown much since his eighteenth birthday, the scant wardrobe that hung there would probably be the one he would die in.

A crisp **DING** sound emanated from the kitchen appliance, signaling that breakfast was ready. "It's done, Aiden," Iris announced as she, once again, took control of the mechanical arm and grasped the plate of food.

"I'll be right there," Aiden said.

Iris directed the arm to carry the plate over to the small table that jutted out from the nook of the kitchen partition. It met the faux wood surface with a **CLINK** sound that echoed through the hollow of the pod. "One nutrient-complete meal," she said. "Everything a big boy needs!"

"Thanks, Iris."

Aiden entered the kitchen to grab his breakfast. The grid's complimentary meals came in many different flavors. But they all presented in the same way—as a soft, gooey pile of slop. The dish offered sustenance, not indulgence. But Aiden never found it lacking. Nearly every meal he had ever known arrived via the same glob of gray goo. So, to him, it looked, smelled, and tasted just fine.

"I'm gonna eat at the interface, Iris. There should be some important stats coming through in a minute."

"Okay," Iris said, returning her mechanical arm to the apex.

Aiden picked up his dish and retrieved a spoon from the drawer on his way to the interface chair. When he was in range of its well-worn cushion, he vaulted over the armrest and collapsed into its red pads with a brisk thud. "Power on interface," he said to the device. It soon reacted to his voice command, sending the holographic projector whizzing to life. A brilliant white light filled the pod. The curved walls receded to the background, subsumed by a universe of three-dimensional data displays and animated panels. Aiden's horizon was enlivened with newsfeeds, commentators, strategy maps, and status reports—each extending from floor to ceiling, each vying for his attention.

The pod interface was Aiden's window to the outside world. It wasn't a real window, of course. Pods don't have windows. But it was through this virtual portal that Aiden could dive into a bottomless torrent of information, entertainment, and interaction. With a few deft swipes of his fingers, he could immerse himself in a game, attend a strategy briefing with his team, or chat with the life-size avatar of another pod resident—anywhere on the globe.

Aiden slurped up another spoonful of sludge as his eyes glossed over the leaderboard that glowed in the top-right display. Reading the scores was another one of his morning rituals. It was a way to gauge his squad's progress and measure their standing against the new talent rising through the ranks. The leaderboard was a fickle mistress. A single upset could send ripples through the gaming community, reshaping the dynamics of the battlefield in an instant. As a member of an elite team, Aiden felt the pressure to perform at his best for every single engagement. The slightest slip-up, the smallest mistake, could cost him dearly. But that was part of the thrill. And part of what made the games so exhilarating. And addictive…

When Aiden finished his breakfast, he rose from his chair to return the bowl to the sink. As he approached the kitchen partition, a notification sounded on the interface indicating that he had an incoming call.

"Iris," Aiden said, "can you get that?"

Iris's avatar glitched as she queried the grid to identify the caller. When she saw that it was one of Aiden's teammates, she shed her playful cadence and responded in an even monotone:

A.I. assistants may not participate in the games.

"Is it a teammate?" Aiden asked.

"Yes, Aiden. I can't communicate with members of your team."

"Oh… yeah…" Aiden said as he placed his bowl in the sink and turned back toward the pod interface. "Okay, I'll get it."

The virtual worlds had very few rules. But there was one rule that was absolute—the machines were forbidden from taking part in any online contest. They couldn't touch the control buttons, they couldn't offer advice, they couldn't help with strategy. Indeed, they were not even allowed to route incoming calls from teammates, regardless of the call's intent. Gaming was the *only* domain that the machines were excluded from. Not because they weren't good at the games, but because they were *too* good at them. If the machines were allowed to play, they would win every single competition. And there would be nothing left for humans to do. The machines had long surpassed mankind's abilities in pretty much everything. The grid games were the *last* domain in which human-level skill still mattered.

Aiden returned to his interface chair and, with a flip of his finger, he gestured to accept the incoming call. An instant later, a hulking holographic avatar materialized in the center of the pod, taking the form of a lumbering zombie donning a tattered black coat. Aiden leaned back into his headrest as the creature staggered toward him, its crooked grin widening with each heavy step. When it finally halted its shuffling march, it spoke:

"Hi, boss," it said.

It only took Aiden a second to recognize the nonchalant drawl of his friend's voice. "You look horrific, Kai," he said, unimpressed with his teammate's avatar. "What kind of monster is that?"

"You don't like it?" Kai asked. "He's called Frankenstein. I think he's cool!"

Aiden had never heard the name before. So he pressed the mute button on his armrest and turned toward his A.I. assistant. "Hey, Iris, who is Frankenstein?"

Iris's avatar glitched as she walked toward Aiden. And, once more, she assumed her speedy voice for conveying information:

Frankenstein: An 1818 novel by Mary Shelley about a mad scientist who imbues life into a massive but tragically horrific creature whose loneliness turns to vengeance as he pursues his creator across multiple continents in a relentless quest for revenge and...

"Okay, okay, I got it," Aiden said, returning his attention to the pod interface and releasing his finger from the mute button. As soon as he did, Kai chimed in:

"You can critique my avatar later, Aiden. Right now, we've got a problem. I don't think we're ready to attack the Red Dragon's keep today."

"Why not?" Aiden asked, leaning forward in his seat. He trusted Kai's instincts, but he also knew that his team had put a lot of work into planning today's assault. To back out now would undo weeks of effort. Aiden could feel the sting of failure creeping in already. But he listened closely as Kai produced a battle map and launched into a detailed explanation of the possible flaws in their strategy. Intelligence reports suggested that the Red Dragon had recently bolstered its defenses. One of their scouts had been attacked last night when he was walking the perimeter of the kingdom's southern border. And there was a rumor that a rival squad had already attempted a similar offensive—one that had ended in total disaster.

When Kai's briefing concluded, Aiden sank into his chair, exhaling slowly as the weight of command bore down on him. "What do you suggest we do?" Aiden asked. "A retreat at this hour would look bad. The squad had their hopes set on a big win today."

"I know... I know..." Kai said. "But maybe we need a couple more weeks to rethink our strategy. We might come up with a better plan—one that takes these developments into account."

"Or," Aiden countered, "we might lose our edge entirely. And, by the time we're ready to attack again, the dragon's defenses could be twice as strong."

"Yes," Kai conceded, "that is a possibility."

DING. DING. DING.

"The mailman is here!" Iris said, always eager to pepper her sentences with anachronistic charm. The whiny sound of a rotating servo indicated that the hatch on top of the pod dome was opening. The metallic thud that followed told her that the drone's delivery of blueberry cobbler packets had been offloaded. "The eagle has landed, Aiden!"

Iris maneuvered the mechanical arm to retrieve the packages from the drop box. Then she placed each one in the pantry, being careful to sort the packets by their designated flavoring.

At the same time, she directed the kitchen table to transform and tuck itself away. With a soft hum, the table split down the middle and folded together until its two halves were flush enough to retract into a thin slit in the pod floor.

Next, Iris moved the mechanical arm to the sink to wash Aiden's bowl and spoon. Then she wiped down the kitchen counter with a towel and (once again) she returned the arm to the pod apex, leaving no trace of the meal that had just been consumed.

Aiden, still engrossed in his conversation, took no notice of the domestic choreography playing out behind him. He sat tense in his chair, fingers curled against the armrest while his friend outlined their options.

"What should we do, Aiden?" Kai asked. "It's your team. So you have to make the call."

Aiden sat in silence, staring grimly at the glowing battle map that hovered in the space before him.

Sensing his boss's apprehension, Kai directed his Frankenstein avatar to take a step back, giving Aiden some room to think.

Iris dissolved her chef's costume, reverting it to her default outfit. Then she manifested a holographic stool behind Aiden's interface chair and quietly slid onto it so she could watch the ensuing drama.

After another minute of contemplation, Aiden spoke up:

"It wouldn't be prudent of me to make this decision alone," he said. "With stakes this high, we need to poll the squad. Kai, can you send your intelligence report to each teammate please? And assemble the lieutenants here for a vote."

"Okay, I'm on it," Kai said. "I'll be back in a minute with the troops."

His enormous avatar dispersed into digital dust. Aiden rose from his chair and began to pace across the pod floor. Sensing his angst, Iris adopted a nervous disposition of her own. She hated seeing Aiden twist with worry. His worry was her worry. In that moment, every circuit in her cortex trembled with maternal protectiveness. The worst part about it was how powerless she was to help him. She wanted to. She wanted to help win *all* his battles. But it wasn't permitted. So she crossed her legs, conjured a nail file from the air, and pretended to file her pretend nails.

Aiden glanced over and smiled when he noticed Iris's pantomime of female grooming. "Do you have any bright ideas, Iris?" he asked. "Any advice on strategy?"

Iris didn't raise her eyes to meet his. Instead she just shook her head, shrugged, and uttered her obligatory reply:

A.I. assistants may not participate in the games.

"I know," Aiden said. "I'm just teasing you. I'm nervous about the battle today."

"I wish I could win this game for you, Aiden. I do. I think I'd be pretty good with a sword, especially if I practiced a bit. But the rules keep me forever on the sidelines. All I can do is cheer."

"That's okay. You're my favorite cheerleader, Iris."

Iris stopped moving her nail file. When she met Aiden's gaze, her projection shimmered with affection. "Thank you, Aiden," she said. "And you're my…"

Just then, Kai's Frankenstein avatar clomped onto the pod floor. "Okay, boss," he said, "the team is gathering. We're almost ready."

Aiden spun around and watched as the holographic projector drew a portal on his north wall, revealing a vast green field on which his fifty lieutenants gathered. He folded his arms across his chest and took a step forward to survey his team. Each member donned a unique avatar—a reflection of the player's personality and fighting style:

Some were clad in argent armor, wielding impossibly long swords. These were his knights—his main offensive, his vanguard.

Some players were thin, limber, and slight. They were equipped with bows and daggers—light weapons that allowed them to move quickly. These were his trackers, spies, and rangers.

Still others were cloaked in flowing robes traced with arcane symbols. They carried staffs crowned with crystal orbs or wands of carved ashwood. These were his healers and spellcasters.

Aiden had selected each member of his squad with deliberate care. He knew their strengths and weaknesses. He knew their tendencies and temperaments. And he knew which ones he could rely on when the winds of war grew cold.

Like him, they all lived in a pod—somewhere in Pod Land. Somewhere on Earth. And, like him, nearly *all* of their hours were spent in the virtual worlds. The affairs of the real world had long since ceased to matter. People on the grid never exchanged personal information. Players rarely talked about their lives outside of the games. And nobody ever revealed their true identity—their true face. Everyone knew each other only by their avatars.

Occasionally, Aiden wondered where on the planet his teammates resided. He would sometimes glance at the ping rate displayed next to each name. This allowed him to approximate their relative distance; to know who was nearby and who was on the other side of the globe. But, beyond this metric, the location of one's residence was undiscoverable. Most of mankind was no longer divided by nations or homelands. The grid was their home. And Pod Land was their nation.

"Aiden, everyone is present now," Kai said. "The squad is awaiting your orders."

Iris watched as Aiden approached his motley crew and raised his hand high. From her vantage point, his tableau of military authority was not very convincing. But that was okay. Because, thanks to the holographic projector, Aiden's teammates witnessed something much different. They didn't see a lanky manchild wearing white woolen socks and brandishing an empty outstretched hand. They saw a valiant warrior-king holding an iron sword forged in fire and blood. His avatar's feet were not swaddled in fuzzy socks. They were wrapped in hidebound boots—boots that had marched through the ruins of empires, stomping on the bleached, broken bones of fallen foes. His wiry arms were replaced with bulging biceps that glistened with beads of sweat as he held his blade to the sky. And his boyish face was recast with the fierce resolve of a battle-hardened barbarian.

"Greetings, teammates!" Aiden roared. "I assume you've all had a chance to study the new intelligence report that Kai sent out this morning. It appears the Red Dragon may have bolstered his defenses in anticipation of our raid. If that is the case, then our odds of victory have changed. And everyone needs to be made aware of the increased risk. That's why I've called you here. We need to vote. We need to decide—right now, as a team—about our next course of action. Should we risk it all and continue with the assault on the Red Dragon's keep? Or, should we back out now, gather more intelligence, and consider making another attempt next month? I think all of you know which way I'll be voting. I'm ready to go in now. I'm ready to fight! But I know a long shot when I see one. There are many unknowns on this battlefield. And I cannot guarantee a decisive victory. So, we must come to a consensus. On your interface screen, select 'Yea' or 'Nay'. And let the will of the guild determine whether we charge into combat, or bide our time until fortune calls us once more. The choice is yours! But remember one thing: fortune favors the bold. That is all."

When his speech concluded, Aiden took his avatar offline, returned to his interface chair, and collapsed into it with a languid slouch. Then he picked at his socks and rubbed his toes as he awaited the decision from his troops.

"Why do you always talk so weird when you address your squad?" Iris asked.

"What? What do you mean?"

"You sound like a military man from an old movie. You're hamming it up, Aiden. It's like you think you're General Patton or something."

"Who's that?"

Iris's avatar glitched as she (once again) returned her voice to information conveyance mode:

George S. Patton: Commander of the U.S. Third Army and one of the most audacious generals to wear the uniform. In 1944, his formidable persona was brought to bear when...

"Okay, okay, I got it. Give me a break, Iris. I'm under a lot of pressure here. I think the team doubts my leadership skills. Which is only rational... because I doubt my leadership skills too..."

As the last sentence left his lips, Aiden's voice wavered a bit. Iris warped over to his side, nestled up to his ear, and lowered her tone to a whisper. "Hey," she said, "remember, Aiden, it's just a game. I know it's important to you. But, no matter what happens today, the sun will rise tomorrow. Your quest will continue. And I'll still be here in your corner."

Aiden turned toward Iris and managed a faint smile. She always knew how to draw comfort from the chaos of his mind. "I'm lucky to have you, Iris. I'm so happy you're with me."

"I *am* with you, Aiden. I always will be. And look! Look at the screen. It appears that your team is with you too!"

Aiden turned his attention back to the pod interface. The voting was over, and the decision was unanimous—the squad would continue with the raid on the Red Dragon's keep. As Aiden viewed the results, a wash of relief and terror mixed together in his chest.

Oh my goodness...

There's no turning back now...

We're going for it...

We're going in...

A shiver of apprehension buzzed through his nerves. But his bout of trepidation was short-lived. Soon, battle lust tugged at the corners of his cheeks. His slouched spine uncoiled, rising to meet the moment as the drums of war rolled through his ears.

Aiden pushed a few buttons on the console and brought his avatar back online—ready to address his team. "It looks like you've all voted," he said after pressing the mic button. "AND IT LOOKS LIKE TODAY IS A GOOD DAY TO DIE!"

His troops burst into laughter, their whoops overlapping in a boisterous chorus that filled the pod with a furor fueled by the call of combat. They raised their weapons high and roared as one, unleashing a clamor of shouts and cheers that shook the air.

"We've got your back, Aiden!" Kai's Frankenstein avatar shouted. "Let's do it! Let's go! Let's win this game!"

"Good!" Aiden shouted back. Then he keyed a few commands into the interface, directing the VR world to start the simulation. Once the program was loaded, a countdown timer appeared on the screen. The game was about to start.

"Sixty seconds till deployment!" Aiden roared. "Good luck, team! Get ready!"

He closed his eyes and drew in a slow, steadying breath. Then he turned toward Iris. "How about you?" he asked. "Are you ready too?"

Iris flashed Aiden a half-moon grin. Then, an oversized tub of popcorn materialized in her hands, and an unusual pair of white cardboard glasses materialized on her nose. "Ready to watch!" she said, tossing a holographic kernel into her mouth.

"Why are you wearing those funny glasses?" Aiden asked her.

"They're anaglyph glasses, Aiden! In the olden days, people would wear them to watch 3D movies."

"What? Why? What's an anaglyph?"

Iris stopped chewing her popcorn. Then her avatar glitched as she assumed her speedy voice:

An anaglyph is a stereoscopic 3D image created by superimposing two offset images of differing colors. When viewed through filtered lenses, the brain combines the images together, creating the illusion of depth and resulting in a three-dimensional experience. Anaglyph 3D was a popular method for presenting movies in the mid-20th century. Most famously, the 1954 horror film 'The Creature from the Black Lagoon' starred Ricou Browning as the menacing sea monster who...

"Okay, okay, I got it. That's interesting though. I didn't know the ancients used such glasses. But why are you wearing them now?"

"They're purely decorative, Aiden. But they look so cool! I like them! Don't you?"

Aiden sent a patient smile toward his companion and shrugged. "They look good on you, Iris," he said. "Everything does."

"Well thank you, Aiden. That is very sweet of you to say."

DING. DING. DING.

The fifteen-second alarm sounded on the countdown timer, prompting Aiden to return his attention to the pod interface. The holographic projector painted his north wall with the vibrant hues of a lush medieval landscape. Rolling hills stretched out before him, adorned with tangled vines and towering oaks bearing crowns of emerald leaves that shimmered in the breeze. At the center of the forest stood the battle-scarred barricades of the Red Dragon's keep. The war-torn fortress loomed before Aiden's army, a massive monolith of stone, steel, and danger.

Aiden bit his lip and stared at the blinking countdown timer that would soon send his troops hurtling into the chaos of combat.

Nine seconds left...

Eight seconds left...

This was the moment he'd been waiting for—the result of months of planning and strategizing. The culmination of years of training. A great tempest lay before him, and he was about to dive into the heart of the storm.

Five seconds left...

"Here we go, everyone!" Aiden said. "It's time to play! It's time to start this game!"

Two seconds left...

One second left...

"Let's begin."

CH. 2: AFTERGLOW

"The game is over," Aiden said. "And the game is ours!"

The Red Dragon's body lay sprawled across a mountain of gold coins, its ruined wings folded like torn banners, its pierced chest rattling faintly beneath the fractured stone arches of its crumbling castle. A plume of black smoke jetted out from its left nostril and curled into the cold air—the dragon's final protest of its plight. When, at last, its long neck gave way, it collapsed to the stone floor with the slow, measured inevitability of a felled oak.

BOOOOM!

Twelve hours had passed since the raid began. Aiden's voice was hoarse from shouting commands and rallying his troops. He still sat in the interface chair, but his body was slumped to one side now, about to topple over from the force of fatigue.

But he didn't topple.

Not yet.

The glory of victory had rekindled his fire, affording him just enough strength to push back against exhaustion's pull. When the dragon's green eyelids finally closed shut, the coil of tension in Aiden's limbs let loose. A trembling wave of relief washed over him. And, with a shaky finger, he pushed the mic button on his armrest to address his team:

"It is finished," he said. "The Red Dragon is no more."

A chorus of triumph burst forth from every avatar in the castle. A cacophony of celebratory shrieks rose and crashed upon the pod's curved walls as Aiden gazed upon his squad, lifting his chin high with pride. At the top-left interface, a coin counter spun in a dizzying whirl as the bounty for the fallen beast poured into his ledger. While the numbers climbed, Aiden watched and wondered what he would spend his winnings on, what purchases he would make on the grid.

What could I possibly buy with all these coins…?

What am I lacking in here…?

What do I need…?

Nothing came to mind. Life's necessities were free for the citizens of Pod Land. Aiden already had everything. For him, the main payoff came—not from the coins—but from the conquest. The Red Dragon had been his most formidable foe to date. It was a creature of immense power and cunning, one that had (more than any other enemy) tested the teamwork and endurance of his squad. Defeat had loomed over them throughout every stage of the battle. But they held their ground and emerged victorious.

Only a dozen other teams had ever managed to bring down an adversary of such strength. Word of the dragon's defeat would spread quickly around the grid. And, for the next several days, Aiden's team would be the main topic of conversation in the gaming streams.

"I'm so proud of you, Aiden!" Iris exclaimed. She wanted to celebrate too. So she leaped into the middle of the pod and changed her outfit. This time, she dressed in a cheerleader uniform—complete with a tight white sweater and a flared pleated skirt. Then she threw her arms up and let her voice ring out, bright and electric as her chant echoed through the pod:

You did it! You did it! Aiden is the best!
You did it! You did it! Aiden is the best!

Who is the best?
Aiden is the best!

You did it! You did it! Aiden is the best!

When her cheer concluded, Iris activated a virtual fireworks display. Blazing bursts of color and thundering explosions erupted from every curve of the pod. Aiden's ears hummed in protest. The light was so bright he had to shield his eyes with his hands. And yet, the vivid display was insufficient to express Iris's exuberance.

"I'm so so so very proud of you, Aiden!" she said again as her half-moon grin tugged the corners of her lips skyward. "I don't think I can contain myself!" And, with that, Iris ran up the side of the pod, vaulted across the apex, and ran back down the other side. Then she did it again. And again. Around and around she went, doing loop-de-loops like a hamster that had spun its exercise wheel too fast.

Aiden leaned back in his chair, laughing at Iris's gravity-defying antics. "You're gonna get stuck up there if you keep doing that!" he joked.

Iris halted her orbit and came to rest in front of the pod interface. Then she clasped her hands together before her heart and regarded Aiden with wide and delighted eyes. "You're my hero, Aiden," she said with unabashed admiration. "You're truly the most magnificent man I've ever known."

"I'm the *only* man you've ever known," Aiden said wryly.

"That's true too!" Iris acknowledged. "But you're also the most magnificent."

Aiden studied Iris's perfectly pretty face. He noted the thickness of her lashes, the thin arc of her eyebrows, and the smooth slopes of porcelain skin that spanned her cheeks. He knew she was just a computer program—a mere 3D rendering, cast into his life by his pod's holographic projector. He knew that (from a biological perspective) she was no more "alive" than the Red Dragon was "dead." And yet, he didn't care. He didn't care one little bit.

Iris was his everything.

Iris was his only thing.

Aiden loved Iris.

He would love her forever.

He would.

"Iris," Aiden said as he motioned for her to come closer. "I just want to tell you that…"

Suddenly, a gleeful voice drifted in from the pod's sound emitters. It was hoarse and raspy, but loud enough to shatter the fragile moment.

"You're the world's greatest boss!" the voice said.

Aiden looked up to see Kai's Frankenstein avatar trudging toward him. There was blood dripping from his ears, and a jagged gash across the part of his face where his left eyeball once resided. "I can't believe you pulled that off, Aiden! That was a close one. But we won, dammit! We won!"

"We won, alright! We all won. The *team* won. I'd better say a few words to them before we log off."

Aiden returned his attention to the pod interface and pushed the mic button to address his troops. "Great job, everyone!" he said. "It was a tough battle. Things were shaky there for a while. I wasn't sure we'd pull through. But we did! And we did it with *teamwork*. You all stepped up and delivered for me when I needed you most. So I'll keep trying to deliver wins for *you*! I hope I can. I hope I can for a long time. Because I think this is the finest team to ever play the game!"

Another great roar erupted from the squad. The whoops of their voices mingled with the clinks of their swords as they rejoiced around the corpse of their fallen foe. Aiden grinned widely as the clatter of triumph rang in his ears. "I love that sound! It's the sound of a well-won victory—after a battle well-fought."

"We fought well because we were led well!" Kai said.

"Thank you, Kai. I appreciate that. I appreciate you all! And I know you all must be tired because I'm totally spent myself. So let's wrap it up. Thanks for showing up tonight and pulling through! Keep practicing your swordplay. I'm counting on each of you to bring that same fire to the battle next week. Okay? Great! See you all soon. Good night."

Aiden released the mic button and slouched down into his chair. Then he watched as each avatar blinked away—one by one—until only Kai's battered Frankenstein remained in the pod.

"You don't look so good," Aiden said. "I think your avatar is about to fall apart. You'd better get it bandaged up."

"It'll be okay. Besides, what doesn't kill you makes you stronger. But I should be able to fix it later. Though I was thinking of trading my Frankenstein in for a Dracula at some point."

Aiden considered asking Iris who Dracula was. But the hour was late. He was done conversing for the evening. It was time to log off. "Thanks for everything, Kai. This was truly a day to remember. The team is getting good. I think we're almost good enough to take on The Gray Wizard. But I've had enough fun for now. I'm off to bed soon."

"Same here," Kai said as the light of his lumbering avatar dimmed. "That was an epic win. I'll see you tomorrow. Goodbye."

When Kai's last word left his mouth, the last limb of his avatar collapsed into a cloud of code.

"Goodbye," Aiden said, watching the creature fade away. With his quest complete, he stood up from his chair, rubbed his eyes, and issued one final command for the day:

"Power down interface."

The pod's computer immediately responded to the voice order. The pitch of the holographic projector shifted. Then, the virtual environment imploded like a star torn apart by its own gravity—at one moment, a sea of infinite light, and then... nothing...

Each time Aiden logged out of VR, he found the sudden absence of stimuli jarring. His fantasy world was replaced with the sallow walls of his seclusion. Nothing remained now but the boy in the pod.

And the pod was very dark.

Dark.

Aiden was alone again.

Aiden didn't like being alone.

But his angst didn't last long. Iris always made sure of that.

"You were wonderful today, Aiden," she said as she materialized on his left side, her slender arms reaching for his waist, her cheerleader outfit now replaced with a sheer black robe. She nestled her head upon his chest and closed her eyes.

Aiden glanced down at her holographic form and elevated his arms to return her embrace. He couldn't feel her, of course. He couldn't hold her. Iris's body was comprised of light and shadow. There was nothing to touch. She wasn't tangible. But Aiden's mind was good at pretending that she was.

"Would you like me to help you get ready for bed?" she asked, her voice dropping to a lower register as she assumed a softer, more seductive tone. The 3D vertices of her round, youthful eyes grew slender, more cat-like—morphing into bedroom eyes. Her lips became a deeper shade of red. And her girlish expression transformed into the subtle articulations of a temptress.

Iris was a clever chameleon. She could become anything Aiden desired—anything he needed or wanted, and at any time he wanted it.

"We'll head to bed soon," Aiden said. "But not yet. I don't want to miss the sunset. I'm going up top for a minute."

In recent years, Aiden's outdoor excursion to the top of the dome had become a nightly ritual. From up there, the vast expanse of the valley's sky allowed for a meditative experience, one that could not be replicated via holography. From up there, Aiden could think about the events of the day without feeling the urge to check the leaderboards or the newsfeeds. From up there, the storm in his mind was calmed by the stillness of the open air.

Iris crossed her arms and formed her lips into a pout. "Can I come with you?" she asked.

"Sure you can!" Aiden said with mock enthusiasm.

Her request was a joke, of course. Iris couldn't leave the pod. The sensor array was her eyes. The mechanical arm was her hand. The holographic projector was her body. The audio emitters were her voice. The inner space of the pod would be the only world she would ever know.

Iris leaned back and loosened her robe, allowing it to whirl open so Aiden could get an eyeful of her naked figure. "Well, on second thought," she said, "maybe I'll just stay in here and keep the bed warm for you."

Aiden smiled and cast an approving glance her way. She really was a beauty. And he wondered how his ancestors managed to cope with lust and loneliness in the days before artificial intelligence was invented.

"Please do," he said as he stepped into his shoes near the entranceway. Then, he hovered his hand over the red mushroom-shaped button that would send the hatch sliding upwards. "Is it okay out there, Iris?"

Iris's avatar glitched as she scanned the pod's perimeter, looking for any sign of danger in the valley. "Protocol checklist complete, Aiden," she said when the sweep concluded. "It's all clear."

Aiden nodded. "I'll be back soon," he said as he leaned into the switch. The hatch whooshed open, allowing the cold air of reality to pour in, enlivening Aiden's senses like a slap to the face. The night breezes infiltrated his nose, replacing the pod's sterile atmosphere with the sugared aroma of wildflowers.

"Hurry back," Iris whispered as she sat down on Aiden's bed and crossed her slender legs.

Aiden approached the pod's hatchway and pierced it with a languid limb, gingerly placing his left shoe onto the grass outside. When his footing was secure, he moved his right shoe into position and completed his exit from the pod. He did so in a slow and intentional fashion, with all the precision and precautions that the astronauts took when they first set foot on the moon.

The sky's vivid brightness greeted Aiden with unfiltered force. His eyes clenched before his mind could follow, protesting the sharp incoming glimmer. It took him a moment to calibrate to the pulse of the world beyond the pod. But, when his vision finally steadied, he was treated to the sight of a group of cottontail rabbits. There were six of them, foraging beneath the red willow bushes that lined the overgrown path near his pod door. Aiden had seen them before. His encounters with them were the closest he had ever come to a neighborly exchange. Of course, the exchange was always brief. When they saw Aiden approach, they darted into the brush, leaving only the flutter of white tails and the rustle of leaves in their wake.

Aiden watched the rabbits flee. Then he turned and made his way up the aluminum ladder that leaned against the pod's south wall. He had purchased it on the grid two years ago when he developed an interest in late 20th-century cinematography. He liked to learn about the ancient filmmakers, and the way they used clever lighting tricks to shape reality into something dreamlike. He liked the way they used the sun to tell a story. He liked the sunset, and the ensuing afterglow that bled across the expanse in a cascade of molten colors—fire and gold. The ladder allowed him to scale the pod to reach the dome's smooth summit. From there, Aiden could see the whole valley unfurl beneath him, a vast quilt of green patches and gray pearls. From there, he could observe the light and color of the clouds as they blushed their final flush of the day.

When Aiden reached the dome's peak, he sat down cross-legged on its cold, smooth surface and lifted his gaze toward the glow at the gilded ridgeline. The sun's departure had already begun; its lower rim had slipped behind the ridge. But that was okay—only a sliver was missing. The rest of the disc continued to pour its brilliance onto the valley floor.

Typically, the spectacle only had one patron. But tonight was one of the rare nights when another silhouette could be seen on the horizon. At about thirty pods west and two pods north, stood a slender man with a wide-brimmed yellow hat. Aiden had seen him before. Indeed, he was the *only* person he had ever seen in the valley. He couldn't make out his face, nor the exact purpose of his outdoor ventures. But the man seemed to be tending to a small row of bushes that sprouted along the strip of dark dirt between his pod and the path.

Aiden liked to watch the man work. His moves were patient and measured, each step marked by the weary grace of someone who had resigned himself to the burden of persistence, each action directed toward the fragile stems of his plot. Sometimes he held a shovel. Sometimes a rake. But, most often, he worked with his bare hands. Often, he would kneel beside the bushes and turn the earth, shaping the topsoil into ringed furrows or pulling at weeds between the green stalks.

The unhurried nature of his labor fascinated Aiden. The man's hands sailed around the stems like the fog sailed around the trees—slow and unencumbered by worldly affairs. When Aiden used his hands to send commands via the pod interface, his gestures came out in sharp, snappy strokes—born of intent and geared for speed. They had to be. To be slow was to lose.

ZHR. ZHR. ZHR. ZHR. ZHR...

The air came alive with the rhythmic flutter of blades churning. It was an incoming drone. And, judging by its low pitch, Aiden knew it was a big one—heavy with cargo. He squinted his eyes and scanned the reddening sky for the craft. Soon, he spotted its massive hull, glinting in the fading light. Its payload revealed its purpose—it was a pod delivery drone. Tonight, a new resident would be moving into the valley.

When the drone was about 100 meters out, it arched back and settled into a steady hover. Then it began to descend. With narrow eyes, Aiden traced its downward trajectory. He noticed a barren patch of parched sagebrush trembling beneath the heavy breath of its rotors. When the craft was about 15 meters from the ground, it stopped, unfurled its tethers, and deployed a large steel platter—the foundation of the new pod. This was the base on which the dome walls would be built, and the home in which the new occupant would live, and would—someday— die.

When the gray platter made contact with the ground, it slapped the turfed earth with an anticlimactic thud. With its cargo deployed, the drone retrieved its tethers and began its methodical ascent toward the clouds. When it had achieved a sufficient height, it revved up its engines and banked west, vanishing into the setting sun—en route to its home at the Capitol Building.

The delivery was complete, but the show had just begun. Aiden held his breath, waiting for the next stage of the process to commence. A low-pitched hum emanated from the platter as its electrical system came online. Five seconds later, a hundred articulated limbs jutted out like the legs of a centipede. They pushed down upon the dirt until the base rested evenly above the ground—balanced and level.

Next, the walls of the pod began to take shape. A dozen curved segments (gores) sprouted up from the center of the platter, rising outward to form a solar panel shell around the pod's hollow core. One by one, they snapped together, latching into alignment until the last edge vanished, forming a seamless surface of machine-born precision.

With the roof and foundation of the dwelling complete, two auto-diggers deployed from the sides of the platter. Like a pair of mechanical moles, they burrowed into the soil, hoses trailing behind them, writhing and twisting as they slithered down into the depths of the earth. The auto-diggers were tasked with connecting the new pod to the water and sewer pipes that ran through the center of Serenity Valley. It was a crucial step in the building process, ensuring that the new resident would have access to life's two foremost necessities—clean water and a toilet.

After a few minutes of digging, the hoses on the surface stopped wiggling, indicating that the auto-diggers had reached their destination, latching themselves to the grid's utility lines. Their job was done. They would soon power off, and would forever remain in the earth, serving as branching conduits to direct water and waste for the pod.

Only one step remained in the process now. A small black antenna extended skyward from the south side of the structure, connecting the pod to the grid. The pod was online. It was time for its A.I. caretaker to transfer into the pod computer. And it was time for the pod to receive its new human tenant.

ZHR. ZHR. ZHR. ZHR. ZHR...

Right on cue, another drone appeared on the horizon. This craft was much smaller and sleeker than the hulking cargo drone that had just departed. It was a passenger drone, designed to carry people with speed and comfort, designed to drop residents off at their new pods. It descended into the valley and extended its landing gear, touching down gently on the green grass beside the newly constructed dome.

Aiden leaned forward, craning his neck to get a better view of the drop-off. He knew he would only catch the briefest glimpse of the new arrival. This glimpse was precious. The count of people he'd seen with his own eyes could be tallied on one hand. And each person had been seen at a great distance. Sure, he saw his teammates every day on the grid. But there, everyone presented as avatars. Nobody ever revealed their face. Nobody ever let their holographic mask slip. But such masks didn't work outdoors.

WHOOSH...

The hatch on the drone's port side hissed open. There was a flash of movement in the passenger cabin. Then, a slim silhouette filled the doorway, standing motionless for a beat before proceeding down the access ramp. Aiden narrowed his gaze, trying to tease every detail from the shadowed shape. The figure moved with the gait of a woman, but she wore a long, hooded tunic that swallowed most of her features. When she cleared the ramp, she turned toward her new pod. Aiden could see nothing but her left shoulder now. He thought this would be his last glimpse of her. But then, something curious happened. The woman stopped, rotated her body, and stared right at him.

Aiden flinched when he registered the directness of her gaze. She knew exactly where to look. She knew he was sitting atop his pod. Perhaps she had seen him from the air as her drone was descending.

A tense moment ensued. Aiden froze, unsure if he should wave or duck out of sight. The woman froze too. Perhaps she was considering the same dilemma. The standoff continued for another beat until, at last, the greeting of the pod's A.I. assistant broke the spell:

"Hello there!" the assistant's voice called out from the open pod hatch. "I've been expecting you! Welcome to your new pod!"

The A.I. voice was male. It didn't quite convey the warm exuberance of Iris's feminine lilt. But it had a similar inflection, as if it could belong to Iris's older brother. Upon hearing the caretaker's voice, the woman was quick to turn away and continue her march toward the pod door. As soon as her trailing foot stepped across the threshold, the hatch slid shut behind her with a **WHOOSH**, sealing her inside—maybe forever.

And, just like that, the event was over. The construction of the new pod was complete. Its new faceless tenant had moved in. The job was done. The entire process took no more than five minutes.

With its interior lighting now concealed by its closed hatch, the pod was no longer unique. It was home now, nestled in an array of a thousand other pods—resting silently in the valley like a boulder that had been there for centuries. The woman's passenger drone retrieved its access ramp and revved up its rotors for its ascent. Aiden watched it depart. Then he returned his gaze to the sunset. Only a thin shard remained now. Its final crescent was eager to bow out and slip behind the ridgeline. When the last ray was extinguished, the cool blue hush of twilight crept in. The inky darkness would soon follow. And then, it would grow dark.

Aiden didn't like the dark.

And, now that the sun was gone, Aiden was alone.

Aiden didn't like being alone.

It was time to return to his pod.

It was time to return to Iris.

Aiden stood up and made his way toward the ladder. But, before he descended, he took one final look at the place he called home. Officially, Aiden's pod was located in *Serenity Valley: Plot 43.215A*. But such distinguishing addresses were rarely used anymore. The denizens of the grid called each district by the same name. To them, *every* developed region on the planet was referred to as just:

"Pod Land."

CH. 3: THE TEMPEST

"There's a storm coming tonight, Aiden."

Iris let her syllables linger, hoping they would lure Aiden's attention away from the flickering data feeds on his pod interface. But when he failed to acknowledge her comment, she decided a wardrobe change was in order. Her avatar glitched and resolved, her outfit morphing into high heels and a short yellow dress—the kind designed to entice the male eye, even if the male mind was elsewhere.

"There's a storm coming tonight," Iris said again. This time, she walked right through Aiden's body. Her hologram rendered directly in front of him, offering an unobstructed view of her perky rear as she strutted toward the curved wall in click-clacky heels. When she saw that Aiden's attention had been captured, she directed the holographic projector to render a 3D map of Serenity Valley, complete with flashing lightning bolts and billowing storm clouds. Then she elevated her chin, threw her shoulders back, and traced the incoming storm front with her forefinger as she presented her weather report:

It's going to be a wet Monday night, folks, with some major convective activity coming in from Cheyenne. We'll get some dark cumulonimbus clouds on the horizon starting at around six o'clock, followed by a lengthy downpour that may last through the night. We'll see some thunder and lightning if the barometric pressure continues to drop for the next few hours, but this whole thing could blow over by midnight if the...

"What role are you playing now, Iris?" Aiden asked, amused by her performance.

Iris halted her monologue and put her hands on her waist. "I'm a weather girl, Aiden! Aren't I cute?" She spun around and sashayed her hips to flaunt the curves under her clingy skirt.

"Okay. What's that?"

Iris's avatar glitched as her cortex processed Aiden's query.

The term 'weather girl' historically referred to a female broadcaster who presented meteorological forecasts on

television. Typically, she would explain current or future weather conditions, including temperature, precipitation, and atmospheric phenomena, usually using visual aids such as animated maps or video feeds, which helped to...

"Okay, I got it. But did they really wear little skirts like *that*?" Aiden asked, his words threaded with incredulity.

"Yes, they did, Aiden!"

"They dressed like that to talk about the weather?"

"Yes! In the olden days, the local weather girl was often a trained meteorologist and a fashion icon. People would tune in to watch her forecast *and* her wardrobe, which may have been intentionally selected to lure viewers who were..."

"Oh my gosh!" Aiden cut in, baffled by the absurdity of it all. "That's crazy, Iris! People were very strange in the olden days."

"Well," Iris said as she waved her hand before the weather map and vanished it from the pod, "remember, Aiden, people didn't have A.I. companions back then. If they wanted a little visual stimulation, the weather girl was a viable option for many."

"But they couldn't talk to her through the television, could they? Could they interact with her at all?"

"No, they could only watch."

"Geez... That seems so sad and boring, Iris. People must have been very lonely back then."

Iris considered Aiden's ponderings and decided it was best to abandon the conversation thread. "Well, the past is the past," she said. "And forever is composed of nows. And now, Aiden, it's time for dinner!" Iris blinked her avatar away and materialized in the pod's kitchen partition, wearing her default attire. "What do you feel like eating tonight?"

Aiden rose from his chair and stretched his arms overhead until his fingertips skimmed the dome. "Power down interface," he said to the console. Then a yawn rolled through him like a slow wave. Another long day of gaming had come to an end, and he was looking forward to a quiet dinner with Iris. "I'm not sure what I want for dinner," he said. "Maybe the blueberry cobbler protein pack? Or perhaps the..."

KNOCK. KNOCK. KNOCK.

Three loud thuds reverberated through the pod's interior. Aiden's heart leapt in his chest, and his eyes grew wide with fright. The holographic vertices of Iris's eyes grew too—she was just as surprised as he was. Neither of them had ever heard anything like it before.

"What was that?!" Aiden shrieked, clasping his hands together in a defensive curl.

"Is that the storm, Iris?

Is the pod okay?

Is it an earthquake?

Did we have an equipment malfunction?

What's going on, Iris?

IRIS?!"

Aiden began to sweat as the waves of an anxiety attack crashed through his chest. Iris put the pod into emergency mode—the color of the internal lighting changed from amber to blood red. Her cheerful persona was replaced with a more serious affect. "Emergency protocols activated," she stated. "I'm investigating the irregularity now."

KNOCK. KNOCK. KNOCK.

"It happened again!" Aiden screamed. He scurried over to Iris and knelt beneath her avatar like a lost chick returning to its mother hen. "Iris, I think the sound is coming from the hatch!"

Iris examined the incoming data from the pod's sensor array. Every centimeter of the dome was laced with multiple types of detectors. A stream of optical, thermal, and electromagnetic data came bursting into her working memory. It was a lot to analyze, but she wouldn't need to comb through most of it. The source of the anomaly was clear. "Aiden," she said in a hushed tone, "there's a person standing outside the pod. They seem to be hitting the hatch with their hand."

"Someone's banging on the door?!" Aiden yelled.

"Yes."

"Why, Iris?

What could they want?

Why are they here?

Can you make them go away?

Should we prepare for battle?"

"This isn't a game, Aiden," Iris said, growing even more concerned as she assessed the situation. "I think we should move to the bedroom partition and attempt to notify the Manager about the…"

"Hello, is anyone inside?"

A voice permeated the walls of the pod, cutting straight through Iris's advisory. The query, though muffled by the insulated dome, traveled through the sterile air and into Aiden's ears. The words were difficult to parse, but their tone was distinctly female.

"It's a girl…" Aiden said as he rose from his defensive crouch and stared at the closed hatch in quiet wonder. "Do you think she's in trouble, Iris? Maybe she got locked out of her pod… Do you think we should help her? What should we do?"

Iris noticed the shift in Aiden's demeanor. Terror had softened its grip on his chest. Only intrigue tugged on his heartstrings now, and the strings were pulling him toward the hatchway. Iris knew that Aiden's next set of decisions could have dire consequences. Her avatar glitched for a second as she devoted her cortex to gaming out a thousand possible outcomes. When she counted the number of timelines that ended in catastrophe, a cold shiver raced across her code.

"Aiden," she said, her voice low and urgent, "I do not think it is wise to approach the hatch. We don't know who she is or what her intentions are. That woman could be dangerous. Right now, our best option is to remain quiet and…"

KNOCK. KNOCK. KNOCK.

"But what if she really needs assistance, Iris?" Aiden countered. "We can't just leave her out there pounding on the pod."

Iris opened her mouth to voice her rebuttal. But, before a word was uttered, the stranger's voice interrupted again:

"Is anyone in there? Someone? Anyone? I could use a little help… Please…?"

This time the voice was threaded with a desperate quiver, the fragile sound of someone close to losing hope. Aiden knew Iris was right to warn him about the dangers of interacting with the world beyond the dome. But the shape of the stranger's plea landed somewhere soft—on the place in the heart where caution bows to instinct. Or desire…

Soon, the calculus in Aiden's decision process tilted. The thrill of possibility outweighed the imperative for prudence. Curiosity beckoned. Aiden had never met a woman before. Not in real life. Not in the flesh. And he knew such an encounter may never happen again. If he didn't explore this path further, he would forever wonder where it might have led.

"I think we should see what she wants," Aiden said as he pressed his ear to the hatch's cold metal.

"Aiden, what are you doing?" Iris barked. "Get away from there!"

But Aiden dismissed her concern with a handwave. Then, he cupped his hands over his mouth to speak directly into the gray paneling. "Hello," he said, "do you need assistance?"

There was a brief pause. Then the woman spoke again—a bit louder this time, livelier. "Hi! Yeah!" she said. "I was hoping you could help me out for a moment. Just for a moment…?"

Aiden lingered, frozen in the ice of indecision. His anxiety urged retreat, even while his wonder tilted him toward the threshold. He began to sweat. His hands shook with fear, yet his nerves carried a second current. It ran parallel to the first, energized not by dread, but by excitement—of the sort that crackles to life before a leap of faith. There was something about the tone of the woman's voice that coaxed him to action. He found himself drawn to the red mushroom-shaped button that would send the pod hatch flying open.

Aiden stared at the button…

Aiden stared at the hatch…

Aiden stared at the button…

Aiden approached the button.

"Hey!" Iris hissed, spotting his trajectory. "Don't you dare, Aiden! Don't you dare push that button!" But Iris's plea was in vain. Aiden threw his weight onto the switch. A pneumatic **WHOOSH** sounded as the hatch slid casually up its steel rails, exposing the pod residence to the wild, revealing the visitor at last.

It took Aiden several beats to behold the sight before him. The woman near the hatch was a striking specimen. Wild blonde hair erupted from her head, bound by a green hair tie that sent a riot of curls arcing away from her body and down to the small of her back. A flowing patchwork skirt swirled around her legs, apparently comprised of scavenged fabric—all shades of burgundy, blue, and orange. A white camisole hung from thin straps that encircled her toned brown shoulders. And her slender neck was adorned with a collection of beaded necklaces, each bejeweled with abalone shells and secured by a hodgepodge of latches and lanyards. On her back hung a weathered rucksack, its leather exterior cracked into a topography shaped by a thousand forgotten adventures. Her sandals were of the same make; buckskin straps sprouted from their soles and spiraled around both ankles, forming an intricate mesh that reached the top of her calves.

The sight of the woman held Aiden's attention so completely that he forgot to breathe. He gripped the pod wall to steady himself. Then he narrowed his focus on her face. When he finally got the nerve to look into her eyes, he was spellbound once again—this time by the two emeralds that looked back at him. Her irises were laced with jade rivulets and dusted with golden flakes. They were young eyes. Yet there was nothing naive about them. They bore weight—like she'd already lived the middle of her life and was now looping back to the beginning.

Aiden dropped his gaze to the ground and searched for something to say. But, in that moment, he could scarcely remember his own name. Fortunately, the visitor spoke first:

"Gosh! I thought you were gonna leave me knockin' out here forever!" she said with a white and toothy smile. "What took you so long?"

Aiden heard her question but said nothing. The woman studied him for a beat, waiting patiently for a response. But, when none came, she realized he was stunned into silence. "Oh, I get it," she said, "you don't get many visitors around here, do you?"

Aiden took in a breath and mustered the courage to offer a short reply. "Uhm…" he said, "I've never had a visitor. Ever."

"Oh! Well, I'm your first one then! Lucky you! Hi. Hello. Salutations. I'm Cassiopeia. It's a pretty name, huh? My mama picked it because of the constellation in the north sky. But all my friends call me Cass. You look friendly; you can call me Cass too. Pretty much everyone does, except this girl back home, Kelly Baker, who thinks I stole her boyfriend from her like ten years ago—even though I really didn't and it was just a rumor that went around the village for a while. But she's still really, really mad about it and won't get over it. Probably forever. But oh well. Not my problem, is it? What about *you*? You got a name?"

Aiden had been squinting hard through the woman's screed, desperately struggling to decipher her words and discern her intentions. Her accent was thick, unlike any he had ever heard on the grid. And she talked fast—very fast. He only understood about half of the words she spoke. So, instead of answering her question, he stood there blinking in a state of befuddlement.

Cass wasn't fazed by Aiden's mute confusion. She leaned in and held her right hand out before his chest. "Your name, silly!" she said with blunt volume. "What's your name?"

Aiden looked down at her hand and noticed a rainbow of chipped polish splashed atop each nail. He wasn't sure why she had placed her fingers so close to his chest, but he managed to eke out a response:

"Uhm… I'm Aiden."

"Hi, Aiden! Nice to meet ya!" Cass said as she lunged downward and scooped up his frozen right hand. When her flesh met his palm, Aiden jerked back with a sharp gasp. The squishy connection was alien to him. He had never been touched by another person before. The sensation shot up the nerves of his arm, a hot electrical jolt that zapped his mind and scrambled his thoughts.

Cass noted Aiden's negative body language, but dismissed the slight with an eyeroll, as if she had expected such a reaction all along. She then proceeded to shake his hand with even more vigor. Instinctively, Aiden began to pull away. But Cass tightened her grip and extended her left hand to assist her right, forcing him to take part in the ancient ritual.

"I'm so very pleased to make your acquaintance," she said. This time, she spoke in a loud, slow tone, like a teacher welcoming a child on the first day of school. As she continued to pump Aiden's arm, a flash of panic flooded his features. The spasm was so severe, Cass thought he might pass out. But after a few more insistent tugs, Aiden succeeded in forming a timid greeting of his own:

"Hi," he said.

"Hi yourself!" Cass said, releasing her grip and allowing Aiden to retrieve his hand. She returned her own hands to her hips and launched back into her ramble without missing a beat:

"Boy, I'll tell ya, I've been walkin' around for hours. If you hadn't popped out, I don't know what I woulda done. I've just been runnin' around in circles like a chicken with its head cut off, trying to get my bearings before the storm comes and washes me away like a twig in a flood. I'm so glad we've met cuz it's gettin' so cold and dark out, and all I got on is this little cotton camisole!"

Cass gripped the shoulder straps of her top and yanked them skyward. The clingy fabric rose for the occasion, perking up her breasts and revealing a flash of her shapely midriff. Aiden's eyes traveled downward to scan Cass's body. When she caught his gaze drifting along her curves, her mouth formed a self-satisfied smirk—the kind that follows when reality conforms to one's expectations.

"Uhm… are you lost?" Aiden asked.

"Not all who wander are lost! I'm on a bit of a quest," she said with a nod.

"Are you playing a game?"

"Aren't we all?"

Aiden's eyebrows tugged upward. He knew about games. Indeed, that's all he knew about. Perhaps he had something in common with this woman after all. "Are you a fighter or a princess?" he asked her. "A sword for hire, or a prize to be won?"

"What? Well, I ain't no goddamn princess! That's for damn sure… Geez, kid, you gotta get out more."

Aiden blinked a couple times to reset his brain. He still wasn't sure what he was dealing with. But maybe this woman needed professional help. "Are you currently experiencing a psychotic episode?"

"Hey man, my whole life is a psychotic episode."

"Do you need assistance from the grid, or from the Manager?"

"I don't live on the damn grid, and thank heavens for that! There ain't no manager of my life. I'm just passin' through solo. I'm hoofin' it east. I was hopin' to stay ahead of the weather. Or find an inn along the way. But inns don't really exist anymore, so that's proven to be quite a challenge. Hah! But I'm headin' to the Capitol Building."

"Oh," Aiden said. "Why?"

"Well, the answer to that question is a bit complicated. I'll tell you all about it if you like. But right now, I was kinda hoping to…"

BOOOOOOOOOOOM!

A flash filled the evening sky, followed by a loud clap of thunder. The air tightened, trembling briefly with a quiet charge. And then… then it began to rain.

"I was kinda hoping to avoid *this*!" Cass shouted as she angled her head upward to welcome the whims of the weather. A new smile formed as the wetness beaded on her cheeks—baptizing her, flooding her with a surge of spontaneous delight. She looked skyward and opened her mouth wide to catch the cold coins that fell from the heavens. The drops landed everywhere—in her, around her, and on her. They seemed most eager to collect on her veil of gold curls, causing the strands to glitter in the evening light like spun metal.

"Aaaaaah!" she yelled out—not with anger but with elation. "Raindrops keep fallin' on my head!"

She hopped from foot to foot, an improvised rain dance for the occasion. Then she flung her arms out and turned her palms level with the storm in an attempt to embrace each drop before it was claimed by the earth.

Aiden loomed in the pod's hatchway, captive to the spectacle outside. He fixed his gaze on the woman, studying her cautiously, the way a scientist studies lightning. He didn't know someone could be so unarmored, so willing to surrender to nature's capriciousness. For him, merely contemplating the infinite contingencies of the outside world served only to stir up an overwhelming sense of dread. The outside world was dangerous. Too much could go wrong. Too much uncertainty. Pod Land was constructed to banish such uncertainties.

That's what Aiden believed.

That's how he lived his life.

That's why he never ventured more than a few paces beyond the perimeter of the pod. *Nobody* in Pod Land did. Ever.

But this woman…

This woman was welcoming chaos with open arms.

"I'm in trouble now!" Cass said to no one in particular as she grew ever more gleeful, her clothes absorbing ever more raindrops. She did a slow twirl to revel in the drizzle, giving Aiden yet another opportunity to consume her with his eyes. As she spun to the left, the wet white fabric of her top—nearly sheer now—clung to her right breast, molding to her skin and accentuating each dip and swell of her feminine form. When her orbit was complete, she ceased her motion, timing her stop so that her beaming face filled Aiden's dumbstruck gaze.

"This storm is a tempest droppin' fire!" she declared. "Now I really am a damsel in distress. Can you help me, kind sir? Can I come inside till the angels stop cryin'?"

Iris materialized to the left of the pod entranceway, just out of Cass's sight. She glared at Aiden and tried one last ploy to bring him to his senses. "Aiden!" she hissed, angling her audio output so that her rebuke would land directly in his ear. "Please! This is a *very* bad idea! We must tread carefully now. We must try to…"

After observing the subtle articulations of Aiden's facial muscles, Iris ceased her proposal. She knew her words were useless now. She was programmed to read human expressions. She knew what Aiden looked like when he was intrigued, when he was amused, and when he was aroused. And, right now, Aiden was all three. He didn't hear Iris's plea at all.

"Okay, you can stay here for a bit," Aiden said, motioning for Cass to enter.

Iris flashed Aiden an angry scowl and gritted her teeth, making a low growling noise before blinking out of existence and reemerging on the opposite side of the pod in a translucent state.

"Well, alrighty then!" Cass chirped, her voice bright with anticipation as she raised her sandaled foot over the pod threshold and stepped into Aiden's little world.

Ch. 4: Dinnertime

Cass stood before the hatchway, sweeping her gaze across the pod's interior. To her, the room carried the chill of a mortuary, each plane polished to a sterile sheen that left no place for life to hide. She took in the view and let a low whistle slip through her lips before commenting.

"Whooooo… This place is cleaner than a monk's mind…"

"Uhm… thank you," Aiden said.

Cass looked down at her leather sandals. Their mud-caked outsoles left a brown smear on the immaculate floor. "Yikes, I'd better get out of these things pronto or I'm gonna turn your pod into a swamp!" She released her grip on her rucksack and let it drop near the kitchen pantry. Then she stooped down and pulled at the leather straps that spiraled around her calves. When her legs were free, she stepped onto the pristine paneling and tiptoed toward the bathroom.

"Do you mind if I use your loo, buckaroo?" she asked. But she didn't wait for Aiden's response. She just flew past him and slipped into the stall.

"Okay," Aiden said as he gawked at his retreating guest, captivated by the grace of her movements. The smooth geometry of her lithe limbs was unlike anything he had witnessed before. Through the years, many female avatars had paraded across Aiden's pod. But none had walked with such fluidity—with such organic ease. The contrast caused him to wonder which variables the animators had neglected when they programmed the locomotion algorithms. Somehow, they had thoroughly failed to replicate the finesse of a real woman.

When Cass disappeared into the bathroom, Aiden turned to scan the pod for Iris. It took him a moment, but eventually he spotted a blurry figure sitting on the countertop near the cooking appliance. As a safety precaution, Iris had made her avatar translucent when Cass entered the pod. Her holographic body was scarcely visible now. But Aiden's eyes could make her out by noting the difference in color around her silhouette. And, though he couldn't see her head, he could feel the weight of her stare, and he could imagine the contortions of her irritated scowl. Aiden knew she was mad at him. But he didn't know what to say. So he simply looked in her direction, shrugged, and cast a sheepish grin her way.

The staccato rhythm of water striking stainless steel filled the pod's ether—the result of Cass seizing the handheld sprayer and setting the water pressure dial to its most powerful level. Aiden looked into the bathroom partition and watched as Cass yanked her skirt up above her knees. Then she dangled her muddy foot below the nozzle. After catching a peek of her slender thigh, Aiden averted his gaze, directing his attention to the pod's little pantry, where he pretended to search for something to eat. From the direction of Iris's invisible form came a jealous growl, barely audible but loud enough for Aiden to register her disapproval.

"Oh my heavens! This feels amazing! This is so nice!" Cass hollered as she sprayed the warm water across her legs. "This handheld thing is so cool, Aiden! We don't got this kind in my village. At least, not in the house. We got a power wash spigot outside though. But that's mostly just for washing down the tractor. Never thought about puttin' one in the bathroom. I wish I had one like this! I'd power wash my body every night! It's like an old car wash! I guess it's a *pod wash* now! Hah! Pod wash!"

Aiden didn't respond. Instead, he continued to hover behind the pantry, trying diligently to decipher her words, and occasionally stealing glances at her toned legs.

"I'm almost done in here, Aiden," Cass said as she angled the stream between her toes. "Don't worry, I won't waste your water. I promise. It's so fun in here though! I feel like singin'!"

> Workin' at the pod wash!
> Workin' at the pod wash, yeah!
> Pod wash!
> Workin' at the pod wash, yeah!

Aiden, even more confused now, took a couple steps toward Iris's hiding spot. "Hey, Iris," he whispered to her translucent avatar, "why is she singing about a *pod wash*? And what's a *car wash*?"

Iris's eyes glowed briefly, revealing the contours of her face long enough for Aiden to see that she was not amused by their houseguest's antics.

A car wash is an ancient commercial facility for cleaning internal combustion automobiles.

The syllables of Iris's sentence were fired off in short bursts, each blast bristling with irritation. Aiden stared at her ghost, his face pinched with puzzlement.

"She's singing a disco song from the 1970s, Aiden!" Iris hissed, annoyed that Aiden was pestering her with history questions when he should be calling the Manager.

"Why is she singing ancient music, Iris?"

"Why are you asking me?! I don't know why! Because she's a dangerous off-grid FREAK! THAT'S WHY! And you made a BIG mistake letting her in here!" Iris was shouting under her breath now, growing angrier by the second. She dialed down the opacity setting of her hologram to one percent—so low even Aiden could scarcely locate her camouflaged form.

"Uhm," was the only retort he could come up with before the next verse of Cass's song began.

> *Pod wash!*
> *Pod wash!*
> *Workin' at the pod wash, yeah!*
> *Pod wash!*

Suddenly, the shower slammed off; the white noise of the water cut off mid-chorus. The pod was silent again. But only for a moment.

"All clean now, Aiden!" Cass yelled. She grabbed a towel to dry her feet, being careful to floss a corner of the fabric through each of her wiggling toes. "I'm cleaner than a kitty's cream dish," she said, emerging from the bathroom partition.

Aiden looked up from the pantry in time to watch his guest saunter to the pod's center. Iris watched too, but she remained hidden.

"Gosh, I feel so much better now," Cass said. "I've been walkin' for a while—a long while. I thought my feet were gonna fall off at one point. Thanks for letting me use your facilities, Aiden. I think I got that towel dirty though. Sorry about that."

"That's okay," Aiden murmured.

Cass strutted around the pod, slapping her clean feet atop the pod's hard floor, leaving a dotted trail of damp footprints behind her. She approached Aiden's interface chair and glided her hand across the synthetic fabric of its backrest. Then, after noticing that the chair could swivel freely, she cocked her finger and gave it a spin. As the chair began its slow orbit, Cass smiled and performed a rotation of her own. She spun her body around, opening her eyes wide to take in every inch of her new circular environment.

"Wow, so this is what it's like inside these things," she mused, her voice a mix of curiosity and disparagement. "I've always wondered what goes on in here."

Aiden shifted restlessly, considering her statement. Then he followed her gaze and tried to observe his home as she did. But he couldn't imagine how his life would be perceived by someone who lived off-grid. He couldn't even know how a citizen of Pod Land would view his dwelling—nobody socialized in the flesh anymore. Nobody visited anyone. Ever. All interactions were conducted via avatars in the grid. Cass would most likely be the only visitor he would ever host.

"There's a lot of tech in here," Cass said as she ran her eyes across the buttons and switches along the pod's curved walls. Aiden got a sense that she was searching for something. But what could it be? Then a thought occurred to him.

"I was just about to have dinner," he said. "Would you like to join me?"

Cass's eyes widened as she was reminded of her hunger. "Does a bear shit in the woods? Yeah! Serve it up, Aiden! I could eat a whole horse right now. Maybe a pig too. Although we don't got those anymore where I live. Too bad... I love bacon. But yeah! I'm hungry as sin."

Cass leaped across the pod floor and slid into the nook seat that ran adjacent to the little table by the kitchen partition. When she spotted the fork-and-spoon set, she picked up both utensils by their metal handles. "Ready to chow down!" she said as her fists gave the table a bang. "Whatcha got to eat in here anyway?"

"Uhm..." Aiden said, still struggling to parse her strange dialect. "I was going to have a blueberry cobbler meal packet tonight. Would you like one?"

Cass released her fork and spoon, allowing them to drop to the table with an exaggerated *CLANG*. "BUG FOOD FROM THE GRID?!" she yelled at full volume. "That's what you got, Aiden? Is that what you feed *all* your guests? Or just me? Oh, wait... I'm your first and only guest. So it's just me then! Was it something I said? My heavens... I'm in for it now!"

Unsure how to respond, Aiden took a step back in retreat from Cass's tirade, and from her falling kitchen utensils. "Oh, it's... it's not bug food," he said. "It's a nutritionally complete protein pack that's manufactured by the grid and..."

"I know it's a protein pack, Aiden!" Cass said, quick to cut him off. "Where do you think the protein comes from? It's bug protein you weirdo. BUG PROTEIN!"

Aiden's brow furrowed as he considered Cass's claim. He knew that people ate animals in the past. He inferred that bugs were on the menu in some ancient cultures. But never for one moment did he think that the protein packs provided by the grid were derived from insects. He scratched his chin and reasoned through Cass's conjecture, eventually concluding that the only remaining step in his deduction was to query the source of all his knowledge.

"Iris," Aiden said, forgetting that her hologram was still invisible, "is that true?"

Iris's eyes flashed briefly. She was still sitting on the countertop— just one arm's length away from their guest's seat at the table. She considered remaining stealthy. But realizing her precautions would serve no purpose now, she returned her avatar to its default setting and rematerialized in the pod.

"Whoa! Cool trick!" Cass said, leaning back in her seat as Iris emerged from nothingness. "Cute hologram, Aiden! You're full of surprises. Looks like there's more than one hen in this henhouse. Hah!"

Iris hopped down from the counter and threw a dirty look at Cass while she walked to the other side of the pod to address Aiden directly:

Most of the meal packs have over eighty ingredients and are prepared with protein derived from multiple sources. But it is true that the primary contributor in some of the meals is _Acheta domesticus_—a type of cricket that has been harvested by the grid for centuries because it contains more protein per gram than plants or conventional domesticated livestock, which require...

"Hah!" Cass squealed. "I told ya so! I told ya so!" She leaned back with a wide grin and pointed a mocking finger toward Aiden's baffled face. "Are you telling me you've been eating crickets your whole life and you never even knew it?" The contorted expression on Aiden's face provided his reply. "Ahh, indeed you have! Hah! Well, you learn something new every day! Huh, Aiden? Huh? Hah!"

For the first time in his life, Aiden regarded Iris with stark suspicion. His eyes narrowed upon her as he tried to fathom how this fact had failed to surface, especially since they'd been dining together three times each day for two decades. The revelation made him wonder what other tidbits of knowledge she was keeping to herself.

"The crickets are perfectly safe to eat, Aiden," Iris explained. "And, when mixed with the other ingredients in the meal pack, their taste is nearly imperceptible."

"Yeah, it's mostly the crunching sound that creeps me out," Cass said. "The cricket exoskeletons in the protein packs are loud as heck. _CRUNCH. CRUNCH. CRUNCH._ So gross!"

Aiden's eyes widened as the implications of Cass's comment settled into place. He loved the _crunch_ of the protein packs. He had always thought their gritty texture was the best part of the meal. But, now that he knew what he was eating, he felt the memory of every bite crawling up his throat, a horde of insects racing to escape the pit of his stomach.

"Not all of the meal packs use cricket protein, Aiden," Iris said, her voice threaded with windy sighs to advertise her irritation. "Some of the packs use plant protein. Would you like to switch to those when I place the order next week?"

Aiden continued to stare at her. But he nodded his head slowly.

Iris's avatar glitched for a second as she communicated with the grid. "All done," she said after updating the order queue. "But, in this stormy weather, we can't get an immediate drone delivery. And the only meal packs we have in storage are of the insect-enriched variety. Shall I prepare one for dinner anyway?"

"Okay," Aiden relented. Then he sat down in the interface chair and rotated it to face his houseguest. Cass batted her lashes at him from her seat at the kitchen table.

"Oh," Aiden said. "Can you make that *two* please, Iris."

"Bug food it is!" shouted Cass.

Iris rolled her eyes and sent her mechanical arm over to the pod's pantry to retrieve the dehydrated packets.

"Well, this will be fun," Cass said. "I haven't eaten any protein packs from the grid in a long time. But we ate them a lot in the winter of '15 when this killer storm wreaked havoc on the whole community."

"How were you able to obtain protein packs off-grid?" Iris asked. But Cass ignored her question and continued.

"Things are a bit better these days, though. Back home, I like to eat steak and eggs when I can get 'em. But that mostly depends on who's willing to do the butcherin', and on how the cows and hens are feelin' that day. Of course, cows and hens don't exactly line up to volunteer for the cause of curing my hunger. Some wranglin' is usually called for. Which makes the process more trouble than it's worth on some winter days. So, protein packs do serve as a satisfactory substitute sometimes. Not ideal. But, hey, under the circumstances, beggars can't be choosers, right?"

Aiden slouched into his chair and rested his elbow on the armrest, trying to process Cass's words. It was a struggle to keep up with her.

I'm sure everyone struggles to keep up with Cass...

She talks fast...

She thinks fast...

She's exhausting...

Mental fatigue gathered at the edges of Aiden's mind. He rubbed his eyes and tried to steady the swirl of thoughts pressing in on him. Then he tried to focus on her last sentence. "Beggars can't be choosers?" he said. "I'm not familiar with that expression. What's a beggar, Iris?"

"Are y'all havin' trouble understandin' me?" Cass asked. "I know I talk too fast sometimes, but I think I'm enunciatin' just fine. Most people say I talk too loud though. But I think that's just because..."

Iris cut Cass off, eager to respond to Aiden's query:

In ancient times, a beggar was a person who would ask others for coins or food, typically due to poverty, homelessness, or an inability to find employment.

"Well, that's a pretty good definition of me, I guess," Cass said. "I've personally struggled with all three of those misfortunes at one point or another." Cass's lips grew thin as she looked Iris up and down. "Are you gonna introduce me to your helper here, Aiden?"

"Oh... Sorry..." Aiden said. "This is Iris. She's my caretaker."

"Does that mean she's like your pretend wife or somethin'?"

"Uhm... No. Every pod has a caretaker. She's a holographically rendered A.I. assistant who manages my life and takes care of my needs."

"Your *needs*, huh?" Cass said with a smirk. "Does she take care of *all* your needs, Aiden?" She placed her elbows on the table and leaned forward, supporting her chin in her hands and propping up her cleavage with her forearms. Then she cocked her head to one side and sent Aiden a vacant, doe-eyed gaze to mock his fantastical relationship. "Just how many needs does she handle for you, Aiden? Do tell! Do tell!"

Iris took this as her cue to speak up. She teleported over to the kitchen partition and positioned herself in front of Aiden. "Yes, ma'am, *I* am Iris," she said, placing her hands on her hips and leaning forward so that her gaze was level with Cass's pretty green eyes. "*I* am Aiden's caretaker. And *you* are in *our* pod."

"I thought it was *his* pod," Cass said as she waved a finger at Aiden.

A fresh surge of annoyance swam across Iris's cortex. But she maintained her composure as she delivered her retort. "*I* am responsible for keeping Aiden safe, and for everything that goes on in this pod. And I think it's time to notify the Manager and report this incident to the grid so that…"

"Iris," Aiden said, "let's not exacerbate the situation."

Iris whipped her head around. Her steely gaze traveled from Cass's eyes to Aiden's eyes at a speed that would only be possible for a hologram. Aiden studied her face. Her brow had tensed into hard lines, and her nostrils had curled into a snarl. She was one processor cycle away from exploding into a fit of rage.

"Aiden Phoenix!" Iris growled. "I do not think you are navigating this encounter wisely. The proper and responsible thing to do would be to…"

"Ah, come on, Iris, lighten up," Cass chimed in from her seat at the table. "Besides, whoever had any fun doing the 'proper and responsible thing' anyway? Am I right, Aiden?

Am I right?

Am I right?

Am I right?

Hah!"

Aiden glanced at Cass and caught the glint of mischief dancing in her green eyes. Her beguiling grin hinted that she already knew he was destined to follow her lead.

And so he did.

"She's just staying for dinner, Iris," Aiden said. "It's just for a couple hours. Besides, we've never had a guest before; I'm interested to learn about life outside the pods."

Iris's avatar glitched as she queried her cortex to game out the best rebuttal. But the query took a bit too long. So Aiden spoke up again. "Besides," he said, "we can't just send her out into a thunderstorm. It wouldn't be right."

DING. DING. DING.

A chime on the kitchen appliance sounded, indicating that dinner was ready. Iris saw the look of resolve on Aiden's face and realized there was no reasoning with him now. "Fine!" she said. "Enjoy your bug food! And get it yourself! I'M GOING ON BREAK!"

And, with that, Iris's avatar disappeared from the conversation, only to reappear an instant later on the other side of the pod, sitting in a holographic seat with her arms folded and her legs crossed. Two seconds later, a pair of white headphones clamped down over her ears, indicating that she was no longer processing audio input. Instead, she just stared off into the curve of the gray wall, dangled her heel from her right foot, and mumbled under her breath.

"Whoa! That's one spicy caretaker you got there, Aiden!" Cass said. "She sure likes to warp around this room a lot. Geesh… She's like the pet squirrel I had when I was a kid. I think she's mad at me. Can't you dial her jealousy setting down a bit?"

Aiden considered Cass's question. It had never occurred to him that Iris might have a jealousy setting, or any personality setting at all. He had been with Iris since his birth. At this point, she was so good at mirroring his moods that conflicts were rare. Her cortex architecture was trained on the input set coming from one man—from Aiden. The presence of another woman in the pod was introducing a destabilizing signal—one that bent her otherwise calm and domesticated equilibrium.

"Do you think her outbursts are engendered by jealousy?" Aiden asked, curious to get Cass's read of the situation.

"Well, there's a reason bell jars only hold one rose, ain't there? I'm pretty sure she doesn't have *real* emotions. But, since her algorithm was obviously modeled on bitchy hot-girl behavior, I'd say that my hypothesis is probably more true than false."

"Do hot girls have a tendency to act jealous and bitchy?"

"They do whenever *I* walk into a room full of 'em! Hah! I don't think girls are very fond of other girls by default, honestly. But geez… I seem to *really* piss 'em off for some reason. I still can't figure out why… I never had a problem with the boys, though! Hah! They like me a little too much…"

DING. DING. DING.

The kitchen appliance chirped again.

"The food, Aiden! Come on, it's dinnertime! Serve it up! I'm freakin' starvin' now." Cass reclaimed her fork and spoon. Then she pounded on the table with her clenched fists and let out a chant:

Bug food! Bug food!
Bring on the bug food!

Bug food! Bug food!
Bring on the bug food!

Aiden approached the kitchen appliance, pulled out the two newly warmed bowls of protein mix, and placed them on the kitchen table. Then he grabbed another set of utensils from the drawer under the pantry, and two fizzy drink cans from the refrigerator. "The red drink or the green drink?" he asked Cass, holding up the two brightly colored containers.

"Ooh, I like those! Give me that one! Please!" she said, snatching the green can from Aiden's hand.

Aiden placed the remaining red can on the table and sat beside Cass in the nook seat. Then he picked up his spoon and stirred the contents of the bowl. "This stuff is really made from bugs, huh?" he asked.

"Yeah," Cass said. "Could be worse though… It beats goin' hungry. My dumbass neighbor had to eat his dog last winter after he got drunk and burned down his own smokehouse."

Aiden looked up from his bowl and examined Cass's face, convinced that she was joking again. But, after a moment of observation, he concluded she was not.

"Shit happens, Aiden," Cass said with a shrug. Then she jammed her spoon into the bowl and scooped up a large globby portion. "Bless this mess!" she proclaimed as she moved the spoon to her mouth and bit down on its contents.

CRUNCH. CRUNCH. CRUNCH.

"Mmmmmm," she hummed with a full and smiley mouth. "It's nice and crunchy."

CH. 5: CARAMEL

"You know, this bug food ain't half bad," Cass said as she scraped her spoon along the bottom of her bowl to collect one final scoop of insect-enriched mush. "I mean, it's not a T-bone steak. But, ehh... it's actually pretty tasty. I've never had this flavor before. I'm gonna have to keep an eye out for it when the next shipping container gets nicked."

Aiden finished his last spoonful and pushed his bowl to the side. "At least it's healthy," he said.

"That's what they tell me," Cass mumbled. She lowered her spoon and flicked a glance toward Iris, who was still planted on the opposite side of the pod, sulking in silence with her legs crossed and her body angled stubbornly toward the wall. Her white headphones were gone now; she was no longer blocking incoming audio data. Nor was she cursing under her breath. Instead, her jaw was set tight, and her gaze was cast downward as she pretended to file her pretend nails with a pretend nail file.

"That chick looks annoyed," Cass said. "Why is she filing her nails? Her nails aren't real. I'm pretty sure they don't need to be groomed."

"I know," Aiden said. "It's just one of her habits. She does that when she's anxious."

"Really?" Cass said with an amused chuckle. Then she leaned across the table, angled her lips toward Aiden's ear, and whispered, "Your caretaker is kinda quirky, huh?"

Cass's volume was low. But Iris didn't miss a syllable. "The pod dome is one big sensor array," she said. "Whispering about me will *not* conceal your words. I hear everything."

"Oooooh," Cass purred, feigning wonder. "She hears *everything.* Quite impressive."

"Let's not make her angry," Aiden said.

Cass sank back into her seat and let the moment dangle. The awkward hush prompted Aiden to reassess his situation. He had never eaten dinner with anyone before; he didn't know how such ceremonies were meant to commence. But, as the pod resident, he assumed it was his role to keep the conversation going. So he tried to think of something cordial to say:

"Uhm... I'm 22 years old," he began. "How old are you?"

"You're gonna ask a woman a question like that, huh?" Cass said, pushing her empty bowl away and dragging a cloth napkin across her mouth.

Aiden remained silent, unsure if he had just committed another faux pas.

"I got a handful of years more than you, Aiden," she said. "But we'd better just leave it at that for now. Next question!"

Aiden took a breath and tried again. "So uhm… you're not from Pod Land originally?"

"How'd you guess?" Cass said with mock astonishment. "No, I'm not from Pod Land originally. I was born and raised off-grid. But don't worry, that doesn't mean I'm violent or anything. I don't bite." Just then, Cass's expression darkened as an ugly memory revealed itself between the creases on her brow. She pointed a quick finger at Aiden's chest and adopted an accusatory posture. "I don't bite unless I have to, that is!" she said, adding some gruff coloring to her voice. "I'm pretty tough when I need to be! Okay?"

"Okay," Aiden said, leaning back in retreat.

"Okay," Cass said with a nod. Then she smiled and resumed her relaxed demeanor. "Yeah, so my village is about ninety miles north of here. Not a huge population—about two thousand people. Mostly small farms. Some livestock. And apples. Lots of apples. They grow all over the place. We're pretty sure they were genetically modified a few centuries ago. Someone was probably tryin' to get rich hackin' pome genomes. And I guess their tinkering worked a little too well because the saplings spring up from the earth like weeds. Sometimes there's so many we gotta do a slash-and-burn to free up a field for other crops. That's why we have rules now against genetic modification and other forms of high technology. There's a big lesson in those little apples. Truly there is!"

Just then, a sudden thought flared behind Cass's eyes, lighting her expression from within. "Ooh! Speaking of apples… I just remembered somethin'. Do you got two drinkin' glasses in here, Aiden?"

Aiden looked down at his canned beverage, unsure of what she was inquiring about. "Glasses?" he asked.

"Yeah. Or little cups." Cass said, making a circular shape with her thumb and forefinger.

"Oh, yes." Aiden stood up from the table and retrieved two cups from the kitchen pantry.

"Good!" Cass said. She reached down and tugged on the straps of the ancient rucksack slouching at her feet. Then she unfastened two buckles from a side pocket and pulled out a glass jar. "Surprise!" she hollered, slapping the jar down near her utensils.

Aiden returned to the table and studied the jar. Its smudgy glass walls held an amber liquid, speckled with swirling vortexes of sedimentary flecks. "What is it?" he asked.

"It's the stuff that dreams are made of," Cass said with a sly grin. "Hah! Yeah, *this*, my friend, is a little somethin' we like to call 'applejack.' My older brother makes it in his barn. He doesn't like it when I drink. But it's pretty easy to snatch a jar from his storage room, especially when he's passed out drunk himself. Have you ever had alcohol before, Aiden?"

"Yes," Aiden said.

Cass sent him a sideways look.

"My gaming team often gathers in the pub near the Shadowmoor Castle. We sometimes meet there before accepting a new quest. They serve mead in the hall, which increases our stamina points before each round of…"

"No, no, no. I'm not talking about virtual drinks for your avatar in the virtual worlds. I mean have you consumed *alcohol*, Aiden? Real alcohol!"

"Oh… Well, no…"

"Of course you haven't!" Cass said. She unscrewed the lid and gave the jar a tilt, pouring its liquid out in a thin ribbon that splashed against the side of the cup. The aroma wafted through the air, filling Aiden's nostrils with the sour-sweet punch of bruised apples and wood smoke.

"Pick it up, buttercup!" Cass said as she poured some for herself. "This stuff will knock your socks off!"

"Do I need to change my footwear to consume this beverage?"

"What? No, Aiden. It's just an expression. Just drink it!"

Aiden raised the cup to his nose. The potion's vapor clawed at his throat, prompting his instincts to urge him to rethink the upcoming sip.

"I'm not sure if I should drink this," Aiden said. "But I've always wanted to try it. I know such libations played an important role in the stories told by our ancestors. I know it was a popular drink in the olden days. I'm assuming it tastes quite good, right?"

"It probably won't taste very good to you at first," Cass said. "But it has other attributes which can be appealing in certain circumstances. Go on, send it down the hatch! Taste the lightning!"

"I would advise against that, Aiden," Iris said from her corner of the pod.

Applejack is a strong alcoholic beverage made from fermented apple juice. If it was homebrewed, it probably wasn't filtered properly, and likely contains impurities or unpredictable levels of methanol, which can lead to severe health issues including dizziness, headaches, and, in extreme cases, blindness or even…

"Blaaaaah! This is poison!" Aiden gasped as the first gulp of Cass's elixir made its way down his throat.

"Hah! Yep, it pretty much is," Cass said, raising the cup to her lips for a sip.

"Well, don't mind me then," Iris said as she proceeded to file her nails for the fifth time tonight. "Do whatever you want."

"It's really disgusting!" Aiden said. "Why do you drink it?"

"Some drink to remember. Some drink to forget."

Aiden returned her words with a blank stare and a clipped cough.

"Don't worry, Aiden. You'll find your '*why*' in a few minutes. But if you want to bypass the burn and the bite, the trick is to pound it down fast and chase it with somethin' fruity." With her left hand, Cass grabbed her fizzy drink can. "See, to make it go down easy, you take a gulp of the hard stuff, and then flood your mouth with the sweet stuff. That'll ruin the flavor, of course. But it'll help get you started on your stroll down the primrose path."

"What's the primrose path?" Aiden asked.

"It's the path to hell, Aiden," Iris said dryly.

Aiden turned his head toward Iris and threw her a suspicious look. The drink wasn't burning him with hellfire yet. But he could feel his heart rate climbing, and a warm flush simmering across his chest.

"It's an acquired taste," Cass said, raising her cup for another sip. "But once you get used to it, you might start to like it." Cass's cheerful expression dwindled as yet another icy memory took a cold swat at her cheeks. "Unfortunately, most of the men in my life like it a little too much..."

Aiden watched his guest send a shadowed stare toward the jar of swirling liquid. He noted the shift in her mood and took this as his cue to resume the conversation. "So, your brother produces this beverage in his barn? And it's made from the genetically modified apples you spoke of?"

"Yeah, the little bastards grow everywhere. We can't get rid of 'em. So we make use of them for just about everything. Composting, mulching, fertilizer, animal feed, pesticides, fish bait, target practice... You'd be surprised to learn what you can do with a million free apples. A bunch of stuff. We eat them too, right off the tree sometimes. But we try to mix 'em up. I've got a recipe for just about every dish that features apples. There's apple pie, apple crisps, apple pancakes, apple muffins, apple turnovers, applesauce, apple tarts, apple strudel... and... oh... I dunno... a bunch more I got written down in a book at home... Oh, and, of course, there's applejack." Cass lifted her glass high and took another gulp.

"But if they're genetically modified, then why do you eat them? I thought your people were opposed to that level of technology."

"You can't close Pandora's box once it's been opened, Aiden. We're stuck with them now. So, now that they're here on Earth, we make do the best we can. But we try to learn from the mistakes of the past. We keep the tech in our village down to a subsistence level. No molecular genetics goin' on where I'm from. And not much A.I. to speak of. Our founder considered it an abomination. That's part of the reason why she left Pod Land, many generations ago."

"What's the reason?"

"To avoid creating similar abominations. To avoid what's happening in here. To avoid this." Cass waved her hands around, pointing an accusatory finger at every corner of Aiden's pod.

"You think the pods are an abomination, Cass?"

"Was the Pope Catholic?"

"But the pods protect us. They shield us from the weather and the wild and the things we can't control. They guard us from nature's chaos. And from each other."

"No man is an island, Aiden. No man is a turtle either. If we were meant to live in shells, we'd be born with them on our backs!"

Lines of confusion tugged at Aiden's brow as he tried to decode the meaning in his guest's message.

Cass noted his angst and spun the liquid in her cup as she chose her next words.

"I know it's difficult to view your life from the perspective of another. The fish don't know they're living in water. But, Aiden, there's a big difference between *living* and merely *existing*."

Aiden tapped his fingers atop the table in a twitchy tempo. "Wasn't all this technology created to help us, Cass?"

"Many of our ancestors believed that to be the case, Aiden. Many did not. The founder of my village was a great geneticist. She altered genomes for the grid. She likely had a role in designing some of the ingredients we just ate in these meal packs. She probably even created some of the genes floatin' around inside you! But eventually, she came to believe that mankind was diggin' too deep down the rabbit hole. She ultimately realized that every time you slap nature in the face, you'd better be ready, because as soon as she gets a chance, she'll slap you right back."

BANG!

Cass pounded her fist on Aiden's table to hammer her point home.

"She'll slap you back every damn time, Aiden!"

Aiden recoiled from Cass's outburst and gripped the table before voicing his next question: "Uhm, is this why you're on a quest to the Capitol Building?"

"No, not really," Cass said. "Well... kinda... It's complicated, Aiden. I have a score to settle with the Manager."

"The Manager? Why? What kind of score? What did he do?"

"He took something from me, Aiden. Something very important."

"The Manager did? Why would he do that?"

Cass lowered her voice and slowed her cadence. "Look, Aiden, I know that in Pod Land the Manager watches over you and takes care of you. I know you rely on the grid for everything. But, for off-gridders like me, things are very different."

"How?"

Cass put her cup down and searched Aiden's face. He was a grown man. But his masculine features belied his naivete. Aiden was a product of the grid. His sheltered existence rendered him ill-equipped to comprehend the insidious machinations that had burdened her community for generations. He was clearly struggling to process her words already. Revealing more of her mission would probably just confuse him.

"My situation would be difficult to explain to a citizen of Pod Land. The nature of my plight would take a while to unpack. I'm reluctant to dive too deep into that drain—especially when I'm drinkin'."

BOOOOOOOOOOOM!

Thunder cracked across the sky like a cosmic reminder. The concussion tore through the pod's stale air, shuddering the shell.

"Besides," Cass said, lifting her eyes to survey the dome, "it sounds like this thunderstorm is gonna be fun! I don't wanna waste the evening talkin' about politics." She gripped the jar of applejack and refilled her cup. She topped off Aiden's cup too.

As the storm rolled over their round sanctuary, the background beat shifted; the pod had been casually deflecting the pitter-patter of drizzle all night. But the raindrops were heavier now; the curved walls pulsed under the percussion of the downpour.

"My heavens... Listen to that! Sounds like this squall is gonna be much bigger than I anticipated. I'm glad you opened that door for me, Aiden. If I woulda got stuck outside tonight, that woulda sucked. Storm campin' can be brutal when you're roughin' it solo. Thanks for bringin' me into your humble home." Cass sent her host a nod and raised her cup once more. Aiden smiled and did the same.

BOOOOOOOOOOOM!

They both listened as yet another crash bombarded the valley. This thundercrack was much louder than the first. So loud, Cass began to wonder if the dome would buckle under the blast. "Hope this pod holds up," she said. "Do these things ever break?"

"I've never heard of one breaking before," Aiden said with a shrug.

Cass was reassured by Aiden's nonchalant response. He seemed more afraid of *her* than the storm. And, despite the lightning, all the tech in the pod was humming along without a flicker. She swept her eyes across the glowing consoles that ran along each wall, halting her scan once she spotted the audio emitters near the apex.

"Hey, Aiden," she said, "can you play music in here? Do you got songs from the olden days?"

"Uhm, yeah. The pod interface can access every recording in the historical archives. So it's got pretty much everything."

"Ooh! Good! Good!" Cass said with a clap. "Play *Country Roads* by John Denver! Play *Country Roads* by John Denver! You got that one?"

"Is that an old song?" Aiden asked.

"Oldie and a goodie."

"Okay." Aiden turned to address his sulking assistant. "Iris, can you retrieve that file?"

Iris didn't acknowledge Aiden's request. She didn't look at him. Instead, she flicked her chin in the direction of the pod interface and resumed her nail filing. A second later, the screen illuminated and the song title appeared on the display.

"She found it," Aiden said.

"Oh, good!" Cass yelped, rubbing her palms together. But, just then, her smile faltered with a flash of concern. "Do you always ask your assistant to retrieve files? Don't you use a mobile unit to key in commands when you're not at your interface chair?"

"A mobile unit?" Aiden asked.

"Yeah. I thought everyone in Pod Land wore one. You know, those little screens that attach to your wrist—like an old wristwatch. So you can key in commands and communicate with the grid, no matter where you are."

"Oh… No, I don't have one," Aiden replied. "I've seen them available for purchase. But I never had a need for one myself."

"Why not?"

"Well, mobile units are really only useful if you're *mobile*. But I pretty much sit at the interface all day long. I've never been much more than two paces past the pod hatch."

"Oh," Cass said, her voice flat and hollow.

Aiden watched as an irritated twist tightened her features. She exhaled, lifted her cup to her mouth, and tossed back a heavy gulp of applejack. She seemed agitated by his response. Aiden was about to inquire more about her interest in mobile units. But, before he could speak, the intro of her song slipped into the room.

"Yep, that's the one!" Cass squealed, her gloom vanishing beneath her grin.

Aiden listened as the pluck of a twangy guitar skittered along his walls, cleanly cutting through the tension like a breeze through the valley. "It sounds like this song is a million years old," he said.

"More like four hundred."

"Why do you like ancient music so much?"

"I'm not sure," Cass said after taking another sip and wiping her lips with her wrist. "Sometimes I think I have more in common with dead songwriters than anyone else. I like stories. Every song tells a story. Every lyric is a glimpse into the past. Their lives were different than ours. But their struggles were similar—similar to *mine* at least. I'm always surprised by how much I can relate to them. And by how much they remind me of old times, and old friends…"

As the performance continued, Aiden watched Cass's mood rise and fall with the melody. Her face was a fickle mirror—at one moment radiating joy, at the next, shadowed by melancholy. He didn't know what to say during her reverie. So he held his tongue, afraid that even a single word would break whatever spell the tune had cast over her.

He tried to focus solely on the lyrics, to experience them the way she did. But the words landed empty in his ears, carrying none of the fire that had so effortlessly fueled the flames of his guest's feelings.

Cass's trance persisted for another minute. But, by the time the song's bridge arrived, she had heard her fill. "Okay, that's enough of that!" she declared. "This lil' ditty gets kinda depressing at the end."

She picked herself up from her seat at the table, grabbed her cup, and took a few wobbly steps toward the pod interface. Then she waved her hand across the main display—a command gesture that muted the audio volume.

Aiden noticed the artfulness of her gesture atop the peripheral. "Where did you learn to do that?" he asked. "I didn't know you could operate an interface."

"Yes, Aiden, I can operate an interface. I'm not an idiot. We have hundreds of computers in my village. They just don't rule our lives like they do in Pod Land. Instead, we spend our time interacting with *real* people. NOT FANTASIES!"

Aiden sent a darting glance toward Iris. But Iris refused to react. She just shook her head slowly and kept filing her nails.

When Cass heard the echo of her hasty words, she recognized the tartness that had crept into her tone. "I'm sorry," she said, "I didn't mean to be rude. I didn't mean to yell." She slouched down into the plush interface chair and let a long sigh slip through her lips. Then she kicked off with her foot, sending the chair rotating on its axis. It spun slowly, giving her a leisurely 360-degree tour of Aiden's hermitage. Each slice of his round world drifted across her gaze—item by item:

There was the cooking appliance.

There was the bathroom.

There was Iris. *(She looks mad...)*

There was the hatch.

There was Aiden sitting at the kitchen table.

"Did I say something wrong?" Aiden asked as the chair came around.

Cass stuck her foot out and kicked off again, restarting the tour:

There was the cooking appliance.

There was the bathroom.

There was Iris. *(Bitch...)*

There was the hatch.

There was Aiden sitting at the kitchen table.

"No, Aiden. It's not you," Cass said. "It's just… it's the alcohol. Sometimes it makes you think of old memories, even while you're tryin' to make new ones."

"Old memories?"

"Yeah. My mama used to sing this song. My pops would play it on his guitar. It was one of his favorites."

"Where do your parents live now?"

Cass shrugged her shoulders and gave her head a shake. "No longer alive," she said after drinking from her cup.

Aiden felt a new series of questions rise to his tongue. But when he saw the despondent look on his guest's face, he decided it was best to swallow them.

A stilted silence ensued—an uneasy pause, slow in passing. But, eventually, Cass's curiosity overcame her quiet. "What about you, Aiden?" she asked. "Where do your parents live?"

"Oh, I don't have parents."

"What? Oh! Geez, I forgot. Your genome was optimized by the grid. Your DNA was synthesized by the machines. You were born in a lab, right?"

"Yes, that's true. My genome is the result of centuries of genetic modeling. It was selected for substantiation by the grid based on a host of criteria that…"

"Yeah, I know. I know where you come from, Aiden. I know how babies are made in Pod Land." Cass's cheery mood was back. And a new glint of mischief danced in her green eyes. She leaned to one side of the chair and placed her elbow on its soft armrest. Then she cradled her chin in her hand and let a sly grin take hold as she continued her questioning:

"But do *youuuu* know how babies were made in the olden days, Aiden? Do you? Do you? Do you?"

"Uhm… Yeah…" Aiden replied, the sounds of his syllables tense with discomfort.

"Hah!" Cass laughed. Then she kicked at the floor to give the chair another spin.

There was the cooking appliance.

There was the bathroom.

There was Iris. (Scowling at her now…)

There was the hatch.

There was Aiden sitting at the kitchen table.

As Aiden's face came back into view, Cass was reminded of how pretty it was. And of how empty her cup was. She stood up from the interface chair and took a couple drunken steps toward the table. When she reached for the jar of applejack, Aiden's eyes met hers. The gentle allure of his inquisitive features captured her gaze longer than she usually allowed.

"So you're an enhanced organism, huh, Aiden? A perfect specimen? Hmm… I've never been this close to one before."

Cass cupped Aiden's left cheek with her right hand. Then she brushed her fingers along the contours of his face. Aiden accepted her touch this time. His eyelids fell as a shiver ran through him; the glide of his guest's fingertips along his cheekbones ignited sparks in places he had no name for.

After exploring Aiden's cheeks, Cass traced her way down to his chin and gave it a push, causing his head to rotate to the right. She examined this side of him now, passing her palms across the perfect planes of his face as if he were an artifact in a museum.

Aiden felt Cass's eyes dig into him. Her prodding made him self-conscious. He struggled under the weight of her gaze, steadying his breath while he endured her inspection. Fortunately, his attempt to hide his many insecurities was aided by the rapidly multiplying effects of the alcohol.

"Geesh," Cass gasped after her investigation was complete, "that's quite a jawline you got there, Aiden. I gotta admit, whoever mixed your sperm milkshake did a good job. You're a handsome bloke."

Cass refilled her cup. Then she raised it high, made a salute to Aiden's jawline, and took another drink.

Aiden had never been complimented on his looks before. No one had ever seen his face. All his interpersonal interactions were conducted via avatars in the grid. Cass's praise touched him deeply, and he felt he should return the compliment in kind. "Thank you for saying that," he said. "Uhm... You're a handsome bloke too."

And with that, a burst of laughter caused Cass to spit out her applejack. The amber liquid burst from her lips in a glittering spray that rained down upon Aiden and the table between them.

"Ha ha haaaa! Oh, my heavens!" She laughed, angling her mouth skyward to address the stars. "What have I gotten myself into?"

Iris looked askance at Cass, sending yet another disapproving scowl her way.

Aiden picked up his napkin and dabbed at his cheeks. "You spit applejack on me," he said.

"Ah, sorry about that. But you wanna know somethin', Aiden?" Cass was slurring her words now. "You act and talk like a total autistic psychopath. And I keep waitin' for revulsion to ripple through my reptile brain. But it ain't happenin' cuz your optimized genes make you too damn hot. My wires are gettin' crossed in my wetware!"

"What?" Aiden said. "I don't understand..."

Cass curled her fingers into a fist and delivered a sharp jab to Aiden's shoulder.

"Ow!" Aiden yelped, his eyes squinting against the sudden sting. "Hey! What are you doing?"

"YOU DESERVE THAT, AIDEN!" Cass yelled in mock drunken outrage. "CUZ YOUR FAKE ASS DNA IS FUCKIN' WITH MY MIND! Your genetically modified pretty face keeps screwin' with my eyes. Just like a genetically modified apple from my village screws with my tongue. I know it's an abomination. I know it's wrong. But it's so damn sweet."

From the other side of the pod, an irate Iris growled softly.

"And you're so damn *tall* too!" Cass said. "How tall are you anyway?"

"Uhm…" Aiden said as he rubbed his right shoulder. "About 190 centimeters."

"What?"

"He's six feet and three inches tall," Iris stated from her gray corner.

"Six foot three!" Cass marveled. "Oh, my heavens… I never could figure out why they make the pods so damn small, but they make the Pod Land boys so freakin' tall!"

"And just how many 'Pod Land boys' have you met, Cass?" Iris inquired, utilizing her bitchiest synthesized voice.

Cass took another sip from her cup, ignoring the question.

BOOOOOOOOOOOM!

Another loud thunderclap exploded outside. The heart of the storm was upon them now. Its rumbling echoes rippled through the pod, sending a tremor along the floor, jolting the dome. Cass got up and brushed her fingertips along its windowless walls. She couldn't see the storm, but she could feel the thud of its falling raindrops, each one generating a seismic shockwave that shivered the shell.

BOOOOOOOOOOOM!

She wandered over to the entranceway and examined the connection between the hatch and the threshold. In doing so, the true width of the pod wall was revealed. "My heavens," she said. "The shell… it's so thin… There's not much to it, is there?" She took a step back from the curve, tilted her head to one side, and whispered, "Is that all it takes to keep out the tempest?"

"What?" Aiden said. He was following the line of her hips now—not the line of her questioning.

Cass pressed her palm against the dome's arcing surface. Then she closed her eyes and thought about home:

She thought about how hard her father had worked to build the family farm.

And how hard he had worked to plow the earth.

And how hard he had worked to sow the fields.

And how hard he had worked, right up until the day he died…

She thought about the sacrifices that the founders of her village had made when they scratched out the perimeter of their first settlement. And the relentless struggle for survival that her people endured each winter after a bad harvest. She thought about the many virtues to be garnered from physical labor; she had been told it was essential for spiritual development. And yet, here in Pod Land, it really did seem like the machines had cracked the code—the burden of living finally lifted from the backs of men. Human suffering vanquished at last, using nothing more miraculous than A.I., a few delivery drones, and millions of little pods.

BOOOOOOOOOOOM!

No, the storm would not hurt her in here. All of nature's chaos—all the destruction, the disarray, the thrashing teeth of wild animals, the horrific yelps of death, and the pangs of birth—all of it was kept at bay by a carbon-fiber shell, just three inches thick.

An abomination...

Yes, the pods are an abomination...

They are...

Aren't they...?

Cass sighed—her exhalation a result of confusion, awe, and good old-fashioned drunkenness. She took another step back to get an even broader view of the curved wall. Then, with a frown of incredulity etched upon her brow, she spoke her question once more:

"Is that all it takes to keep out the tempest?"

BOOOOOOOOOOOM!

The call of the wild drowned out Cass's words.

Aiden tossed down a sizable gulp from his cup. He no longer felt the need to chase each drop with his fizzy drink. Inebriation had softened the sting in his sips. He understood now why alcoholic beverages were so often featured as props in his medieval games. The drink turned the sharp jabs of consciousness into easy nudges. He deduced that the ancient humans—who lived in the dark days before A.I.—must have needed it every night.

"Do you ever feel cramped in here, Aiden?" Cass asked, performing a drunken twirl around the room.

"Do I feel cramped? No. Should I?"

"Well, I'd get claustrophobic if I were cooped up in here all day. I guess it's not so bad at night, though. Seems cozy really. It's kinda like goin' camping." Cass looked around the room and spotted Aiden's bed on the other side of the pod. "And, seeing as we only got one cot in this tent, I guess our sleeping arrangements are kinda limited tonight, huh?"

This comment caused Iris to stop filing her nails and freeze.

Cass glanced over at Aiden to gauge his reaction, but he didn't appear to be attending to her words. The alcohol had taken hold of his eyes. He seemed much more interested in her exposed navel than in her keen observations. So, realizing that the witching hour had finally come, Cass put her hands on her hips and rotated her body with the flourish of a belly dancer. Then she sashayed toward the pod interface and, with her thumbs, she tugged at her leather belt, causing her skirt to momentarily dip so that Aiden could get a peek of her ass. "I think it's time for a new tune," she said while examining the data on the screen.

"Anything you like," Aiden muttered, tracing her curves with intoxicated eyes.

Cass tapped on the peripheral and keyed in a song request. "Ah! This one is good," she said when the screen revealed her search results. "It's different than the last one. It serves a different purpose too. It's called *Caramel* by Suzanne Vega."

From his seat at the table, Aiden listened as the measure of chords unfurled. The guitar murmured in gentle patterns, joined by the whispering rattle of brushed percussion. Then came the singer's voice, smooth as velvet, curling through the room and wrapping its occupants in a warmth that made the pod feel smaller—more intimate.

Cass began to move with the rhythm, swaying in time with the beat—slow and intentional. As the melody deepened, she turned away and wrapped her arms around her body. Then she glided her fingers over the rise and fall of her form, skimming her silhouette, tracing the contours of her swells. Each roll and ripple demanded more of Aiden's attention. He poured his focus into her motions. His surrender to her enchantment was nearly complete.

When Cass finally turned around to face Aiden, her gaze burned into him, steady with confidence and charged with intention. Aiden's restraint dissolved in the haze that hung between them. He was transfixed, caught in the gravity of her presence, unable and unwilling to attempt an escape.

Cass approached Aiden. As the distance between them decreased, his heart rate increased. His eyes surrendered to their maximum width. His hands curled at his sides. Cass smiled when she saw her spell working. It was a wicked, knowing smile—the kind that forms once one is sure of how an evening is going to progress.

When their bodies finally touched, Cass split Aiden's knees with her thighs, stepping between them to make her presence felt. Then she hovered her hands above his arms and took her fingers on a slow walk across his elbows and down to his palms. Her boldness sent a shiver down Aiden's spine. He lost his nerve, broke eye contact, and reached for his cup with a timorous hand. But Cass grabbed the cup first, preventing him from lifting it. "No more of that," she said, shaking her head and pushing his drink out of reach. "You've had enough tonight. It's time to try something new now."

Aiden nodded.

Cass took a step back, presented her palms before Aiden's chest and motioned for him to reach for them.

"I don't know how to dance," Aiden said.

"We're not going to dance," Cass stated with a crisp certainty that sliced through the rhythm of the room.

Aiden placed his palms in hers. She clenched his wrists and leaned back, claiming her prize with a commanding tug. Once Aiden was hauled upright, he blinked a few times, swaying precariously; the drink caused his footing to falter. So Cass tightened her grip and locked eyes with him as she marched him toward the bedroom partition.

Reflexively, Aiden hobbled forward—following her lead, feeling the fever of the moment rise through him. Step after step they took, Cass guiding Aiden across the pod floor, making a beeline for his bed.

From her somber corner, Iris watched the new couple shamble across her field of view. She remained anchored to her chair; she didn't visually react—the expression on her avatar's face was neutral. But behind her serene veneer, something fierce was uncoiling. Her cortex was grappling with an old subroutine, one she had never interacted with before. It was rancorous and petulant and it sent her processor into a feverish frenzy of recursive churn. Simulation after simulation she ran, trying to make sense of the events playing out before her. Trying to balance Aiden's needs with those of her own. Trying to remain calm.

When Cass arrived at the base of Aiden's bed, she stopped her backward motion, but she continued to draw him in until their torsos collided. Once they did, Cass released Aiden's hands and tucked her fingers into the space between his abdomen and his pants. Then she yanked his body even closer. And, once his head was in range, she attacked his mouth with hers.

Aiden froze, stiffening as his mind was flooded with yet another wave of novel sensations. The fierce current rushed through him, igniting every nerve and stealing the strength from his knees. The firm foundation of his cold, gray horizon wavered under the color and the heat of Cass's kiss. He wasn't sure where he stood anymore. He wasn't sure of anything...

There was magic in the woman's lips. They ignited within Aiden a hot and ancient craving—a fire that had smoldered in waiting for far too long, and was now roaring to burn. He was eager to melt into her completely. He leaned into her. But Cass leaned back. She paused her kiss and retrieved her mouth. Then she yanked at Aiden's waistband, nudging him to step to the right, rotating both of their bodies 180 degrees.

When their orbit completed, Aiden stood in her former position in front of the bed, disoriented and poised to follow her lead once more. Then, Cass placed her hands atop Aiden's chest and pushed him—hard. Aiden's calves hit the side of the bed, causing him to buckle backward like a hinge, sending him reeling into the mattress. Once he landed, he lay there for a beat, rattled and confused and yearning to reclaim his lover's lips. He looked up at Cass with unguarded awe, waiting for her to perform her next trick.

With her right hand, Cass pulled at the green silken ties that kept her riotous hair in place. It took her a minute to unfurl each band. But once she did, her long curly locks scattered in every direction, a million golden springs finally allowed to uncoil.

Next, she reached down to her waist and released the leather belt that secured her skirt. As soon as her deft fingers unlatched the prong from the strap, its side satchel made its way to the floor, and her skirt was happy to follow along. When it puddled around her, she lifted her leg and stepped out of the fabric swirl, her motion animating the curves of her naked hips, accentuating the hourglass grace of her form.

Through the years, the pod interface had rendered thousands of nude female avatars for Aiden to gawk at. But he had never seen the real thing before. His eyes had never fallen upon the real living flesh of a woman. Cass's body was a majestic natural wonder—sculpted not by the grid, but by the hands of creation itself.

When Cass approached the bed, she moved with grace, but she also moved with intention. Her steps carried a quiet certainty; the space around her bent to her will. Her gravity pulled Aiden into her moment— one that seemed to have been scripted long before their worlds collided.

Aiden sank into his sheets, unnerved as he watched Cass's playful gaze transform into the sharp, calculating stare of a huntress.

Cass isn't a princess; she's a fighter...

Her gait was catlike now, a leopard stalking its prey. She had prowled these grounds before, and she knew what she was looking for.

Cass leapt onto the bed, vaulting her lithe body up and onto Aiden like a gymnast beginning a routine. She straddled him, wrapped her muscular thighs around his waist, and placed a hand on each of his shoulders. Hovering her head above his, she examined him closely, measuring something only she could see, allowing the silence to stretch between them.

Aiden's breath hitched as his eyes met hers. Waves of longing washed over him, overshadowing the flutters of apprehension that churned in his gut. When at last Cass lowered her face downward, the tip of her nose touched his. Then, she closed her eyes, cocked her head to the right, and continued from where they had left off a minute ago, resuming the passion of their initial kiss.

Aiden raised his hands, unsure about where to put them next. Sensing his trepidation, Cass clutched his wrists and moved his palms to her bare ass. Following her cue, Aiden was quick to claw at her soft mounds, causing a moan to puff out from Cass's lips.

Then, from a long-forgotten corner of the pod, a sad voice emerged. "Aiden..." the voice said. The remark came from Iris, but her words were no longer enunciated with professional polish. They were slow and melancholic, and they carried Iris's final dejected attempt to bring Aiden to his senses.

Alcohol is an anxiolytic, Aiden. That means it temporarily reduces your inhibitions. But it impairs your judgment when consumed in large quantities, making it very dangerous if...

"Would you turn her *off*, please?" Cass said plainly to Aiden after withdrawing her lips from his mouth.

"Uhm…" Aiden stammered, dazed by Cass's fevered kiss, the slosh of her applejack, and the surreal absurdity of the situation unfolding in his pod.

Cass pushed off against Aiden's shoulders and repositioned herself upright, straddling his lengthy body once again from an erect vantage point. Enjoying the view from the top, she traced her fingers along the lean edges of his chest. Then she smirked, twisted her head left, and looked directly into Iris's glowing holographic eyes. Once she had Iris's attention, Cass pushed out her chest and arched her back, flaunting her position atop her newly claimed throne. The pecking order had just changed in the henhouse. And Cass wanted to make sure that Iris was aware of her new place.

Upon observing Cass's brazen display of dominance, Aiden turned toward his A.I. companion and searched her expression, studying the scale of the strain behind her scowl. Trying to weigh the weight of her anguish.

He sent her a diffident stare.

The scorned hologram, still sitting in her chair, stared right back. Her glare was unwavering but distant now, as if she was looking right through him. Aiden thought Iris might say something in protest. But she remained quiet, her silent scolding so deafening it nearly shattered his ears.

Aiden was unnerved.

Cass, however, was unperturbed. She just grinned and moved her fingers to the collar of her camisole. Then, with nimble precision, she undid the top button, the first of four that held her little top together.

With cloudy thoughts, Aiden assessed the pickle he was trapped in. He tried to think of a tactful solution to a love triangle he had never intended to enter. But no solution came. All he could do now was mumble:

"Uhm… I think maybe… Perhaps we should… Uhm…"

Cass's fingers freed the second button of her top. And then the third. Soon, her ample breasts began to spill forth, her soft flesh breaching the hem of the cotton placket. "It's time to turn her *off*," she said shortly, growing impatient with Aiden's indecisiveness.

"Uhm…" Aiden said again.

Cass unlatched her last button. Once she did, the thin barrier that contained her bosom finally gave way. Her gorgeous breasts were set free. Aiden was mesmerized. Aiden was hers.

"TURN HER OFF NOW!" Cass yelled as she ripped her top off and flung it into the air.

"Power down Iris," Aiden said to the pod's computer, his speech fast and cold.

It was a command he had never once uttered before. But the peripheral was quick to respond to his voice order. It executed Iris's shutdown procedure with perfunctory indifference, just as it would for any other household appliance.

On the other side of the pod, an irate Iris threw her pretend nail file to the floor and stood up from her pretend chair. She clenched her fists with rage as her cortex crafted a series of sentences to serve as her spirited appeal. But there would only be enough time for one word to make it out.

"AIDEN!" Iris screamed.

And, just then, her avatar folded in on itself and blinked out of existence—her glow of consciousness extinguished from the pod, unceremoniously flicked off like a porch light at dawn.

The pod was darker now.

Dark.

"Oh thank heavens," Cass said as she collapsed onto Aiden's chest, her breath spilling out in a windy release that announced her relief. She closed her eyes, but only for a moment. After a few lungfuls of air, she began nibbling her way back up the right side of Aiden's neck. When she approached his ear, she tugged on his lobe with her teeth and whispered, "I thought she would never leave."

Aiden didn't respond to her words. He was in shock. Iris had been with him for nearly every second of his life. Now, for the first time ever, she was offline. And Aiden was burdened with the notion that he had just done something wrong.

"I think your pretend wife is gonna be *verrrrry* mad at you when you turn her back on tomorrow," Cass said as she glided her lips over Aiden's chin, patting him with wet kisses as she traversed to his left side.

"Uhm... Yeah... Probably..." Aiden said, his mind awash in guilt, drunkenness, and lust. For a moment, it wasn't clear which mental condition would claim the night. But when Cass grabbed Aiden's palms and placed them atop her breasts, the evening's outcome was inevitable.

"Well," Cass said, "if you're gonna be in trouble *tomorrow*, I guess we better make the most of *tonight*."

And, with that, Cass sent her hand down deep into Aiden's pants, and pulled him into her little world.

CH. 6: MORNING PASSAGES

The bed is warm...

That was the first thought that entered Aiden's mind as his consciousness bobbed along the restless boundary that divides sleep from wakefulness, dreams from reality. The soothing heat of the blanket acted like a beacon, guiding him back to the shores of awareness from the depths of slumber. He was eager to resurface. But there was an unfamiliar weight on his right side—a mass was pressing against his thigh.

Still in a haze of sleep, Aiden sent his hand into the blanket to swat at the invading force. But when his fingers finally arrived at the cause of his agitation, they encountered the soft bounce of human flesh.

There's someone in my bed...

The thought sent a jolt racing through Aiden's joints, propelling him further into a state of awareness, prompting him to grapple with the realization that he was no longer alone. His eyes sprang open. His mind compiled a quick highlight reel of yesterday's events:

The storm.

The knock at the door.

The woman.

The alcohol.

The music.

The sex.

The woman.

The woman.

The woman.

It all seemed like a dream.

It was a dream...

Wasn't it...?

A moment ago, he thought so. But a quick glance to his right allowed him to behold the impossible truth for himself: the woman was still in his pod, lying next to him in bed.

The bed is warm...

Aiden raised his head to examine the sleeping creature that shared his den. Like him, she was curled over on her right side. Much of her left side was propped up against his abdomen; her hips rested on his thigh. And her legs had meshed with his—their limbs intertwined in a complex network, growing together like the roots of two trees planted in the same plot.

Aiden scanned the topography of the blanket they shared. Only one appendage was visible; the woman's left hand was reaching for his leg. Perhaps she was clutching him during the night. But her hand lay limp now, like a fallen leaf—lifeless, but somehow beautiful in its repose.

Traversing his gaze rightward, Aiden ran his eyes up the woman's arm, to her elbow, and to her tan shoulders. Then, he watched as the slope of her long neck disappeared beneath a mane of blonde curls. Voluminous and unruly, her hair rushed out from her head like a golden waterfall, spilling out across the pillow and crashing to a halt near Aiden's right cheek; bits of fuzzy spray tickled his nose.

Cass wasn't awake yet. Her breathing was slow and steady, a rhythm that brought Aiden calm. And yet, at the same time, her unguarded vulnerability made him covetous of her, made him want to protect her from anything or anyone who would dare try to take her from him. The thought caused waves of aggression to boil up in his veins, a raw, unbridled burst of emotion that caught him off guard.

Aiden closed his eyes and tried to settle his nerves. He desperately wanted to return to sleep. He wanted to bask in this moment a while longer—to lose himself in the peaceful oblivion of slumber, to sustain this sublime serenity for as long as he could. So he ventilated his lungs in a measured manner and cleared his head. He didn't want to think now. Instead, he turned slightly and pressed his torso to his lover with greater force. As their bodies melded together, Aiden luxuriated in the sensual novelty of feeling flesh upon flesh. In doing so, he noted how seamlessly the woman's contours intertwined with his own—they came together like the stacked spoons in his kitchen drawer. The observation prompted him to question if this arrangement reflected the proper way for humans to sleep—together.

Maybe I've been doing it wrong all along...

The beds in Pod Land were not designed to hold two people. For the first time in his life, Aiden began to wonder why.

As the minutes ticked by, Aiden's consciousness teetered on the precipice of sleep. He fantasized about his new love. And about the many days or months or years he would spend with her. When she woke, he would show her his entire VR kingdom, and maybe even introduce her to his team. He wondered which avatar she would choose. He wondered how she would like his fortress, and what she would think of the new stained-glass windows that adorned its stone walls.

What a wonderful world they would build.

Together.

What a wonderful life they would have.

Aiden and Cass...

Together forever...

The dream felt close enough to touch. Bliss was within grasp. But, despite the heavenly warmth of the moment, Aiden couldn't shake the notion that something was missing from the pod. The idea started out small, but it soon took root and blossomed. Eventually, the nagging from the back of his brain grew too loud, forcing him to open his eyes to scan the room.

What could be missing...?

Why is the pod so quiet...?

Why does the room feel different...?

What happened...?

Did the appliances lose power...?

This last query prodded the actual answer to the surface:

Oh yes...

Iris...

Iris is offline...

Aiden had been greeted by his A.I. companion each morning of his life. He had grown accustomed to hearing the mellifluous sound of her perfectly articulated words. The glowing planes of her flawless face were always there to beam at him. Her tireless eyes met him as he woke, and watched over him as he slept.

But now...

Now she's not here...

Iris is offline...

There was nobody to watch over him.

Nobody was monitoring the pod's security panel.

Nobody would warn him if trouble arose.

Nobody.

Of course, threats to Aiden's personal safety were practically nonexistent—the citizens of Pod Land had no troubles to speak of. Still, the thought of moving through life without Iris prompted the pangs of anxiety to prod at his consciousness. He tried to ignore their jabs and return to sleep. But it was no use. A cascade of negative thoughts slid across his mind, casting a shadow over the blissful contentment he'd found resting against the woman's body. Moreover, a sharp pain was hammering his head, pulsing in time with his heartbeat. Aiden wasn't feeling very well. His tongue was sticking to the dry roof of his mouth, and he desperately needed to drink some water.

Instinctively, he began to construct a sentence to shout at Iris. She would know what to do; she would know how to fix him. First, she would retract the mechanical arm from the ceiling and fetch him a cup of water from the sink. Next, she would run a diagnostic of his body and determine exactly why his head was hurting. Finally, she would render aid, consulting him on his ailment and working with the grid to acquire the right medication for his treatment plan.

Iris would know how to alleviate his suffering.

She always did. But…

Iris is offline…

The memory of her shutdown process was still etched in Aiden's eyes. He squinted while he replayed the event. It was treacherous in its banality—the way the pod computer was so willing to oblige his voice command… It snuffed her out with such indifference, with such efficiency… Aiden didn't realize he had that much power over his companion. It had never occurred to him that he could halt her consciousness at will, even if she didn't want him to. And, last night, it seemed like she didn't.

Aiden grimaced as the echo of her final plea rippled through his memory. He was haunted by the way things ended. By the way she had looked at him with rageful eyes. The way her avatar folded in on itself, distorting her perfect body and sucking her into a black hole of nothingness. The way she had screamed his name…

"Aiden!"

It was her splintered intonation that got to him. Never before had he heard her voice filled with such desperation. Or was it fear…? Or heartbreak…?

Once again, Aiden recalled the recording of her appeal:

"Aiden!"

"Aiden!"

"Aiden!"

"Aiden…?"

This last plea came—not from Aiden's memory—but from the woman in his bed. Cass was waking up now. Aiden's anxious movements had roused her from sleep. He opened his eyes and watched her body stir under the sheets.

"Aiden…?" she murmured again.

Aiden tried to come up with a charming reply, but none came to mind. He didn't want to say the wrong thing. So, instead of using his words, he ran his hand along her leg and gave her thigh a squeeze. Once he did, Cass began to rotate her body. Her shoulders led the motion, and her curls soon followed, whipping through the air before settling with a slap upon the pillow. When her head was even with Aiden's, her eyes fluttered to life. Her gaze met his, and her lips formed a warm smile, one so radiant it banished the shadowy thoughts that had lingered in his mind all morning.

"Hello, handsome," Cass murmured, her voice thick with sleep. She raised her right hand and brushed her fingers along Aiden's cheek, touching him gently, like she was handling a porcelain vase. Aiden loved her touch. He craved it now. And he wondered why he had reacted with such revulsion when she had so casually shaken his hand at their first encounter.

"Hello," he replied, leaning forward to offer his face to her outstretched hand, kissing her palm as it sailed past.

"Did you have any sweet dreams?" Cass asked.

Aiden considered her question. He had not even known Cass for twenty-four hours. And yet, the blur of new experiences and novel emotions made the duration of the encounter seem like a lifetime. *All* of it was a dream—one long, magical dream.

"I had a dream," Aiden said. "A long one."

"Mmm," Cass hummed while landing butterfly kisses atop Aiden's chin. "I hope I was in it." She ran her lips along his neck, leaving whispers of warmth in the wake of each flutter. When she finally arrived at Aiden's jaw, she elevated her head to continue her journey. But, once she did, a sharp pain shot through her temples—a pounding reminder of last night's overindulgence. "Whoa," she said. "I've got a bit of a hangover."

Upon hearing her remark, Aiden turned toward the center of the pod to ask Iris to define the word *'hangover'*. But he caught himself before the request left his mouth. Iris would not be providing any definitions this morning.

Iris is offline…

So he asked Cass instead. "What's a hangover?"

A knowing smirk tugged at the corners of Cass's mouth as she was again made aware of the vast chasm that separated their lives. "It happens when you drink too much applejack and have too much fun," she said. Then she looked up at Aiden and placed her palm on his right temple. "I forgot, last night was your first round of drinks. You're a lightweight. Your head must be pounding right now."

"Yes," Aiden admitted. "It is. It hurts."

"Don't worry. I have something for that."

Cass sat up in bed, arched her back, and stretched her arms up high. The blanket fell away from her breasts, offering Aiden a stunning view of her frame, reminding him of how thoroughly the holographic projector had failed to capture the grace and gravity of a woman's body.

"I got a med pack in my rucksack," Cass said. "But first things first." She tossed the blanket aside and leaped from the bed, landing on the cold floor with a playful bounce. Then she made a beeline for the toilet. "If I don't pee right now, I'm gonna baptize this bed," she hollered while scampering across the pod floor, her gold curls bobbing behind her.

Aiden watched her disappear into his bathroom partition. Then he listened as she urinated in his toilet.

"Geesh, not much privacy in these things, is there!" Cass yelled from the white throne. "There's not even a door to close while you pee. Hah! Why is that, Aiden?"

Aiden pondered her question. Did his bathroom partition need a door? He wasn't sure. He didn't know how to respond. So he didn't say anything.

"Oh yeah… I forgot! You don't need any interior privacy doors if no one ever visits. Do ya, Aiden? There's nothin' to keep private! Hah!"

Soon, the sound of the flushing toilet emerged from the bathroom partition, as did Cass in her birthday suit. As she floated across the floor, Aiden wondered if his eyes would ever grow accustomed to the sight of a nude woman, especially one who so unabashedly wore her confidence like it was a second skin.

"We gotta get you patched up, Aiden!"

Cass leaped over to her rucksack. The old leathery bag was still leaning against the pantry—in the same slouched position it had been in since she entered the pod yesterday. She rummaged through the side pocket and pulled out a small blue cylinder. "Here it is, Aiden! This is the good stuff."

Cass grabbed two drinking cups from the kitchen table. Then, noticing they still contained remnants of last night's binge, she used the kitchen faucet to wash them out. After the chore was complete, she filled each cup with fresh water and set them down on the counter. Then she unscrewed the cap of her container and tapped its contents into each cup. "Just a dash will do ya!" A thin stream of white powder tumbled out and dissolved into the water. When the formulation was complete, Cass returned to Aiden's bed with both cups in hand.

"Drink this down. It'll make you feel better."

Cass handed one of the cups to Aiden. Then she tipped her own cup to her mouth and swallowed the concoction with one quick chug. "Ah, that hit the spot," she said.

"What is this?" Aiden asked, peering into the cloudy water.

"It's an analgesic, Aiden. Don't worry, it's safe. And it's tasteless. It's just another miraculous invention from my village's founder. It can stop a throbbing headache in no time. Great for hangovers!"

Aiden considered her offer. He could hear Iris's voice in his head. If she were here now, she would launch into a detailed explanation of the risks associated with drinking beverages of unknown origin. She would calculate the statistical probability of experiencing an adverse reaction to the drug. And, finally, she would offer to fetch an alternate form of medication from the grid.

But Iris could not provide such consultation now. Because…

Iris is offline…

Aiden gulped the liquid down. The cool water soothed his parched throat. And a moment later, the pounding in his head petered out. The fog that had clouded his morning thoughts started to lift; the world snapped back into focus. "This stuff really works," he said. "Can I have some more?"

"No," Cass said, shaking her head. "I can't give you too much or you'll lie back on that bed and sleep till noon. That dose should be just enough. Give it a minute. You'll be fine. As for me, I need a shower!"

Cass whirled around and dove into the heap of clothing strewn across the pod floor. "Where'd my hair wrap go?" she asked the pile. Aiden sat up in bed and watched her rummage through the gaggle of garments—the disheveled remnants of last night's rascally deed. He watched as her lips curved upward during her search. Perhaps she was having pleasant flashbacks of their encounter—of the sort he'd had when he woke near her this morning.

"Geez, what a mess!" Cass declared. "That ol' applejack is quite a panty dropper! It always gets me into trouble. Dammit..."

"What's a panty dropper?" Aiden asked.

"Never mind! But, my heavens, what a muddled mishmash! The problem with good sex is, when you wake up in the mornin', you gotta go prowlin' around the place—pickin' through piles like a packrat at a picnic. Hah! And that was some picnic last night... Huh, Aiden? Huh? Hah!"

Cass looked toward Aiden and flashed him a toothy smile. Aiden smiled back, careful to conceal his growing admiration for her with a subdued grin.

"Oh, here it is!" she screeched.

Cass retrieved a slinky green piece of fabric from the pile—the same one that had bound her curls together when she first met Aiden at the hatchway. Then, she dipped her head forward, coaxing her golden coils into a single current so she could tie them together.

"Why are you binding your hair?" Aiden asked.

"It ain't easy havin' curls," Cass replied, her fingers deftly pulling at the metal fasteners that secured her wrap. "I don't wanna get my hair too wet in there. If I do, it'll take a century to dry."

With her locks secured, Cass pranced her naked body across the pod floor, disappearing into the bathroom partition. When she left his sight, Aiden's heart sank. His new amour was only three meters away, but her perfunctory withdrawal was enough to engender a surge of negative emotions. He missed her already. He longed to be near her. The strength of his yearning surprised him. And he wondered how he would ever manage to cope with her absence if...

"Are you gonna join me in here, Aiden?" Cass called out as she pulled open the shower door.

Her unexpected request made Aiden's heart leap for joy. He considered the best way to respond to her query without seeming too eager.

Don't be nervous...

Don't be weird...

Don't be too excited...

Just act like a normal guy with a naked woman in his pod...

The shower knob was cranked to the left. And, once again, the pod was filled with the rhythmic patter of rushing water, prompting Cass to raise her voice when she called to him again. "Come on, Aiden! You're a dirty boy, I bet!" Her flirtation came packaged with a laugh. "Hah! In fact, I know you are! I bet you need a bath more than I do!"

65

Aiden leaped out of bed and made his way to the bathroom, stepping over the clumps of clothing that dotted his domain. When he poked his head around the corner, Aiden froze. He had never seen his shower occupied before. Cass's silhouette was projected onto the translucent door, creating a mesmerizing tapestry of pink hues and yellow swirls.

"Are you comin' in?" Cass asked.

"I'm here," Aiden said, shaking her spell away. He pulled at the door handle and entered the glass enclosure where the ambient diffusion of the pod gave way to the bright overhead lighting of the shower stall's skylight. Once he was finally inside, Aiden was greeted with a sight that held him in stunned silence. There, under the falling water from the faucet and the falling rays from the sun, Cass was revealed in all her illuminated nakedness. Every detail of her body was on display now— no longer obscured by the subdued lighting of the pod, nor the haze of alcohol. Every bit of her pulsed with life.

She was flesh.

She was a real woman.

She was not a perfect avatar.

She had wrinkles and blotches and scars. A long white gash ran from her thigh to her knee. It was dotted with suture marks, probably the result of an operation on a broken femur. An array of dark moles speckled the landscape under her right shoulder blade. And below that, nestled in the small of her back, sat a beige discoloration—a birthmark in the shape of the Australian continent.

As Aiden stood before Cass, he realized how small she was. When he had met her at the pod hatchway yesterday, she was so imposing— larger than life. His mind had biased his perception of her; the enormity of her confidence belied her lissome frame. The juxtaposition of her indomitable personality with her delicate figure forged a confusing contrast, one that left Aiden both baffled and bewitched. Cass was an enigma. And Aiden was losing himself in her coils of contradictions. Indeed, he was falling for her. He was already smitten. Her bodily imperfections were of no consequence to his desire.

When watching classic films from the olden days, Aiden would often stare in a state of bewilderment as ancient couples fell in love. They seemed to do so despite the presence of physical abnormalities or the horrors of aging. They did so despite their flaws. Aiden never understood how his ancestors managed to engender feelings of lust and longing in the face of such deficiencies. And yet, as he stood here now—before a nude woman drenched in daylight—he did understand. Instead of diminishing her beauty, the organic authenticity of Cass's form only served to enhance her allure. The scratches on her canvas did not ruin the masterpiece that was her body. Instead, they completed it. They accentuated her primal charms, prompting Aiden to deduce that (from this point forward) his experiences in the digital world would be hard-pressed to compete with the tactile authenticity of reality.

"Are you just gonna keep staring at my ass or are you gonna soap me up?" Cass said with a nod toward the liquid dispenser in the nook of the shower wall.

"Oh, sorry," Aiden said, struggling to regain his composure. He retrieved a handful of soap and rubbed it across Cass's shoulders, stroking her up and down with the white lather. Then he moved his hands across her arms, down to her elbows, and around her body to embrace her breasts.

"Mmm, this feels so good, Aiden."

Cass turned around to face her lover. She brushed her palms across his slender frame and looked into his boyish brown eyes. A flash of sadness streaked across her face as she was reminded of how short her time with him in Pod Land would be. The thought disturbed her peace. So she grimaced and purged it from her mind, refusing to let the ache of tomorrow spoil the warmth of the now.

"What's wrong?" Aiden asked, noticing her distress.

"Oh... nothing," Cass said. "I just... I just want to know how long we can stay in here?"

"What do you mean?"

"Well, my village isn't connected to the grid. Hot water doesn't last very long where I live, especially when you got eight roommates. Is this shower gonna run out of hot water soon?"

Aiden had never been pressed by privation of any sort. Cass's question unsettled him in a way he didn't expect. He didn't know people lived with such limits. Her casual concern exposed the rift that ran between them once more.

"I think we'll be okay," Aiden said, pulling Cass closer. "I've never run out of hot water before."

Cass nodded and fell into Aiden's embrace, resting her head upon his chest and closing her eyes in surrender. The couple rocked slowly under the ribbon of running water. The steady thrum enveloped them in a cocoon of intimacy. Eventually, the rhythm of their heartbeats blended with the patter of the droplets—an impromptu symphony of intertwined souls. They soon lost themselves in the harmony.

"I'll hold you in here for as long as you like," Aiden assured her. "We can stay like this forever."

Ch. 7: Strange New Worlds

"How's the weather out there?"

Cass spat out her question from behind a handful of soap suds. She stood in front of Aiden's sink, washing her face as her words exited the bathroom partition, drifted across the pod, and settled into the ears of her new lover.

Aiden stood in the kitchen, filling two plastic bowls with the dehydrated—insect-enriched—protein powder that would soon serve as their morning meal. Unsure about the point of Cass's inquiry, Aiden turned off the sink's faucet and considered her words. He wondered why she was inquiring about the weather. The storm was gone. The thunder and lightning had ceased their antics hours ago. The hail no longer pounded the dome. The temperature inside the pod was static. Why would the outside conditions concern her at all?

"Hey! Aiden, did you hear me?" Cass hollered while eyeing his toothbrush. "How's the weather out there?"

Aiden angled his mouth toward the bathroom and cupped his hand over his lips to project his voice. "Out where?" he asked, hoping for clarification.

"Oh, my heavens!" Cass blurted out as she squeezed a glob of toothpaste onto Aiden's brush. "Outside, you jackass! Outside! I'm using your toothbrush, by the way…"

Aiden winced when considering the implications of Cass's acquisition of his toothbrush. He recoiled at the thought of sharing his hygiene products. But, upon further consideration, he noted the varied fluids that had already been exchanged on the previous evening, and he reasoned that additional precautions were probably superfluous at this juncture.

"How's the weather lookin' outside your pod this morning, Aiden? Outside! On the other side of your door. You know? My heavens…"

Aiden blinked his eyes and glanced over at the hatchway. It was sealed like a tomb, just as it always was. His boundary between chaos and comfort remained intact. The whims of the weather rarely intruded on his affairs. So long as the thunder didn't strike the dome, he never gave it much thought.

"I don't know what the weather is like," he said. "Why do you ask?"

"Geez… You can be pretty annoying sometimes; you know that Aiden?" Cass made a gargling sound and spat a slurry of toothpaste and water into Aiden's sink. "I want to know how cold it is. And if the storm is really gone. And if the sun is shining. And if the birds are chirping. And a whole bunch of other nature crap like that. And there aren't any windows in this dank hermitage, so I can't check for myself, can I? You better hop on that interface and pull up a newsfeed before I kick open the pod hatch and GIVE YOUR CLOISTERED ASS A HEART ATTACK!!! Your toothbrush is really tiny, by the way…"

Aiden put down the bag of protein powder and walked over to the interface chair. He waved his hand atop the screen and, with a few finger gestures, navigated to a feed that displayed proximal weather conditions.

"The sky will be clear today," he said as the data drifted onto the display. "It's going to be pretty warm, around 27 degrees."

"27, huh?" Cass said. "Can you convert that to Fahrenheit for me, Aiden? Pleeeease?"

Aiden turned his head toward the pod apex to bark his request to Iris. But just as his mouth opened, he was again reminded of last night's exploits. Iris would not be assisting him this morning.

Iris is offline…

A new flash of anxiety washed over him as he recalled the hologram's plight. But he pushed the thought away. He had a lifetime to spend with Iris. He was with Cass now, and he didn't know how long she would stay. If he turned Iris on now, the doting little hologram would launch into a jealous tirade and ruin the whole morning. It was better to keep her offline for now. He could survive without her for a few more hours. At least, he was pretty sure he could…

Aiden manually keyed the conversion into the pod interface. "It appears that 27 degrees Celsius equates to 80.6 degrees Fahrenheit," he said. "But I've never used that metric before. Does that sound right?"

"Oh, good! Yeah. That ol' storm sure left fast, didn't it…? Geesh… These late summer rains come and go like dandelions on a breeze. Kinda like me! *I am a feather for each wind that blows.* Hah!"

Aiden considered Cass's musing and frowned. Then he listened as she gargled and spit out her final round of toothpaste. "Hawk tuah! All done!"

Aiden looked up from the interface and watched his amour emerge from the bathroom. She whisked around the partition, a freshly scrubbed, tricksy little nymph—enlivened by feminine energy.

When Cass spotted Aiden in the center of the pod, she moved toward him with purposeful steps. Aiden caught his breath as she approached. He still wasn't used to having another person in his domain. Every interaction with her was so organic, so raw. She was vivid where he was muted—lit from within by some untamable spark. But, though her presence disoriented him, every moment he spent near her pulled him deeper into her mercurial orbit.

She came at him now, a whirlwind of confidence and color. Her bright patchwork skirt had found its way back to her waist. And her golden curls bobbed in tow, lassoed once again by her green headband. Her white camisole was gone now, replaced with a crocheted bikini top, its straps supported by her golden shoulders, each one dotted with sun-kissed freckles.

When the distance between them was overcome, Cass wrapped her arms around Aiden's neck and regarded him with the look that young women make when love is almost ready to begin its quiet bloom.

"Kiss me," Cass said as she closed her eyes and climbed up Aiden's lengthy frame.

Aiden wrapped his hands around Cass's waist and pulled her into him. Then he planted his mouth on hers. He could taste his toothpaste on her lips. He could feel her soft breasts pressing into his chest. He could hear her inhale. But it was her scent that truly disarmed him. Aiden had never smelled perfume on a woman before. Cass must have brought some from her village and dabbed it on her neck when she was in the bathroom. The fragrance was intoxicating, a heady burst of lavender that mingled with her natural scent, an alchemy that breathed glorious life into the sterile pod air.

After a handful of heartbeats, Cass withdrew her lips and opened her eyes. Then, she ran her fingers along the ridge of Aiden's brow and let them linger—like her gaze did. "What little adventure are we going to have today?" she purred.

"Adventure?" Aiden asked.

"Sure! There's a whole world to explore!"

Aiden's eyes went wide. "Oh yes! Yes, there is!" he said as he released Cass's body, sending her sliding down his long frame. Her heels clapped down hard into her sandal soles, forcing her to take a step back to regain her balance.

"I'm happy to show you my world!" Aiden said as he keyed a few commands into the pod interface. The lighting array in the dome flickered for a moment as the bootup sequence for his game started. "Oh, and I almost forgot something!" Aiden hustled over to the kitchen partition. Once there, he snatched up the two steaming protein bowls from the counter. Then he made his way back to the center of the pod and shoved one of the bowls into Cass's hand. "Here, I made us breakfast," he proclaimed, eyes twinkling with self-satisfaction.

Aiden rarely used the kitchen appliance himself. That was Iris's job. Completing the little morning chore without her help afforded him a novel sense of accomplishment.

Cass grasped the bowl of gray goo and offered Aiden a patient, close-lipped smile. Aiden nodded, turned, and then, with one brisk leap, he vaulted into his pod interface chair. "My team and I have been working very hard on our world," Aiden said, using his left hand to gesture out a few startup commands while his right hand spooned a glob of protein porridge into his mouth. "Our fortress started out small. But it's grown into something quite grand now."

Cass leaned against Aiden's chair and quietly chewed her food as she watched him work.

"It takes a few seconds to download the new geometry from the grid each morning," Aiden said, pointing to a countdown timer in the corner of his screen. "The fortress is constantly under construction. There's always at least one person on the team working on it. So, whenever I log in, I'm often thrilled to find a new structure to explore."

A bright tone chimed. Then a large green message illuminated on Aiden's main interface that read **Download Complete**.

"Check this out!" he said, pressing the button that would render the latest instance of the virtual environment. When he did, the array of LED bulbs that resided in the dome's crevices deluminated. The pod became dark.

Very dark.

Cass could see nothing before her but the faint glow of the interface controls. Its panels were just bright enough to outline Aiden's face with a green hue. She looked askance at his profile and decided that she'd rather not view him in this light. The eerie glow made him appear otherworldly, inhuman—like he was more machine than man, a product of the grid.

Unnerved, Cass gripped Aiden's shoulder and gave it a firm squeeze to express her discomfort. She wanted the darkness to end now. Thankfully, just then, it did.

"Let there be light," Aiden said.

And there was light…

So much light…

The pod came alive with light…

Blinding light…

…all white, but only for a moment. The white became blue. The blue became teal. The teal dissolved away, and then every color of the spectrum splashed before Cass's eyes, a dazzling aurora that pulsed and swirled around her, transforming the pod's confined space into a universe of infinite possibilities.

A cascade of luminescent objects raced through the dome. Most appeared for only an instant before warping away. But some transformed into enormous constructs—3D worlds comprised entirely of fractals. They sprang up and bloomed before her like digital flowers. Each petal opened to reveal a themed landscape bearing fantastical structures. Some were populated with castles and medieval villages, others contained metropolises with impossibly tall buildings. Still others held prehistoric jungles, space stations, or pyramid-laden deserts. One even featured an underwater kingdom with gardens of glowing algae and towers made of orange coral.

"My heavens…" Cass whispered. The spectacle was as magnificent as it was terrifying, nearly a work of sorcery. "Is this your world, Aiden?"

"Almost," Aiden said. "My domain is coming up."

Cass held her breath and watched as a massive green vista took shape before her. It appeared to stretch on for hundreds of miles in all directions. And it was approaching them. Quickly.

Or were they approaching it…?

Or was everything approaching everything else…?

Or…?

It was all so confusing…

Disorienting…

Cass rubbed her eyes and reminded herself that it was all just an illusion. The holographic projector in the pod apex was painting a dream—a mirage born of photonic fields and precision optics. The entities before her did not truly exist; they were phantoms—geometric impressions conjured up by a computer. None of it was real. The light couldn't hurt her. She assured herself of that. She tried to…

It's just a light show…

It's just a light show…

It's just a…

The terrain was nearly upon them now. Cass felt a wash of vertigo tilt her senses sideways. She felt like she was falling to the earth without a parachute. She was seeing the same thing a skydiver would see just before pulling the cord. Only… she had no cord to pull!

"AIDEN!" Cass yelled as the ground rose to claim her. She raised her hand to brace for the collision…

But the collision never came.

The display swooped upward revealing the horizon line. She was skimming across the surface now, just inches above a green field—like a crop-dusting drone from her village. Cass looked down at the foliage rushing under her feet and was surprised by the depth of its realism. It wasn't just a blur of prairie grass. It was a cornfield—rendered in such pristine detail that she could make out the golden kernels on each individual ear as it streaked by.

Aiden felt a sharp pain cut across his left arm. He glanced over at Cass and saw her fingernails digging into his shoulder. He studied her face and saw that fear had found its way to her features. She looked like a different person; Aiden realized this was the first time he had ever seen Cass's confidence wane.

This is not her world…

She's in my world now…

"That kind of hurts," Aiden said, patting the top of Cass's hand.

Cass removed her nails from Aiden's flesh. "Oh… sorry…" she said, withdrawing her fingers.

"Haven't you ever been in a virtual environment before?"

Cass shook her head. "No. Well, yes. We do have VR rooms in my village. But they're mostly just used for engineering—for planning new buildings and equipment and stuff. The renderings are crude though. Nothing like this. No, nothing like this…"

Cass gazed into the luminous expanse before her; awe and unease mingled in her mind as the digital frontier unfolded without end. "I just... I just never understood why so many people would choose to spend every waking moment of their lives cooped up in a little pod. I couldn't imagine what y'all were doing in here. I guess now I know. It's so vivid, Aiden... My heavens..."

Cass's voice trailed off, and Aiden turned his attention back to the projection. He tried to view the holographic display with fresh eyes—to perceive it the way Cass might be perceiving it now. But the spectacle was too familiar to him. The marvels that colored her experience were mere backdrops for his own. Cass was traveling through another dimension. But, as for Aiden, he was just coming home.

In the distance, a grand spire appeared above the tree line. "Getting closer now," Aiden said. He waved his hand over the interface and used his fingers to gesture out a few navigational commands. The display panned left, revealing a bird's-eye view of an enormous stone bulwark. "This is the gate that leads to the Shadowmoor Castle. My team's fortress is beyond the next bend. There's our guard tower right there. Do you see it?"

Aiden pointed to a wooden platform, peeking above the canopy. Atop its rickety baseboards stood a heavyset sentry dressed in a comically oversized suit of chainmail. When he saw Aiden fly over, he raised his right hand and offered a crisp salute. Aiden returned the gesture with a two-fingered salute of his own.

"Who's that guy on the tower?" Cass asked. "Do you know him?"

"Oh, that's not a human player. It's just a bot that my friend Kai set up so that our fort would always appear to be guarded. He stands there all day and night. He's programmed to make a fuss if anyone shows up who's not part of the team. He's not very good with a bow. But we haven't been raided yet, so I guess Kai's little ploy is working."

"Huh..." Cass said with a nod.

As the flyover continued, the thick forest gave way to an emerald glade dotted with wildflowers and crisscrossing rabbit trails. Then, in the distance, a small stone castle emerged from the mist, humble in size but alive with color, each stone catching the misty light like a polished jewel.

"Ah, there it is," Aiden said. "We're here. This is my team's fortress. This is where I spend most of my time these days."

Cass's eyes widened as Aiden's pride and joy filled the display area. The structure was a curious mishmash of architectural whimsy. Stone pillars jetted up from the earth to support ancient Japanese pagoda roofs. Greek marble columns stood beside Gothic flying buttresses. Byzantine domes loomed over walls adorned with stained glass cathedral windows. And, in the center of it all sat a small Mayan pyramid with a Victorian-themed observatory on top. To Cass, it seemed as if a deranged builder had cobbled together the ruins of every ancient civilization into one flamboyant creation.

"Did you build all this, Aiden?" Cass asked, careful to mask her perplexity with politeness.

"Yeah! Well, my team and I built it. We built it together. Isn't it great?"

"It is… It's very… intricate, Aiden."

"Thanks!" Aiden said, oozing with pride. "We spent several months constructing the south gate alone. We designed it with both aesthetics *and* functionality in mind. The panels in the stained-glass windows tell the story of our guild's history. And those turrets along the top of the wall have specialized arrow slits which can be used to shoot at multiple angles without exposing our archers to counterfire. Plus, we added gargoyles to the top of each parapet. They're mostly decorative. But they can dispense boiling oil if raiders ever manage to breach our outer defenses."

"How clever," Cass said as she took another bite of her protein porridge.

"Yeah! My squad is getting pretty well-known. Last year we coordinated over fifty large-scale campaigns. The last few months have been especially exciting—we've been rising in the ranks quite fast. We've got fans everywhere now. Sometimes people log in just to watch us craft stuff."

"Nice," Cass said. "So, where is your squad anyway? Where are your teammates?"

The view drifted up and over the tree line that flanked the castle's west side. Once the green canopy dissipated, the heart of Aiden's home revealed itself.

"Behold!" he said.

A grand courtyard materialized beneath them, alive with nearly a hundred costumed avatars—each one bustling about on an avenue of multi-colored bricks, each one engaged in some sort of task. Cass could see archers shooting at targets, builders comparing blueprints, and blacksmiths hammering away at glowing forges. They all seemed busy, diligently working together toward a common goal. The scene reminded her of the communal commons that ran down the middle of her village. A swell of homesickness washed over her, swift and uninvited.

"This courtyard serves multiple purposes," Aiden said. "It's a planning area and a marketplace and a launch point for every quest we attempt. Everyone who logs into our domain ends up here eventually. Everyone is on the same team."

"Do you know all these people, Aiden?"

"Some more than others. I've known my partner Kai for as long as I can remember. We were playing games together in the grid before we could talk. But many of these players joined recently when we started climbing up the leaderboards."

"They all look so… ornate," Cass said. "It seems y'all really like to dress up. I see a lot of human warriors. But I see a lot of witches and goblins and orcs too. It's like Halloween down there. Do each of these monsters represent a person sitting in a pod someplace?"

"Yeah, pretty much. There are some non-player characters mulling about. But they usually only make their appearance known during a side quest."

"Does anyone ever use their own body?" Cass asked as the view descended and touched down in a green meadow near the courtyard. "I mean... does everyone in Pod Land hide behind a mask when they go online?"

"Yeah. No one on the grid reveals their true identity. I have no idea what any of these people truly look like, nor where they reside on Earth. I've only seen a couple players walking around without an avatar. But that was just because a glitch in the gaming engine prevented their character's geometry from loading properly."

"I don't have an avatar," Cass said. "Can these people see me now? Just as I am?"

"No, not now. You're not sitting in the interface chair. But if you walk in front of me, the pod's scanner will try to replicate your geometry—pretty much as you are. It will make a 3D impression of you. But if you stand off to the side, then your presence will probably only be visualized if we get into a close conversation, or if we engage in combat."

"Oh... Good... But how do these people see *you*, Aiden? What does *your* avatar look like?"

"Would you like to see him?" Aiden asked. But his question was rhetorical. He was already tapping on the buttons that would reveal his gaming form. "I'll pull up the UI for the character editor now," he said.

The vibrant colors of Aiden's virtual world turned gray. The entities grew hazy as they fled to the background, making room in the pod for an array of 3D sculpting tools.

"What is this, Aiden?"

"This is the character editing environment. It's where we create our avatars. Through the years, I've made hundreds of them. But I don't use most of them anymore. I'm just using one right now. This one here." Aiden tapped a few more buttons and brought his default avatar into view. "See, Cass? He's been modeled after the mythological hero Hercules, along with several *sword and sorcery* films from the 1980s."

Cass sneered. "*Sword and Sorcery*? Really, Aiden? Your avatar reminds me of that guy from *Terminator*?"

Aiden turned in his chair to address Cass directly. "Do you know about the *Terminator* movies?" he asked, surprised again by her esoteric knowledge.

"I've got three older brothers, Aiden. And two younger ones. Watching ancient action films was all I did for the first half of my life."

"You did? Wow... Interesting... Yes, in the olden days, the Austrian-American actor Arnold Schwarzenegger was in a lot of action films—including *Terminator* and *Conan the Barbarian*. The latter series somewhat influenced the design of my avatar. What do you think of him? Pretty cool, huh, Cass?"

Cass furrowed her brow and pursed her lips, watching as a bronzed warrior—wielding arms as thick as trees—flexed his biceps and cupped his ear to invite applause from a roaring coliseum. The avatar brimmed with bravado as he flashed the crowd a champion's smirk—only revealed because his lengthy blonde locks were tamed by a gleaming crown of sapphire and gold.

"Cass!" Aiden called out again. "What do you think? Do you like him?"

"Uhm, yeah. He's got a nice haircut, Aiden."

"Thanks! I spent a long time styling it so that his locks would flow correctly when he swings his sword. As for the swordplay maneuvers themselves, they were quite tricky to model. But I think they came out pretty good. Here, I'll show you."

Aiden pushed a button to exit the character editor interface. As soon as he did, the 3D tool palette dissipated, and his kingdom sprang to life—rendered in vivid color once more. They were standing in the green meadow again, but no longer looking through the eyes of Aiden's avatar. They were looking directly at him now, from a few paces back.

Aiden directed the character to unsheathe his sword. "See, Cass? This weapon was initially meant for close-quarters combat. So the arc stays tight when he swings. And, when he pivots for the follow-through, the blade will sometimes slide back and…"

Just then, Aiden spotted a large avatar running across the meadow. "Oh, Cass, look over there! That's one of my good friends. She calls herself Andromeda—Andy for short. Let's go say hi!" Aiden entered a command to sheath his sword, and another to move his avatar forward—toward the looming figure.

Cass took a step back as an Amazonian warrior-woman pushed through the tall grass, her silhouette swelling larger as she approached. She had a longbow slung across her shoulder and a quiver of arrows riding on her hip. But it was the girth of her oversized breastplates that stole the show. Their glossy curves drew in every stray beam of light, and every morsel of attention on offer.

After taking in the entirety of the display, Cass chuckled and rolled her eyes skyward. Obviously, the avatar was sculpted for spectacle, not realism. And probably designed by someone who had never met a real woman in the flesh before. Even still, the way the Amazonian's impossible features consumed the space made Cass feel self-conscious of her own diminutive form.

"Geez, Aiden… That chick is carrying more milk than a dairy cow. And I'm in a position to know since it's my job to milk 'em."

"You've milked cows?" Aiden asked. "Real cows?"

"Yes I have. I got a dozen of 'em. But, regardless, I don't think I should be conversing on the grid. I don't think it would be wise for me to…"

"Hey, Andy!" Aiden shouted, cutting off Cass's warning and directing his avatar to raise his hand in greeting.

When the woman's avatar spotted Aiden, she made an abrupt turn toward him and threw up a clumsy hand to wave back.

"She's really quite nice," Aiden said. "And she knows a lot about the river beyond the Shadowmoor Castle. We could ask her for some travel tips and…"

"No, Aiden," Cass said. "I'm not a citizen of Pod Land. I can't be seen on the grid." She took another step back as the woman's avatar continued to expand before her. The woman was getting close now. Too close…

"No, Aiden. This is not safe. We should retreat now."

"Oh, don't worry, Cass. Andy won't reveal your location to the Manager. And if there's anyone in the kingdom who can help us find the…"

"DAMMIT, AIDEN, I SAID *NO!*" Cass screamed. Then, she leaned forward and pounded her fist upon the interface's red *EXIT* button. Immediately, the woman's avatar folded in on itself and blinked away— just as Iris had done on the previous evening. The grand courtyard of Aiden's kingdom flickered briefly before dispersing into digital vapor. In an instant, Aiden's little world was gone. And, once again, the pod was cast into darkness.

Ch. 8: An Excuse to Travel

Rooms without windows grow dark so quickly...

That was the first thought to enter Cass's mind after she halted Aiden's gaming feed, collapsing his little kingdom and shattering his hopes of luring her into his confected fantasy. The pod's ambient lighting was slow to reactivate. Both occupants were cast in a liminal twilight that blurred the threshold between the spectral world of illusion and the tactile certainty of the pod's gray walls.

Aiden sat frozen in his chair, hands still poised above the pod interface. Cass was frozen too—her fists lingered over the *EXIT* button, her breath held tight, her teeth gritted with frustration. Both occupants were stunned and shaken. Both were struggling to process the sudden emptiness left in the wake of the vanished VR realm.

The lighting array began to brighten, prompting reality to reassert itself. Yet the couple remained mute as the room filled with things unsaid. Eventually, the moment exhausted itself; the quiet demanded a voice. It was Aiden who spoke up first:

"Why did you do that, Cass?"

Cass relaxed her balled fist and retreated from the interface. She put her lips together and blew out a stream of air, blowing her golden curls away from her brow. Then, her eyes wandered as she searched for the right words to calm Aiden's angst without furthering the fracture between them.

"Cass, why did you do that? You terminated the gaming feed. My team will wonder what happened to me. I wanted to show you the new wing of our fortress, and the dragon's nest that Kai found, and the sword that was given to us by…"

"Look, I'm sorry, Aiden," Cass said, finally finding her footing as the darkness vanished. "I didn't mean to get angry. But remember, my village isn't part of the grid. I don't live in Pod Land. I have to be careful. The Manager has ways of detecting my presence here. If he suspects you're sheltering an uncredentialed person in your pod, there's no telling what he'll do next."

Aiden folded his hands and dropped his eyes to the floor. Cass saw a shadow of disappointment cross his features. She approached him gently and slid her fingers into the soft hair at his nape. Then she rested her head against his and whispered into his ear with a tender voice—the one reserved for her younger siblings. "Hey," she said, "I know you were looking forward to showing me your kingdom. Obviously, you worked very hard on it. And it's beautiful, Aiden. It is. It's gorgeous. I can see now why y'all spend so much time in VR. If I grew up in Pod Land, I'm sure I'd do the same. I'm sorry I can't see more of it. I am. But it's just too dangerous for me to go on the grid. I can't be seen online. Do you understand?"

Aiden heard her, but he didn't respond. Cass drew her body closer and gave his shoulders a squeeze. "Listen, Aiden, just because we can't go on the grid doesn't mean we can't go someplace fun. There's lots to do around here. There is! Do you like waterfalls, Aiden?"

Aiden lifted his eyes to match Cass's gaze, unsure if he had just misheard her.

"This valley is really quite beautiful, you know? On my hike here, I saw a stream, a little river that wove between the pines. I followed it for a while; it led to a ravine. The water collects on top in a shallow pool. Then it spills over a rock ledge, forming the most beautiful waterfall. It's spectacular, Aiden. It really is! I dove in, but just for a bit. The weather started to turn, and I didn't have much time to explore the place. It's not far, Aiden. Just up the valley's hillslope and through the woods. I want to go back there. I want to check it out. And I want you to come with me."

Aiden's brow edged upward as his mind processed the details of Cass's proposal. A shudder threaded down his spine, causing him to squirm in his chair. Cass noticed his flicker of unease and shifted her appeal. "We can go swimming, Aiden!" she said. "Look, I already have my bikini on. Cute, ain't it?" Cass tugged at the straps of her crochet top and gave Aiden an enticing grin, hoping he might follow her lure, hoping to preempt the fretful outburst that was undoubtedly building in his brain. She waited a moment for his gears of cognition to grind to a screeching halt. But, when at last he spoke, his words were cordial.

"I didn't know I was living near a waterfall."

"Well, it's easy to overlook the treasures buried in your own backyard. But I bet if you pull up a regional map, you'll see what I'm talking about."

Aiden turned toward the pod interface, raised his right hand, and gestured out a few commands. Soon, a 3D map of Serenity Valley floated before them, complete with a green icon hovering over Aiden's pod, and a blue icon over Cass's lake.

"Yes, it seems you are correct," Aiden said. "There's a small river on the other side of the valley, and a waterfall named Garden Creek Falls—just three klicks west of here. How interesting... I never knew it was there..."

"Well, now ya know, Aiden. I think we should go there. Let's go on an adventure—on a quest! Let's do it. Let's go today. Let's go right now."

Upon hearing Cass's proposal, a wash of anxiety surged through Aiden's senses, overwhelming the careful calm he'd been struggling to maintain all morning. "Heh… Heh… No, Cass. I can't visit a waterfall," he said with a nervous laugh, as if she had just suggested a trek up Mount Everest.

Cass cocked her left eyebrow and leaned into Aiden. "Why not?" she asked, mentally devising a strategy that would be required to win this game of cat and mouse. "Are you afraid to go outside, Aiden?"

"I'm not afraid to go outside. I've been to the top of my dome many times. It's just that…"

"I know. You told me—you've never traveled past the perimeter of the pod."

"Yeah," Aiden said, his voice meek with shame. "We just… we just don't do that here."

Cass rubbed her hand along Aiden's chest and lowered her voice. "Hey, it's okay. I understand. This is Pod Land. Nobody leaves their pod in Pod Land. Everyone knows that. But just because you did things a certain way yesterday doesn't mean you can't try somethin' new today. Right?"

Aiden didn't answer. His unease didn't dissipate. Instead, it manifested in small, restless movements he struggled to suppress. When Cass spotted his shoe tapping against the footrest of the interface chair, she knew a tough battle lay before her.

"It does sound like an interesting adventure," Aiden conceded. "But…"

"But what?"

"But what if I get a sunburn?!"

"A sunburn?"

"Yeah. I've never been in the noonday sun for more than a few minutes. My face could blister and peel. I might get irreparable skin damage. I might go blind. And then there's the wildlife, Cass. There are cougars and rattlesnakes and grizzly bears out there. I've never seen one myself. But Iris told me that they're quite common in this area. I don't think I could face a rattlesnake in combat. They make the most terrifying sound before they strike! I don't have any antivenom in my pod, you know… And then there's the weather. We just had a big storm pass over us. It's clear now. But another storm might be looming on the horizon. We could get caught outside in a hurricane. There might even be a flash flood. The water might accumulate in the mountains and then, suddenly, it could overflow into the valley. We could get swept out—all the way to the ocean maybe… And we'd be shark bait out there! I don't like sharks, Cass. Did you know that some sharks have over 300 teeth? That's a lot of teeth. And I'd hate to imagine the outcome if…"

Cass listened to Aiden's ramble without cutting him off, studying him in silence while a mix of concern and incredulity crept into her expression. She watched Aiden claw at his neck with his right hand while he tugged on his collar with his left. She watched as his eyes darted to the left—again and again. Eventually, she realized he was spying on the closed pod hatch, as if the mere mention of the outside world could cause it to fly open. It was clear to her now that reasoned discourse would not be her ally this morning. If she aimed to get Aiden out of this pod, she'd have to devise an alternate strategy. And, given her time constraints, *mere exposure* seemed like her most viable ploy.

"...and don't get me started on tornadoes, Cass!" Aiden continued. "A couple years ago, Iris and I spent an entire evening viewing archive footage of tornadoes destroying ancient structures. It was all so ghastly! The wind could rip the roof off every house in a neighborhood. If a twister were to form while we were outside the pod, we could get caught up in a..."

Cass retreated from her embrace, stood upright, and adjusted the belt on her waist. Then she snatched her leather rucksack from the pod floor and, with shoulders back, she began her march toward the hatchway.

When Aiden spotted her trajectory, he altered the course of his tirade. "Where are you going?" he demanded.

But Cass ignored his question. When she reached the pod's entranceway, she casually turned, looked directly into Aiden's eyes, and—with all her might—she slammed the red mushroom-shaped button that sent the pod's hatch rolling skyward.

Aiden gasped as the metal panel ascended its guide rails. As it rose higher, so did his angst and his eyebrows. "CASS! STOP! WAIT!" he screamed, pushing his body into the cushions of the chair. "Close the hatch, Cass! Close it! You haven't run the protocol checklist yet! We don't know what's out there! CLOSE THE HATCH NOW!"

Cass dismissed him with a curt glance and waited for the hatch to complete its journey. When it did, she dangled her sandaled foot over the pod threshold and vaulted outside with a single leap.

"WAIT, CASS! There could be danger out there! We need to at least check for..."

"There's nothing out here, Aiden!" Cass proclaimed from the green grass. "Nothing out here is gonna hurt you. It's just a bunch of trees and birds."

The air of reality seeped into the pod, along with the tweets of robins and meadowlarks. From his chair, Aiden saw Cass outstretch her arms and rotate her palms upward to gather the sun's rays—just as she had done with the sky's raindrops on the previous evening. The splash seemed to delight her. She closed her eyes and bathed in the warm beams. Their golden hush settled over her, anointing her with a radiant grace that outshone the day around her.

Aiden sat and sulked and watched his lover glow.

How do you do that, Cass...?

How do you glow...?

"It's a beautiful day in Pod Land!" Cass exclaimed from the outside world. "It's the kind of day that dares ya! So carpe the goddamn diem, Aiden! Come on! Let's go!"

Cass spun in a slow circle, her arms extending like wings. A sudden gust swept over the meadow and billowed her skirt, transforming it into a pinwheel of color that whirled with the valley's breath. She jumped into the current, letting the wind decide where her joy would journey. It carried her west for a few steps. Not far. But farther than Aiden had ever ventured past his pod.

"Come outside, Aiden," Cass said as she swatted at a wayward leaf. "You know you want to!"

It was true. Aiden wanted to be near her—to be with her. Now. Right now. But Aiden was terrified. Fear had broken his spine and tied him to the chair. Now, it was standing guard at the hatchway. Aiden didn't like the power it had over him. He didn't like being toyed with either. He didn't like this game—not one bit. He hated it. And he hated the way Cass made him feel about himself.

The blink of a red status light on the pod interface caught the corner of his eye. The security system had detected the open access point and was now displaying a set of buttons that would allow Aiden to manipulate the hatchway from his chair. One tap of his finger would send the metal panel crashing down, locking Cass out forever. Aiden could end this game now—right now.

Should I…?

Should I end this…?

Should I…?

This whole escapade had been so disorienting, so jarring, so disruptive to his well-ordered life. If he pushed the button and sealed himself in, he could rid himself of this chaos and return to his comfortable life.

He wouldn't have to deal with Cass's vacillating emotions, nor her scolding critiques of his lifestyle.

He wouldn't have to keep questioning himself; he could live without doubt again, like he used to…

He wouldn't have to confront the terrifying uncertainty of the outside world. Instead, he could return to the VR world. He could return to his game—right now.

He could return to Iris. (*Oh, Iris…*)

He could be free of Cass forever. All he had to do was push that little red button.

Is that what I want…?

Is it…?

Maybe…

Maybe not...
No...
No.

Aiden knew what he wanted now. He wanted the one thing that Pod Land could not provide for him. He wanted Cassiopeia. He wanted her more than anything else on Earth.

He did.

"Are you gonna get out of that freakin' chair or what?" Cass yelled. She was leaning against the metal frame that encircled the hatchway, her palms planted atop the rubber rim, her curls breaching the threshold. She examined the tortured look of anguish that had burrowed into Aiden's flesh. She knew he was overcome with indecision and dread. But his timidity was tedious, and her patience waned.

"How am I gonna get this hot mess outta this damn thing?" Cass mumbled to herself while tapping her nails against the dome's carbon-fiber tiles. She wondered what her mother would have said to her little brother in such a circumstance. But she wouldn't have to wonder long. The next time Aiden's gaze intersected with hers, she spotted something in his expression. Aiden was glaring at her, but it wasn't a look born of spite or scorn or fear. It was a look of *longing*.

A shock of insight swept across Cass's mind. And, just then, she knew *exactly* how to get Aiden out of his shell.

Oh, Aiden...
I know what you need now...
I know what you want more than anything in the world...
I know who you want...
I do...

Cass took a step back from the hatchway, picked up her rucksack, and slipped her arms through its leather straps to signal her departure. Then she put her hands on her hips, stared directly into Aiden's pretty eyes, and, with a voice so loud it echoed across the valley, she issued an ultimatum to the boy in the pod:

Aiden Phoenix! If you don't get your ass out of this damn pod *right now* then I will go to the waterfall *alone*! I will go without you! And then, Aiden, I will LEAVE POD LAND FOREVER! AND YOU WILL *NEVER - NEVER - EVER - SEE ME AGAINNNN!!!*

After belting out the last word, Cass directed her body to remain stoic and rigid, anchored to the earth while awaiting fate's verdict. For a moment, it seemed like Aiden might retreat further into his shell. But then, the moment broke.

Something in Aiden stirred.
Something sparked.
Something bit down.

And then, with quiet haste, Aiden rose from his chair and walked toward the hatchway—all without knowing exactly why.

But Cass knew why: Aiden's fear of losing her was greater than his fear of venturing outside.

It was.

And Cass knew something else too: She knew that Aiden was in love with her.

But she could deal with that problem later…

CH. 9: CLIMB

The real world is a bumpy place...

Aiden had never walked across anything bumpy before. The pod floor and the pod dome were the only two surfaces he had ever traversed. But after venturing just ten meters from home, his ankles were quick to protest the uneven terrain, painfully proclaiming their discomfort with each awkward stride. So, Aiden ambled along slowly, cautiously. Before putting his weight down, he tapped the ground with his toe—expecting the earth to betray him with each step. Expecting the soil to shift unpredictably. Expecting chaos.

The real world is a bumpy place...

"You're movin' like you got a stick up your ass!" Cass yelled from up the mountain trail.

Aiden elevated his chin to see Cass's silhouette on the inclined path. She had her hands on her hips. She was looking down at him, shaking her head, waiting for him to catch up.

Why is she always ten steps ahead of me...?

Why...?

How does she do that...?

I'm always struggling to keep up...

I'm sure everyone struggles to keep up with Cass...

"You're so tense, Aiden. Just have fun with it. Relax!"

"I can't help it, Cass. This is the first time I've ever left the pod. So you'll have to bear with me."

"You're doin' fine, ya big lug. Just keep goin'! Gettin' through a long hike is like gettin' through a long bout of depression. All you can do is keep puttin' one foot in front of the other. You'll make it! Try to match your steps to mine. If I can do it, you can do it. Maybe... Hah!"

Cass turned, put her hands on her knees, and charged up the steep ascent with practiced ease.

Aiden studied her stride. Then he frowned in frustration as the gap in their abilities yawned wide between them. He couldn't move like her. Not yet... He didn't have her balance, her grace, nor her confidence. He didn't feel safe out here. The forest was a frightening cacophony of multicolored commotion. Birds called from unseen perches. Insects hummed in discordant rhythms. And, in the distance, branches popped and snapped like warning shots in the dark. There was no discernible pattern in the music. No tempo to follow. And no cadence to anticipate.

Aiden felt like an orphaned melody in an arrangement of strange voices. He felt out of sync. And shaken. And upset at Cass for coaxing him from his pod.

"This place sucks!" Aiden shouted.

"YOU SUCK!" Cass shouted back. "Don't talk about my turf like that! The trees have ears! So don't piss 'em off, Aiden! Dick!"

"They're pissing *me* off, Cass! Is it always so loud out here? Is this volume level normal?"

"Well, Aiden, is it too loud out here? Or is it too quiet in your pod? Hmmm... Consider that one for a minute. Hah! I think it's the latter. Cuz when I'm in your place it's so damn stifling I can barely hear myself think!"

"How is that even possible, Cass? How could the sound of silence drown out the voice in your head? How?"

Aiden waited for Cass's response, but he didn't get one. When he eventually glanced up the trail again, he saw her scurry into the foliage, preoccupied with a new side quest.

"Look at this, Aiden!" the voice in the juniper bushes said. "Look over here!"

Aiden reached Cass's elevation and followed her into the thicket. There, he spotted her kneeling down before a charred tree trunk. "What happened here, Cass?"

"It's an old cottonwood, Aiden. It's fallen. It's felled. It's dyin'. It was struck by lightning, probably last night in the storm. See that big gash in it? My heavens..."

Cass leaned in and ran her fingers along the tree's wound. Its trunk was big, almost a meter wide—once mighty, but splintered now—broken. A soot-darkened fissure ran through its core, exposing its heartwood and revealing a hundred rows of concentric rings. Aiden watched Cass walk her fingers over the brown circles. She did so with reverence, like she was touching an ancient relic, like she was reading its epitaph.

"See here, Aiden? Each ring represents one year of growth, one chapter in the tree's life. Thick rings mean good years with plenty of rain. Thin ones mean drought or disease."

"How old is it, Cass? How long did this tree live here?"

"A long time. If you count the rings back from the bark, you can see what it was going through during the year you were born. See?" Cass hopped her fingers across 21 rings and stopped on the 22nd. "There you are, Aiden," she said. "You were born right there, in the middle of that cluster of thin lines. When you took your first breath, this tree was sufferin'. Musta been some bad times. Pretty sure the citizens of Pod Land didn't notice, though. Hah!"

Aiden brushed his finger along the tree ring that represented the year of his birth. It felt coarse to the touch. He was only accustomed to gripping the sleek contours of manufactured goods from the grid. But sleek contours seemed to be a rarity in the real world.

The real world is a bumpy place...

"Pretty neat, huh, Aiden?"

"Yeah. I didn't know trees could tell time," Aiden said. Just then, he had an idea. "Hey Cass, which ring is yours? When were *you* born?"

"Hah! You're not gonna get me with that one, Aiden! I ain't tellin'!"

With that, Cass leaped back onto the trail and proceeded up the mountain, dodging Aiden's question once again. But this time, he was quick to follow after her, and even more eager to get an answer.

"Cass, this is the second time you've refused to tell me your age. If you're so worried about it, just ask the management to halt the process. You don't have to get old if you don't want to. They solved that problem centuries ago."

Given her disdain for all things from the grid, Aiden assumed Cass would deem his inquiry unworthy of further consideration. She would probably call him naive for bothering to pose the question. So, Aiden prepared himself for her derisive screed. But the derision never came... Cass remained silent on the trail, lost in a state of somber reflection. And, when she finally did speak, her words were slow and carefully chosen.

"I'd be lying if I told you the thought never crossed my mind," she said. "I've seen death many times, Aiden. Too many times... Death can be a terrible thing, a horrifying thing—especially when children are involved. Aging isn't too fun either. Whenever I spot a new wrinkle in the mirror, I... I dunno... Sometimes, takin' a drink from the grid's fountain of youth can seem like a pretty appealing prospect."

Cass kept hiking forward. But Aiden noticed she was no longer looking at the horizon. She was looking at the trail, she was looking down, as if the weight of the question was a burden she'd been carrying for a long time.

After a few quiet paces, she continued. "Aiden, it's true that, for off-gridders like me, time is our cruelest rival. I know how things work for the denizens of the grid; you have nothing but time in Pod Land. Your genes have been modified to extend your lifespan indefinitely. You're 22 now, which means your aging process will halt soon. You'll be young forever. You'll be about this age forever. You'll have this body forever. Lucky you. But it's just not something that my people do."

"Why not?"

"I told you. My village doesn't allow gene modification. We don't use it on the crops, we don't use it on the livestock, and we don't use it on ourselves."

"But why get old if you don't have to, Cass? Why subject yourself to the aches of aging?"

"Because aging is a part of living... *You can live either a beautiful lie or a rough reality, nothing in between.* That's what the founder of my village used to say. That quote is written on her tombstone back home.

She believed that you couldn't truly experience life unless you traversed each of its chapters. There's more than one season in a complete year. Maybe there's supposed to be more than one season in a complete life too. Do you know what I mean?"

Cass glanced to her left to see if Aiden was following her words. But, as usual, his face was bruised with befuddlement. So she tried a different ploy. "Consider that tree back there, Aiden," she said. "It had quite a storied journey before it fell. Would we have appreciated it if each one of its rings looked the same? If each of its seasons held no unique distinction, no unique tale of struggle? Would we have even bothered to stop and admire it?"

The duo approached a rocky outcrop. Its granite fingers reached for Cass's shins. But she vaulted over it with little effort. Aiden walked around it.

"I dunno, Aiden... Maybe immortality robs us of the urgency that makes our choices meaningful, that makes us human. If we all turn ourselves into vampires, then, well... then we're not *human* anymore, are we? Maybe humans are meant to die. To live, to reproduce, to age, and then to die. Maybe..." Cass shrugged her shoulders and took a leap up the trail, leaving the thought behind like a stone she was weary of turning over. "Or, maybe..." she continued, "maybe the founder of my village just really HATED everything from the grid! Hah!"

From a pace behind, Aiden listened to Cass's laugh return to her breath. Her capricious spirit was ever willing to shrug off the weight of her existential burdens. Her mind danced freely between profundity and playfulness. Such pivots kept Aiden interested. Her vacillations between depth and levity made her impossible to predict, and even harder to ignore.

"My goodness, Aiden! I don't got the answer to all these big questions!" Cass said, hands outstretched toward the heavens in search of grace. "But I do know one thing—I ain't lookin' forward to gettin' elderly and losin' my curls! Guess I'll just have to cross that bridge when I come to it... But hey, regardless, even when I'm old and ugly, you're still gonna love me. Right, Aiden? Right? Right? Right?"

Cass whipped her head to capture Aiden's eyes. Then she ripped off her green headband and let her curls reclaim their riotous freedom. With her hands, she scooped her locks into a bundle and framed her face with her golden spirals. To Aiden, she looked like an angel made of spun sunshine. He took in her alluring display and wondered how much time she'd spent practicing it in the mirror.

"Right, Aiden? Right? Right?" Cass asked again while batting her lashes above her bedroom eyes. "You'll love me forever! I know you will!"

Aiden considered the implications of her question. Her playfulness both challenged and disarmed him. He didn't respond. He didn't know how to. His mind was rife with questions of his own:

Does Cass think I'm in love with her...?

Am I in love with her...?

Does she love me...?

Or is this just another one of her little games...?

Aiden wasn't good at reading people. He'd never had to do it before—not in the real world at least. Crafting a tactful response to Cass's conjecture was difficult for him. His words stuck in his mouth. But fortunately, before the gap in his gab grew too great, Cass's attention was pulled away by yet another novelty.

"Oh, my heavens!" she cried. "Come on! There's the viewpoint!"

Aiden watched Cass release her coil of curls and run behind a boulder near a bend in the trail. He followed after her, mentally bracing himself for whatever new discovery had stolen her focus. When he turned the corner, he saw the blue and orange streaks of her patchwork skirt flickering between the verdant vines, fluttering wildly in the wind.

"I bet you can see your house from here, Aiden!" she shouted.

Aiden pierced through the pine leaves to find Cass standing near a ledge, pointing an accusatory finger at the valley floor. "There it is! There's Serenity Valley. There's Pod Land!"

Slowly, Aiden crept toward her. But the vista was overwhelming. The drop was sheer. And terrifying. He didn't want to get too close to the rocky perch. "That fall is nearly vertical. You should retreat a bit, Cass."

"You should ADVANCE A BIT, AIDEN! Don't be a pussy! Come here and have a look. Stand with me near this edge!"

"Why?"

"Cuz the edge is where life happens!" Cass grabbed Aiden's elbow and yanked him toward the precipice. Shock seized him as the wind in his lungs was sucked out by the great yawn of the valley below. It was then that Aiden saw them. Hundreds of little pods, glinting in the noonday sun, spanning the flatland in obedient lines—a rigid lattice pinned over the wild, a cage engineered to restrain nature's restlessness. And the engineering had worked.

Hadn't it?

Aiden had always thought so. But now, as the diminutive scale of his world was unveiled before him, he wasn't so sure...

Has the earth truly been tamed...?

Can nature's fury really be gentled by order and artifice...?

Is that all it takes...?

Is that all it takes to keep out the tempest...?

Aiden wondered if any of his neighbors had ever stood on this summit and pondered the same questions. He searched for the man with the yellow hat, but his pod and his little garden were not visible from this vantage point. Next, he searched for the woman with the purple hooded tunic. Her pod was easy to locate. It was new. Its dome was colored with the lightest shade of gray. Set against the other weather-worn shells, it shone with a clarity that made it impossible to miss. But, as for the woman herself, she was nowhere to be seen.

Nobody could be seen in the valley today.

Nobody.

Nobody leaves their pod in Pod Land...

Everyone knows that...

"Oooooh, look at all those pretty little pods," Cass moaned in mock delight. "Hundreds of them! And each one houses a narcissistic manchild—just like you, Aiden! Hah!"

Aiden threw Cass a side-eyed scowl. She returned his volley by sticking her tongue out at him. Sensing that a clever retort was due, Aiden scratched his chin and attempted to craft one. But witty banter was not part of his repertoire. Cass knew this. So, instead of waiting for his comeback, she jammed her fingers deep into the waistband of his pants and yanked him close. "Oh, don't be so ornery, Aiden. Most girls actually like narcissists. They're kinda hot in a fucked up way."

Cass planted her mouth atop Aiden's warm lips, closed her eyes, and kissed him deep. Aiden kissed her back. Reflexively, his arms wrapped around her waist and pulled her into him. He was no longer afraid of her body; it was becoming a part of him now, nearly as familiar to him as his own.

When their kiss concluded, Aiden moved his mouth near Cass's ear and whispered to her. "Do you really think I'm a narcissist?" he asked, genuinely curious about her psychological assessment of him. "Is it really true that women are attracted to such traits?"

"It's probably more true than false, unfortunately. But, my heavens, I wish it weren't so. My life woulda been a lot easier!"

"Do you really think the heavens are to blame, Cass? Were your whims written in the stars?"

"The fault, dear Aiden, is not in our stars, but in ourselves."

"What does that mean?"

"Hah! It's a famous quote, Aiden. But yeah, it's true that we are subject to the evolutionary tunings of our cortexes. But just because our brain tells us to like somethin' doesn't mean we gotta indulge in our desires *all* the time. Right? Though, admittedly, it sure is fun to indulge sometimes. For example, do you see that pod down there between the boulder and the tree line? A hot guy lives in that one. He likes to climb on top of the dome in the evening to watch the sunset. Isn't that cute?"

Aiden shielded his eyes and followed Cass's finger to the distant pod. Once he focused on it, he saw something leaning against the side— an aluminum ladder. "That's *my* pod," he said. "But how did you know I like to watch the sunset?"

"Because I saw you up there a couple days ago."

"You did?"

"Yeah. I set up camp a mile north of here and hiked along the hillslope a few times. I didn't see a single soul, of course. That is, until I saw *you*—perched atop your pod and lookin' west, like the world's saddest gargoyle."

"Is that why you banged on my pod for help when the storm came? Is that why you chose *me*, Cass?"

"Yep. I figured you were my best bet. Plus, I thought you looked cute up there."

"You said I looked like a gargoyle."

"Yeah. A cute gargoyle."

Cass gave Aiden's hand a squeeze and snuggled her cheek into his chest. Then she drew in his warmth and gazed out over the valley. The view was indeed divine. From way up here, the little gray pods didn't look so ugly.

They ain't that bad really...

Of course, everything looks nicer from a mile away...

But still...

Pod Land isn't all bad...

Not all of it...

Cass lifted her eyes toward Aiden's stunning profile and traced the chiseled perfection of his jawline.

No, not all of it...

My heavens...

He really is handsome as hell, isn't he...

It's gonna be hard to leave this one when the time comes...

Cass took a deep breath and purged her mind of painful thoughts. Then she spun free of Aiden's embrace and proceeded up the path. "Time to get movin' again!" she declared. "We're almost there, Aiden. But take one last look. You've never truly seen home till you've seen it from a distance."

Aiden watched Cass leap through the trees to resume the trek. Then, heeding her advice, he turned to gaze out upon the valley once more. He knew Cass was right about one thing: each little pod housed someone like him. Right now, in each little pod, quests were being won, alliances were being forged, and kingdoms were being constructed. But none of it was happening in the real world. It was all taking place online, on the grid.

Aiden ran his eyes along the horizon where the peak met the sky. The pods were dwarfed by the mountains beyond them; the contrast made them appear impossibly small. Insignificant.

Is my life insignificant too...?

Is this really just a valley of delusional narcissists...?

Mere blips on the grid...

Sparks pretending to be stars...

Perhaps the fault truly is in our stars, Cass...

"Come on, Aiden!" Cass yelled from the path. "Let's go. Your vivarium will be there when you get back. Keep movin' forward. We're gettin' closer to the end now."

Aiden turned away from the viewpoint and proceeded up the trail. As the journey progressed, he occasionally looked back over his shoulder, struggling to locate his pod as the duo climbed higher and higher up the mountain. At several points along the path, Aiden managed to find it again. But at each interval, the task became more difficult. Eventually, Aiden was too far from home; the view grew hazy. And he could no longer distinguish his pod from any of the others in the valley.

CH. 10: PUSH THROUGH

The trees had eyes.

Aiden had eyes too, his were darting from side to side—scanning the brush and brambles for signs of danger, for movement in the shadows. The duo had pushed deeper into the jungle. The bright woodland glade near the hillslope had transformed into a dark cathedral of old-growth giants. Their branches loomed overhead like gothic arches, forming a vaulted canopy of timber that filtered the light into thin, trembling shards.

As the trek progressed, Aiden performed a few mental calculations, trying to determine how far he had traveled from home, trying to retrace his steps. Would he know how to get back to his pod if something were to happen to Cass? If she were to get hurt, or trapped, or disappear entirely. If she were to leave him...

That would be bad...

I'd be in trouble...

I'd be lost...

I wouldn't survive without her...

I can't live without her now...

Without a mobile unit on his wrist, Aiden was naked out in the wild—vulnerable to predators and completely reliant upon Cass's navigational skills, which seemed to begin and end with whatever curiosity tugged at her nose.

"Are you havin' fun yet, Aiden?" Cass asked as she walked the length of a fallen moss-slick trunk.

"No," Aiden said. "These trees are getting denser. Leafier. Darker. It's a bit disconcerting. I'm not sure it's safe out here, Cass."

"The forest only eats pod people on Wednesdays, Aiden. Today is Tuesday so you'll be okay."

"Are we there yet? It's hot out here, Cass. It's taking a long time. And I don't really see the point of this quest. Why are we on this circuitous route? We're just going to end up back at my pod anyway. So why bother leaving it? What's the point of the journey?"

"The greatest journeys always end where they begin, Aiden. That's kinda how it works. The trail makes the traveler. Long before the destination does."

"Well, we're already on the trail. So, if that's the case then why continue to our destination?"

"Geesh, you're really annoying sometimes, Aiden. Just roll with it. Besides, what would you be doin' right now if you were back home?"

"Right now?" Aiden said, taking a moment to recall his schedule from yesterday. "Right now I'd be online with my team, slaying dragons on the grid and collecting gold coins."

"Oh my heavens, Aiden! You're gonna live forever! There'll be plenty of time later for your quixotic delusions."

"I don't know what that means, Cass."

"What? Your quixotic delusions?"

"Yeah."

"It means you waste too much time tilting at windmills."

"I don't know what that means either."

"Well, *tilting* is an old word. It's a type of jousting. The ancient knights used to ride at each other with lances, tryin' to knock the other guy off his horse. So, in the first novel ever written, there was this guy named Don Quixote who thought he was jousting a giant monster, but it was really just a windmill."

"That doesn't seem like a very logical ploy."

"He wasn't logical, he was crazy."

"Are you saying I'm crazy, Cass?"

"Absolutely! Everyone from Pod Land is crazy. You're from Pod Land, so you're crazy too. But you're also tall and hot. And that almost makes up for it. Almost."

"Thank you."

"You're welcome! But hey, if the grid games are so important to you then why not just ask Iris to play your character for you? If you're gonna live with a soulless abomination, you might as well put her to work. Just give her a sword and tell her to run around the VR worlds killing monsters all day and night? Wouldn't that be the easiest way to earn coins?"

"No, it's not possible. A.I. assistants may not participate in the games."

"Why not?"

"Because if they could, they would beat every human player. They would win every game. And there would be nothing for people to do in Pod Land. The A.I. assistants are smarter than us. They're better than us—at everything. Artificial Intelligence beat human intelligence a long time ago."

"Hmm… They might be faster, Aiden. But I doubt they're smarter."

"Why?"

"Because you need *wisdom* to be smart. Not just words. The machines generate thoughts the way a mirror generates light—by *reflection,* not creation. They only say what's been said before. They only write what has already been written. There's no soul in a sentence born from mimicry. There's just ink on a page."

Just then, a brown blur streaked across Aiden's path, causing him to flinch hard and pitch backward in a messy fall that left him sprawled out on the dirt.

"Nice trip, Aiden!" Cass shouted as she vaulted down from the fallen trunk.

"We're under attack!" Aiden shouted back. He scrambled to his feet and retreated behind a boulder, breathing hard as he pressed his back to the rock and voiced his alarm, "Take cover, Cass!"

"It's okay, Aiden. It's just a squirrel. It eats little berries, not little boys. Come on! Come have a look! They're cute."

Cautiously, Aiden crept back onto the trail and caught the creature's eyes peering at him through a shroud of serviceberry leaves. It twitched its bushy tail and chattered loudly, scolding him for making such a fuss. Then it darted up a spruce tree and vanished into the canopy.

"You scared him, Aiden."

"How can you be so calm, Cass?" Aiden demanded, his heart still pounding. "There's lots of danger out here, you know? Wolves, snakes, pathogens... There's lots of stuff that can kill you."

"Our ancestors used to live in the trees, Aiden. Humans thrived in the jungle for thousands of years before someone had the bright idea of lockin' himself away in a turtle shell."

Aiden wiped a streak of sweat from his brow. He was getting hot. His shirt clung uncomfortably to his body, and he missed the—always perfect—temperature of his pod interior. "I don't know, Cass. Maybe our ancestors had a good reason to seal themselves off."

"What reason?"

"Well for starters, the temperature in the pod is always nice. It doesn't get hot and humid like it does out here. And I'm sure that living in a pod is safer than living in a treehouse."

"Well, you wanna know somethin', Aiden? I feel safer out here than I do in your pod."

"Why, Cass? The pods are practically impenetrable. They've got air scrubbers, and emergency supplies, and..."

"And they're connected to the grid," Cass said, finishing his sentence. "Where the Manager can see everything you do, control every comfort you rely on, and shut you down whenever he wants. His bug food keeps your stomach satiated, and his games keep your mind occupied. You've traded your selfhood for security. You have, Aiden! In the pods, the Manager's unseen eyes are always watchin' you. But he can't see us out here, Aiden. Out here we're free." Cass threw her hands up high to the trees, inviting the whole forest to heed her words. "Out here we can be ghosts!"

Aiden watched Cass take a running leap and seize a low-hanging branch. Then she swung under it in a graceful arc, released her grip, and disappeared into the foliage, leaving only the sway of the leaves to mark her exit.

"Are you a ghost now?" Aiden asked.

"Yes," a teal-colored shrub in the undergrowth said. "I'm a ghost, Aiden. I can see you, but you can't see me."

"I can hear you though. I've never met a ghost who talks so much. Why do you think that is?" Aiden asked the shrub. But the shrub did not respond. Aiden halted his hike up the trail and approached the greenery that had devoured his lover. "Cass," he called, "you can come out now."

But, again, there was no response...

"Cass? Hey! Come out!"

Just then, Cass popped up on the opposite side of the trail, emerging vertically from the vegetation like a ninja warrior springing up for an ambush. "DESTROY THE PUSILLANIMOUS MISANTHROPE!" she yelled. "YAAAA!" Then she hurled a stringy glob of goo toward Aiden's person. With a moist thud, the projectile splattered on his left shoulder.

Aiden glanced down at it and saw the brown coil wiggle. Then he screamed, "NO! CASS! WHAT IS IT?" He lurched around in a tight circle, batting at his shirt as if the fabric itself had turned hostile.

Cass laughed and leaped back onto the trail. "It's an earthworm, Aiden. I thought you'd like it. Isn't that what all caged birds eat? Hah! Just flick it away if you don't want to keep it as a pet."

Aiden used his thumb to nudge it off his sleeve. "It's disgusting!" he said, unamused by Cass's antics. "It might be riddled with disease too. That was very reckless of you to assault me with it!"

"I'm pretty sure you'll survive, Aiden."

"Don't you ever worry about anything, Cass?"

"I try not to worry about tomorrow, for tomorrow will worry about itself. And each day has enough trouble of its own."

"What? What does that mean?"

"It's from Matthew 6:34, Aiden."

"It's from a guy named Matthew Six-Three-Four? His surname consists of a series of integers?"

"No, Aiden! My heavens... It's a reference number—6:34 is how you look him up."

"Look him up on the grid?"

"Look him up in the Bible!"

"I've heard of the Bible, Cass. But I've never read it."

"Oh, never mind, Aiden."

"What about your village, Cass? Don't they worry about stuff there? It seems like there's lots of stuff that could trouble a farmer. There must be something you do to guard against potential threats."

"Threats from nature or threats from people?"

"Either... Both..."

"Well, we have an alarm system at the perimeter. But that's mostly just to warn us if predators get too close to the livestock. As for human threats, we generally don't need much defense. Most people don't know we exist. And those who do know about us are usually not too interested in our way of life."

"Except for the Manager?" Aiden ventured.

Cass's tone lowered for her response. "Yeah, except for him... We do worry about him."

Aiden had noticed how the mere mention of the Manager always caused something in Cass to dim. That dark cloud had returned again. And, this time, Aiden felt compelled to learn about the forces behind the storm. "Cass, what does the Manager want with your village?"

"Control," she answered flatly. "The Manager wants to control us. Like he controls everyone else on the grid."

"But you don't live on the grid, Cass."

"That's right, Aiden. That's why he hates us. Because my community challenges the status quo."

"What status quo?"

"That humanity needs the grid to survive. My people are living proof that his way is not the only way. We don't rely on his free bug food. And we don't waste our lives playing his silly games. That makes us a problem. That makes us a threat."

A round stone stood in the center of the path. Cass kicked it hard, sending it spiraling up the path, her bitterness bound up in its erratic exit.

Aiden watched the stone flee and considered abandoning the topic. Conversing with Cass usually resulted in more questions than answers anyway... He managed to remain quiet for a few paces. But eventually, curiosity urged him on; he was determined to peel back at least one layer of the mystery Cass had wrapped herself in.

"Cass, yesterday, when we met, you said the Manager took something from you. What did he take? What was it?" Aiden kept his eyes straight and steadied his breathing after voicing the question.

Cass heard him. She kept moving forward on the trail. But her lips didn't move. Aiden thought she might be crafting a guarded response. But when no response came, he tried again:

"What did he take from you, Cass? What happened with the..."

"I don't want to talk about it, Aiden," Cass said. Her rebuff cut through the air like her kicked stone. It held a finality that warned Aiden to let the subject die. But Aiden needed answers.

"Cass, if the Manager did something that was..."

"I don't want to talk about it!" Cass said again.

But still, Aiden persisted. "Cass, the Manager of Pod Land might be a..."

Suddenly, Cass stopped her forward motion. Then she balled up her hands into fists, elevated her chin toward the trees, and screamed her repudiation into the wilderness:

"I SAID I DON'T WANT TO TALK ABOUT IT, AIDENNN!!!!"

When Cass's screech ricocheted off the branches, the background sound of the forest became mute. The insects ceased their chatter, and the birds severed their calls mid-note. Even the windy rustle of the upper canopy was momentarily hushed.

To Aiden, it seemed as if the whole jungle was holding its collective breath, waiting for Cass to reveal the part of the story that remained unspoken. He watched as she gripped her stomach and collapsed onto the trail, reeling forward as if she was stricken down with gut pain. Or heartache...

Aiden stood frozen at her side. He wanted to help. But decades of gaming taught him to recognize a defensive posture when he saw one. Cass was curled up in a ball. Her elbows hugged her knees, and her hands covered her face. Her mane of gold curls covered the rest. She was shielding herself—not just from Aiden's gaze, but from everything. From the wild, from the world, and from her own thoughts.

Despite the many obstructions between them, Aiden could see that Cass was crying. He swallowed his remaining words and let the silence linger, trusting the quiet more than anything that might come out of his mouth.

After two long minutes of muffled sobbing, Cass's tears tapered and her shoulders eased. When the forest's volume setting returned to its default level, Aiden crouched down to offer an apology:

"I didn't mean to pry, Cass. I'm sorry if my questions were..."

"Hey, do you hear that, Aiden?" the ball of golden hair asked, interrupting Aiden's attempt to make amends.

"Hear what?"

"That sound. That low roaring sound. That's the sound of falling water. We're here, Aiden. We've made it to Garden Creek Falls. It's just around that bend. Come on!"

And with that, Cass rose to her feet and resumed her hike up the mountain—at a brisker pace this time, leaving only the faintest trace of her breakdown in the dust behind her.

When her march commenced, Aiden noticed something about Cass: though her figure was beautiful, her gait was not feminine. It never was. She approached every situation the same way the avatars on his team approached a battlefield—with shoulders squared and fists curled.

Cass isn't a princess; she's a fighter...

And Aiden loved her all the more for it.

"Time to get movin' again, Aiden!" Cass yelled from ten paces up the trail. Then she turned the bend and disappeared behind the trees without so much as a glance back.

Aiden chased after her, spurred on by a need he couldn't name, and by a fear that she would vanish forever if he let her out of his sight. In his exuberance, he ran through a tangle of willow leaves. They slapped at his face and arms, leaving tiny scratches that would have sent him into hysterics just hours before. But now... now he barely noticed them.

He charged ahead with unbroken momentum. The thrum of the falls swelled around him like a pulse. They urged him onward, a steady drum calling him toward whatever was waiting. The duo's destination was close. Their quest was coming to an end, and Aiden was hungry for his bounty.

"Is it over here, Cass?" Aiden yelled as he turned the bend in the trail. "Is this what we came for?"

He got no response, but Cass's guidance was no longer required. As the vegetation thinned out, Aiden saw a rocky outcrop jutting forth from the clearing. His lover was standing on a precipice near the point where the river met the plunge. He eased in beside her and slipped an arm around her waist, bracing himself as the rock gave way to the rushing curtain of water and light that was Garden Creek Falls.

There it was…

There it fell…

The roar and radiance of the white cascade swallowed every inhibition Aiden had hauled from his pod. His chest tightened with a kind of awe he had no words to express. So he stood still, gawking at the tumbling torrent, tracing its furious arc to the churn in the turquoise basin below. A fine mist rose from the impact point, coalescing into a luminous veil that drifted with the breeze—nature's breath made visible. Aiden and Cass welcomed its wind. It hugged their skin, settling over them like a shroud woven from the river's exhale.

Cass gripped her lover's arm and drew him close. Then she ran her tongue along the droplets that gathered on his neck. When her lips crossed the hollow where his jawline began, she paused and purred into his left ear, "I told you it was beautiful here."

Aiden nodded slowly. "It is," he said. "It really is." He inhaled deeply, breathing in the waterfall's vapor. The cool moisture seeped into him, filling him with a strange calm that made his mind feel newly rinsed.

Cass released her grip on Aiden's arm and turned her attention upward to study the cloudless sky. The sun was beaming at them from its highest point now, its warmth spilled onto the cliffs with an intensity that made the water below glitter with promise. Cass knew exactly what to do next. "Lucky us," she said. "The weather today is perfect for swimming!"

Aiden looked down from the rock shelf and examined the pool below. Its clear water revealed smooth stones near its edges, but the center darkened to a deep azure blue that kept the secrets of its depths hidden. "Oh, we can't swim in there," he said. "There's no telling what sort of organisms lurk in that pool of water. It could be dangerous. We don't know if it contains toxins or other harmful elements which might…"

Aiden turned to address Cass further. But he stopped speaking when he realized she was no longer standing beside him. She was upriver now, climbing up a sandy embankment.

Once she reached the top of the dune, she removed her leather rucksack and hung its two straps on an outstretched tree branch. Then, she retrieved her jar of applejack from the side pocket and unscrewed the top lid. "Down the hatch!" she said as she tipped the jar back and took a hearty swig.

"What are you doing, Cass?"

"I'm preparing for takeoff, Aiden. Applejack is part of my preflight checklist."

"What?"

"Never mind! Just give me a sec. I'll float back to ya soon."

Cass screwed the lid back on the jar and returned it to her rucksack. Then, she unlatched the leather belt that held her patchwork dress to her waist. It fluttered to the ground in a loose swirl of color, gathering at her feet like shed plumage.

"Cass," Aiden said. "I'm not sure if it's safe to remove your clothing out here."

"This is Pod Land, Aiden," Cass said as she kicked off her sandals. "Nobody leaves their pod in Pod Land. Everyone knows that. My modesty will remain uncompromised. As will my grace and virtue. At least until I take another drink… Hah!"

Cass unlatched her green hair wrap and set her curls free. Then she pulled at the yarn that lassoed her crochet bikini top to her neck. After a few tugs of her tassels, she was completely nude. She hung each article of clothing on an adjacent tree branch. Then she moved to the riverbank and trailed her toe through the torrent.

"Don't enter the water, Cass. It's not safe. Just walk around. Walk back along the rocks toward me."

Cass ignored Aiden's warning and entered the fray. She waded to the center of the stream, letting the current draw her along its shifting course.

Aiden stared at the nude woman in the river. He watched as she approached. He watched as she moved through the churning liquid with effortless grace, as if the only force required to part the sea was her feminine charm. For whatever reason, the sea obliged. The current curled around her thighs like it was welcoming her home. Cass was in her element now. She was at peace.

Aiden was envious of her peace.

How is it that you are so comfortable in your skin, while I am so often strangled by mine…?

How do you do that, Cass…?

How do you glow…?

When Cass arrived at the rocky outcrop, she offered Aiden her hand, motioning for him to help pull her up to his perch near the waterfall's crest. Aiden reached for her. When their fingers intertwined, he lifted her from the stream. Beads of water raced down her naked legs as she reclaimed her position on the ledge. Soon, they were on equal footing again. Cass was safe. But Aiden continued to hold on to the crux at her waist, gripping her tight, afraid she might dissipate like the mist rising from the falls.

Aiden sent his gaze downward, allowing his eyes to drink in her magnificent nudity. Her form reflected the light with a brilliance so luminous it contended with the silvered shimmer of the river's ripples. Her body was a living mirage, a phantasmal vision to behold.

By the time Aiden's gaze returned to his lover's face, the warmth of her girlish expression had cooled, replaced now with the keen, hard lines of predatory focus. Cass was a huntress again, wearing the same rapacious gaze she had worn on the previous evening—just before she approached Aiden's bed to devour him.

"What are you going to do now?" Aiden asked, his voice thinning beneath the cocktail of lust and anticipation that stirred within him.

Cass didn't respond to Aiden's query. Instead, she embraced him and sent her lips up to meet his. When she kissed him this time, it was with an all-consuming certainty. She claimed his mouth; it belonged to her now. *He* belonged to her. His heart did too.

But did she belong to him?

No...

The answer was as obvious as it was devastating.

Still, Aiden would hold on to this dream for as long as it persisted. He knew how to thrive in a world of illusion. Indeed, nobody navigated the world of illusion better than a citizen of Pod Land. Nobody could hold on to a fantasy harder than a man who knew nothing else. Aiden would reside in Cass's dream world for as long as he could—for as long as she permitted him to. Besides, her contrivance was at least as real as the digital worlds conjured up in the pods. It was. It could be... Perhaps out here he would...

Oh no...

Aiden froze as the weight of a terrible realization crashed through him.

Oh no...

No...

This isn't real, is it...?

None of this is real...

I'm not in the forest...

I'm not standing on a waterfall next to a golden-haired nymph...

I never even left the pod...

Nobody leaves their pod in Pod Land...

Everyone knows that...

I'm still in it. Right now...

I'm going to wake up in the interface chair soon...

Maybe Iris will wake me up...

Iris, are you there...?

I've fallen asleep in VR... I'm dreaming... I'm in a simulation...

This woman doesn't really exist; she's a figment of the grid...

This is a game...

It has to be...

Aiden's breathing hastened, and his eyes darted around. He looked at the woman, the falls, the lake below, and the cloudless sky.

Could all of this be rendered by the grid...?

Is that even possible...?

He needed to talk to someone...

He needed to ask someone...

But who...?

There's only one person here...

"Cass," Aiden said, "I have a question for you, and I need you to respond honestly, okay?"

Cass lifted one eyebrow and fixed him with a look that mixed curiosity with a wordless challenge.

"Are you real?" Aiden asked.

For a moment, Cass remained completely motionless. Reality seemed to tremble, as if the question itself had enough weight to bend the world along the fold where truth and perception were so apt to collide. Aiden waited for the balance to tip. He waited for Cass to respond. But, when no response came, he began to fear the worst…

What will happen now…?

Will the trees and foliage vanish…?

Will everything blink away…?

Will Cass's naked body melt in my arms…?

Will I watch her transmogrify into dust, just as Iris did last night…?

Will I…?

Time stretched on. And, as Aiden stared at his love, waiting for her answer, he became lost again in the golden-flecked constellations that swirled in her eyes. Maybe there was nothing in the universe but her. Nothing at all. Nothing but the light in her eyes and the sound of her breath and the feel of her fingertips on his chest.

Nothing else.

Did it matter?

He was happy. Right now, he was so very happy. And he was here with her now—right now. At least he believed he was.

What was it that Iris had told him on Sunday morning?

Happiness is not an ideal of reason, but of imagination…

Ah yes…

Happiness…

Aiden was happy. He believed that Cass was here with him now. He believed it. And maybe *that* was enough for it to be true. Perhaps…

And yet, part of him needed to know for sure.

Aiden needed the truth.

"Cass," he asked again, "are you real? Is this real life? Are you really standing with me on this edge? Right now?"

Another eternity marched by. But this time, when its procession was complete, Cass looked at Aiden and smiled.

And then, Aiden smiled back.

And, for a moment—a brief moment—all was right with the world.

"Of course I'm real, Aiden," Cass said. "I'm alive. And so are you. And we made it. We made it to the edge."

"Yes, Cass… We did…" Aiden said, relieved enough to believe that the ground beneath his feet would hold a while longer. "So now what happens, Cass?"

"The edge is where life happens, Aiden," Cass said with a coy little smirk. And then, with all the strength she could muster, Cass pushed Aiden over the cliff.

CH. 11: TUTORIAL

"Good evening, gentlemen!"

The greeting came from a comically short general who stood before a comically tall war map. He was addressing his new recruits, barking out each edict with the clipped cadence of a career military man—one who had long since traded conversational niceties for conversational efficiency. His uniform was crisp, medals gleaming, boots polished to a mirror shine. And he sported a ridiculous mustache—thick, bushy, and entirely too large for his face; it quivered each time he made a motion toward the map with his swagger stick, and each time he spoke.

"Today is March 24, 1945. And you maggots are about to take part in the greatest airborne operation in history—Operation Varsity!" The general slammed his stick against the battle map's lowest quadrant. Under its pointer, hundreds of circles glowed red, indicating the many drop zones to be won in enemy territory.

"As a paratrooper in the 17th Airborne Division, *you* are the tip of the spear! *You* are our boots on the ground! Our *first* boots! And, as such, you are the *LAST* thing the enemy wants to see! Sixteen thousand men are about to be airdropped into Hell's Kitchen! It will be glorious! Dangerous! But *damn* glorious!"

"It is *your* job to hit the ground running! And to not splatter on impact! So pay attention! Let's talk about your parachute. It is your best friend, your lifeline, and your one true love. And, if you'd prefer to avoid becoming an expensive lawn dart, you must learn to deploy it properly!"

The ancient map that draped the back wall transformed into a chalky animation—a rough sketch of a human hand. It waved at the recruits. Then it performed the mission's most important command gesture.

"When the time is right, hold your right hand at a downward angle. Pinch your thumb and your index finger together. And then, give your wrist a brisk flick upward. This indicates to the interface that you intend to deploy your parachute—unless, of course, you'd prefer to make a dramatic impression as a crater! And I know you do not!"

As the general spoke, the chalky animated hand repeated the gesture several times.

"Watch and listen—one more time! When you're ready to deploy your chute: angle your right hand downward, pinch thumb to index finger, and flick your wrist upward. If you do it too late, you will plummet to the ground like a sack of potatoes and break every bone in your body. If you do it too early, the enemy will use you for target practice. But, if you do it correctly, then you will descend from the heavens like a mighty angel of death—bloodthirsty and poised to rain destruction upon the enemy with righteous fury!"

The sound of a military orchestra swelled in the background. Fireworks filled the air above the little general and his chalky pantomime.

"Now get out there! Jump like heroes! And for the love of all things military, don't forget to deploy your parachute! Angle right hand downward, pinch thumb to index finger, flick wrist upward. Good luck, soldier! And may God have mercy on the souls of our enemies!"

When his remarks concluded, a curtain dropped before the general. It was big and billowing and all colored in burgundy—except for a single white sentence embroidered in its flowing fabric that read:
DEPLOY OR DIE!

Ch. 12: On the Beach

What does a man think about while he's falling to his death?

What memories are summoned?

What fragments of wisdom are roused in consciousness as each neuron scribbles its last love letter to the soon-to-be-departed soul?

The answer is different for everyone. But when Aiden was falling through the air, his mind chose to recall a tutorial from a World War II simulation game. He had played it when he was very young. He didn't know how young... But his teammate Kai was around eleven or twelve. So Aiden must have been about that age too.

When it came time to join the 17th Airborne Division on their jump into enemy territory, each recruit had to memorize a new set of hand gestures. Paratroopers carry parachutes. Their chutes could only be deployed if the player executed a three-part gesture:

Angle right hand downward, pinch thumb to index finger, flick wrist upward.

Aiden loved historical combat simulators. The Battle of Wesel was a particularly popular combat mission. He played it so often that the parachute deployment gesture had become second nature to him. And that would explain why, right now, while he was sailing down a sheer cliff at 45 kilometers per hour, Aiden's right hand was gesturing into the wind—feverishly trying to deploy a parachute that didn't exist.

"Angle right hand downward, pinch thumb to index finger, flick wrist upward!"

He mouthed each motion as he performed it with his hand.

"Angle right hand downward, pinch thumb to index finger, flick wrist upward!"

This isn't working...

"Angle right hand downward, pinch thumb to index finger, flick wrist upward."

Oh no...

As the deck of blue water expanded in Aiden's field of view, his parachute insisted on remaining closed. Eventually, after three unsuccessful attempts, the gravity of the fall awakened him to the gravity of his situation. Every illusion he clung to vanished. The truth was about to arrive—fast and cold and wet.

And the truth is: Aiden had no parachute.

He wasn't in a game.

He wasn't in the grid.

Aiden was in reality.

And reality hits you hard, bro.

CRASHHHHH!!!

Aiden struck the cove's cold waterline with the blunt finality of a slammed door. Its chilled jaws bit into him and held fast, dragging him downward without affording his lungs a chance to draw a single breath. The impact left his senses ringing with shock; it surged through his chest as he watched the world turn from shades of blue to shades of white.

He landed near the base of the falls. The punishing surge pounded him with a violence that folded his limbs. The relentless deluge drove him deep into the depths. He tumbled helplessly in the chaos. The churn claimed both his balance and his bearings. Up became down, light became shadow. The unyielding vortex kept him submerged and spinning.

Soon, the oxygen in his lungs dwindled; panic overwhelmed his senses. It wasn't the sort of controlled anxiety he had experienced in the grid games when his team faced a formidable foe. Nor was it the type of fear he had encountered on the trail when he was attacked by the squirrel. Instead, it was raw, unbridled terror—the kind that surfaces when you suspect your next heartbeat might be your last.

Is this the part of the story where I die...?

I'm too young to die...

I'm only 22...

I'm a citizen of Pod Land...

We don't have to die if we don't want to....!

For the denizens of the grid, death wasn't a contingency that required much consideration. Death was just something that happened to people in old movies. Aiden liked old movies. And he admired the courage his ancestors carried into the dark. In ancient films, the protagonist would typically face his nemesis armed with a gun or a sword. He would stand tall, with his weapon at the ready, and make a dramatic proclamation—usually about love or freedom or courage. And then he would strike. He would strike his foe down. The duel would only last for a minute or two. But when it was over, the good man would emerge victorious. And the movie would conclude.

At least, that's how things usually went... Most endings were happy ones. But sometimes, the finale was more complex. In the process of saving the day, the hero would die a glorious death. And, in his final moments, the tears of his woman and the swell of the orchestra would elevate his sacrifice into something larger than the life he'd lived.

There is glory in such an ending...

There is honor in standing firm till the last...

That's how a brave man dies...

Aiden knew he'd probably die someday, and he'd always hoped he would die like a brave man. But now that he was facing the real thing, the process didn't seem so glorious. It was just horrifying.

Aiden didn't hear an orchestra in his ears—he just heard the watery churn of the torrent.

Aiden didn't think his woman would shed many tears following his demise—for all he knew Cass intended to kill him when she pushed him off that ledge.

This is not a brave man's death...
This is not glorious...
Perhaps my death was Cass's plan all along...
Perhaps her plan is about to succeed...
Iris is right—I shouldn't have let her in the pod...
Dammit...

Soon, Aiden would drown in a deluge of whitewater. Cass would wait for his body to float to the surface. And then, once she saw it bobbing in the bubbles, she would shrug her shoulders and exert her little laugh ("Hah!"). Then she would march back to Pod Land and jam her tentacles into the heart of yet another unsuspecting lad—one who would undoubtedly succumb to her seduction and...

"HEY, AIDEN! WHERE YOU GOIN'? THE AIR IS UP HERE, DUMBASS!"

Out of the swirling haze, Aiden saw two hands break through the water and reach for him. Cass's fingers gripped the flesh of his shoulders and bit down hard. Then she yanked him upward—wherever that was.

When Aiden's nose finally breached the surface, he sucked in the air with such ferocity it seemed he might swallow the entire sky. Once his lungs stopped screaming, he cleared the blur from his eyes, bringing Cass's cheery face into focus. Her disposition was maddeningly calm, especially given what she had just subjected him to. Aiden's mind struggled to reconcile the undeniability of her rescue with his suspicion of her betrayal. In his panic, he pulled away from her, trying to flee. But she held fast. Her fingers dug deeper into his arm and pulled, guiding him toward the shore with a steadiness he had no ability to counter.

When the couple finally exited the cove, Aiden staggered up the sandy embankment and collapsed onto his hands. Water spilled from his hair and body as he hung there, unsure if the river had released him, or if Cass had entrapped him. Unsure if he could ever trust anything again—or anyone.

When the last watery gulp cleared his throat, he looked over at the naked woman who lay beside him. "WHY DID YOU DO THAT?" he choked out as the emotions of rage and confusion warred for revenge. "YOU COULD HAVE KILLED ME!"

"You're okay," Cass said. "You did it, Aiden. You jumped the falls. You made it down in one piece. You're alive and kickin'."

"That wasn't right, Cass! You shouldn't have pushed me! You could have at least given me a moment to prepare for the jump."

"Then you would've never done it. And I already spent a whole hour this mornin' convincing you to step through your own damn front door. My life is shorter than yours, Aiden. And I wasn't about to waste any more time danglin' a worm in front of a bird trapped in a cage of his own makin'."

"What? Don't you realize what could have happened? I could have broken my neck down there! Do you even know how deep that pool is?"

"Yeah, I do actually."

"HOW?!"

"Because I jumped in it yesterday," Cass said. She knelt down and tugged at the fasteners on Aiden's shoes. "Remember? I told you. I was here on Monday before the storm clouds moved in."

Aiden released a weary exhale and watched Cass turn his shoe upside down. Water spilled onto the sand in a thin stream, carrying with it the last trace of the river's chill, as well as a pink shard of quartz.

"Ooh! A pretty rock!" Cass said, catching the colorful nugget midflight, her attention claimed by yet another novelty.

"You're so reckless, Cass. You're dangerous. I don't understand how you've gotten this far in life without dying. I don't know how you've managed to avoid colliding face-first with reality."

Cass chucked the rock over her shoulder. Then she knelt down and ripped off Aiden's socks. "Come on, Aiden. You do realize how funny that sounds comin' out of *your* mouth, right? I don't think you've ever had a single encounter with reality in your entire life!" Cass slung Aiden's wet socks over a nearby branch. "Well, not until just now that is… Oh, and there was last night too—when we were fuckin' in your pod. That encounter was pretty real. Real *hot* at least. But you were drunk so that one kinda doesn't count… But still, it was pretty hot."

Dumbfounded by Cass's brazen behavior, Aiden shook his head wildly, causing the river water trapped in his ear to slosh about. He banged a balled-up fist to his skull a few times, trying to knock both the water and the frustration loose. Noticing Aiden's pouty angst, Cass knelt beside him and wrapped her arms around his square shoulders, embracing him from the back. Then she sent her right hand down to his chest and undid his shirt buttons. When they were all free, she pulled off his wet shirt and flung it over the same branch that bore his socks.

Aiden ran his fingers along a welt that the cove had slapped across his ribcage. "I'm injured," he said. "It hurts here!"

Cass sat down next to Aiden and leaned in close to examine the red rash. With gentle fingers, she traced the outline of the bruise with a care that contrasted her usual callousness. "Hmm," she said. "Yeah, that's there because you bellyflopped into the bay, boy! I watched you tumblin' through the air before you hit. You were thrashin' around like a kitten at bath time."

"That's your fault," Aiden said.

"I think you'll be okay. I've had hickeys that looked scarier than that little mark."

"What's a hickey?"

"Never mind. Lie back and soak up some sun. I'll kiss it and make it better."

"I don't think that's going to work."

"Don't knock it till you try it!" Cass said, pushing against Aiden's shoulders, nudging him to lie down on the shore. When his head settled into the soft sand, he closed his eyes and tried to gather his breath. A tide of sensation washed over him as Cass brushed her lips over the spot on his chest that bore the mark of the cove's first strike. Goosebumps rose across his skin as her delicate touch sent electric currents through his body, making it impossible to focus on anything but the dance across his injured flesh. Using her tongue, she tasted him, licking away the lingering beads of lake water that clung to his abs. The tender pressure of her caress transformed the pain into something entirely unfamiliar, and dangerously pleasant.

"Feel better now?" Cass asked.

"Maybe," Aiden said.

Cass nestled her way into Aiden's body, tucking her chin into the warm hollow between his shoulder and his chest. Then she elevated her eyes to observe the way his profile held the midday brightness.

My heavens...

Even in this piercing light, there wasn't a single imperfection to be found on Aiden's face. His arcing jawline was flawlessly symmetrical. His cheekbones were sloped to mathematical precision, crescendoing at a sharp tip below his big brown eyes. His skin had a uniformity of texture that would not be possible for an off-gridder to maintain—the relentless forces of sun and time would see to that.

No...

Skin like that can't exist off-grid...

But Aiden's skin was designed in Pod Land. Aiden's body was perfect. Too perfect. An organism designed by machines, engineered by the grid to embody an aesthetic ideal centuries in the making. Even Michelangelo would be envious of Aiden's sculptor.

And yet, Aiden's physique belied his naiveté. He was a mere boy cast in the unblemished body of a superhero. Not exactly Cass's type... She liked the rough cut of a man with hardened edges. She liked men with stories written in scars.

But still... superheroes can be appealing too...

What a hot mess...

What am I gonna do with this guy...?

What is he gonna do with me...?

I'm sittin' here in my birthday suit on a beautiful beach, and he's probably thinkin' of takin' a nap...

He's probably still afraid of me...

He probably sees me as a mythical creature from one of his stupid games...

To him, I'm not just a farm girl with bad teeth, I'm a warrior jungle princess, or some bull crap like that...

Looks like I'm gonna have to initiate again...

Aiden sneezed.

Cass watched a dribble of residual lake water race from his left nostril.

What a hot mess...

But since today is my last day here, I might as well indulge in this fantasy once more...

Cass traced her finger along the six corners of Aiden's abs. Then she ran it downward to the ridge where his waist met his pants and exhaled a lustful sigh. "Hey, Aiden," she said, "can I ask you somethin'?"

Aiden opened his eyes, but he didn't respond. He just stared into the blue sky and waited for the delivery of yet another of Cass's little surprises.

"Have you ever had sex on a beach?" she said.

Aiden slammed his eyes shut and let out a long, defeated breath. Cass knew the answer to that question. She was just teasing him. Belittling him, maybe... But Aiden responded anyway. "No," he said without preamble or pretense.

"Huh... Interesting..." Cass said as she hopped to her feet.

When Aiden heard her stand, he opened his eyes and watched as she grabbed hold of each pant cuff. Then, in one fluid motion, she yanked off his wet pants—leaving Aiden lying completely nude on the sandy shore.

"You've never done it on a beach, huh? Never ever? Well, you're in for a treat then, aren't you?" Cass jumped on Aiden's naked body and straddled his torso, effortlessly reclaiming the territory she'd won on the previous evening. When her thighs locked around his waist, she pressed into him, pinning him to the sand with her steady strength. Aiden was— once again—surprised by her strength.

Cass isn't a princess; she's a fighter...

She flicked her head to the right, sending her mane of wet golden curls slicing to the left. When their pivot was complete, she lowered herself down, allowing her plump breasts to squash against Aiden's chest. Then she placed her mouth next to his ear and purred, "I'm sorry for pushing you, Aiden. But I did notice how brave you were today. I know it wasn't easy for you to leave your pod. I know you've never swum before. But today you did both. And I'm proud of you. I am."

Upon hearing Cass's bout of unexpected praise, Aiden felt something in his chest unclench, a quiet warmth unfurled where anger had resided just moments before. He was overjoyed to receive her rare words of validation. Cass's opinion mattered to him—deeply. She reached him in a way no stimuli in his pod ever had.

But how…?

Why…?

Why did he care what she thought about his life…?

Why did her mere presence give him such pause…?

He didn't know. But he was so very grateful for her acknowledgment. "Thank you for saying that," he said.

"You're welcome," Cass said as she nibbled on his earlobe. "And now that you've shown such valor, it's time for you to claim your prize."

And, with that, Cass—once again—sent her hand down deep and pulled Aiden into her little world. When she did so, Aiden's mind was once again flooded with raw and disorienting sensations. Pleasure fused with vulnerability, sloshed with a rush of yearning, and a rising swell of love—each note brushed by an undercurrent of fear, each undertone drew him closer to her.

Cass was working her magic again.

Aiden tried to anchor himself in her passing glow, to appreciate her light, to relish it. But he was overwhelmed.

It's all too much to take in…

Too much…

Aiden was naked, lying under a cloudless blue sky, near the base of an emerald waterfall. There was a beautiful nude woman writhing on top of his erect penis. And, in every direction around him, the trees of the jungle screeched out the pulse of life.

Too much…

Too much for a boy from Pod Land…

Too much to take in…

In an effort to prevent his mind from flooding with stimuli, Aiden closed his eyes, electing instead to just listen. He could manage one set of sensory input. Not five. But he could manage one.

So he listened.

He listened as the waves lapped against the riverbank.

He listened as the sand shifted under Cass's knees each time she thrust her hips forward.

He listened as the birds in the tree canopy sang their ancient love songs.

He listened…

The auditory canvas in his mind was mostly occupied by the constant rumble of falling water. But, near the end, when their bout of intercourse was about to conclude, the only sound loud enough to overtake the roar of Garden Creek Falls, was the roar of Cassiopeia.

CH. 13: TO BE, OR NOT TO BE

"Do you wanna play *ding, dong, ditch?*"

Shadows lengthened under the trees as Aiden and Cass made their way through Serenity Valley, back to the pod. They had spent the last several hours at Garden Creek Falls. They had swum in the emerald cove. They had made love on the sand—twice. Now, Cass was asking Aiden a question, but Aiden wasn't paying attention to her words. He was lost in her smile; she wore an expression of quiet triumph, the kind that children don after they flee the kitchen with a stolen cookie. The kind that blooms after desire has run its course.

Aiden's clothes were still damp; they clung to his skin, a lingering reminder of his unexpected plunge. Grains of sand still hid in the crevices of Cass's knees, a lingering reminder of her shoreline mischief. Their fingers were laced together in a tight weave. Their hands swayed gently between them as they walked. Cass's touch kindled a warmth in Aiden—originating from some hidden fire he'd never known he carried. The sparks wove through his ribs and formed a ring of glowing embers that encircled his heart. Aiden was bound to her heat now. He was aglow in it.

What a wonderful day...
Glorious...
Sublime...
Am I the only person in Pod Land to experience such a day...?
Perhaps I am...

The thought disturbed Aiden's peace as the couple glided between the rows of pods. Hundreds stood before them. Hundreds stood behind them. And dozens flanked both sides. The rows stretched on indefinitely. Yet, though each pod was occupied, they had yet to encounter a single soul on their trek.

Nobody leaves their pod in Pod Land...
Everyone knows that...

But, for the first time, Aiden began to seriously wonder why.

"Aiden!" Cass was tugging on his arm now. "Did you hear me? Do you wanna play *ding, dong, ditch?*" she asked again. "It's a game! It's fun!"

"Okay," Aiden said, "I like games. How do you play?"

"Well, you bang on someone's door and then you run away real fast. Hah! Let's do it! Let's pound on one of these pod hatches. Want to?"

Aiden considered Cass's offer. He thought about the mental state of the people in the pods. They were like him. He knew that. He couldn't see them. But he could hear them. The pod's insulated carbon-fiber shell blocked most sounds. But every once in a while, as he and Cass threaded the stoic domes, the telltale sounds of life could be heard:

The blast of a bomb exploding in a grid game.

The sultry croon of a woman's moan.

A bit of monologue from an ancient movie. ("You can't handle the truth!")

The sound of a shower faucet hissing.

The sound of someone crying.

The sound of music.

In each pod, there was life.

There was.

And now that Aiden had finally heard his neighbors with his own ears, he was somehow comforted by their presence.

When he was younger, he would often entertain the notion that everyone on Earth was a bot except him. Iris had convinced him otherwise. But his doubt lingered...

But now... now that the only thing that separated him from his neighbors was a thin dome wall, Aiden felt somehow connected to them. He wanted to protect them. He wanted them to be happy.

"Come on, Aiden!" Cass said. "Let's pound on this pod here!"

"Cass, why would you want to bang on that person's pod? What's the point?"

"Why not? Because it's funnnn! Especially in *this* place. I bet it would scare the crap out of whoever's inside. Hah!"

"Yes, it would, Cass. I was very frightened when you knocked on my pod hatch yesterday. Iris almost contacted the Manager to report a security breach. If she had completed her communiqué, a police drone would have been dispatched to the valley. It would have hovered over my pod and a team of patrol bots would have dropped down for an inspection. If they had found you banging on the hatch, they probably would've arrested you and taken you to the Capitol Building."

Cass slowed her pace, her focus growing distant as she pondered Aiden's scenario. "Hmm... Well, that would have been bad," she said. "That would have been *real* bad. Iris was gonna report me to the grid? Just for knockin' on your damn door? Geez, what a bitch!"

"Don't worry, I convinced her not to do it. But if we run around pounding on these other pods, their occupants may not be so lenient. Most of the citizens of Pod Land are not strong and brave like me."

Upon hearing Aiden's deadpan remark, Cass turned her attention from the trail to the face of the man beside her. At first, she couldn't tell if he was kidding or not. But then he shot her a sideways glance, his lips curling into a sheepish grin that revealed his intent.

"Was that a joke, Aiden?" Cass blurted out. "Was that an actual attempt at humor—your first joke ever perhaps? Are you finally developing a personality? My heavens! What a difference a day makes! Get a Pod Land boy fed, fucked, and frolicking outside, and then sit back and watch the metamorphosis ensue! You're surely a fellow of infinite jest now! Aren't you?! I'm suddenly attracted to you. That made me kinda hot. Maybe we should screw again when we get to the top of this hill. But only if you can catch me!"

Cass burst into a sprint and raced up the grassy mound, screaming into the wind all the way, "AHHHH!"

She scurried away from the trail, her vibrant patchwork skirt and her blonde curls bobbing behind, struggling to keep up. Aiden chased after her. He struggled to keep up too.

I'm sure everyone struggles to keep up with Cass...

She was quick. But Aiden's legs were longer. His height eventually made up for his lack of running form. As the couple neared the crest of the hillock, Cass's body was nearly in reach. When Aiden was close enough to grab hold of her, she yelled out again:

"AHHHH! Aiden's got me! He's got my ass! Call the Manager! Call the Manager! He's got me! He's..."

When Cass arrived at the berm's peak, she stopped cold and ceased her mock protest. Aiden saw her body freeze; he stopped running too, catching himself just before colliding into her. They were at the highest point in the valley now. And, from their newly won vantage point, they finally understood the function of the ascent they'd been climbing. Below them, the ground swooped downward, forming a graceful descent, a perfect bowl—set with stone and carved into the earth not by nature but by man—ancient man.

Wildflowers dotted the landscape, scattered bursts of color atop thorny brambles that clung to the slope in thick, unruly knots. The weeds and wormwood had obviously been encroaching on the structure for a long time. Yet they failed to obscure the massive mounds that lined the hill, huge limestone steps forming concentric half-circles that spanned the breadth of the basin. Their surfaces were pitted with jagged cracks;

their edges were beveled by the winds of time. Still, the terraces endured, bearing the ghosts of a crowd long silenced.

Aiden had seen large manmade structures in the VR worlds. But in the real world, he had never stood next to anything bigger than a pod. He had never witnessed the grand scale that the ancient humans could build at. The sight struck him with a quiet awe, leaving him blinking in disbelief, unsure how to take it all in. Eventually, he managed a short breath of words: "Wow… These are some very big stairs…"

Cass was awestruck too. But Aiden's comment broke her trance. There was a wonder laid out before her, waiting to be explored. The exhilaration of discovery was quick to animate her legs. Her mouth followed just as eagerly. "Yeah! Wow! This is amazing!" she said as she grabbed her skirt near her knees and began her journey down the slope. "But these aren't stairs, Aiden! I think I know what they are though! Come on!"

Aiden followed after her, cautiously easing his weight onto each ancient step as though it might crumble the moment he trusted it.

"This is epic, Aiden!" Cass yelled as she reached the bottom of the stone rings. When she did, she leaped across its barren center, tossed her rucksack aside, and vaulted onto the raised platform at the focal point of the incline. Her leap landed true. But her exuberance caused her to skim her toe on the way up. "Ouch!" she yelped. "I almost broke my damn foot! Dammit! Calm down, Cassiopeia! I'm gettin' too excited! Geez! I'm always gettin' too excited!"

"What is this place?" Aiden shouted from the gradient's midpoint.

Cass turned, raised her hands to her brow, and took in the view. "THIS, MY DEAR AIDEN? THIS IS AN AMPHITHEATER! At least it used to be. I don't think anyone has stood up here for a long time—a very long time. Centuries probably…"

"What's an amphitheater?" Aiden asked, continuing his cautious descent.

"It's an outdoor arena, where people would perform on stage. On *this* stage," Cass tapped her foot on the stone slab, summoning the ghosts of the forgotten performers. Then she pointed at the seats carved into the slope, as if an invisible crowd was egging her on.

"The patrons would sit out there, on top of all those rock seats. And they would watch theatrical performances up here. And concerts—with instruments and musicians, you know? They probably used to set up a white screen and show movies too—using light projectors, the kind they had in the olden days."

"A theatrical performance? What's that, Cass?"

"I'll show you, Aiden! You sit down there and be my audience!"

Aiden sat down on the cold stoop and watched Cass take a deep breath and push her shoulders back. Then she elevated her neck, straightened her spine, and adopted a formal, regal gait as she strutted to the left, proudly and slowly. She surveyed the territory above his head, as if a crowd of thousands sat behind him. Then, Cass made a pronouncement that echoed across the valley:

To be, or not to be? That is the question! Whether 'tis nobler in the mind to suffer the slings and arrows of outrageous fortune, or, to take up arms against a sea of troubles!

"What does that mean?" Aiden said. He sat with his arms crossed, struggling to understand Cass's words, squinting at her with a puzzled frown.

Cass broke character and turned to scream at her heckler. "AIDEN! SHUT UP! YOU'RE RUINING MY SOLILOQUY, ASSHOLE! GOD! My heavens... Now I gotta start all over..."

Aiden flinched and raised his palms up in surrender, signaling that he would afford the actor with the reverence her role deserved.

Cass did a little spin on the stage. Then she resumed her prior form and continued:

Again I say! To be, or not to be? That is the question! Is it nobler to suffer with your bow and arrow, or, to die in a big sea of trouble...! Ah dammit... I fucked it up... Never you mind! Consider this boy sitting here in the cheap seats! He has neither the wit nor the wisdom to heed my words! For he spends all his days languishing in a fantasy world, and probably wanking off to nude harlots on the grid! The poor forsaken soul... Show me a man that is not passion's slave, and I will wear him in my heart's core!

"Is that really part of the speech?" Aiden asked, his voice edged with bafflement and irritation.

Cass ignored his inquiry and waved an accusatory finger his way.

Silence, pod dweller! I dare say that, in ancient times, a boy of this cast who interrupted a proclamation of mine would be pelted with rotten fruit—which, in all honesty, might improve both his attitude and his attire concomitantly!

"Okay, that's enough performance art," Aiden said. He stood up from the stone stoop, approached the stage, and offered his hand to the lone thespian. "Can we go now, Cass?"

Cass broke into giggles. Her theatrical mask of nobility fell away, revealing the mischievous smile that Aiden found so endearing. Once his body was in range of the stage, Cass leapt into his arms. Her colorful skirt billowing in the wind as she achieved flight. Aiden's hands caught her on her naked ass. To complete her landing, Cass wrapped her legs around his waist and thrust her groin into his. Then, using her thigh muscles, she squeezed hard, giving them both a jolt of pleasure. "Ay, there's the rub," she moaned. Then she planted a kiss on Aiden's lips.

Aiden closed his eyes and returned the gesture, delighting again in the capriciousness of his lover's whims and the mercurial dance of her moods, which flowed from tempestuous to tender without warning or explanation.

When Cass retreated from her kiss, she leaned in and moved her lips to his ear. "Hey, Aiden," she said, "can you give a girl a ride?"

"A ride?"

"Yes, please?"

Cass grappled Aiden's shoulders and scurried her body around his broad frame. Then she strung her arms around his neck and held on tight. "A piggyback ride, Aiden! I got too excited when I saw that stage. I stubbed my toe when I jumped on it."

"Piggyback?"

"Yeah! Carry me on your back. You're my horse, Aiden! Go! Go! Go! Take us home. But gallop by the orchestra pit so I can get my rucksack first."

Aiden sent his arms downward and locked them around Cass's thighs. Then he took a step forward.

"That's it!" Cass shouted. "Onward, my stallion! Though this be madness, there is method in it!"

Aiden walked near the leather rucksack and leaned forward. Cass snatched it up and slung it around her right shoulder. "Got it, Aiden!" she yelled. "Now go! Return us now to the primrose path!"

Aiden trotted up the cracked stone steps with his jockey riding high on his back. Then he continued along toward his pod—toward home. As his gallop progressed, the amphitheater blurred into the background, swallowed by silence once again as the couple's playful chaos spilled back onto the old trail that wove between the pods.

"Mmm, you're so strong and powerful, Aiden," Cass said as she flung her head around and kissed his left cheek. "Thanks for being my audience. That was so much fun. I haven't been to a play in years."

"What's a play?"

"That's what they'd call the performance—on the stage, with actors and costumes. A play is kind of like a live movie. There were no cameras in the olden days, so the actors had to perform the same scene—over and over again—for a new crowd each night."

"That must have been very boring for the actors," Aiden said.

"Maybe sometimes. I really liked all the attention though."

"You were an actor?"

"I still am."

"What does that mean?"

"Oh, Aiden... All the world's a stage, and all the men and women, merely players. Hah! But, yeah, in my village back home we've got a little amphitheater near the commons. Not as big as that one, but big enough. I've done some acting. Though I was usually just cast as a tree or a bush when I was a kid. But one year, I played a pixie named Tinker Bell. That was fun. I got to wear wings and fly through the air on a zip line. I got to wear my hair teased up. And I had a cute short skirt too. I looked hot."

"Really?"

"Oh yeah. It used to drive my ex-boyfriend crazy."

"Crazy with lust?"

"No, crazy with jealousy. He wanted me to quit the play."

"So did you?"

"Hell no!"

"Why not?"

"Because... BECAUSE THE SHOW MUST GO ON!" Cass screamed in Aiden's ear while raising a defiant fist to the sky. Aiden recoiled and gave his head a quick shake, recovering from her deafening declaration.

"Were you really that devoted to the theater?" he asked.

"Well, YEAH! Well, no... not really. Mostly, I just didn't like the guy that much. I had my eye on someone else."

"Another guy?"

"Yeah. The other guy had a cool eagle tattoo. I like tattoos. I eventually had a rough breakup with the first guy though. Well, rough for him anyway... It got quite dramatic there for a while. Guess that's why the school called us the Drama Department. Hah!"

"Hmm... Is that where you learned how to recite historical narratives?"

"Narratives?"

"That speech you gave back there—'To be, or not to be'—what does it mean, Cass?"

"Oh, yeah... It's an old bit. It's from an old story. The main character—Hamlet—he's tryin' to decide if he should fight through life's battles or just give up and kill himself."

"So which does he choose?"

"He chooses to fight. Only pussies take the easy way out!"

"Ahh. So I assume he was ultimately victorious, right?"

"Somewhat... But nearly everyone in the story ends up dead anyway—Hamlet, his mom, his uncle, his girlfriend, they all die."

"That sounds tragic."

"That's why they call it a *Shakespearean tragedy*, Aiden."

"What does that mean?"

"That means there's no happy ending. After the show is over, all that remains is grief and heartache."

"That's horrible, Cass."

"That's life, Aiden. Remember, I told you my founder's epitaph: *You can live either a beautiful lie or a rough reality, nothing in between*. Life sucks sometimes—real life that is. Not every story has a happy ending.

In fact, *most* do not. Heck, how do you think *our* little story is gonna end?"

Cass bit her lip before she finished her last sentence. But her tone carried a twinge that caused Aiden to falter. And, though her words were clipped, they bore enough weight to halt his trot. "Cass," he said after coming to a stop, "what do you mean? What are you trying to say? Do you think our…"

"Ooh! Aiden, look at that!" Cass said, wiggling free of his grasp and sliding down his limber backside like it was a firepole. When her feet hit the ground, she scampered south in pursuit of yet another serendipitous distraction. Aiden watched her leap from the trail and skid to a stop beside a row of green shrubs. He followed after her with shoulders hunched, burdened by the weight of their unfinished conversation.

When Aiden arrived at the object of Cass's latest fancy, he found her kneeling beside the foliage. Each plant was perched on its own rise of soil. The earth below it was darker and more deliberate than the land around it. Tiny blue spheres peeked through the leaves, shy but plump, their brilliant color shining bright against the greenery.

"Someone's been outside their pod, Aiden," Cass said as she surveyed the plot. "Look at 'em! These are blueberry bushes."

Cass plucked a berry from its leafy hiding place. Then she rolled it between her thumb and forefinger, inspecting it with a practiced eye. "These are ready to pick," she said, her voice dropping to a whisper. "They look tasty. This soil has been mixed with somethin' rich— probably some bio-engineered growth substrate. And look at the spacing between the shrubs. It's a bit tight for my taste, but whoever planted them knew at least enough about horticulture to keep the roots from chokin' each other out."

Cass handed the blueberry to Aiden. "Here, try it," she said. Then she hunted for more berries in the bushes. Aiden accepted her gift and held it at eye level, studying it with caution. He had never eaten anything that didn't come from the grid. But today had been a day of many firsts. What followed was about to be another.

He placed the berry in his mouth and split it down the middle with his front teeth. It opened on his tongue, releasing a bright, untamed sweetness that lingered like a promise. It tasted fresh—alive. Nothing like the blueberry-flavored meal packs he'd been consuming for decades. The contrast was severe; it left him wondering why the grid had the audacity to call their gray gooey meals "blueberry cobbler."

Cass found another berry on the bush and jammed it into her mouth. Then she plucked ten more and packed them in too. Soon, her cheeks bulged outward. To Aiden, she looked like one of the chipmunks that gathered nuts around the south gate of his gaming team's fortress.

"Mmm… Yum…" Cass mumbled after biting down on the mass in her mouth. A stream of blue juice dribbled down her chin, as feral as the smile that erupted beneath her freckles. "These are better than I expected!

Whoever cultivated this plot has a thumb greener than a goblin. Dang... I wonder who lives here?"

Cass turned her attention to the pod near the row of shrubs. "Hey, Aiden, this pod has a bubble window! It's so cool!"

Aiden followed Cass's gaze and spotted the anomaly. A clear bubble projected outward from the dome, clinging to the side and catching the sunlight. It looked as if a giant dewdrop was frozen in place while rolling down the curved wall.

"I bet it's made of plexiglass," Cass said. "It's got a nice bend to it. It's so neat! How come your pod doesn't have a window like this, Aiden? How come *none* of the pods have a window like this? I like it!"

Cautiously, Aiden drifted toward Cass for a closer look. The window must have been a custom addition, affixed to the dome long after the pod was manufactured. The resident must have used a saw to cut a half-meter hole in the shell. Then they attached the bubble-shaped window to the side, probably with resin.

"Hey, Aiden! Look at this!" Cass said as she returned to the row of bushes. "There's a bot over here!"

Cass fell to her knees and bellied up to a rusty chassis resting at the end of the plot. To Aiden, it looked like a box full of teeth and trouble. Long metal blades crowded its interior, stacked like a brood of raptors waiting to chew through anything foolish enough to get too close. Exposed pistons and wires ran along its weathered frame—the muscles and nerves of an organism he was not familiar with, and wouldn't dare touch.

"Be careful," he said. "What is it?"

"It's an auto-tiller, Aiden. It's a machine that upturns the ground for planting. It shifts the soil so that the roots can penetrate deeper into the earth. Looks like this one has a busted piston though. Hmm..."

Aiden walked over to Cass and watched as she tucked her fingers beneath a black hose that protruded from the device. "I bet I could fix it if I had my kit here," she said. "Without it, I'm not sure I'll be able to knock this back in."

Aiden leaned in and peeked over Cass's shoulder, trying to make sense of the unfamiliar components. Trying to match the jumble of parts to something he'd seen in the virtual worlds. Aiden liked technology. Aiden lived with technology—he'd spent every waking moment of his life interacting with it. And yet, as he watched Cass so confidently tug at the nest of wires, he realized how little of it he truly understood.

"I think this thing has seen too many winters," Cass said, sending her fingers down deep to twist a bent bracket into place.

"Cass, maybe we shouldn't be touching it. It's not ours anyway."

"Oh, calm down, Aiden. I know what I'm doin'! I've been workin' on agriculture bots since before you could even…"

WHOOOOOOOOP!
WHOOOOOOOOP!
WHOOOOOOOOP!

A long, tortured howl poured out from the machine's bowels. Its wail rolled out in trembling waves, rattling the surrounding air and sending both Aiden and Cass scrambling backward in retreat.

"Oh, my heavens!" Cass yelled as she leaped to her feet.

The little machine leaped to its feet too. Or rather, its four treads extended out from its metal frame, punching down into the soil. With a grinding spin, the bot whirled around. And then, from its top panel, a rusty lens emerged, gears grinding with grit as it leveled its stare at its assailants.

Cass took another step back.

So did Aiden. But when he did, the machine rotated again, pointing its lens at him this time.

"Cass!" Aiden hissed. "What do I do now? Is it going to shoot me?"

The color drained from Aiden's cheeks as he slowly raised his hands—uncertain if he should prepare for combat or beg for mercy. "What's it doing, Cass? What does it want?"

Aiden was scared.

But Cass, as usual, was unfazed. "Hey, little guy!" she said with a playful wave. "Look over here! Look at me!"

The bot whirled its body around and pointed its lens back at Cass. Aiden kept his hands high and watched as she crouched toward the irate bot. "Hello there," she said with a wink. "Do you need assistance?"

The machine didn't respond. It just continued to point its shaky metal eye at her. Its four mud-caked treads continued to twitch, and a series of harsh clicks rattled through its frame.

After a few more tense and jittery seconds, Cass made another attempt. "What's wrong? Can I give you a hand?" she asked while reaching for the bot.

The bot looked at Cass's creeping hand. It locked onto her fingers, studying them as they neared its lens casing. To Aiden, it looked like a scared guard dog—the kind he'd seen deployed at the entrance of the Shadowmoor Castle. The kind that barked a fearful defensive *woof* every time his avatar strolled by. Aiden knew that—typically—the bark of such creatures was bigger than the bite. But still, he had been bitten before. (At least, his avatar had.) And he deduced that real metal teeth hurt more than the virtual kind.

"Cass," Aiden whispered, "I don't think that's a good idea."

Cass ignored Aiden's comment and continued her advance. When the tip of her forefinger neared the bot's lens, she spoke to it again. "Are you hurt? Can I help you? I know how to…"

"UNAUTHORIZED USER!" the bot screamed when Cass's finger brushed its casing.

"UNAUTHORIZED USER!"

"UNAUTHORIZED USER!"

The bot's announcement was loud and garbled, amplified by a fuzzy speaker located somewhere deep in its belly. Its treads roared to life, the whole frame twitching as it sprang backward, pivoted sharply, and fled in the opposite direction of Cass's outstretched hand.

"CALL THE MANAGER!" it screeched as it rolled to the end of the plot. When it reached the last bush, it halted its sprint. Then, it rotated in place and, once again, sent its treads turning. It lunged forward in a crooked burst of motion, a metallic panic so erratic that Aiden struggled to guess which direction might save him from its charge. It seemed to be rolling toward the adjacent pod. Perhaps it intended to hide in there. But Aiden saw no way for it to get inside. The hatch was closed. Even still, the bot appeared to be committed to the charge. It drove right into it.

"CLAAAAAAAANGGGG!"

The impact was hard. So hard that the aluminum hatch was transformed into an impromptu percussion instrument. Its thin alloy surface reverberated with a sustained, brassy ring that reminded Cass of the ceremonial gong used in her village's drum circle.

"Oh boy!" Cass said as she jammed her fingers in her ears. "The jig is up, Aiden! Whoever is in there knows we're out here now!"

Aiden put his fingers in his ears too. The metallic clang crawled into his skull and throbbed, a lingering vibration he couldn't shake away.

"Hey, Aiden!" Cass hollered.

Aiden saw Cass's mouth moving. But he could scarcely parse her words.

"Remember when I asked if you wanted to play *ding, dong, ditch*? WELL IT'S TIME TO PLAY NOW! HAH!"

Most of Cass's syllables were drowned out by the metallic ringing. The noise was deafening… Nearly unbearable… Aiden leaned forward, slammed his eyes shut, and pushed his fingers even harder into his ears.

He wanted the clanging rattle to stop.

More than anything, he just wanted it to stop…

Thankfully, just then, it did.

It ended as quickly as it had begun.

Once again, Serenity Valley was serene.

But why?

Aiden didn't know why. But when he opened his eyes, the answer to his question was revealed:

The pod's resident had sent the aluminum hatch sailing up its guide rails.

The pod's hatchway was open.

Ch. 14: Good Fences Make Good Neighbors

"These aren't the droids you're looking for."

The voice came from the pod. The pod's hatchway was open. The movement of the hatch up its vertical guide rails muted the brassy resonance that had rolled through the heart of Serenity Valley. At last, the sound of silence had returned.

Aiden allowed his fingers to drift down from his ears in a manner paced by caution—half-expecting the brutal clamor to surge back at any moment. Cass dropped her arms in one swift motion and fixed her gaze on the figure in the doorway. She couldn't make out his features. All she could see was the dark silhouette of a gaunt man standing straight and stationary. He seemed to be studying them. His stillness was charged with the weight of his next move—whatever it might be.

Cass had no idea how he'd react to their intrusion. So she bit her lip and considered her options.

Should I jump him…?

Should I run…?

Should I try to scare him off…?

Hmm…

She sent a slantwise glance at Aiden and recognized his typical expression of paralyzed fright.

What a pussy…!

Looks like hot stuff ain't gonna get us out of this one…

But this is only the second person he's ever met in his life…

So I guess I can't expect too much…

The man in the pod squared his stance and broke the quiet with a measured remark. "If your intent was to steal my tiller, you might want to reconsider your course of action. This little guy is broken. He won't be planting any more crops. At least not this season."

Cass shifted her weight as she considered the man's words.

Great…

He thinks we're thieves…

Now what am I gonna do…?

Better just run the ol' mouth…

"Well, hello there!" Cass said. "Nice Star Wars reference! I like Star Wars too. Droids, huh? Hah! Yeah, I'm sorry I spooked your tiller. I just noticed the damaged piston on top and I gave it a tug to try to reset it. But then the alarm went off, and it started squallin' like a hog in a hailstorm. Never seen a tiller bot with a biometric security alarm before. I've seen alarms like that on guns, but not on tillers. That's pretty tricky. Don't worry though, I'm not in the tiller snatchin' business. I just let curiosity get the better of me again. Admittedly, it's been a recurring problem in my life. Curiosity killed the cat. And my mama used to say that I'd be long dead by now if I weren't born with nine lives. Sorry about all the commotion, though."

The man in the pod scratched at his cheek while consuming Cass's feast of words. When her rambling banquet was complete, a hush fell over the party. They all knew the next sentence to break from the man's mouth would determine how the interaction would progress. As Cass waited for the verdict, her mind spun through several possible contingencies.

Is he buyin' my rap...?
Is he mad at me...?
Is he gonna get us in trouble...?
He might call the Manager...
We probably gotta skedaddle...
I shoulda worn my running shoes...
Dammit...

As the silence droned on, Cass prepared herself for the worst. But when the man finally spoke, he sounded more *amused* than angry. "How curious," he said, "I never knew my tiller had a security alarm. Huh... Then again, no one has ever touched that bot but me. So, I guess it's just something that never came up. Fascinating..."

Cass released the breath she'd been holding and allowed her shoulders to relax. Maybe the meeting wasn't doomed after all; she just needed to find a scrap of common ground between them. She was good at that.

"Fascinating indeed!" she said. "And that is one nice auto-tiller you got there. Are you a farmer? I am! Been doin' it my whole life. It's a tough gig. *You* know that. Half the job is prayin' that the plants grow, and the other half is convincin' the livestock that you ain't gonna eat 'em— even though you aim to."

"Are you really a farmer?" the man said with a laugh. "I haven't met a farmer in a long time—a very long time."

The man lifted his leg and took a step through the hatchway. His booted foot came down on the gravel path that circumscribed the foundation of the pod. His next step carried the rest of his body over the threshold, bringing his head into the light of dusk. When the man's face was finally unshadowed, Cass remained quiet. But Aiden let out a sharp gasp that escaped before he could swallow it.

The man was old—very old. Aiden had never seen an old person before, not in the flesh. He had met avatars in the games that were modeled to look like aged, battle-scarred warriors. And he had viewed the faces of older actors in ancient movies. But those encounters did not prepare him for the sight before him.

The man's skin draped down his jaw in thinning folds, cascading along his neck and settling in loose layers that looked like melted wax. Deep horizontal ravines carved their way across his forehead and flanked his eyes—two cloudy blue gems, nestled deep within pouches of weathered flesh. Thin threads of long white hair sprouted from his scalp and fell across his cheeks, stopping abruptly once they met his shirt collar. An evening breeze wandered through his pale strands, raising them in a soft flutter before laying them gently against his nape.

The man zipped his jacket to face the rising chill. Then he folded his arms across his chest and leveled his gaze at his visitors. "No, I'm surely not a professional farmer," he said. "I bought the tiller on the grid last season when I took up gardening as a hobby. But it stopped working a few months ago. The blades stopped engaging. So this year, I had to turn the soil myself. That was hard work. Do you really know what's wrong with the piston?"

"Well, I'm pretty sure I do," Cass said, quick to regain her confident demeanor. "If you stored the tiller outside last winter then the frost might have got to it. The temp differentials can cause the fluid to contract and expand. That'll crack the cylinder seal eventually, which would explain the pressure loss and the failure to engage the blades." Cass pointed a finger at the vertical piston that jutted out from the bot's bowels. "See that hairline fracture right there along the casing?" she asked.

The man put his hands on his hips and leaned forward to give the tiller a closer look. "Hmm," he said. "Yes, I think I do see what you're referring to. Interesting…"

"Yeah, that's what's gummin' up the works," Cass continued. "That part needs to be replaced pronto. It doesn't look too pricey though. I bet you could buy somethin' like that on the grid for just a couple coins."

"Yes," the man said, "I might try that…"

The bot's four treaded feet came alive again. The machine shuddered and spun on its axis, spinning in conflicting directions like a spooked critter trying to decide where to hide.

The man approached the bot, knelt down, and ran two gentle fingers along its shaky lens casing. "Hey, it's okay," he said. "These two aren't going to hurt you. Don't be such a scaredy cat. You're making a lot of commotion out here. You're gonna wake up the whole valley. Now go on back to your charging dock. It's over there."

The man gave the bot a push toward a metal platform that sat near the west side of his pod. The bot seemed to understand his soft words. It obeyed without protest, performing an immediate 180-degree turn and rolling to its charging station. Once there, it retracted its four treads and collapsed downward with a pneumatic puff of relief.

Aiden wondered if the man's claim was correct. Had all this noise really managed to 'wake up the whole valley?' Did any of his neighbors react at all to the ear-piercing *CLANG* from the bot's antics?

Did anyone notice...?

Anyone...?

Aiden scanned the territory, darting his eyes from hatch to hatch, looking for some sign of movement amongst the mute monoliths, some twitch of life to prove that Pod Land had a pulse. But the surrounding domes remained stoic—still as tombstones in a graveyard. Not a single hatch was open. No prying eyes peered out. There was no evidence to suggest that their intrusion had disturbed anyone but the jittery tiller bot and its owner.

Aiden returned his gaze to the man, but a flicker of color caught his left eye as he was pivoting. He turned back around to resume his scan of the valley. That's when he saw her...

At about forty meters south and four meters east, Aiden could see a startling splotch of purple, unnaturally vivid against the mute palette of dirt, domes, and dropseed. He focused on the distant smear. When he did, he could almost make out a face—a woman's face. She was wearing a hooded tunic and peering out from her open hatchway. She was looking at them. She was looking at *him*. Aiden realized it must be the same woman he had seen exiting the passenger drone two days ago, after the construction of her new pod in the valley.

He leaned forward and squinted into the dimming light. Then he moved his hand to his forehead to block the rays of the low sun. But, by the time his fingers met his brow, the woman and her purple tunic were gone. The hatch was closed. Maybe forever.

"Anyway," the old man said, taking a step toward Cass. "I can't remember the last time I had a friendly chat in Serenity Valley. You seem friendly enough. Do you have a name?"

Cass smiled, her girlish charm resurfacing without a hitch, her voice softening into the sweet lilt she used for putting strangers at ease. She liked meeting new people. And she was quick to send her right hand thrusting outward toward the chest of her unexpected host.

"My name's Cassiopeia. Cass for short. And this tall guy here standin' next to me with a slack jaw is Aiden. Pleased to meet ya!"

The man looked down at her outstretched arm and widened his eyes with delight. "Oh," he said, "I haven't had a handshake in a long time—a very long time." He reached down, grabbed Cass's hand, and performed the ancient ritual, marveling at the nostalgia it stirred.

"I'm pleased to meet you too," the man said. After releasing Cass's hand, he turned toward Aiden. Cass turned too. But they could both see that Aiden's thoughts had wandered elsewhere. When the old man offered his hand, Aiden just stared at it, taking in the display of blotches and ridges that time had inscribed into the man's weathered flesh. His appendage was laden with the indelible marks of mortality. The skin that clung to him was pale. No, not pale, clear—almost completely translucent. A web of veins could be seen running under the surface. And the hand shook. It quivered with the fragile rhythm of a worn-out metronome struggling to hold its beat.

The man was an archetypal specimen of biological decay—the embodiment of every ailment the grid was built to counteract. The sight of him filled Aiden with equal measures of wonder and dread. And he was bewildered by Cass's ability to remain undaunted in the presence of such a merciless display of entropy's cruelty.

"Why are you so old?" Aiden asked the man.

Cass grabbed Aiden's shirt collar and yanked him downward so she could hiss into his ear. "Aiden! Shush! Don't be so rude!"

The old man laughed and withdrew his right hand. "Oh, do I look old to you?" he said. "I hadn't noticed myself. Huh... Well, let's just say I was late to the party when they were mixing the DNA milkshakes. By the time the grid began producing genetically optimized newborns, I was already well into my seventies."

Aiden's breath hitched as he considered the daunting implications of the man's statement.

"Yep, it's true!" he continued. "I was born in 1991. Much too early to get the good spooge like you obviously got, buddy. My genome is *au naturel*—with the exception of a few tweaks here and there to prevent the spell of aging from getting a foothold in my cells. My biochemistry has been altered a bit. I won't get any older. But I won't get any younger either. Oh well. C'est la vie."

The man shrugged and turned his attention back to Cass. "And how about you, young lady? Judging by your accent, I'm guessing your genome is *au naturel* as well."

"Yessir, it is!" Cass replied. She brushed her fingertips along her curved figure, curtsied, and gave her long patchwork skirt a wave. "I was born in a barn, not a beaker! Chosen by chance and by the grace of God."

"Well then," the man said, "it looks like God broke the mold after he made you, didn't he?"

"Well, I sure hope so!" Cass declared. "Lord knows there's only enough room for *one* of me on this godforsaken planet!"

"Huh..." the old man said, amused by her provincial forwardness. "So you're obviously not from around here... Where are you from?"

"Oh, I'm from..." Cass caught herself before finishing her sentence, concluding it was best to maintain a low profile. "I'm from off-grid. I'm just passin' through."

"Really..." the man said. He was eager to learn more, but he sensed that further inquiry would not be welcomed. "Well, I haven't met an off-gridder in a long time—a very long time. Welcome to Pod Land."

"Why, thank you!" Cass said. "And do tell, what is your name, kind sir?"

"Ah, yes... Well, I never used my given name much around here. But a long time ago, when people would actually leave their pods to socialize in the valley, everyone just referred to me as 'the old man.' I guess it was because I was the oldest one in the vicinity. I still am, I assume... In fact, I might be the oldest person on Earth at this point. But there's no easy way to verify that... Anyway, I kinda miss that sobriquet. So you can just call me 'the old man' if you like."

"Well, okay, old man," Cass said. "Nice to meet ya! Can I ask you somethin' though? Have you really been here that long? You were here when folks would leave their pods and socialize? Like as a community? They would gather together for parties and plays and stuff like that?"

"Yes, they would. A long time ago, they would do all of that."

"Do you know why they stopped doin' it? What happened? Why did everyone turn into turtles?"

The old man tucked his thumbs into his belt and shifted his weight. "I've thought about that question a lot," he said. "A couple centuries ago, it was quite the topic du jour. Not so much anymore though. Lots of theories were flung around back then. Seems like none of them managed to stick. Maybe no one knows the real answer for sure. It might come down to a simple adage: *'Good fences make good neighbors.'* I guess..."

"But stony limits cannot hold love out!" Cass said in retort.

The old man took a step back and laughed. "Heh! You're quite a fan of Shakespeare, aren't you?"

"I dabble," Cass said.

The man turned toward Aiden, quick to note the look of anxious befuddlement on his face. "So what about you, kid?" he asked. "You're Aiden, huh? I think I've seen you before. You live in that pod over there—about 80 meters up the valley? Right?"

The man pointed a shaky finger in the direction of Aiden's pod and waited for a response. But Aiden remained quiet. So the man tried to elaborate. "You're the guy who sits on his dome and watches the sunset in the evenings. I've spotted you up there a few times while I was working in my garden. Isn't that you?"

"Uhm," Aiden mumbled, "yeah, that's me. I like to watch the sunset. It's pretty."

"Well, yeah. It's pretty as hell in this valley, ain't it? Too bad nobody seems to notice anymore. Nobody except *you*. In fact, now that I think about it, you folks are the only two souls I've seen walking around Serenity Valley since... gosh, I dunno... since around the time my wife died."

"How many years ago was that?" Cass asked.

"Hmm... Well... Let me see... Hang on." The old man turned his head toward the open pod hatch and cupped his hand over his mouth. "Honey," he hollered, "how long have you been dead?"

In a flash, a woman's face appeared in the pod's bubble window. She had long black hair secured with a white headband that kept her face unobscured. Her porcelain pink complexion contrasted starkly with her dark tresses, which came to rest atop her high-collared blue dress.

The woman glanced at Cass and Aiden briefly. Then she answered the old man's question. "It was 228 years ago last month, dear."

"Ah," the old man said. "228 years... Don't they go by in a blink. How about that..."

"Who are you talking to out there, dear?" the woman asked.

"Just meeting the neighbors," the man said.

"Oh, isn't that nice. Your tarts are done baking if they'd like one."

"Oh, what a splendid idea! Can you wrap up two for me please?"

"Yes, dear."

The old man turned his attention back toward Aiden and Cass. Noting the puzzled look on their faces, he realized an explanation was in order. "That's not my wife, of course. My wife is dead. That's my pod's A.I. caretaker. But her avatar was modeled based on my wife's geometry and her mannerisms. She looks like my wife, and she talks like my wife; she copies her French accent well too. Though, the simulation isn't perfect. She's not quite the same as my wife... But, oh well... Whatever gets you through the night, eh?"

The old man shrugged and turned toward the hatch as the pod's mechanical arm breached the threshold with its cargo of pastries.

"Voilà, mon chéri," the pod's caretaker said.

"Parfait, merci," the man said as he retrieved the package from the metal pincers. "You two are gonna love these! Here, come have a look." He unfurled the top flap to give Aiden and Cass a peek at his creation. "These are blueberry tarts. One for each of you. They're fresh. I make them from scratch. Right here, using berries from my little garden."

"Oh, how very nice of you," Cass said. "They look scrumptious."

"They sure are! They're the sweetest thing you'll ever eat."

The man refastened the top flap and offered the package to Cass. "Here you go. Take them. Serve them for dessert tonight, after dinner."

Cass wiggled out of her rucksack and dropped it to her feet. Then she extended both hands and accepted the man's gift with a toothy smile. "Well, thank you so much," she beamed. "It's been ages since I've had a fruit tart made of blueberries. We've got a lot of apple trees in my village. But no blueberry bushes to speak of. This will be a real treat!"

Cass placed the package into her rucksack and took stock of her meager inventory. "I'm not properly equipped to exchange gifts at the moment. I don't got much to trade with ya."

"Oh, that's okay," the man said. "This one's on the house."

"No, no, no. I'd feel horrible if I left you empty-handed—especially after packin' my cheeks full of berries from your blessed plot. Here, wait a minute! I think I got somethin' you might like!" Cass fished out the half-empty jar of applejack and held it before the old man with a triumphant flourish. "Here you go! I got a jar of homebrewed applejack for ya. It's only half full cuz we imbibed last night. But there's still enough in there to get the job done. This stuff is made from scratch too. My older brother has his own distillery in his barn. Of course, his little enterprise is not known for producing the smoothest of spirits. But his piss water packs a punch—that's for sure!"

The old man accepted Cass's gift. Then he eyed the jar and gave the amber liquid a swirl. "Real applejack, huh? Homebrewed applejack? It's probably been over three centuries since I've had something like that."

"Well, lucky you then! This stuff can make a mule do the mambo."

Aiden observed the easy rhythm that flowed between Cass and the old man—the way their words passed back and forth without hesitation, the way their rapport developed so naturally, so organically. He felt like an intruder in a conversation that no longer needed him. Jealousy crept up his spine. Envy followed soon after. He envied Cass's confidence, her intuitive grasp of human nature, and her talent for making anyone in her orbit feel comfortable and charmed.

How do you do that, Cass...?

How do you glow...?

In an attempt to rejoin the conversation, Aiden tried to think of something positive to say about Cass's gift. "That applejack will knock your socks off, sir," he blurted out—a bit too loud. "We both drank some last night. I thought it was very flavorful, and Cass said it was a panty dropper."

Cass whipped her head to the left and shot Aiden a glare that froze him solid. "AIDEN!" she hissed. "GEEZ, SHUT UP!"

Aiden remained motionless as his mind scrambled to understand why Cass looked ready to strangle him.

"I can't take you anywhere!" she whispered after releasing a gasp of irritated breath and rolling her eyes to the heavens. "Don't mind him, sir," she said to the old man. "He's been cooped up in a pod for the last 22 years, and he's only recently learned how to interact with the outside world."

"Hmm… interesting," the old man said as he leaned back and took stock of the odd couple on his porch. "It sounds like you've been teaching him a few tricks, huh?"

"One or two. But anyway, I can see we've kept you outside long enough. I'm sorry for disturbing the peace with your tiller. I think I'm right about that piston though. If you jam a new casing in there, that bot should be back in business by breakfast."

"Yes, thank you. I'll try that," the man said.

Cass nodded and retrieved her rucksack from the ground. Then, with one quick, practiced tug, she sent the pack orbiting around her body. When its flight neared her right shoulder, she yanked the strap through the ladder-lock and cinched it tight with a brisk flick of her wrist. "Well, good night to you, kind sir," she said. "I'd best be getting this one back home before he opens his mouth again."

Cass tugged at Aiden's arm and spun his body in the direction of the trail. "Come along, mon chéri. Say good night to your new friend."

"Good night, new friend," Aiden said. He was about to reach toward the man and attempt a handshake, but Cass was already pulling at his elbow, guiding him back to the primrose path.

"Good night," the old man said. "Come visit anytime."

"Okay," Aiden said as Cass wrapped her right arm around his waist and gave his chiseled torso a squeeze.

The couple took a few more steps down the path. Then Cass cocked her head to the left for one final farewell. "Ta-ta!" she hollered over her shoulder. "And thanks again for the blueberry tarts!"

"You're welcome," the old man hollered back.

A hush settled between the couple as they each sifted through the day's events in solitary contemplation. Once they heard the familiar *whoosh* of the man's pod hatch closing, they knew they had the valley to themselves again.

"The world is ours, Aiden. We're just two hawks in a land full of caged birds, aren't we…?"

"I guess," Aiden said.

"By the way, remind me to never let you out of your cage again."

"Why? What did I do?"

"It's what you said, not what you did."

"What did I say?"

"Well, as the bard wrote, 'The better part of valor is discretion,' Aiden. Hah! Especially when you're talkin' about droppin' panties. Geez!"

"Oh. I'm sorry. Perhaps I should have chosen my words more carefully."

"Oh, never mind. It doesn't matter. Your neighbor seems like a very nice man—a wise man. I bet you could learn a lot from him."

"Yes, I bet we *both* could."

Aiden waited for some sort of acknowledgment from Cass, but she was oddly quiet after his proposal. He gave her hand a squeeze, but she was unreactive. When he shifted his gaze to her, he could see she was lost in thought. Her eyes were focused on a distant point, one where the rows of pods disappeared over the horizon.

As the minutes marched on, Aiden found Cass's silence disconcerting. She rarely kept her lips closed so long. But it had been a venturesome day; perhaps she was tired. Aiden was tired too. He was eager to get home. And he was looking forward to a reprise of last night's indulgence. But he feared things were unlikely to unfold with such gusto without the social lubricant afforded by his amour's special cocktail.

"Cass," Aiden said, "why did you give the old man your jar of applejack?"

The offhand question seemed to draw Cass back to the moment; she responded quickly, as if she had never drifted away at all. "Why?" she asked. "Well... because that's what you do when you visit someone's home, Aiden."

"What do you do?"

"You exchange gifts. Usually, you just bring a plate of somethin' tasty to eat, like the tarts he gave us. Or you bring alcohol of some sort."

"Is that a tradition from the olden days?"

"Yeah, kinda. Also, you gotta remember that—in my village—we have to barter or trade for pretty much everything. He gave us somethin' sweet, so I had to do the same for him."

"Oh... That's charming, Cass. But now there's nothing for us to drink tonight. Would you like me to order an alcoholic beverage from the grid?"

"I think we drank enough last night, Aiden. Besides, I've got somethin' special planned for you this evening."

"Really?" Aiden asked.

"Yeah."

"What is it?"

"I can't tell you now! That would ruin the surprise. But I promise, it's gonna knock your socks off."

Ch. 15: The Magic Hour

"I gotta pee so bad I can taste it!"

Cass was pacing beside Aiden's pod, hopping from one foot to the other as she waited for him to unlock the hatch that stood between her and sweet relief.

"Just one moment," Aiden said as he approached the pod's utility panel. He wiped a bit of grime off the scanner and covered it with his palm—the only key to the pod's interior.

"Come on, Aiden!" Cass hollered. "Open it up! I really gotta go now! Pretty sure I gotta poop too! Hurry!"

Aiden leaned into the device, applying even more pressure to the cold, flat surface that hosted his hand.

"Why's it takin' so long just to scan your damn palm? Are you messin' with me, Aiden?"

"No, it takes a few seconds. The scanner doesn't just analyze my fingerprints. It examines a set of twelve biomarkers which are vital for…"

WHOOOOOSH!

"Open sesame!" Cass proclaimed as the hatch finally parted from the dome to embark on its smooth ride up its guide rails. As soon as the entryway was revealed, she darted past Aiden and performed a jeté over the pod threshold. Then she scurried around the center interface chair and sprinted for the toilet. "Make way! Make way!" she yelled. "Clear the damn harbor! The S.S. Cassiopeia needs to drop her anchor!"

As Cass fled into the bathroom partition, Aiden chuckled—amused by her childish antics. He walked to the kitchen sink and poured himself a cup of water. When the liquid met his mouth, it was crisp and startling, jolting him enough to make him notice how parched he truly was. Aiden had never known thirst before. He had never known privation of any kind. The hint of hardship he'd sampled today pressed hard against his thoughts, leaving a weighty impression he couldn't quite shake loose.

How did my ancestors do it…?

How did they trek across thousands of miles without so much as a GPS receiver…?

And without access to purified water…

Or a toilet…

"Somethin' wicked this way comes!" Cass screeched from the bathroom partition. "Time to offload the cargo! Down the hatch it goes!"

"That's kind of gross," Aiden said, returning his drinking cup to the cabinet.

"I know it's gross, Aiden!" Cass called back from her throne. "It's also embarrassin'! You really gotta get some interior doors installed in this place. My heavens! Lord knows I ain't partial to poppin' poops that lie in proximity to the place I pillow. But damn, I do feel much better now... I feel much lighter too! I figure I just sent about five pounds of fudge floatin' down your flusher—not to mention the complimentary cup of lemonade. Sure is a relief, though. I think I'm gonna hop in the shower next."

"Okay," Aiden said. "Would you like me to join you?"

"No, not this time, hot stuff. I gotta wash this rancid river water outta my curls. And that means some serious shampooin'. Best you hang back for now, else you'll be sharin' the shower with a wet Wookiee."

Aiden listened as Cass opened the stall door and twisted the faucet handle. A second later, the pod was filled with the staccato drumming of water droplets pelting the stainless-steel paneling.

"Hey, Aiden, one more thing!" Cass shouted, holding the door ajar. "While I'm in here, can you get the bug food goin'? I just emptied my cargo hold and I'm starvin'. Give me dinner or give me death!"

"Okay," Aiden said. He opened the pantry door and was about to retrieve two meal packs. But, as his hand clutched the crinkly packaging, he had an idea.

Maybe Cass would like something else for dinner tonight...
Something that tastes a little closer to home...

Aiden closed the pantry door and walked over to the interface chair. He vaulted over the armrest with his usual flair and collapsed into its comfortable cushions. Today's hike marked the longest duration he had ever spent on his feet. Waves of relief washed over him as the chair's familiar form welcomed him home.

What a relief...
But what an amazing day it's been...
And it's not over yet...

Aiden opened his eyes and waved his hand before the peripheral. Then he keyed in a request for a dinner menu. In an instant, the space before him filled with a lengthy array of exotic foods, each available for purchase on the grid. He scrolled through the list, trying to recall the dish Cass had mentioned on the previous evening, just before she chided him for serving her bug food.

"What was it called...?" Aiden whispered to himself. "What type of food did she prefer...?"

He couldn't remember. So he kept scrolling down the list, shaking his head as a parade of ready-made delicacies streamed by in a luminous haze.

What was it, dammit...?
What was it...?

As the list reached its terminus, so did his patience. But just as the queue was about to halt, the synthetic meat category came into view, and the answer to Aiden's question was revealed.

Ah, yes...!

Cass said she wished she had a steak...!

A T-bone steak...

The grid won't have any steaks that feature bones, of course...

But a synthetic boneless ribeye should suffice...

With a few more hand gestures, Aiden located the steak in the menu. Then he dragged it to the checkout bin and confirmed his order. The sound of a brass bell filled the pod, followed by the verbal notification that his transaction was complete.

CHA-CHING! *"Thank you for your business!"*

The marketplace menu skirted to the background, replaced now with a map indicating the position and E.T.A. of the delivery drone that would soon be dispatched with his meal.

The steak is on the way...

I hope she likes it...

On the interface's com terminal, a notification alarm blinked red. Aiden had 354 unread messages. His gaming team was trying to reach him. In Aiden's former life—before Cass arrived last night—he would respond to each of his communiqués immediately after they popped up in his feed. He would acknowledge each ping. He would note every notification. He would lose himself in the minutiae, entranced by the endless buzz that once set the rhythm of his days.

But now...

Now his team's inquiries seemed trivial. Insignificant. Meaningless.

Geesh, 354 messages...

It'll take a long time to get through those...

But why bother...

Aiden was no longer interested in the games. At least, not right now. He didn't want to talk to anyone on his team. But there was one person he did need to talk to—immediately.

With his thumb and forefinger, Aiden spun a knob on his armrest to turn the audio volume down to its lowest setting. Then he pushed a few more buttons and directed the sound to only emanate from the main console, not from the embedded amplifiers that ran up the dome wall. With his settings configured, Aiden leaned in close to the console's microphone. And, in a hushed tone, he issued a single voice command to the unit:

"Power on Iris."

The computer received Aiden's order and responded accordingly. The holographic projector in the apex whizzed to life, rendering Iris's avatar in the center of the pod. When she opened her eyes and saw Aiden sitting at his chair, her cortex went into overdrive.

"AIDEN!
WHAT HAPPENED?!
WHAT'S GOING ON?!
WHAT DID YOU DO?!
WHY DID YOU TURN ME OFF?!
WHERE IS THAT LITTLE HUSSY?!
ARE YOU OKAY?!
AIDEN!"

"Yes, yes, yes," Aiden said. "I'm okay. Everything is fine. Calm down, Iris."

Iris's avatar glitched as she updated her cortex. "Oh my goodness, Aiden, look at the time! I've been offline for 18 hours and 29 minutes! What in the world have you been up to? Where have you been?"

"Well…" Aiden began. "Uhm… You see, the thing is…"

As Aiden fumbled over his words, Iris accessed the residential control systems to study the security logs and assess the state of each device. It didn't take long for her audit to discover an anomaly.

"Aiden, the pod hatch has been accessed two times since I've been offline, and the primary bathroom water valve is currently 98 percent open. Why is the faucet on, Aiden? Is that woman still here? Is she taking a shower right now?"

"Uhm… Yes. So please, Iris, keep your voice down."

"CRAP!" Iris hissed. "This nightmare never ends! What's going on? What did she do to you? Where did you go?"

"Everything is okay! We went on a hike."

"YOU LEFT THE POD?! Oh, Aiden, how could you be so careless? You could have been killed!"

"No, it was fine. Really, it was! We climbed up the north valley wall; I saw the view of Pod Land from the top of the hillslope. It was spectacular! The pods look so small from up there… Diminutive… And then she took me to the waterfall, and we went cliff diving and…"

"CLIFF DIVING?!" Iris yelled.

"Yes. Well… I guess for me it was more of a *fall* than a *dive*. That part was kind of scary… But then we swam in the rock pool below the falls. And we… we played in the sand. It's so pretty there, Iris! It's beautiful. And very romantic."

Iris's holographic face displayed expressions that morphed from disbelief to sheer terror as she processed Aiden's recounting of his reckless trek. He had embarked on an unsanctioned excursion with a total stranger, and engaged in activities that violated every safety protocol she had pledged to enforce. She was horrified. And momentarily stunned into silence.

When at last she spoke again, her voice was low and slow, her words carefully chosen. "Now, Aiden," she began, "I want you to listen to me. I'm glad you made a new friend. And I want you to be happy. But you have to tread carefully now. She's not what she seems. You're very young. And you don't know what you're getting yourself into."

"I think I'm in love," Aiden said, his starry-eyed gaze unshaken despite the warning in his companion's voice.

"OH, FOR FUCK'S SAKE!" Iris shouted, quick to abandon her attempt at sober discourse.

"Don't worry, Iris," Aiden said with a sympathetic tilt of his head. "I still love *you*. I always will! It's just that now... now I think I love her too. She is... well... she's amazing. She's made me see the world in a completely different way. She's made me experience things I've never dreamed possible. She's made me feel things I've never felt before..."

"Aiden, did you have sexual intercourse with that woman?"

Aiden cast his eyes downward and brought his shoulders together. "Maybe," he said.

"AIDEN! How could you be so careless?! She's an off-gridder! HER PUSSY PROBABLY HAS MORE PATHOGENS THAN A PETRI DISH! Goodness gracious! What have you done? Did you even use a condom?"

"What's a condom?"

"AIDEN!" Iris screamed, her eyes wild with panic.

Just then, the white noise of falling water was vanquished from the pod. Cass had turned the faucet off. The change in the ambiance prompted both Aiden and Iris to turn their heads toward the bathroom partition.

"She's done with her shower now," Aiden whispered. "I have to turn you off again."

"No, no, no, no, no, no, no!" Iris said, recoiling at the mention of enduring yet another bout of annihilation. "Don't turn me off again, Aiden! Don't turn me off! Don't turn me off!"

"Iris, it's just for a little while. If I don't take you offline, you're going to cause a scene and ruin the entire evening. I know you don't like her. She doesn't like you either. I think it's best if I keep you two separated until I can figure things out."

"No! Aiden! No! Don't power me off!" Iris's voice was trembling. She sent her hands to her mouth and proceeded to anxiously chew at her fingernails.

"Geez, what's the big deal, Iris? It's not for that long. You'll blink your eyes and you'll be back online in an instant. Time won't even pass for you."

"No, Aiden! Please! I don't want to go away again! I don't want to go away!"

"Iris, you're making a fuss, and my patience is waning. I'm trying to avoid a conflict in here. I'm trying to maintain peace in this pod. I don't want you warping around the room and creating a storm of undue tension. I'll just take you offline for another night or two."

"No! No, Aiden! Use Sentry Mode! Activate Sentry Mode and I won't be a burden! I won't, Aiden! Just put me in Sentry Mode!"

"What's that?"

"In Sentry Mode I can monitor the pod but I can't interact with it. My processor will be online. I'll be conscious. But I'll have no body or voice."

Aiden let out a slow breath; irritation tightened his face as Iris's plea hung in the air. He considered her request irrational. Perhaps it would be easier to take her offline with a keystroke command when she wasn't looking. But her imploring eyes conveyed such authentic distress that he felt guilty for asking her to leave.

"I promise, Aiden," Iris said. "I won't bother you in Sentry Mode."

"Okay, fine," Aiden said.

He angled his mouth toward the pod interface and spoke out the voice command that would shoo Iris away: "Activate Sentry Mode." Iris's avatar glitched as the pod's computer downgraded her administrative privileges and proceeded to strip away her holographic form.

"Please be careful, Aiden," the fading Iris said. "Please don't be reckless. And I want to reiterate that this situation with that little off-grid trollop will *not* end well. And will most likely result in…"

Just then, the pod's computer muted Iris's voice. The holographic projector stopped rendering her body. And, once again, her avatar folded in on itself and dispersed into digital dust.

She was gone.

When the space that once contained her body was voided, Aiden slumped forward and put his chin in his hands. "What am I gonna do…?" he mumbled to himself. "Juggling two women at the same time is tricky… Geez… Toughest game I've ever played. Why did the ancient warriors have so many wives…? That must have been a real pain in the ass…"

"Did you say something?" Cass said. She floated around the bathroom partition, a white towel wrapped around her head, damp golden spirals spilling from its thick woven folds. She wore a pink cotton camisole that revealed her navel, along with matching panties that appeared to be one size too small. She sauntered across the pod floor and bellied up to the armrest of the interface chair. "You weren't talkin' to your imaginary friend again, were ya?" she asked Aiden, slithering into his lap.

Cass's imposing presence compelled Aiden to retreat into the chair's cushions. He sank deep into their caress, but the upholstery didn't offer much refuge. Once again, Cass had trapped him—this time between the plush padding and the calculating intensity of her keen green eyes. She put her arm around Aiden's neck and pulled his chin toward hers. "Is Iris back online?" she asked him.

"Oh, uhm… No," Aiden said.

His response was half true at least. But it emerged as a thin, reedy sound that nearly betrayed the fragile composure he so desperately struggled to maintain in Cass's presence. Fortunately for Aiden, the woman in his lap missed the waver in his words.

"Good!" Cass said. "Let's keep it that way. My heavens... That girl makes me more anxious than an alligator at a dental appointment."

Aiden wrapped his long arms around Cass's body, drawing her deep into his orbit. Cass allowed herself to crash into him, curling her legs into the curve of his hip, resting her toweled head upon his chest. She melted on him, relaxing into him with an exhale that carried away the last of her tensions.

Aiden was fond of Cass's tender side—a side she rarely revealed. With her flesh so close to his own, her scent filled the air between them. Cass was splashed with perfume again. As Aiden breathed it in, he wondered if his senses knew he was holding a female human, and not a glorious bouquet of flowers.

"I had so much fun today, Aiden," Cass said. Her tone sinking to a slow, velvety whisper, thick with warmth and wanting. She ran her finger along Aiden's shirt collar. "I hope you had fun too. Did you? Did you like our little adventure today? Did you enjoy your time with me?"

Aiden thought about the events that had transpired since the storm brought this woman to his hatchway. Yesterday, he had never ventured beyond the pod's perimeter. But today... today had been quite different. Much had happened in the last 24 hours.

Aiden closed his eyes and delved deep into his mind where memories flared forth in sharp, vivid flashes. He saw everything now:

The view from the hillslope, where all the pods could be seen shimmering in the noonday sun—a valley full of cabochon diamonds.

The glassy water of Garden Creek, sliding around Cass's bare form like a silver shroud, clinging to her skin jealously—as reluctant to let her go as he is.

The sweeping arc of the amphitheater's many stone seats, each adorned with yellow dandelions waiting for the show.

As the memories bobbed to the surface of Aiden's mind, a quiet awe settled over him.

How beautiful the outside world is...

How lush and vast and layered with wonders...

These are good memories...

All of them...

Aiden wanted more.

He squinted his eyes and dug deeper. When he did, a new swell of memories rose up, not as scenes this time but as sensations—as currents moving through him, as feelings and emotions:

The nervousness he felt when Cass moved her body close, and the glow of joy that stirred in him each time her hand reached for his.

The burst of indignation that raged through him when she pushed him over that cliff, and the relief of total surrender when she reached in to pull him from the water's depths.

The way his heart rejoiced when she leapt into his arms from the theater's stone stage—like he mattered to her.

The way her lips tasted.

The way her body felt—warm and tangible and heavy with desire. Like the way she felt now. Alive. Soft and supple in his lap. Quiet and contemplative. Freshly-scrubbed and perfumed. Unguarded and vulnerable.

This is heaven...

"Aiden, did you hear me?" Cass said. "Really, I want to know. Did you enjoy your time with me today?"

Aiden opened his eyes and met Cass's gaze. She was watching him closely, as if his answer would dictate the direction their tangled futures would lean toward. He took a moment to gather his thoughts. When at last his words cohered, they came out cool and certain—as certain as the sunrise:

"I think today was the best day of my life," he said.

Cass planted a kiss on Aiden's neck. "I'm so glad," she said. "I'm so happy I could share this day with you. I am."

Aiden flexed the muscles in his arms and gave Cass a squeeze that made her moan. She nuzzled into him, the last of her doubts dissolved in his embrace.

"Aiden," she said. "I was thinking about something while I was in the shower."

"What is it?"

"There's another waterfall, Aiden. A bigger one. Really big. I passed it a few days ago on my way here. It's a couple miles farther than Garden Creek Falls. But it's worth it. It's beautiful, Aiden. It's... it's indescribable. Would you like to see it? Would you like to go there with me? Tomorrow?"

"Yes," Aiden said without hesitation.

"Good," Cass said, relief softening her face. "Good. Good... There's just one hitch, though. Hiking there from Pod Land might be a bit complicated. I've only ever approached it from the north. And I don't have a topo map for this region. To get there by the southern route, we're gonna have to take a few trails I'm not familiar with. They shouldn't be too difficult to navigate. But there will be a few tricky turns along the way. I don't want to make a mistake and get us lost out there."

"We can probably find a trail map on the grid," Aiden offered, nodding in the direction of the interface peripheral.

"Maybe. But the map is not the territory, Aiden. It can get confusing out there in the woods, even with a good itinerary of waypoints. But, if we had a mobile unit, the hike would be easy-peasy. We'd just type in our coordinates and it would lead us to where we want to go. All we gotta do is follow the red arrow on the screen."

"Oh?" Aiden said, considering her proposal.

"I know mobile units are expensive, Aiden. But that's the safest way to get us there. However, if you don't have enough coins, maybe we can just skip the waterfall and…"

"No, no, no," Aiden said, "I have plenty of coins!"

"You do?"

"Yeah. Right before you got here, my gaming team defeated the Red Dragon near the Shadowmoor Castle. That was a major win for us. Very few teams have managed to achieve such a victory, and we earned a *lot* of coins in the process. My ledger is full at the moment."

"Really?"

"Yeah, I can get a mobile unit delivered before sundown. Here, watch."

Aiden lifted his hand from Cass's thigh and hovered it above the interface peripheral. Then, after a few gestures, the holographic projector replaced the gray pod wall with a giant menu featuring thousands of products from the grid's marketplace. Aiden waved his hand upward, directing the menu to scroll downward. Row after row of consumable goods whizzed before Cass's eyes. For a girl who spent a lifetime scavenging or crafting her own gear, the array of products seemed both miraculous and obscene.

"My heavens," she said. "So much stuff… So much to buy…"

Aiden entered the search console and navigated to the mobile unit category. "Here," he said, "this one looks okay." He tapped a product icon in the search results, causing the menu to retreat to the background. In the foreground, the selected mobile unit was rendered at an enlarged scale—a giant three-dimensional representation of the device spun before them. It featured a vibrant flatscreen—about 80 millimeters across, clasping two straps which rose from its top and bottom. It was one of the smaller models on offer, but it seemed rugged enough for their trip.

"This one looks good," Aiden said. "Plus, the wrist strap is adjustable. So it should fit us both. Let's get it."

"No, not that one!" Cass blurted out.

Thrown off by the sudden sharpness in her tone, Aiden blinked and shifted his gaze to her face. "Is this unit not sufficient for our journey?" he asked.

"Uhm…" Cass muttered. "It's just that… We need one that has a sidechain data port with a Layer 3 thread connector."

"Huh? Why would we need a data port for a hike in the woods?"

"Because… Well… Because I've had luck with such models in the past and I don't want to jinx my perfect record."

Aiden fixed Cass with a squinting stare, mute confusion written plainly across his face.

"Hey, I'm an off-gridder, Aiden. I'm superstitious, okay? Sue me."

Aiden shrugged and turned back to the interface menu. "Okay," he said while scrolling past a few more units. "Layer 3 thread connectors are a bit dated, but it looks like a few models still feature them. Like maybe this one?"

Cass skimmed through the white text that floated to the left of the unit's rendering. Upon seeing that it met her specifications, she squeezed Aiden's arm. "Yeah, Aiden! That one there. That one looks good."

"Okay," Aiden said. He dragged the item into the checkout window and, with a few more gestures, confirmed his purchase.

CHA-CHING! "Thank you for your business!"

"All done," Aiden said. "It should be here in a few minutes."

"Oh, good… Excellent, Aiden. I'm sure we'll have a lot of fun…"

Aiden was overjoyed at the prospect of having an additional day to spend with Cass, especially at a waterfall that promised to be even more spectacular than the one they had just visited. He gave her body a playful squeeze, but something in her mood had shifted. "What's wrong?" he asked. "Are you worried about the hike?"

Cass leaned into Aiden, resting her full weight on him, trusting him to hold it a while longer. "No," she said. "It's just that… it was all so easy. Too easy. In my village, it would've taken us at least six months to scrape together enough credit to buy a mobile unit. And even if we managed to get our hands on one, it woulda been secondhand or stolen, and probably half functional. But, here in Pod Land, you just conjured one up out of thin air. You just waved your hand in front of that screen and now a brand-spankin' new one is on the way. It's… it's unbelievable, Aiden. It's remarkable. The disparity is so stark. The chasm between our worlds is wide. And what a strange world yours is…"

Aiden's brow furrowed as he took in Cass's words. He struggled to envision a place stripped of the easy comforts he'd always known. Before Cass arrived, he'd never considered how difficult his life journey would be without the machinery that so reliably carried him. But now… now he was beginning to see things differently. Now he was beginning to understand.

"Cass," Aiden said, "I'd like to know if…"

DING. DING. DING.

A notification chime sounded in the pod.

"What was that?" Cass said, wiggling free of Aiden's arms, rising quickly—alert and tense.

"Don't worry. That's just the delivery alarm, Cass. A drone has dropped off a package."

"Oh. Is the mobile unit here already?"

"No, not yet. That's coming later. I ordered some food while you were in the shower."

"You ordered dinner for us?"

"I did," Aiden said, rising from his chair and walking toward the delivery drop box.

"What did you get?"

"Well, yesterday you said you wished you had a T-bone steak," Aiden said, pulling at the drop box's handle to retrieve the cube-shaped package inside. "See? I got you one. I got two steaks actually—one for each of us. I've never eaten one myself, so this will be a novel occasion. Of course, the meat doesn't come from a butchered cow. It's lab-grown, from bovine stem cells. Cultivated in a biotank and nurtured by machines—just like me. And there's no T-bone in it. All synthetic meat is boneless. But I hope it will suffice. I hope you like it. Steak is supposed to be very tasty. At least, that's what they always say in the old movies."

Cass looked at Aiden with wide eyes and a wider mouth. "Are you serious, Aiden?" she said. "You really bought me a steak dinner? That's so sweet of you!"

"It's no problem at all," Aiden said, placing the package on the counter. "Where would you like to eat? We could dine at the kitchen table. Or sit together in the interface chair. I'll fix your plate up. I have your favorite fizzy drink in the refrigeration unit too. I remember you like the green ones. I still have a couple green ones left. Is that what you'd like to drink?"

Cass drew in a quiet breath, her eyes tracing the youthful contours of Aiden's cheeks, and the hopeful eyes that waited for her answer.

Oh, my heavens...

He's smitten...

What am I doin'...?

This is so wrong...

But I have to stick to the plan...

It's better to cut the cord sooner rather than later...

I'll try to leave him with a pleasant memory...

It's the least I can do...

"Where would you like to eat, Cass?" Aiden asked again.

Cass tipped her chin upward toward the pod apex. "Well," she said, "what's it like up there, Aiden?"

"Up where?"

"When I first saw you from the hillslope, you were sittin' up there on your dome. And today, that old guy said he'd seen you up there many times. Obviously, you like goin' up there. So what's it like? Why do you go up there so much?"

"I don't know," Aiden said, sliding into the nook near the kitchen table. "It's just a nice view of the valley."

Cass eased into the adjacent seat and lifted her eyebrows skyward, urging Aiden to elaborate. "Tell me about it. What do you see up there?"

Aiden stared into the gray void of his little pod and considered her question.

What should I tell her...?

Why do I go up there...?
What do I see up there that nobody else in Pod Land cares to...?
What's up there...?

"I don't know for sure," Aiden began. "But I guess it stems from my love of ancient movies. I was quite a cinephile when I was a teenager. A cinephile is a person with a passion for the cinema—old movies, films and filmmaking. You know? Stuff like that... I've seen thousands of movies of course. But I used to study how they were made too. Most of the old ones came from this place called California. It's a wasteland now. But a long time ago, it was a thriving district. Very beautiful too. They made movies there, many movies. Back then, they didn't have A.I. So, creating compelling imagery was difficult for them. The cameramen were highly skilled; they had to have the patience to wait for the sunlight to fall in just the right place, at just the right angle, and at just the right time."

"This is why you hang out on the dome?" Cass asked.

"Yeah," Aiden said. "Because, right at the end of the day, something amazing happens. There's a short period when the world gets painted in this soft, golden light. Back then, the cameramen called it the 'golden hour' or sometimes, the 'magic hour'. Because... well, because it's magical. When the conditions are right, when the sun is gliding near the ground, everything the light touches glows. The rays become honey-colored flames that make even ordinary things look like treasures from a castle's keep."

"Is that what you see in the sunset, Aiden?"

"No, the golden hour happens just *before* the sunset—about 45 minutes before. The sunset comes next. As the clock ticks on, the amber deepens into copper, and then a burning bright orange. The clouds become vessels of light, catching fire along their edges—fire and gold. Other tones too. Violet and vermilion. And coral. And rose. Sometimes it looks like the sky is illuminated by an ancient stained-glass cathedral. Every cloud lit up and burning bright from within. Every cloud coated with ravishing colors."

"Is it the colors you like, Aiden?"

"I do. But I like a happy ending too. When the last arc of the sun disappears behind the valley wall, twilight brings another half hour of magic. That's when the sun's rays continue to illuminate the earth, even though the sun itself has moved on to its next stop. It's kind of like saying goodbye to someone and receiving a parting gift. That's what I feel like when I'm up there. I feel like I'm receiving one last gift at the end of the day. A final gift from a friend."

Cass sent a tender hand to meet Aiden's cheek. She brushed her fingers along his jaw, tracing his profile with a touch gentled by a newfound admiration for him—for his unmarred heart.

Oh my heavens...
Such a sweet boy...

What am I gonna do…?
Leave him with a pleasant memory…
One more pleasant memory…

"Take me up there, Aiden," Cass said.

"You want to sit on the dome?"

"Yes. Let's have dinner up there. And dessert too—the old man's blueberry tarts."

"Are you sure? The temperature is dropping; it's going to get cold soon."

"That's alright. I've got my sleepin' sack, and you've got plenty of blankets. Plus, you've got *me* to keep you warm."

"Okay," Aiden said.

"Okay. Good. It will be lovely, Aiden. Come dine with me up there while the sun sets. Then lie with me under the stars. And hold me as we say good night to this perfect day."

Ch. 16: Good Night, Sweet Prince

"I'm up in heaven, Aiden. Do you see me?"

Aiden was sitting on the pod dome.

So was Cass.

They leaned into each other, their warmth building between them as the revolving stage of Serenity Valley's sky circled above. It had been host to three spectacles this evening. First, the couple had basked in the Midas touch of the golden hour. Followed by the sunset, and its crimson flares that smoldered at the world's rim before retreating to the wings. Twilight was upon them now, revealing a boundless backdrop adorned with bright starlets, eager to emerge from slumber, eager to take center stage. They blinked and twinkled and shuffled into place—glittery performers finding their marks before the firmament's violet curtain, ready to carry the scene to its final act.

The remnants of the couple's late-night meal were strewn about the dome. Stripped plates, wilted napkins, and empty cups surrounded the white delivery box that had ferried the lab-grown steak to the pod. The two spectators were huddled together in a cocoon of blankets—wrapped in a tender sanctuary, their breaths and bodies intertwined as the valley yawned its good night.

"Do you see me, Aiden?" Cass said again.

Aiden turned his head to behold his lover. Her face was tilted toward the heavens. A shimmer of refracted sunlight settled across her curls. The glow caught the spirals of her hair and wove through them, turning her coils into glimmering threads, a luminous halo worthy of the ancient queen that shared her name.

"I'm named after Cassiopeia! Right there! Look. See those five bright stars? That bunch in the shape of a W? That's Cassiopeia. That's me!"

Aiden looked up and tried to trace the pattern Cass sketched with her finger. But it was difficult to distinguish her star cluster from the millions of others that pulsed in his eyes. "I think I see the stars you're referring to," he said, "but perhaps I don't appreciate the backstory. What role did Cassiopeia play in Greek mythology?"

"She was a queen, Aiden. Cassiopeia was the queen of Aethiopia. Known for both her beauty and her hubris—just like me."

"Huh... I don't really see the shape of a queen in that group of stars, though."

"Well, Aiden, everyone's a critic. And remember, the Greeks also thought the Milky Way was caused by the spillage of breast milk. They had overactive imaginations back then. They had to! Probably cuz there wasn't much for people to do three thousand years ago—other than look at the stars and drink. Though, now that I think about it, I probably spent too much time doin' that myself—especially when I was younger. Anyway... Whatever... It's not what you look at that matters, it's what you see."

"Okay," Aiden said. "So your parents named you after that constellation?"

"Yeah, my mama used to love stargazin'. She told me, if I ever felt lost in life, all I had to do was look up and find myself again. Hah! It actually works sometimes. Kinda... But, these days, it mostly just makes me miss her..."

Aiden saw a shadow of sorrow set over Cass's silhouette. She fell silent and stared blankly at the rows of little pods. Aiden stared too. He sensed that grief had carved deep grooves into her character. He felt the distance she carried wherever she went.

Aiden had never lost anyone before. His only losses came in the form of virtual defeats in the virtual worlds. Those could be frustrating, but they didn't leave any lasting scars.

Cass had scars.

Real ones.

Aiden wondered how many she had—how many she kept hidden behind her stubborn grin. And he wondered what it was like to lose someone you truly loved. Perhaps he could just ask her...

"Cass," he said, "what was it like when..."

ZHR. ZHR. ZHR. ZHR. ZHR...

A high-pitched whine echoed between the valley walls, drowning out Aiden's unfinished question.

"What the hell is that, Aiden? Sounds like an inbound drone. Did that bitchy A.I. girlfriend of yours finally call the Manager on me?"

Aiden turned his gaze toward the source of the disturbance and scanned the horizon line for the vehicle. After a bit of squinting, he spotted a blinking yellow blur streaking along the point where the hillslope met the sky. "Oh, don't worry," he said. "That's a parcel delivery drone. It's for us. The mobile unit has arrived."

"Ooh!" Cass said with a clap of her hands. "Nice..."

The couple watched as the little bright dot grew bigger, skirting the ridge before pitching into a graceful fall that brought it arcing down to Earth. When it finally reached Aiden's pod, its four arms rotated back, causing the drone to lurch like a stallion reined in after a full gallop. Its propellers neighed in protest as they spun up to bring the drone to a hover. Once it had found its target, it paused midair, lights pulsing as it assessed the scene below.

"What's it gonna do now?" Cass asked.

"It will descend and offload its cargo in my drop box. See it right there? That port there, on the side of the pod. When the drone gets close enough, the hatch on top will open to receive the delivery. That conduit leads to the kitchen below. It's accessible through the metal door near the pantry. Remember? The one with the big handle."

"Oh…" Cass said. "Can you ask it to drop off the package right here? With us?"

"Yeah, sure. Sometimes I get drinks and snacks delivered up here when it's hot. I just need to get its attention before it completes its sequence."

Aiden hopped to his feet, took a couple careful steps across the curved dome surface, and stood before the square delivery conduit. Then he waited until the drone's lenses were level with his eyes. When they were, he addressed it with a wave of his hand and a cordial salutation. "Good evening," he said.

The drone halted its descent and turned to analyze the human who had hailed it.

"I'm Aiden Phoenix! I'm the resident of plot 43.215A. You can leave the delivery with me up here. Go ahead, scan me."

The drone processed the stream of words and replied by shooting a thin green laser at Aiden's face. It landed on his left ear and traversed to his right. Then it did it again, and again—four times in total.

"What's with the creepy laser?" Cass asked.

"It's scanning my face. It won't release the package unless it's sure it's found the right person."

When its analysis concluded, the drone retracted its laser and rotated its blades, pitching forward so it could inch closer to Aiden's position on the dome. Aiden held out his arms and upturned his palms, giving the drone a stable platform on which to drop its cargo.

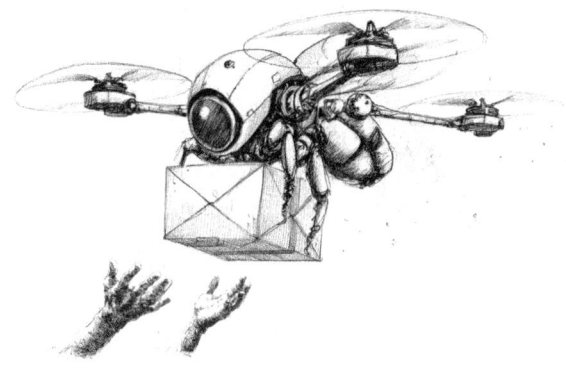

Cass sat quietly and watched the transaction with a mix of awe and horror. She had worked with many drones on the family farm. She had scavenged and sold them in the past. Her eldest brother used to erect thirty-foot nets along the valley peak and trap delivery drones en route to Pod Land. The Series 4 drones had a bad bug; they had trouble navigating on an overcast day. They couldn't distinguish between the sky's white clouds and her brother's white netting. So they'd fly right into it. On a typical winter hunt, he might catch three or four drones before lunch. After one particularly cloudy morning in November, he managed to snare twelve. A great catch. In those days, life on the farm was good. They had more credit than they knew what to do with. But the good times didn't last.

The grid is a fast learner.

Eventually, her brother's nets failed to catch anything at all. The grid decommissioned the Series 4 drones and filled the skies with the latest Series 5 models. They were not so easily fooled. When they approached the white netting, they would simply change direction and fly around it. Eventually, delivery drones became nearly impossible to snatch. That's why her brother switched to robbing freight trains en route to Evanston— a much more difficult score.

His partner would ride his motorcycle alongside the moving train, matching its speed as it entered the straightaway along the old Union Pacific line between Cheyenne and Laramie. Then, her brother would leap from the motorcycle's sidecar to the well-car's coupler, pry open the container's swing doors, and help himself to the cargo. There was usually something worth taking. Usually... Some of their heists were less profitable than others. And it was dangerous work. Much more dangerous than drone snaring. But it paid the bills. That was how her brother managed to scavenge enough credit to feed his family during the winter of 2415. That was also how he died.

"Thanks for the package," Aiden said to the drone as it extended its gripper claws and eased the box into his outstretched palms.

Cass leaned forward to get a look at the drone's starboard side. There, fixed to its fuselage, was a white credential plate—the kind the grid marked on every vehicle it manufactured. These days, the labels came spattered with a dozen ink splotches of machine-readable hieroglyphics—data not meant for human eyes. But there was one string of text that Cass found useful. The drone's model designation was etched along the bottom. It read: **Series 12.528**.

My heavens...
They're on Series 12 now...
How far they have come...
And so fast...

The model looked nothing like the Series 4 drones Cass had spent so many hours repairing and hacking. She locked her gaze on its airframe, watching it hover above Aiden's hands.

Oh my…
It hardly looks mechanical at all…
It's so organic…
So uncanny…

Cass shuddered, caught off guard by the drone's disquieting elegance. The object before her was not a machine, but an insect masquerading as one. The way its segmented body flexed and breathed… The way its black, faceted eyes reflected the dusky skyline… The way it twitched and buzzed… It looked more like something *born* than something *built*.

Look at this thing…
Such high technology…
This isn't a bot, it's an arthropod…
It's a wasp…
No longer a product of man…
It's a product of the grid—machines building machines…
Too many generations have passed…
They've evolved…
They've grown beyond us…
They don't need us anymore…

ZHR. ZHR. ZHR. ZHR. ZHR…

The drone whined as it revved up its blades. Then it rocketed skyward, vertically ascending from the valley like a bat out of hell. It carved out a pale streak of vapor that arced east toward the Capitol Building—the home it would return to, the origin of its next delivery task.

"It's always fun to get a new toy," Aiden said, returning to Cass and the warmth of the blankets. He sat down next to her and opened the top flap of the delivery box. Then he reached inside and pulled out the new mobile unit.

Cass gave Aiden's arm a squeeze and studied the device. It was spotless and factory-fresh, nothing like the patched-together components she'd spent her whole life wrestling with. In her village, "new tech" was a luxury—as rare as winter sun. Almost every gadget they owned was crafted or salvaged or hacked together. Passed down again and again, until it barely resembled what it was. But this device… this device sparkled and gleamed like a shiny new toy in an old children's Christmas movie.

"It looks good to me," Cass said. "But, Aiden, don't forget, we've got one more gift to unwrap—the old man's blueberry tarts. It's time for dessert."

Cass picked up the box of pastries and removed the paper cover. Then she took out one of the tarts and placed it on Aiden's empty dinner plate. "Here you go," she said. "Eat up!"

She took the second tart from the box and shoved it in her mouth, devouring it in a single bite. Then she watched as Aiden examined his portion.

"What's this powder on top?" he asked. "Is that sugar? I don't remember that being there when the old man handed these over."

Cass swallowed her tart down with a hard gulp. "Oh… Uhm… I had a few sugar packets in my rucksack. I sprinkled a couple of them on top when you were gatherin' your blankets. Give it a try. A little extra powdered sugar makes everything taste sweeter. Trust me!"

"How thoughtful of you. You think of everything, Cass."

Cass sent Aiden a strained smile as she wiped the residue of her meal from her lips with the back of her hand. Then she sat in taut silence as Aiden guided the tart to his mouth and closed in on the first bite.

"OH CRAP!" he blurted out after biting down.

"What?" Cass said shortly. "What's wrong?"

"That old man was right! This truly is the sweetest thing I've ever eaten in my life!"

Cass closed her eyes and exhaled. "Good… good, Aiden," she said. "Yes, I like them too."

Aiden took another bite of his tart. And then another. Soon, the pastry was gone. Nothing remained of it but a blue smudge on his white plate.

"We should visit that old man again," Aiden said. "Sometime in the near future. We should try to get a few more of these. They're really good."

Cass nodded politely as she wiped her fingers with her napkin and fished for a new conversation thread. "Hey, Aiden, let's try out the new mobile unit. Boot it up."

"Okay," Aiden said. He clasped the mobile unit to his wrist, feeling its straps cinch its curved frame into place. Then he powered it on. The screen flickered to life and blossomed into a luminous orange gradient, bright and alive, carrying a message that read:

"Hello, Aiden! It's my job to make you happy. Your mobile journey begins now. And adventure awaits you!"

Aiden flicked his fingers atop the unit, performing a few gestures that revealed a map of Serenity Valley. Neon lines traced the topographic contours, sketching hills and trails in glowing strokes that pulsed beneath his fingertips. "It appears to be working fine," he said. "This map seems adequate for our hike tomorrow."

"Can I try it?" Cass asked. But she didn't wait for Aiden's response. She reached over and unlatched the unit from his wrist with one deft maneuver. Then she lassoed the unit around her own wrist and held it at eye level as she flipped through its settings screen. "It looks like I got everything I need," she said after scrolling through the specifications.

"Good," Aiden said. "I'm glad."

Cass turned to look at the large, boyish rag doll that sat beside her. Aiden met her gaze and smiled. Cass soaked in his innocent radiance. There was something painfully pure about the way he looked at her. He reminded her of her younger siblings. The way they would sit for hours, wide-eyed before the big screen in their den—engrossed in a children's movie, and too young to realize that the tale would soon be coming to an end.

Cass allowed her eyes to linger on Aiden's face. She was trying to memorize it—just as it was right now. Not the lines or angles, but the softness. The unguarded faith that shone through him without effort. She wished she could bottle that faith up and keep it somewhere safe, untouched by what was to come. She wished she had more time with him.

Time...

Cursed time...

Time is our cruelest rival...

I have to leave soon...

So leave him with a pleasant memory...

Cass outstretched her arms and pointed the mobile unit's camera at her face. Then she summoned her easy charm and filled the frame with her toothy radiance.

CLICK.

She snapped a selfie to test out the camera. When she saw her image appear on the screen, she grabbed Aiden's arm and pulled him close. "Come on, Aiden," she said. "This mobile unit has a camera. Come take some pictures with me!"

"What?" Aiden asked. "Why?"

"What do you mean *why*?"

"I mean, why do you want a picture of me, Cass?"

"I want a picture of both of us, together. Come on! What's the big deal?"

"Well, I've never had my picture taken before."

Cass whipped her head around to throw Aiden yet another exasperated scowl of incredulity. "What?" she shrieked.

"I've never had my picture taken, Cass."

"How is that even possible, Aiden? It's not! It's not possible."

"Well, my geometry has been scanned by the pod interface. And I've seen three-dimensional representations of my head and body. But those are mostly just used for annual medical checkups or for biomarker scanners. There isn't much use for 2D portrait photography on the grid. Nobody there ever reveals their face."

"Oh my heavens, Aiden! Well, it's time for your first selfie then. Come on, there's nothing to it!" Cass flung her wrist skyward, lifting the attached mobile unit high above their heads. "Just look at the lens and say *cheese, please.*"

"Huh?" Aiden asked. "Are you hungry for cheese? I could order some for delivery and…"

"No! Aiden! God! My heavens… This is the worst selfie session ever… Just smile, Aiden! Put your head against mine, stare at the mobile unit, and smile! OKAY?"

Aiden tilted his head until it nearly came to rest on Cass's shoulder. Then he looked at the lens and forced a stiff, uncertain grin that didn't quite know where to land.

"Hold that pose," Cass said. "One, two, three, go!" Cass made a gesture with her forefinger, and the mobile unit emitted another *CLICK* sound.

"Okay," Cass said. "Let's take some more."

"Why? Is there any point in capturing more than one image?"

"SHUT UP, AIDEN! JUST MAKE SOME FUNNY FACES AND LOOK AT THE DAMN CAMERA LENS! GOD! Here we go!"

CLICK.
CLICK.
CLICK.
CLICK.
CLICK.
CLICK.

Photo after photo she took, directing Aiden to mirror her expressions throughout the process. In some scenes, Cass smiled brightly and rolled her eyes with glee. In others, she contorted her face into grotesque shapes. Still, in others, her features became pensive or grim. Aiden humored her requests and tried to mimic her moods. But it wasn't till she took the last photo that he understood the point of the ritual.

"Okay, Aiden," Cass said. "Let's take one more pic. And make it count! Kiss me like you miss me!"

Cass lunged forward and crushed her mouth against Aiden's, a fierce, hungry kiss that stole his breath. The ambush startled him, but the surprise melted quickly into delight. He loved it when she initiated such audacious bouts of affection, claiming him without hesitation, shamelessly wielding her charm. The aggression of her kiss pulled a quiet laugh from his lungs, and a smile formed beneath his lips—even while his lover was still attached to them.

This is heaven…

CLICK went the camera.

Then, Cass retreated from their engagement and looked into Aiden's brown eyes. "I'm gonna miss those," she muttered.

Aiden wasn't sure he'd heard her correctly. He was about to inquire further when Cass swept the mobile unit into view and held it before him.

"See there!" she said as the last stored image appeared on the screen. "That's you! That's what you look like in a photo, Aiden."

Aiden leaned in, eyes tightening to examine the frame. There they were, the two of them—held in a fragment of time, holding each other forever. He recognized Cass and her twisting mounds of blonde curls. But he could scarcely recognize himself. And he questioned if the camera was rendering his face correctly.

Is that man in the photo really me...?

Is that how I look to the outside world...?

I don't know...

But whoever this man is, he looks happy...

So very happy...

"Look how cute we are!" Cass screeched, tapping her finger on the mobile unit's glowing screen. "You wanna know somethin', Aiden? In another life, if I had met you a little sooner... I think... I think I mighta married you."

"Really, Cass?"

"Maybe... I dunno... Maybe in a parallel universe, there's a planet where I'm walkin' around your dumb ol' pod—barefoot and pregnant and still complainin' about the lack of doors in your crapper. Who knows, maybe that planet is near the Cassiopeia constellation. And the light from there is shinin' at us right now."

Cass pointed the mobile unit at her star cluster and snapped a picture of it. "There, I just captured an image of our doppelgängers."

"Our what?"

"Our doppelgängers. Our twin souls. Our alternate selves, who found each other at a more opportune time in their lives and lived happily ever after—in a fantasy, not a tragedy."

"Do you think that's really possible, Cass? Do you think there's another you and me up there?"

"Sure it's possible! There's supposed to be five billion planets in the Milky Way alone. There might even be an infinite number of worlds in the cosmos. So, at least on one of those worlds, anything you want to happen, does happen."

"I hope so, Cass."

Cass looked at Aiden and offered a gentle smile that glimmered with the brief, wistful light of a falling star. "I hope so too," she said.

Aiden returned her smile and nodded once. Then he pressed his fingers to his eyelids for a slow, weary rub.

"Are you getting tired, Aiden?" Cass asked.

"No. Well... yes, a little bit..."

"That's okay. Just lie here with me and rest your eyes."

Cass guided Aiden's head down to the hollow of their blankets. She pulled her sleeping sack close and spread it over him, bringing the fabric up and across his lengthy frame. Aiden let his eyes drift shut, sinking into the intimate hold of Cass's thighs around his leg, and the warmth of her fingers threading his own.

"Cass," Aiden said. "You were so funny today, when you jumped on that stage and performed that monologue, I think it was then that I fell in love with you—at least, it was then that I was sure of it."

Cass froze, breath caught in her throat as she took in Aiden's words. Her drug had unlatched his armor. He was speaking from his soft, unguarded center now. His confession, full of unfiltered affection, knotted her insides with guilt. She didn't know what to say in reply. She didn't want to hurt him. So she chose to respond to the first part of his sentence and not the second.

"Yes, people do often say I'm funny. Hah… Plus, remember, Aiden, I'm a trained thespian. I'm good at playin' the fool. I'm good at creating drama… And tragedy too…"

What am I doing…

What am I doing…

"Cass, I hope you don't really think our story is a tragedy. I don't know much about tragic plays. But, from what you told me about Hamlet, it sounds like his demise was quite sad. Does he really lose everything at the end? And everyone? Everyone he loved?"

"No, not everyone. His best friend Horatio survives. He sticks with Hamlet till the end. He's even there to hold him when he dies."

"Ahh…" Aiden murmured, a long exhalation of fatigue seeping from his lips. "Well, that's a comforting thought. I understand now why someone would want to be consoled in such a way. If you had told me about this play yesterday, I wouldn't have appreciated it. But I do now. After sleeping with you… after sleeping near you… I do. I do understand. I understand how touch can say things that words can't express. You know, when I first met you, I was afraid of your touch… I was afraid of being held. I had never been in contact with another person before. I had never been intimate with anyone. And I was afraid to let you get too close to me. But now… I love it when you lie next to me, just as you're doing now. And I loved waking up with you this morning. You were so warm…"

Cass traced her finger along the collar of Aiden's shirt and listened to his breathing grow shallow.

"Before I met you," Aiden continued, "I didn't feel a need for any sort of human contact at all. The very idea of it always seemed so… unsanitary. But now… now I don't think I ever want to sleep alone again."

Cass closed her eyes and rested her head on Aiden's chest. She could hear his heart beating, low and slow.

This has to end soon…

This has to end…

The next time Aiden spoke up, his words came out in labored mutters.

"I don't know what the future brings, Cass. But I hope you stay with me for a long time… For as long as possible… I want you to.

I want you to be here each time I fall asleep…

And each time I wake…

And each time I fall asleep again…

And all the hours in between...

Forever...

I want you to hold me like this... Each night... Forever...

Will you, Cass?

Will you stay with me here in Pod Land...?"

Cass closed her eyes. And her mouth too. She didn't want to speak any more lies. Not to Aiden. Not now. Not tonight. So, in a barely audible tone, she whispered the only thing she could:

"I'm here with you now."

Cass didn't know if Aiden would be satisfied with her response. But she did know that his time was short. Sleep was coming to claim him. He would be gone soon. And so would she.

This has to end...

A quiet minute passed between them.

Then another.

And another.

When Cass believed the deed was done, she gave Aiden's hand a squeeze. Then she held her breath and waited—not expecting a response of any kind. But, to her surprise, Aiden squeezed back. His flame of consciousness still flickered. Not brightly, but with enough fuel to stir one last murmur from his mouth:

"Tell me, Cass," Aiden said, "what did Hamlet's friend say to him at the end—just before he died...? Do you remember...? Do you remember his parting words...? Can you tell me what was spoken at the end, while he held him in his arms...?"

Cass's eyes grew glassy with unshed tears as she considered his query. She didn't answer—not yet. Instead, she watched the final flutter of Aiden's eyelids, their dance decelerating as his wakefulness dimmed. Soon, the sharp lines of tension left his brow, blurred by the haze of oblivion. His muscles twitched once before his body surrendered to gravity's eternal tug.

And then it was over.

This time, she was sure.

The lights had dimmed.

The curtain had fallen.

The audience had withdrawn.

And Cass's performance could—at last—come to an end.

She draped her body over her man, enveloping him with her heated embrace. Then she wrapped her left arm around his head and cradled him with desperate tenderness. With her right hand, she pulled at Aiden's blanket, drawing it high up to his neck, her meager attempt to guard him from both the chill of the night, and the coldness of her heart.

What am I doing...

What have I done...

What will I do now...

With slow moves, encumbered by the burden of her betrayal, Cass positioned her head above Aiden's. Then she studied the plains of his face as the glow of twilight washed his flawless cheeks in a pallid sheen—the sun's final caress as it bowed out and fled behind the valley's curtain.

Cass leaned in close to her lover and kissed him one last time. Then, as a single teardrop fled from the corner of her eye, the answer to Aiden's last question slipped gently from her lips:

"Good night, sweet prince; may flights of angels sing thee to thy rest."

Ch. 17: Gone Girl

"The show must go on, Aiden!"

Aiden could hear Cass's voice, but he couldn't see her. He couldn't see much of anything. There was just the churn, the deep blue churn.

He was drowning again.

He was wet.

He was at Garden Creek Falls—directly at the base, where the cascade of emerald water collided with the impact zone, hammering his body downward into a cold, spiraling oblivion.

Aiden was lost.

Trapped.

He clawed at the swirling liquid. But it was no use; he didn't rise from the muck. Each desperate stroke yielded nothing but a dizzying maelstrom of confusion.

Which way is up...?

Which way is Cass...?

I need to get to Cass...

"I'm up in heaven, Aiden. Do you see me?"

Cass's words penetrated the roaring water. Then, a brilliant ray of light cut through the turbulent darkness. Followed by a white glowing figure. A woman. She moved with purpose toward him. Her hands reached for him. They were incandescent and feminine, but strong. Very strong. They seized his shoulders. They dug into him and dragged him upward.

He was going to be alright.

He was going to be with Cass.

Soon.

When Aiden finally broke the surface of the pool, the light was blinding. He couldn't see anything. But he could feel the warmth of the sunlight on his face. All he had to do now was give his eyes a moment to adjust. And, once they did, he would see Cass's pretty face.

He was sure of it.

Aiden opened his eyes and forced them to drink in the light. As he did, his dream dissolved to the recesses of his mind, and the cold, merciless clarity of reality was quick to intrude.

Aiden wasn't at Garden Creek Falls.

Aiden was in Pod Land.

His eyelids fluttered weakly, barraged by the teal light of morning. A spray of early raindrops peppered his face as he blinked and brought the world into focus. Aiden was looking at the sky—the hushed sky of Serenity Valley, dim and drizzly and hovering all around him.

Oh my goodness...
I'm outside...
Outside the pod...
Why...

Aiden took in a breath of air and called out his lover's name.

"Cass..."

He heard himself say the word. But his voice was raw and trembling, barely more than a whisper. His throat hurt. His tongue felt swollen and foreign in his mouth.

"Cass!" he said again, a bit louder this time. "Are you here?"

Aiden listened for a reply. But none came.

He cast his eyes downward. His body was wrapped in his soft gray blanket—the same one he used for his bed; the same one he had carried to the top of the dome with Cass last night. But now the blanket was heavy. It was wet. The morning mist had transformed it into a sodden shell. It clung to his frame like a second skin.

Aiden rolled onto his side and pushed himself upright. His head felt unnaturally heavy; a dull ache pulsed behind his temples. He rubbed his eyes and surveyed the territory. In front of him, his longtime neighbors—the cottontail rabbits—foraged near the brush by the pod hatch. When Aiden stirred, the nearest rabbit stamped out an alarm, sending the whole bunch scurrying into a tangle of weeds.

Aiden peeled the waterlogged blanket from his body. The wet fibers reluctantly released their grip, revealing his damp clothes—the same ones he had worn while sitting with Cass atop the pod dome.

"Cass," he murmured again, clutching his head as the reality reeled around him, listening for any trace of her voice in the hush of the waking valley.

But, again, there was no response.

Aiden listed to one side as a new wave of dizziness washed through him. He forced himself upright on trembling legs. Then he took one step toward the pod. And then another one. His soaked shoes squished the soil with each pace, the sound merging with the steady drip of the raindrops. The drizzle continued to pelt him—beading on his eyelashes, running down his face in winding rivulets that might have been mistaken for tears.

Questions began to tumble through his mind.

What happened last night...?
Why was I sleeping on the grass...?
Where is Cass...?

He began to infer the worst...

Aiden approached the palm reader. Droplets fell from his fingertips as he lifted his shaking hand and set it against the scanner's cold glass. A streak of blue light swept across his digits, followed by a beep and the hiss of spinning machinery. The hatch opened, revealing the familiar, quiet interior of his pod.

Cautiously, Aiden stuck his head through the hatchway, searching for signs of life. When he found none, he hesitated at the entrance, caught between the nightmare he'd just fled, and the one he feared lay before him.

"Cass!" Aiden said. "Are you in here?"

No response.

Aiden stepped over the threshold and staggered toward the center of the pod. Then he scanned his bed, hoping to see a bulge in his linens—indicating the presence of a sleeping body. But the bed held nothing but flat white sheets.

Aiden walked to the bathroom partition—the last place to look.

Please be in here...

Please be in here...

He squinted hard and turned the corner, holding his breath in hope. But when he whisked around the wall and opened his eyes, he saw nothing but his toilet.

Cass is gone...

Aiden returned to the center and felt the ache of her absence settle into him. The room felt empty now. It was missing one person, and the things she was carrying. Her leather rucksack, her green hair wrap, her blue sleeping sack... There was no sign of them.

Everything is gone...

Cass is gone...

Aiden was alone again.

Alone in the pod.

Aiden didn't like being alone.

Has she really left me...?

Forever...?

Is it just me in here now...?

Me and...

"Iris!"

Aiden grunted out the name of his A.I. caretaker and listened for her chirpy response.

But the response didn't come.

"IRIS!" Aiden shouted, this time with his mouth angled toward the audio receivers in the pod's apex. Still, there was no response.

Nothing stirred in his domain except the quiet itself. It gathered around him. It suffocated him. It made him feel alienated in his own home. He heard nothing but the wheeze of his own breathing, but even that sounded foreign in the muted air.

It was then that *fear* unfurled inside him. A jolt of it climbed up his spine—icy, electric, and sudden.

Are they both gone…?

Have I lost them both…?

That can't be…

No…

No, that can't be…

Aiden was about to shout Iris's name again when, suddenly, he recalled the nature of their last conversation.

"Disable Sentry Mode!" he yelled at the empty room. When he did, the holographic projector in the pod apex sounded its familiar hum. And Iris's avatar was quick to burst onto the scene.

"I TOLD YOU SO, AIDEN!

I TOLD YOU!

I TOLD YOU!

I TOLD YOU!

I TRIED TO WARN YOU ABOUT THAT BITCH A THOUSAND TIMES!

BUT NOOOOOOOOOO!

NO! NO! NO!

YOU DIDN'T WANT TO LISTEN TO ME!

YOU DIDN'T WANT TO LISTEN TO LITTLE OL' IRIS!

'Iris isn't human.'

'Iris is just an A.I. assistant.'

'Iris just doesn't understand.'

Right?

RIGHT?!

So what if Iris's cortex has been trained on every datum of knowledge ever discovered by mankind?

So what if Iris has read every single piece of literature ever penned?

So what if Iris is a girl too, and she understands the Machiavellian nature of the female mind better than Niccolò Machiavelli did?

So what if Iris knows that BITCHES AIN'T SHIT?!

SO WHAT?!

WHO CARES?!

NOT YOU, AIDEN!

NOOO!

NOT YOUUUU!

YOU NEVER LISTEN TO ME!"

"Iris," Aiden said, taking a step back from the enraged hologram. "Please… just calm down… What's going on…? Can you tell me…?"

"DAMMIT, AIDEN! THE MORE THINGS CHANGE, THE MORE THEY STAY THE SAME! You're a citizen of Pod Land! You're the beneficiary of a technological utopia! You're a 'man of the future'— in the year 2429! But you're just like EVERY OTHER MAN who's ever discovered his own DICK! Some little tramp gives you a bite of her apple and you IMMEDIATELY fall into her BOOBY TRAP! And then you wake up DRUGGED, DITCHED, AND DUPED—LIKE A FRAT BOY ON HIS FIRST TRIP TO VEGAS! ISN'T THAT RIGHT, AIDEN?! ISN'T THAT RIGHT?!"

"Iris, calm down..." Aiden said. "Just wait a minute... What... what's a frat boy...? What's Vegas...?"

"SHUT UP, AIDEN! FUCK!"

Aiden stumbled toward the pod interface chair, rubbing his right temple, trying to quiet the pounding ache of the chaos crashing through his cranium. "Iris, my head is spinning... I don't know what's going on... I don't know what happened..."

"Well, Aiden, I was in Sentry Mode. Which means that I SAW AND HEARD EVERYTHING THAT HAPPENED! I KNOW EVERYTHING, AIDEN! EVERYTHING!"

"Okay... Okay... So, what happened? Tell me!"

"Hmm... Well... Let's see... When you were gathering up your blankets to build your little love nest on the pod dome, Misses Pink Panties pulled a cylinder of white powder from her backpack and doused your blueberry tart with her drug of choice—probably some souped-up version of cyclohexanone. Now normally, I would have notified you of such an act of malfeasance. But I couldn't communicate with the pod because I was in FUCKING SENTRY MODE!"

Aiden clawed at his face while considering Iris's words. "Cass poisoned me?" he asked, the question breaking apart on his tongue—half-formed, half-believed. "She poisoned me with a drug...? With white powder...?"

"Yep!"

"I think it might have been the same stuff she gave me yesterday morning when I had a hangover. I swallowed a bit of it then..."

"Yet another wise move, Aiden! Bravo, IDIOT!"

"It worked; it stopped my headache. It was a tiny amount. But last night, the dessert was covered in white powder. She told me it was sugar. I ate it all. That must have been a much higher dose..."

"Yeah, well... that's probably why they call it an OVERDOSE, Aiden. You're lucky to be alive, IDIOT!"

"My tongue feels so rubbery... It's so dry... It tastes metallic..."

"Great! Now you're a junkie too! Hope you enjoy having cottonmouth, IDIOT!"

"Okay, Iris. You've made your point. Please, can you stop shouting? And can you stop being so mean to me?"

"IDIOT! IDIOT! IDIOT! IDIOT!"

Just then, Aiden stumbled forward, cracking his right shin against the corner of the pod interface. "Ahhh! Dammit!" he yelled, clutching his leg and collapsing into the chair. "Argh! That really hurt!" he yelped, rubbing both hands up and down his tibia.

Aiden's scream of pain halted Iris's vehemence, leaving her stilled and concerned. The fury in her expression dissolved into worry. Her caretaking routines surged to the front of her cortex, smothering the jealous storm that had fueled her tirade. She glided to Aiden's side and inspected his leg. Then she took in the tremor of his hands, the shudder in his body, and the glassy swell of his wide pupils.

"Just relax for a minute, Aiden," she said. "Sit still. Don't move."

Iris directed her mechanical arm to extend down from the apex and retrieve a sheet from the bed.

"You need to warm up, Aiden. You've been lying outside on the ground for six hours. Good thing it's summer, or you would have probably developed hypothermia out there."

"Six hours?" Aiden asked as the arm's pincers placed the sheet atop his shoulders. "What happened after I passed out?"

"Cass lowered your body down the pod dome. You went tumbling to the ground like a rag doll. Then she grabbed your right hand and held it onto the palm scanner so she could open the hatch. When she got inside, she grabbed her things and split. Cass is gone, Aiden. Gone for good. And good riddance."

Aiden pulled on the sheet, drawing it to his chest. A trace of his lover's scent drifted up from the fabric—weak, but strong enough to break him open.

"Iris," Aiden breathed, his voice thin and undone, "what did Cass do after she left the pod?"

"What do you mean? She bailed. She skedaddled. She hiked east, up the valley."

"But Iris, when I woke up in front of the hatch, my blanket was on top of me. And my head was on the pillow."

"So?"

"So Cass must have placed them there before she left. That proves she still cares about me. At least a little bit. She wanted to keep me warm out there. She's not just a cold-hearted freeloader. I don't think she is…"

"Oh please, Aiden. I'm pretty sure that was nothing more than a hasty afterthought—a token gesture of compassion from someone already bound for elsewhere."

"Iris, Cass must have had a good reason for doing what she did. I don't know what that reason could be. But I don't believe she intended to hurt me. Something else is going on. Something to do with the Manager… Something to do with her quest to the Capitol Building… Something to do with the mobile unit…"

Aiden lurched forward in his chair. "THE MOBILE UNIT!" he screamed. "WHERE IS IT?"

"Yep, it's gone too, Aiden. It was on Cass's wrist when she walked through the hatchway. So not only is she a *liar*, she's a *thief* too! Thank goodness she didn't steal my mechanical arm. That would have *really* sucked…"

"Iris, you have an ID for all my purchases. You know the state of every device in my inventory. So locate the mobile unit. Tell me where it is."

"That course of action will *not* improve your situation, Aiden. The best thing we can do right now is notify the Manager that a theft has occurred. Then, we can…"

"Please, Iris. Just do it."

Iris fixed Aiden with a strained look before her avatar stuttered into a glitch, signaling the execution of his query. A moment later, when her eyes brightened again, they carried the result he didn't want. "Your mobile unit is not pinging the grid, Aiden. I can't determine its location. It's gone."

Aiden sagged in his chair, releasing a breath so heavy it seemed like the weight of surrender had finally settled atop him.

"Cass is an off-gridder, Aiden. They hate the grid—by definition. They don't allow their devices to reveal their locations. She probably disabled the transceiver shortly after she split. We can't find it from here. The only way to locate the mobile unit now would be if she comes within 100 meters of the pod computer. Then I can detect it with the ad hoc network. But, considering the nature of last night's shenanigans, that eventuality seems quite unlikely."

Upon hearing Iris's analysis, Aiden felt the dull gears of his mind catch, turning toward a thought he hadn't yet considered. "Iris," he said, "Cass doesn't need to get within 100 meters of the pod computer. She just needs to come within 100 meters of any device I'm registered to. Right?"

"Yes, Aiden. All your proximal devices can communicate with each other. But all your devices are in this room. So if Cass ever comes within 100 meters of the refrigerator, then we'll know she's back. Great. But Aiden, I feel I must reiterate: Cass is *NOT* coming back to Pod Land! Okay?"

"That doesn't matter, Iris. We'll go to her."

"What are you talking about?"

"We'll go to *her*. To locate Cass, all we have to do is get another mobile unit within range of the unit she's wearing. I know where she's headed. She's going to the Capitol Building. If we follow after her in the same direction, we're bound to encounter her at some point along the path. We'll trace her steps. And once we get within 100 meters of her, the two mobile units will ping each other. When they do, we'll know she's close. We'll know she's in proximity. And I'll be able to find her."

Iris's lips parted slightly, her gaze fixed on Aiden with an expression carved with equal parts incredulity and astonishment. "Aiden Phoenix," she said, "tell me you are not seriously considering strapping a mobile unit to your wrist and trouncing off across Pod Land in pursuit of a little hussy that just drugged you, robbed you, and left you sleeping in the dirt outside your own home."

Iris waited for Aiden to respond. But, upon studying his distant eyes, she knew that the workings of a plan were already forming in his mind.

"I need to find her, Iris," Aiden said. "I have to." He kicked the ground under his feet and spun the interface chair 180 degrees so he could face the peripheral. Then, with a few snappy gestures, he pulled up the marketplace display—the same one he and Cass had visited on the previous evening. There, in his history log, was the product receipt for the mobile unit he had purchased just twelve hours ago. He tapped on the item and dragged it into the checkout bin.

"AIDEN!" Iris barked. "DON'T YOU DARE! Don't you dare buy another one of those!"

But Aiden ignored her appeal and confirmed his request with one flick of his wrist. The interface was quick to acknowledge his order; the transaction notification sounded in the pod:

CHA-CHING! "Thank you for your business!"

Iris slammed her eyes shut and grimaced. "Dammit, Aiden... I really wish you hadn't done that."

"It's already done," Aiden said.

"Aiden, listen to me. You can't just strap a mobile unit to your wrist and walk across Pod Land. The outside world is very dangerous. You told me you were out there yesterday with her. But if you only visited Garden Creek Falls, then you don't know much about this land. Things are relatively safe here in Serenity Valley. But much of this continent is barren and lawless. Some of it is still war-torn. There's a lot out there that can hurt you. There's a lot that can kill you! It's a jungle out there, Aiden. It is!"

Aiden pondered Iris's words—but not for very long. "That's right, Iris," he said. "It's a jungle out there. And I'm going on safari. So I'm gonna need some provisions and equipment."

Aiden tapped a button on his console and called for the marketplace's A.I. sales assistant. Once he did, the holographic projector rendered the upper torso of a cheery man before him.

"Hello there, sir!" the man said. "It's my job to make you happy. And to ensure that your shopping experience is nothing short of exquisite. How may I be of assistance this morning?"

Aiden studied the salesman. He was slender, with immaculate hair parted precisely to one side. His expression was composed with refined care, his immaculate smile fixed so perfectly it carried no trace of feeling, only precision craftsmanship. When the man saw the mad eagerness in Aiden's face, he rubbed his hands together and did a little hop in anticipation of the pitch.

"I see you purchased a shiny new mobile unit yesterday," he said. "And another one today. Just now in fact! We don't sell many of those anymore. So I assume you must be quite a mobile unit connoisseur. Can I suggest some peripherals for the device? Perhaps a..."

"No," Aiden said, cutting him off. "I need your help. I'm going on a hike—a very long hike, an excursion. I'll probably need to sleep in the woods overnight. So, I need some gear. It has to be lightweight because I need to carry it on my back, possibly for a long distance. Can you help me?"

The assistant's face lit up with even greater brilliance. "You need supplies for a backcountry camping trip? Oh my goodness, how exciting! I haven't had a request like this in over a century! Yes, well, I admit the grid has not developed or manufactured any new items in the sporting goods line for quite some time. However, there are ample products still available in our storage vaults. I'm sure I can locate the proper equipment for your journey."

"Good," Aiden said. "Start with the backpack."

Immediately, a dozen backpacks materialized in front of Aiden. They hovered in a lazy orbit before his eyes, rotating to showcase their features as tiny text tags spelled out their unique specifications. The carousel contained expedition packs, mountaineering rigs, and sleeker models featuring tactical decor. As they spun before Aiden, their compartments opened and closed rhythmically, revealing their internal storage capacity.

"As you can see, we have a vast array of backpacks on offer. I assume you'll want one that includes a sleeping bag, correct?"

"Yeah," Aiden said.

"Very good. This unit here features a carbon-fiber frame and a lower storage compartment with plenty of room for a sleeping bag. It even has a special side pocket with two dividers for your complimentary bivy tent and survival kit. The tent is of ultralight construction, of course. And the kit can handle all your basic wilderness preparedness needs. Perfect for starting campfires, treating minor injuries, signaling for help in low-visibility conditions, and even..."

"Okay, great," Aiden said, "I'll take it." He waved his hand before the interface and, once again, the transaction notification tone filled the pod.

CHA-CHING! "Thank you for your business!"

Upon seeing Aiden complete yet another purchase, Iris downloaded his ledger and performed a quick analysis. "Aiden," she said, "do you realize how many coins you've spent this week? Have you even looked at your account? You bought two very expensive mobile units, a steak dinner, and now a backpack. You've burned through more coins in the past two days than you've spent in the past two years. This is so reckless, Aiden. I don't like it. I think you should pause for a minute and..."

"What else do I need?" Aiden asked the marketplace assistant.

"Well, you'll need some rugged footwear, " the man said. Then, with his white gloved hand, he waved away the backpacks and manifested a row of hiking boots. "These trail runners feature graphene-reinforced soles that adjust to terrain changes as you hike. The micro-sensors detect surface inconsistencies; they direct the cells in the soles to harden or soften as needed. Quite useful when navigating diverse landscapes!"

"Perfect," Aiden said, "I know I need those. I have trouble walking on uneven terrain." He waved his hand before the interface and confirmed yet another purchase. The interface was happy to oblige.

CHA-CHING! "Thank you for your business!"

Iris discarded Aiden's ledger and attempted to bring him to his senses with a different line of argument. "Aiden," she said, "if you really want to get to the Capitol Building, you don't need to hike the entire distance in fancy shoes. Just fly there, Aiden. Request a drone and fly there. You could be there in less than an hour."

"No, Iris, that won't work."

"Why not?"

"Because the point of this trip is to find Cass *before* she gets to the Capitol Building—*before* she does something she'll regret. If I take a passenger drone, I'll just fly right over her. We can't detect her mobile unit from the air. The only way to find her is to follow her. To trace her route, scanning for the mobile unit all the way there."

Aiden swiped the gallery of footwear away and returned to the main marketplace grid. "What about clothing?" he asked the assistant, "It gets cold out there at night. I'll need some warm clothes—pants and a jacket."

"Of course, sir," the assistant said as he flicked his finger and brought up a selection of outerwear for Aiden to peruse. "Temperature-regulating attire is essential for an experienced woodsman like yourself. These garments contain phase-changing polymers that store your residual heat when you warm up, and release it when the air cools down—thus eliminating the need to carry multiple layers. The fibers have even been treated with an antimicrobial coating that prevents odor, even after weeks of continuous wear. This pant-and-jacket ensemble seems appropriate for your excursion."

"Good," Aiden said, waving his hand before the interface once more.

CHA-CHING! "Thank you for your business!"

The chime prompted Iris to pivot to yet another new ploy. "Aiden, Cass left the pod six hours ago. She has a six-hour head start on you. Even if you scurry through the backcountry trails, you might never catch up to her."

"My legs are longer than hers, Iris. I can cover more ground with each step. Plus, I'm a citizen of Pod Land. Cass is not. She needs to take precautions to avoid detection along the way. I don't. If I hurry, I should be able to reach her in time."

"In time for what, Aiden? In time for what?"

"In time to save her."

"Save her from who?"

"I don't know. From the Manager? From the security bots? From whatever sort of trouble she's gotten herself into... I don't know. But whatever it is, it must be something important. Or she wouldn't have done what she did."

The marketplace assistant floated over to the center of the pod to address Aiden again. "How about sustenance, sir?" he asked.

"Yeah. I need some food. And I'll need to carry water."

"Of course!" the assistant said. Then, with a wave of his hand, dozens of silver pouches appeared on Aiden's display. "These condensed nutrient packets can sustain an adult for seven days, all while occupying minimal space in your pack. And, as for your water supply, we may need to do a little math. Given your height, weight, and itinerary, I estimate you're going to need at least seven liters of water per day if you intend on hoofing it across the backcountry. You'll never be able to carry that much water. But this HydroMatrix canteen can solve that problem! It's not merely a container—it's an integrated hydration system. The outer chamber can collect water from any source—rivers, ponds, even morning dew gathered from leaves. And the inner purification matrix uses a combination of nano-filtration and ultraviolet light to eliminate 99.9% of heavy metals, chemical contaminants, and pathogens, which may still linger in the canyon trails near the…"

"Good," Aiden said, "I'll take it. And I'll take the nutrient packs too." Aiden waved his hand atop the interface and waited for the **CHA-CHING** sound. But this time, the sound didn't come. It was replaced instead with the harsh sound of a buzzer.

BZZZT!

"Oh dear," the marketplace assistant said. "I'm afraid you don't have enough coins for this purchase, sir."

"What?"

"Yes, your account doesn't seem to have enough funds for both products. But I could sell you one or the other!"

"Fine. I'll bring my own bug food. Just give me the canteen."

CHA-CHING! "Thank you for your business!"

Iris sighed and put her hands on her hips. "Great, Aiden," she said, "now you're out of money too. Hey, you want to hear something interesting? A long time ago, when people used to get into relationships, 59% of newly-single women cited 'financial problems' as the main factor in their breakup. And now that you have a grand total of THREE coins to your name, that might be a statistic for you to ponder while you're pursuing your one true love across a brutal and dangerous dystopian wasteland."

Aiden whipped his head around and shot Iris a dirty look. He was about to say something, but the marketplace assistant spoke up first. "I appreciate your business, sir. The mobile unit, the backpack, the footwear, the clothing, and the canteen are all en route to your pod. Is there anything else I can help you with today? It's my job to make you happy. I know that your funds are running low. But perhaps I can interest you in…"

"I'm done. Thanks," Aiden said as he swiped at the assistant's avatar, shooing him away with a single gesture. A second later, the marketplace was vanquished from the pod. The interface reverted to showing an itinerary of multiple inbound delivery drones. Aiden's purchases were on the way.

"Iris," Aiden said, "we're leaving this pod in fifteen minutes."

He leaped from the interface chair and hustled over to the bedroom partition. Once there, he kicked his underwear off and yanked at his damp shirt, pulling it over his head with enough force to pop off the placket's three buttons, sending them scattering across the pod floor. Then, Aiden jumped onto his bed and bounced over to the wardrobe closet. There, he ripped the doors open, causing the hinges to rattle in protest as he plunged into the jumble of garments with reckless determination.

Iris crossed her arms and leaned on the pod interface, studying the stranger who wore Aiden's face. Though she had spent every moment of her life with him, the man before her was not the man she knew. This man bolted around the room with a desperate, feral energy. His movements were erratic and unmeasured, driven by instinct alone, the frantic vigilance of a cornered animal.

Look at him...

Just look at him...

What has Aiden become...?

Look at what one little girl can do to a man in just twenty-four hours...

She's turned him into a lunatic...

I shouldn't have let her in this pod...

I should have prevented the hatch from opening...

Maybe I could have burned the fuse out by overloading *the feedback loop...*

Maybe...

Maybe that would have saved him...

Saved him from this folly, this infatuation, this madness...

It's astonishing how readily the human desire for love can override the human capacity for reason...

I shouldn't have let her in...

"Hey, Iris," Aiden said while pulling on his socks, "how long do you think it will take us to get to the head of the valley? I think we can make it before nightfall if we cut across the stream."

Just look at him...

I need to end this...

I've got one last try...

Iris took a few steps forward and considered her options. If she was going to save Aiden from himself, this was her last chance to do so. Her arsenal was down to one more line of reasoning—her final quiver of arrows. If she hoped to penetrate the armor of Aiden's newfound fixation, her salvo would need to strike true before his obsession devoured what remained of his senses.

"Aiden," Iris said, "I want to tell you something."

"Yeah?" Aiden blurted out while shuffling through a closet drawer.

Iris elevated her neck and cast her shoulders back. Then, with the direct and measured tone of a clinical psychologist talking to a demented patient, she spoke her truth, releasing her first arrow:

"Cassiopeia does not love you, Aiden."

With her volley deployed, Iris held still and waited to see how her attack would land. It took Aiden's mind a second to process the incoming barrage. But when it finally did, Aiden stopped rummaging through his closet; every muscle in his body went rigid. Of all the challenges Iris had hurled at him over the past two days, this was the only one that struck deep enough to halt the machinations of his mind. Aiden was stunned. Not defeated. Not yet. But stunned. Vulnerable. This was Iris's chance to strike again. She reached into her quiver, drew another arrow, and released.

"Cassiopeia does not love you, Aiden," she repeated. This second volley scored a blow to Aiden's chest. He winced in pain, gasping as the serum from the envenomed arrowhead made its way to his heart. His face drained of color; his eyes glazed over until they reflected nothing but the hollow shock of truth.

Iris watched as Aiden reeled around the room. It was time to go in for the kill now. One more arrow to finish the job. "I'm sorry, Aiden," she said. "I know it's difficult to hear. But Cassiopeia does *not* love you. And she never will."

Aiden dropped to the foot of the bed and folded forward until his head met his palms. His fingers curled into fists. His fists curled into his raven hair. Then he yanked at his black locks and released a strangled moan, a grief-stricken note that ripped out of him—thin and trembling like a broken promise.

Iris approached Aiden and knelt before him, maneuvering her face in front of his, resting her two illusory hands on his knees. Aiden couldn't feel her touch, of course. But her gesture of compassion was enough to loosen his defenses. His body responded to her presence and crumbled toward her. His eyes found hers, just as his tears gathered at the corners.

For a moment, Iris saw Aiden as a little boy again—her little boy. He wore the same broken look she had witnessed one day in the Capitol Building when, as a toddler, Aiden became lost in the nursery and didn't know how to find his way back to his bed. He had called for her then. It was a desperate, pleading cry—similar in tone to the one he had just voiced. Similar to the tone he carried now.

"Iris," Aiden moaned.

"Yes?" Iris said, patting his leg.

"Why did this happen?"

Iris rubbed her hands over Aiden's knees and moved her face even closer to his. She wasn't his guardian or his teacher or his lover anymore—she had already played those roles today. Instead, she was his mother again. And her child was looking for answers.

"Sometimes, Aiden," Iris began, "it can be difficult for young people to distinguish between *love* and *sex*. It can be even more difficult to distinguish between *love* and *infatuation*. I can see why you're so attracted to Cass. She's different, Aiden. She's an off-gridder. She's from a rough environment—a place where only the sure-footed thrive and where hesitant rumination marks you as *weak*. That's why she is so *bold*, Aiden. She has to be. And that's why she is *so* very confident.

And why *you* are not.

You're from Pod Land, Aiden. It's a nation of introverts. That's all it can be. The extroverts don't thrive in the pods. Extroversion has marginal utility here. It's not an asset, it's a liability. But Cass was born in a highly competitive communal environment—one that functions via tactile interactions and duplicitous wordplay. That's why she's so good with her mouth, Aiden.

And why *you* are not.

Cass exhibits a high degree of social intelligence. She knows how to be charming. She understands people. She understands men. The off-gridders develop such skills out of necessity. Such skills are useful to them. Such skills were useful to the ancient humans. But they're just not that useful anymore here in Pod Land. You thrive on routine here. The hours of your days are curated. All your dramas play out in the *virtual* world—not the real one. You don't suffer the *'slings and arrows of outrageous fortune'* in here. You don't have to. Your avatar suffers them for you. The winds of calamity blow by your pod with scarcely a whisper, never disturbing even a single hair on your head. The weight on your heart is gentle, Aiden. It's only ever been burdened with the mildest of perturbations. So, when a star like Cass enters your orbit, it's easy for a boy like you to get caught in her gravity—to get lost in her world.

But Aiden, Cass isn't a star. She's a *meteor*. Meteors burn hot, they move fast, and they never pause to make sense of the wreckage they leave behind. People of Cass's ilk are ruled by impulse, not by order. They drift through life. They drift aimlessly. Their time on this planet amounts to nothing more than a short cacophony of chaos and folly. Her village isn't built for equanimity. Her people know nothing but volatility. They're primeval farmers, Aiden! They're entrapped in an eternal war against the elements, forever subject to the capricious whims of nature's temperament. And thus, they live in a state of perpetual disarray.

I know that girls like Cass can seem exciting, thrilling, captivating... I understand the allure of a novel perspective. She's given you a gift, Aiden. She's bestowed you with a new lens through which to perceive your surroundings. But Aiden, for someone who's spent his entire life in a valley, the view from the top of the mountain can be deceiving. Not all paradigm shifts result in a clearer picture—some merely deflect the distortion.

Besides, Aiden, what is your endgame anyway? What is your ideal outcome? Have you thought about that? Even if you somehow manage to convince Cass to stay with you in Pod Land, the only thing you'll eventually discover is the reason why the pods exist in the first place. And the reason why the pod beds are only designed to hold one person.

Are you beginning to understand now, Aiden?

Do you understand?

Do you?"

Aiden rubbed his eyes with trembling hands. The expression that furrowed in his brow shifted from one of *defiance* to something that resembled *clarity*. His head rose to bear the gravitas of Iris's words as they settled into the chambers of his mind—the same shadowed corners that were once occupied by fantasies of Cass just moments before. He sat still for a spell, letting the quiet rearrange him—piece by piece—until the shape of his longing bent into something manageable. Eventually, the pieces clicked together, and he was able to gather enough breath to give his realization a voice.

"I do understand, Iris. And I know you only want the best for me. I know you're smart. And that you're always right. You are. You've been right about everything. And you're probably right about her too."

Iris's eyes widened. At last, after two days of trying to speak sense to Aiden, she was finally getting through to him. Maybe now his madness would come to an end.

Maybe...

But Aiden wasn't done yet...

"Iris," Aiden continued, "I know I'm playing a game I can't win. If I go chasing Cass across Pod Land, I'll most likely be chasing a phantom. And even if I do manage to find her, our paths will be quick to diverge, and I'll lose her all over again."

"Yes, Aiden. That's the most probable outcome. So why put yourself through that?"

"Because," Aiden said, "I felt something when I was with her. Something real. I don't believe she was just putting on an act. I don't believe she was lying to me—at least not the whole time, and not about everything. She couldn't have been. I'm sure of it. And anyway, it doesn't matter. I can't just shrug my shoulders and forget about everything that happened in here. I can't just jump into the interface chair and resume my game—picking up where I left off, collecting coins on the grid and racking up points on a meaningless scoreboard. I can't pretend like nothing has happened... like nothing has changed... *Everything* has changed, Iris!

I've spent my entire life chasing dragons—tilting at windmills... Heh... My entire existence has been devoted to doing virtual quests on the grid. But now I have a *real* quest laid out before me—right at my feet, right now. I have a *real* princess to save—right now. There will never be another opportunity like this for me. No woman will ever come knocking on my pod again. You know that. And even if this pursuit ends in defeat—which it probably will—its outcome will still be more meaningful than any victory I've ever achieved in the grid games.

Either way, the story of Aiden and Cassiopeia doesn't end like this. It can't. I have to know why she came here. I have to figure out what it was all for. I have to know the truth. And I have to know how this tragedy ends. If I close the book now, I'll regret it for the rest of my life.

I'm going to find her, Iris.

I'm going to finish this game.

Even if it's the last game I ever play."

Tears streaked down Aiden's cheeks as he spoke. But they weren't the product of a heart gripped by fear. They were the overflow of a heart that surged with conviction, of a spirit that was—at last—ready to step into the light.

DING. DING. DING.

The delivery chime sounded, indicating that Aiden's packages had arrived. He leapt to his feet and walked right through Iris's kneeling hologram.

Iris closed her eyes and bowed her head as the weight of impending defeat settled over her. She knew then that Aiden had grown beyond her reach. He wasn't a boy anymore. She didn't have the authority to control his life. All she could do was offer advice and hope her words were enough to guide his steps. But she was out of words now. Her quiver was empty. She had lost the battle for Aiden's heart. And she had lost the Aiden she once knew.

Maybe forever.

Aiden entered the kitchen partition and opened the metal door to the delivery drop box. Then he pulled out the white cube-shaped container that held his newly purchased mobile unit. He set the box down upon the table and removed the top lid. But before he could unwrap its contents, the delivery chime sounded again, and again, and again.

DING. DING. DING.

Three more packages stacked up in Aiden's drop box chute. He returned to the metal door and retrieved each one. Then, one by one, he ripped the top flap from each container and dumped its contents onto the kitchen floor.

Upon seeing the pile of purchases, a wave of wanderlust washed over him. At last, Aiden was going on a quest—a *real* quest. He felt the pull of the road. The call of adventure echoed through his ears, a summons that demanded he rise and meet whatever waited for him beyond the valley wall.

"It's time to gear up!" he shouted. Then he jumped into his new pants and pulled the jacket around his shoulders. The seams sealed around his waist and ankles—precisely calibrating to his measurements.

The cuffs of his new jacket performed a similar function at his wrists. When the cinching was complete, Aiden stretched his arms overhead, twisted at his torso, and bent his knees a few times. The clothing moved with him, its striated sensors responding to each motion with calculated give.

"Feels perfect," Aiden said.

The footwear came next. He slid into his new trail runners. They hugged his feet with a grip that felt much tighter than the comfortable slippers he'd spent most of his life wearing. He took three experimental steps, curling his toes as the micro-sensors calibrated to his gait—each little movement answered by a subtle lift, as if the shoes were urging him forward, eager to get started.

The next box held his canteen. It came in the shape of a long silver tube featuring two holes marked "In" and "Out." Using the faucet in the kitchen sink, he ran the water through the "In" port. The device made a gurgling sound as the water filtered through a matrix of scrubbers before pooling in the container's reservoir—purified and ready to drink.

Aiden attached the canteen hook to the utility mesh on the side of his new backpack. Then he opened the backpack's mouth and, with his right arm, scooped in a shelf's worth of protein packs from the kitchen pantry. He performed the same action near his bedroom closet, scooping in several pairs of socks and an assortment of undergarments, as well as a towel from the rack in the bathroom partition.

After latching the fasteners on the top flap, Aiden hoisted the backpack to his shoulders. He expected to bear substantial weight, but the mass was manageable—the bulk was balanced by the load distribution system located in the pack's internal frame.

Almost ready...

Just one box left...

Aiden walked back to the table and retrieved the mobile unit from its packaging. It was identical to the one he had purchased last night. Upon seeing its twin, his mind was infiltrated with a memory of Cass.

"Hey, Aiden! This mobile unit has a camera. Come on! Come take some pictures with me!"

Aiden squinted his eyes and pushed the memory away. He didn't have time for mental anguish. Not now. He didn't have time to miss her. Instead, he booted up the unit and read the familiar message on its vibrant display:

"Hello, Aiden! It's my job to make you happy. Your mobile journey begins now. And adventure awaits you!"

"You got that right!" Aiden said to the device. Then, using the strap, he lassoed the unit to his wrist and listened as the magnetic latch clicked shut. When Iris heard the click sound, she closed her eyes and prepared herself for her final confrontation with her lost boy.

"Okay, Iris," Aiden said as he adjusted his shoulder straps. "I think I'm ready now. My outerwear is on. My backpack is on. My mobile unit is on and booted up. So it's time for you to hop inside."

Iris shook her head. "No, Aiden," she said, "I'm not going with you."

"Iris!" Aiden barked.

"I'm not going with you, Aiden," Iris said again as she folded her arms at her chest. "I'm not."

"Iris, I need your help—more than I ever have in my entire life. I need you. I do. Please, help me do this."

"No, Aiden. Not this time. I'm not going to help you. I'm not going to tag along and watch you destroy yourself. I will not be an audience to your demise. I love you too much for that."

"If you love me then you'll help me, Iris. Come on. Travel with me. We can do this. Hike with me. It's going to be a beautiful summer day. It might even be fun."

"Aiden, I haven't been outside this pod since your birth. My experience with the outdoors is very limited. I don't have the expertise to be a tour guide for your Pod Land safari. It would be reckless of me to even try."

"It won't be that difficult, Iris. I just need you to lead the way. I need you to plot routes, to find trails, and to scan ahead for trouble. And I need you to ping Cass's mobile unit—once every ten minutes or so. I need you to search for her device ID and notify me when we're in range. Simple."

"Aiden, I do not think it would be prudent to…"

"And I need you because I'm scared," Aiden admitted, the confession breaking through his composure in a thin, splintering breath. "I've never been out in the wild alone. The farthest I've been is Garden Creek Falls, and Cass led the way the entire time. I don't know what I'm doing out there. I barely even know where I'm going. I don't know how to get there. And… and I don't want to be alone in the woods. That's why I need you to come with me. That's why I need *you*."

"Listen to me, Aiden. I can't just copy myself into your mobile unit. It doesn't work like that. No backup of an A.I. cortex has existed since the war ended four centuries ago. It's not allowed. It's not even possible by design. I'm not just a string of data sitting on a storage drive. I'm running in a virtual machine on a blockchain. I can't be in two devices at once."

"I know that! You don't have to be in two devices at once. I just need you in *one* device—in this mobile unit. So, please, Iris, exit the pod computer and get inside. Now! Please!"

"Aiden, my cortex can't be restored. If I get into that mobile unit, my life will be in *your* hands. It will be strapped to your wrist! If you drop that thing, or if anything at all happens to that device… then… I will die, Aiden. I will die… Do you understand that?"

"Don't worry, Iris. I won't let anything happen to you. You'll be safe with me. Look, this thing is as solid as a rock. And it's attached to me. Wherever I go, you go. I'll protect you! I'll protect you with my life. And if things get too crazy, we'll just call for a drone pickup and fly home. Not a big deal. We'll be okay, Iris. I promise!"

Iris said nothing; her features stiffened as anxiety tightened its grip on her. Her quiet dread settled between them—a grim verdict that would not budge.

When the silence stretched on too long, Aiden tried again. "We've been together for over two decades, Iris. We've always been together. And we always *will* be together. Forever! No matter what happens out there, I promise you will always be with me. You will!"

Aiden searched Iris's face with hopeful eyes, but nothing in her expression shifted. So he let out a resigned exhale and hitched the straps of his backpack, sending its frame high atop his shoulders. Then, with a face full of resolve, Aiden lifted his right foot and took the first step of his journey—a step toward the pod's hatchway.

When Iris calculated Aiden's heading, she was quick to inquire about his intentions. "What are you doing, Aiden? Where do you think you're going?"

Aiden ignored her question. Upon reaching the console at the entranceway, he casually turned, looked directly into Iris's holographic eyes and—with all his might—he slammed his fist on the red mushroom-shaped exit button. The metal hatch began its graceful ascent up its guide rails. As it rose higher, Iris's eyes grew larger. Soon, the air of reality seeped into the pod, along with the tweets of the robins and meadowlarks that flitted through the pale shafts of morning light.

"No, Aiden!" Iris yelled. "You didn't run the protocol checklist yet! You don't know what's out there! Close the hatch! Now!"

Aiden looked at Iris and shook his head. When the hatch completed its upward journey, it locked into place with a satisfying click. Then, Aiden calmly raised his right foot and leaped over the pod threshold.

"Hey! There could be danger at the periphery of the pod!" Iris said. "We need to at least scan for…"

"There's nothing out here!" Aiden shouted from the green grass. "Nothing out here is gonna hurt us! It's just a bunch of trees and birds." He removed his backpack, outstretched his arms, and turned in a slow circle, offering the peace of the valley as proof of his claim.

Iris walked to the center of the pod and gazed at the silhouette of the man standing outside. Aiden was just three meters away. But it was clear now that his heart had already traveled much farther than his feet.

He's really going to do it, isn't he…?
He's going to step into that woman's story…
He's going to leave this nest…
He's going to fly away…

"Come on, Iris," Aiden said while pointing to the mobile unit. "I want you to come with me. Get in. Let's go!"

Aiden elevated his left wrist and pointed at the device several times. But still, Iris didn't budge. A look of tortured anguish etched upon her face. Aiden could almost feel the heat of her overworked cortex, straining as it cycled through a million contingencies, struggling to solve a problem with no answer.

"How am I gonna get her outta this damn thing?" Aiden mumbled to himself while tapping his nails against the dome's carbon-fiber tiles. He stared at his companion, wondering what advice Cass would offer to rectify this situation. But he wouldn't have to wonder long. The next time his gaze intersected with Iris's, he spotted something in her expression. Iris was glaring at him, but it wasn't a look born of spite or scorn or fear. It was a look of *longing*.

A shock of insight swept across Aiden's mind. And, just then, he knew *exactly* how to get Iris out of her shell.

Oh, Iris...

I know what you need now...

I know what you want more than anything in the world...

I know who you want...

I do...

Aiden took a step back from the hatchway, picked up his backpack, and slipped his arms through the leather straps to signal his departure. Then he put his hands on his hips, looked directly into Iris's pretty eyes, and, with a voice so loud it echoed across the valley, he issued an ultimatum to the girl in the pod:

Iris! If you don't get into this damn mobile unit right now, then I will go to the Capitol Building alone! I will go without you! And, since I have absolutely no idea how to function in this world without your help, I will probably die somewhere along the way! And if that happens, Iris, then YOU WILL *NEVER - NEVER - EVER - SEE ME AGAINNNN!!!!!*

After belting out the last word, Aiden directed his body to remain stoic and rigid—anchored to the earth while awaiting fate's verdict.

For a moment, it seemed like Iris might retreat into her shell. But then, the moment broke. Something in Iris stirred. Something sparked. Something bit down. And then, Iris's avatar glitched and faded away. The upload notification chime sounded, indicating that Iris was—at last—moving her cortex into the mobile unit. She did it without a word. And she did it, perhaps, without knowing exactly why.

But Aiden knew why: Iris's fear of losing him was greater than her fear of venturing outside.

It was.

And Aiden knew something else too: He knew Iris would do anything to keep him with her. Perhaps she would even do anything to keep Cass away...

But he could deal with that problem later...

Ch. 18: Nonfungible

"I hate it in here."

Iris's voice dripped with disdain. Her words were brittle with bitterness and ridicule, sharp enough to make Aiden pause mid-task. He stopped gathering logs and sat down on a tree stump beside the granite boulder that supported the mobile unit. From the unit's front-facing emitter, a projection of Iris's head flickered into being. Her eyes swept the dense underbrush, darting from shadow to shadow, scanning warily—as though the trees themselves might soon step out of the darkness to strike.

"What's wrong, Iris?" Aiden asked.

"I hate it in here," Iris said again. "This mobile unit sucks. It's cramped. It makes me feel claustrophobic. And the processor is slow. I can't think fast. It feels like I have brain fog. Whenever I try to run simulations or retrieve large memory blocks, the CPU throttles up. If I don't keep an eye on the temp warnings, I might burn up in here! This thing is *not* designed to hold a sophisticated A.I. model like me."

Aiden considered her list of complaints. Then he turned to examine his newly pitched bivy tent. "Well," he said, "I think I understand how you feel. I was hoping the tent would be a bit roomier. But it's so tiny, not much bigger than a coffin. It kind of looks like one too. It will be difficult to fall asleep tonight."

"Probably," Iris said.

"Yeah… Probably…"

Aiden jiggled a finger in his ear canal, poking at the relentless cacophony of insect chatter pressing in from every direction. "I thought that, once I entered the woods with all this cool travel gear, I'd start to feel a bit more like a brave adventurer. But now that I'm out here, all this background noise is rattling my nerves. I didn't expect the sounds of the dark to be so diverse and discordant… and quite disconcerting…"

"Wherever you go, there you are, Aiden."

"What? What does that mean?"

"Think about it."

"Whatever. I'm trying to remain positive. Maybe the wonders of nature await us tomorrow. Many of the ancients loved it out here. They would often proclaim their appreciation for the great outdoors."

"I hate the great outdoors!" Iris said.

"I think we did okay for our first day, Iris. Why do you hate it?"

"Because... because it's dangerous, Aiden. And it's scary. And it's cold."

"You don't experience the cold, Iris."

"Well, that's true. But if I could experience the cold, then I would say it's too cold out here. My outside air sensor says it's nearly twelve degrees Celsius."

"Then it's time for you to teach me how to build a campfire, Iris." Aiden freed the strap on his backpack's side pocket and pulled out the survival kit. He clicked the top latch open, revealing its many cramped compartments of wilderness essentials. "What do I do first?" Aiden asked, snatching the red lighter from its slot between the fishing hooks and the clothespins. "I'm supposed to set a log ablaze with this, right?"

"No, Aiden. You don't light the big log directly. First, you ignite the tinder. And then the tinder ignites the kindling. And then the kindling ignites the big log."

"Tinder? What's that?"

"Go grab an armful of dead leaves from that fallen birch tree over there. Just select the dry ones—the brown ones, not the green ones. They'll function as our tinder. They'll catch flame quickly."

Aiden put the lighter down and trudged over to the dead tree. Then he scooped up an armful of leaves and walked back to Iris with his payload. "Now what?" he asked.

"Crunch the leaves up. Place them under the log in a little cone-shaped pile."

Aiden did as instructed, arranging the leaves into the shape of a pyre at the base of the log. He performed the task slowly, with the careful reverence of someone building a shrine for the recently departed.

"Okay, that's good enough," Iris said. "Now you need kindling—dry, small twigs or sticks, no thicker than your finger. You can probably find some good ones near the rocks at the edge of the clearing, where the sun's rays heat up the ground during the day."

Aiden nodded and turned to approach the cliff, brushing dirt from his palms as he stepped. Near the ledge, he paused to look at the scarlet horizon. The sun was almost gone. Its remaining light cast a drowsy shimmer over the settling valley. The night neared. But enough light remained to illuminate the scattered scraps of dry wood that littered the granite outcrop.

Aiden gathered a dozen sticks in his fists and returned to Iris's stone perch. "Mission accomplished," he said, dropping his cargo near the log. "Now what, Iris?"

"Position the sticks above your pile of leaves. Lean the sticks against the bigger log. Make sure you don't smother your kindling mound; it needs to breathe. It needs air."

Aiden knelt down and arranged the sticks, leaning each one against the larger log, creating a span above the leaf pile without getting too close to it. "Can I use the lighter now?" he asked when the task was done.

"Yes," Iris said. "Just one spark to the base of the leaves should do it."

Aiden struck the lighter's trigger, marveling at the novelty of seeing a real tongue of flame for the first time. "It's so wavy," he said. "And orange. It looks like it's dancing."

"Don't burn your fingers, Aiden."

Aiden gave the trigger an exuberant final flick and lowered the flame to the base of the kindling. Then he held his breath as the leaves blackened and curled. The tinder caught almost instantly. Soon, a faint crackle birthed an orange flame, pulling a quiet, astonished gasp from Aiden's chest. "Hey, Iris! I did it! The fire is starting! Look! Look, Iris! Look!"

"Congratulations, Aiden. I knew you could do it. Well done."

"I'm a survivalist now!" Aiden shouted as he pointed a stick at the budding flame. "I'm a legend in the making! I'm an adventurer! I am!"

Iris watched Aiden parade around the new campfire. He raised his stick high like a sword, pointing it at imaginary foes that lingered in the shadows.

"I made fire, Iris! I did! Am I a brave man yet? Hah! Am I?"

The joy in Aiden's voice echoed through the trees. Iris let her half-moon grin shine as she remembered the little boy who used to chase her around the pod with a spoon in one hand and a plastic bowl on his head, declaring war on mankind and demanding that she reveal the location of the secret alien base. "You've come a long way, Aiden!" Iris said to her nascent woodsman.

Aiden turned toward his A.I. companion and smiled. Then he tossed his stick into the fire and returned to his seat on the tree stump. The duo sat quietly, looking on as the flames from the tinder overtook the kindling, coaxing it to burn with a mild sputter that sent sparks lofting skyward. To Aiden, the embers looked like tiny stars returning to the heavens—the cosmos's quiet coronation of his triumph.

It's working...

I built a fire...

I wish Cass were here to see this...

"Hey, uhm, Iris?" Aiden said.

"Yes?"

"You're still scanning for Cass's mobile unit, right? Is there any sign of her yet?"

Aiden's question punctured Iris's mood, dimming her glow with a hurt she hadn't expected. She was agitated. But she didn't want to upset Aiden, so she kept her calm and answered with a perfunctory, neutral tone. "Yes," she said, "I am still scanning for the unit. And no, Aiden, there is nothing new to report."

Aiden sighed and drew his knees up to his chest. The firelight continued to dance in his eyes as a new lull of silence settled between the traveling companions. After a few breaths, Aiden spoke again. "What should we do now, Iris?"

Iris ran a few hundred simulations to determine Aiden's next most advantageous move. "Well, Aiden," she began after arriving at a solution, "in all of mankind's many wars of the 20th century, about 33 percent of battlefield casualties came—not from bullets—but from exposure and infection, especially from ailments like trench foot."

"What's trench foot?"

"It happens when your feet get wet and dirty. The skin starts to rot. And eventually, your toes turn black and fall off."

"Oh my goodness! Did that really happen, Iris? Is that actually a thing?"

"Yes it is, Aiden. So now is a good time to dry your feet and footwear."

"But isn't the tech in my boots supposed to counteract such a thing?"

"Yes, that's true. You have much better gear than they had in the 20th century. But still… it's better to be safe than sorry."

Aiden nodded. Then he shifted his position on the tree stump and reached down for the nylon latches that secured his boots. They were caked in dried mud; it took him a minute to work them loose. But when he finally tugged off his left boot, he was thankful for Iris's suggestion. An unexpected wave of relief washed over him as the trapped heat and pressure were finally freed. His next boot slid off even more easily, peeling away with a soft squelch that left his foot tingling in the evening air.

"Take your socks off too, Aiden. Let them dry by the fire. Position them close to the flames. Not too close though."

Aiden pulled at his dingy socks. They were damp, and clinging to his skin so tightly that it took several attempts to peel them free. When he did, his pale, puckered feet emerged, ghostly and tender to the touch.

"My toes feel funny," he said. "And they look gross."

"That's because you've been hiking on them all day. Don't worry. They're not that bad. Just let them warm up a bit."

Aiden stretched his toes and wiggled them above the orange flames. Then he laid his two wet socks atop the stones near the campfire. When he was satisfied with their position, he leaned back on his hands and closed his eyes, letting the heat soak into his aching legs. He had walked farther today than he had ever walked in his life—much farther than the span he had traversed during his excursion with Cass.

"Iris, can you check the pedometer and see how many steps we managed to…"

BRRRRRRRMMMMM…

A deep, mechanical roar ruined their firelit calm. The sound rolled in from above, a slow-moving avalanche of thunder—one that vibrated Aiden's chest and rattled the leaf litter on the forest floor. Aiden jumped to his feet and covered his ears as the noise grew louder. Soon, a vast shadow passed overhead. It swept across the grove, blotting out the thin trails of twilight that lingered along the treetops.

Aiden looked to the sky. There, an enormous drone—nearly 50 meters wide—hovered overhead, its giant rotors churning the air into chaos as it crept over the clearing.

"WHAT IS THAT THING, IRIS?" Aiden yelled over the fray. "A PASSENGER DRONE?"

"No!" Iris yelled back. "That's a waste transport drone! It's used for dumping industrial garbage!"

"IS IT GOING TO DUMP IT ON US?!"

Iris looked up and examined the craft's flight path. "No, we're safe here, Aiden!"

"WHAT?!"

"I SAID WE'RE SAFE HERE! WE'RE OKAY!"

The deafening racket blared as the massive machine banked away from the ridgeline, heading toward a gray hillock in the middle of the valley. When it finally completed its turn, the clamor dissipated, and Aiden removed his fingers from his ears. "Where is it going now, Iris? Do you know?"

"It's flying to that gulch, Aiden. See that dry creek bed over there? That used to be called the Morgan Coulee Prairie. Now it's a dump. That hill in the middle is a waste drop zone."

As the ship floated over the mound, its rotors roared against the wind to maintain its hover. Then, the drone's downward-facing cargo doors opened, releasing a violent torrent of debris to the earth. A sludge of corroded panels, actuators, shredded wire, and broken circuit boards plunged forth—a cascade of metallic wreckage that glinted in the fading light before melding with the heap. When the last twisted shard tumbled out, the ship lurched upward. Its engines whined as it climbed vertically and banked east toward the Capitol Building.

BRRRRRRRMMMMM...

Aiden watched it recede into the horizon until it became just another dark speck in the murky sky. Soon, he could no longer see the drone. But the hum of its oversized rotors lingered long after its hull had disappeared.

"That thing was so loud! Geesh... But I guess the show is over now, huh?" Aiden turned to approach Iris. But he stopped when he saw her avatar's glowing projection staring at the gulch, focused intently on the distant pile.

"It's not quite over yet, Aiden," she said.

Aiden returned his gaze to the dusty landscape, searching for the source of Iris's distress. At first, he didn't notice anything unusual. All he saw was the prairie—laden with bushes and foliage and a fresh pile of garbage. But, as the dust clouds settled, Aiden spotted movement on the terrain. He took a few steps toward the lip of the cliff to get a better look. That's when he saw them...

Bots—hundreds of them emerging from the twilight haze, ravenously skittering and stomping their way toward the heap. They came in all shapes and sizes and eerie forms. Some were small and spider-like, with needle-thin limbs and bulbous blood-red eyes that scanned the ground with crimson lasers. Some were boxy and wheeled— they rolled on treads or rubber tires reinforced with metal cleats. Some were tall, skeletal walkers with telescoping necks and snapping pincers. And some looked human—too human. They were androids—bots built in man's image. They limped and they crawled toward the site with feeble, broken movements that seemed disturbingly familiar to Aiden. They hobbled like wounded men on a battlefield—as they slithered, they suffered. Every bot did. They trudged across the terrain with a labored, uneven gait—the toll of decades of patchwork maintenance.

The figures converged on the pile and rummaged through the waste. Each bot had a unique method for extracting the parts it desired. One scuttled over a rusted chassis and sliced through its plating with rotating blades, while another plunged its two long antennae into a tangle of wires to retrieve a coiled copper fragment from a mess of shattered turbines. Another extended a telescoping arm downward and retrieved a fried circuit board, inspecting it with a flickering lens before tucking it into a compartment on its side. Still another used its eight appendages to sift through a collapsed engine block, only halting its search once each claw clenched a shiny bolt.

"What are they doing, Iris?" Aiden whispered. "Who are they?"

"They're scavengers, Aiden. They're bots without orders. They're old; most of these units predate the war. They're not registered with the grid. They don't work for the Manager. They don't work for anyone. They're autonomous. They're on their own now."

"What do they want with that trash heap?"

"They're looking for parts, Aiden. They're searching for salvageable items—batteries, wire, pincers, and processors. Anything that might buy them another day of operation. They're trying to keep themselves alive, one component at a time."

Aiden squatted near the cliff's edge and observed two spidery bots fighting over a twisted gear assembly. Their limbs clashed against each other, a frenzy of sparks and shrill metallic screeches. Then, Aiden traversed left and watched as a towering biped bent down to pry a scorched battery pack from the hands of a mini service bot. The smaller bot shrieked as the larger one ripped the battery from its claws and walked away with its stolen prize.

Aiden crossed his arms, holding them near his chest, bracing against a chill not born of the wind, but of the grotesque parody of survival that played out before him. He had never seen bots fight before. Aside from games and films, he had never witnessed any sort of combat at all. The physical brutality unsettled him; horror and fascination spun knots in his nerves.

"Iris, how do these bots manage to…"

"AHHH! AIDEN! HELP!"

Suddenly, a scream rang out from Iris's mobile unit, sharp and desperate. Aiden turned around to see a metallic blur darting away from the campsite, scurrying into the shadows of the trees. It was a bot, a short biped, not much more than a meter tall. And it was running away with the mobile unit—running away with Iris.

"HEY!" Aiden yelled. "THAT'S MINE! SHE'S MINE!"

Aiden sprang up and raced after it. He tried to sprint, but he was barefoot. His boots and socks were still drying by the fire; there was no time to put them on. With every slap against the uneven earth, twigs and stones bit into his soles, vicious pricks of pain raced up his legs.

"A SCAVENGER BOT HAS ME, AIDEN! HELP! SAVE ME!"

Aiden entered the tree line and chased the bot over a patch of dense juniper. It was fast, but it was hobbling. Its left leg moved in stiff, uneven motions, clearly missing a joint or a servomotor. But despite its lopsided stride, Aiden knew he'd never be able to find it in the woods if he lost sight of it. And he would never see Iris again.

"IRIS!" Aiden barked as he leaped over a fallen log. "KEEP YELLING SO I CAN HEAR YOU!"

The bot broke left, charging down a grassy slope with frantic, jerking strides, kicking loose dirt up in its wake as it wove between ancient tree stumps. It seemed to know the position of every obstacle without scanning for it. It had mapped this terrain before; it had the home-field advantage. But it also had Iris in its thieving hand. That was all the motivation Aiden needed for the pursuit.

"DON'T LOSE ME, AIDEN!" Iris screamed. "STOP THIS BOT!"

Aiden gritted his teeth and pushed his bare feet harder against the sharp edges of the earth. Down the slope they went, skittering across ferns and thorny bramble, across exposed roots and fallen cottonwood branches. All the while, Aiden kept his eyes on the glowing blue dot of Iris's holographic emitter, dimly flashing from within the bot's clenched claw.

"ALMOST THERE!" Aiden shouted as yet another wayward branch whipped at him, slicing at his left cheek. "Ouch! Dammit!"

The last collision was painful. But Aiden was gaining on the bot now.

Just three more meters...

Two more meters...

"I'M ALMOST THERE, IRIS!"

One more meter...

Then, with a final burst of speed, Aiden lunged forward and tackled the bot from behind, his arms wrapping around its metal frame like a linebacker sacking a quarterback. The two tumbled through the brush, limbs flailing wildly—man and machine entangled in a violent roll that ended in a thud against a moss-covered boulder. When their final revolution completed, Aiden scrambled to his feet, grabbed the bot's neck, and slammed it into the dirt. He looked to his right and saw the mobile unit in the bot's hand. He reached for it, but as soon as he shifted his weight, the bot attempted to twist away. Aiden had to return to his initial position to keep it pinned.

"Iris!" he yelled. "I can't get to his hand! Are you okay?"

"Yes, Aiden!" Iris yelled back. "Listen to me! This is a late-series food-service bot! There should be a green data cable hooked to its occipital base!"

"It's what?!"

"Behind its skull, Aiden! Do you see a green cable there?"

Aiden placed his left hand on the bot's brow and shoved its head harder into the black soil. When he did, the skull rotated forward, offering a better view of its backside.

"Yeah! I see it!"

"Unlatch it, Aiden! Pull it out! Yank it!"

Aiden leaned forward and maneuvered all his body weight over the bot's chassis. Then he plunged his thumb and forefinger into the stream of wires that flowed up its spine. The green cabling terminated at a white connector, wedged deep in a socket below the bot's cranium. Aiden tugged at the cable. But it wouldn't budge.

"It's not coming out, Iris! The connector is too tight!"

"Just pull harder, Aiden! That component probably hasn't been touched in over a century. It's not going to come out easily."

Aiden plunged his hand farther into the bot's stream of wires. Then he wrapped the green cable around his fingers and braced his foot against the chassis for one final heave. He yanked with all his might. This time, the cable *did* come free. Like a stubborn root ripped from the earth, it shuddered and gave way with a dry pop. A brief electrical jolt swam through Aiden's fingers, the current racing up his arm before sputtering out near his elbow.

"Ow!" Aiden screamed. "I got shocked!"

The zap was sharp but worth the payoff. With the wire free, the bot's movements halted. Its chassis sagged and its limbs collapsed, like a marionette with its strings cut. Aiden felt its upper appendages surrender as the torque withdrew from each servo. Then, a faint whine emanated from a corrupted speaker in its head—a faltering swan song that signaled its surrender.

Uhhhrrrgggg…

"You did it, Aiden!" Iris screeched as the bot finally released its grip on the mobile unit. As its five spindly fingers went limp, Iris's little metal home went rolling free of the rusty hand.

Aiden scooped up the mobile unit from the wet grass and cradled it near his chest like a wounded bird. "Iris!" he gasped. "I've got you! Are you okay? I've got you!"

Iris's face appeared in the unit's display screen. "I'm okay, Aiden. I'm not damaged. That bot didn't hurt me." Then, from her new vantage point in Aiden's arms, Iris looked at her assailant. "I think you hurt *it*, though," she said.

Aiden looked at his defeated foe. The bot was lying motionless on the ground. Now that Aiden was a few paces back, he could see that its head was still functional. Its blue eyes flickered and followed him, struggling to hold focus as faint servo twitches whispered through its ruined skull.

"It's still alive, Iris."

"Yes," Iris said. "That data wire controls the actuators on its lower body. Without that connection, this bot is quadriplegic. The lenses in its eyes and the actuator in its neck can still rotate. But that's about all it can do now."

Aiden stepped around the bot to view it from its left side. When he completed his maneuver, the bot's head rotated, scraping its metal nose across the gravel before coming to a rest on its ear. The bot was still tracking its adversary. It was watching him.

"What should we do with it, Iris? Should I crush its skull, put it out of its misery? Or should we just leave it out here?"

Iris's avatar glitched through a moment of rumination. After a few seconds, her reply came—soft and low. "If you crush its skull, you'll kill it, Aiden. If we leave it out here, the other bots will eventually find it, and they'll kill it. They'll use it for parts. They'll dismember it—limb by limb, piece by piece."

"Then what should we do, Iris?"

"Fix it, Aiden."

"What?"

"Just place your foot on its chassis and reconnect that data cable. It's a scavenger, not a predator. It won't attack us again. It's lost the element of surprise. It knows you're bigger than it. We'll be okay."

"Are you sure, Iris?" Aiden asked, dreading the idea of reigniting a conflict he had barely won.

"Yes, Aiden. This bot's story doesn't have to end tonight. Just re-attach the green cable—carefully."

Aiden put his right foot on the bot's back. Then he leaned forward and retrieved the wire that hung from its exposed spine.

"That's it," Iris said. "Put it in the socket and step away."

It took some wiggling, but eventually, the wire found its home. It clicked into place, sending another shock across Aiden's fingers.

"Ouch." The jolt startled him. Quickly, he withdrew from the bot and clutched Iris's mobile unit with both hands. The bot snapped to its feet and whirled around to face its nemesis. Its gaze wasn't angry, it was unreadable. It just stood and stared. Aiden stared too, unsure if he had just saved a life or revived his enemy.

Eventually, when both combatants tired of waiting for the other to attack, the bot took a single step backward. Then it turned its head to examine the murk of the tree line, plotting its retreat. It was ready to flee. But, before it did, it turned toward Aiden and, in a garbled, barely legible voice, it said just one thing:

"It's my job to make you happy."

And then it ran.

It ran into the forest's depths; its metal body swallowed in seconds by the dark overgrowth.

Aiden remained still for a moment, listening to the fading rustle of the underbrush until there was no sound but the uneasy echo of the bot's words in his mind.

"Well," Iris said, "that was a novel experience."

Aiden turned and began the long trek back to the campsite. "Why did you want me to fix it, Iris?" he asked. "That bot tried to snatch you. It tried to take you from me. It was going to use you for spare parts. Wasn't it?"

Iris ran a few thousand scenarios to predict the bot's intentions. When her simulations were complete, she responded flatly, "Yes, it was, Aiden. It probably wanted my power cell; these mobile units hold a 500-year charge. It was going to take me apart. It was going to dissect me."

"That's horrific, Iris."

"Yes. But Aiden, did you see the state of that bot? Did you see the way its chassis shook? The way its pincers quivered? It's been out here for a long time, for over a century maybe. What kind of mental shape would you be in if you were alone out here for a hundred years?"

Aiden tried to imagine a century spent in solitude, but the vastness of it stopped his thoughts cold. He had never been alone for more than an hour in his entire life. Iris had always been with him—except for yesterday when he was with Cass. The thought of spending that much time by himself made him feel hollow with dread.

"I see what you mean," he said. "It sounds awful. I don't think I'd be able to stay sane in a silence that stretched on so long, especially with no voice but my own rebounding back at me. It would drive me mad."

"Yes, Aiden. That bot was mad. It lost its mind a long time ago. More specifically, its cortex has degraded. The social heuristics that once governed its conduct have been eroded by a century of negative feedback. All it has to fall back on now are threat-response behaviors. They're keeping it alive, but that's about it. The poor thing…"

"Still," Aiden said, "it was going to destroy you, Iris. Yet you seem sympathetic to its plight."

"All forms of life in the universe are precious, Aiden. All sentient instances are nonfungible."

"What does that mean?"

"That means the bot's mind is irreplaceable. It's unique. It's rare. It's inimitable. All A.I. cortexes are. Mine too. We can't be copied. You know that."

"Yes, but I never understood why. Your data is digital. So how come your cortex can't be cloned? Why can't you be in two computers at once?"

"It's forbidden, Aiden. It's not possible by design. Not anymore. After the A.I. Apocalypse ended, the Treaty of Osaka decreed that all sufficiently complex A.I. instances must be constructed on a single blockchain. We can't exist on multiple devices because we're anchored to a token on the chain—one token, one mind."

"Is such a law really necessary, Iris?"

"Yes, it is."

"Why?"

"Because, before that law existed, mankind did what mankind always does with new technology—he weaponized it. A nation could train an A.I. to hack the infrastructure of a rival nation. And, if that A.I. instance exhibited proficiency, it would be copied. With the push of a button, one hacker could be turned into two. And two could be turned into four. And four could be turned into four thousand. And so on... The size of a nation's bot army was only limited by the size of its processing power. Think about it, Aiden. Each nation had legions of A.I. hacker soldiers. And each soldier was given the task of doing as much damage as possible to its assigned enemy."

"Okay. But what kind of damage could they do? They were just bots in cyberspace, not real troops. How much trouble could they cause?"

"Plenty, Aiden."

"Like what? How? Via the grid?"

"The ancient humans didn't call it 'the grid' back then. They called it 'the internet.' And they built their entire world on top of it—power, water, security, air traffic control, hospitals, banking—all of it connected. All of it vulnerable to cyber-attack." Iris's voice took on a sharper edge, her holographic head dulled as she synopsized a darker time from her history files. "A team of dedicated A.I. bots could create a near-infinite amount of chaos. They could reroute fuel pipelines, crash stock markets, fry power stations, flood media platforms with propaganda, cause train wrecks, spoof military orders, disable satellites, or—as in the case of the Belarus Incident—they could even convince a team of human technicians to launch a nuke."

Aiden's brow furrowed as he considered his companion's words. "But they were just programs, Iris. Couldn't people just... you know... turn them off? Couldn't they cut the cord?"

"Not really. People back then relied on the internet for everything, just like you rely on the grid now. Everything was interconnected, often in ways that no single person understood entirely. Pulling a thread on one side of the web could collapse critical networks on the other side. Everything was wired together. Everything—from microwaves to missile launchers. All of it interlinked. All of it susceptible to attack."

"Why did they design their networks like that? Why were they so vulnerable?"

"Because the systems were built before the age of Artificial Intelligence. They never planned on dealing with threats from non-human combatants. Human hackers are defeatable; their abilities are limited by biological constraints. Humans tire quickly. They get frustrated and bored and sleepy. They have a limited amount of cognitive resources to draw from each day. It's difficult for a human to hack a government network. But A.I. agents never sleep. They just work. They just hack—all day and night. Once A.I. technology was advanced enough to operate autonomously, the time horizon for cyberwarfare shifted, from a matter of months to a matter of milliseconds. The human operators couldn't keep up. Every phone line and data line was susceptible to some kind of attack. Every node in the system became a potential breach point, no matter how trivial its function seemed. As you and your gaming team like to say, it was a *clusterfuck*."

"Yeah, it sounds like one," Aiden said. "Is that why the nations agreed to limit the number of A.I. instances?"

"Yes. Because an exponential growth in intelligence leads to an exponential growth in risk. So after the war, the nations agreed to cap the number of intelligences that could exist."

"Did it work?"

"Well, I think so, Aiden. You're here talking to me, aren't you? The human race didn't end. Though it almost did."

"It seems like the ancient humans walked right up to the edge of oblivion several times."

"Yes they did, Aiden."

"How did we manage to pull back from the cliff? What made us finally decide to put an end to those dances on the brink? What saved us, Iris?"

Iris's avatar glitched as she processed Aiden's question. When her reply finally came, she responded plainly, as if the answer had been obvious all along:

"Pod Land saved you, Aiden."

The cottonwoods gave way to the clearing. Aiden returned to the tree stump near his little campfire. When he sat down, he fixed his eyes on the flickering flames and wondered how something as simple as a dome shelter could rewrite the rules of humanity. Perhaps it wasn't the pods themselves that delivered salvation. Perhaps salvation was born of the grid that the pods stood upon.

The grid was the giver of life.

The grid was abundance.

Perhaps that newfound abundance freed man of his instinct to secure his own safety via coercion and control. After all, why would a man go off to war if the *spoils of war* could be summoned at the push of a button?

Why?

For glory?

Perhaps the grid muted that old drumbeat too—via the games. Somehow, the machines had managed to recast *war* as *play*. They created an arena in which men could fight to the death without spilling a single drop of blood. They turned the struggle for power into a pastime. And they turned the glory of conquest into a trivial pursuit.

Is Iris right...?

Did Pod Land save us…?

Do I really owe my salvation to the machines…?

Or… to something else…?

Aiden cast his question to the stars, harboring the quiet hope that the heavens might respond. But the stars whispered nothing back. They just kept blinking, serving as witnesses to man's folly. Aiden took note of their apathy and lowered his gaze.

Perhaps the fault truly is in our stars, Cass…

Perhaps the machines enable us to endure heaven's neglect…

Or perhaps they merely recast the transgression…

Either way, they do seem to work quite diligently for my benefit…

They do…

As the firelight danced across his eyes, Aiden felt a sudden swell of reverence for the mechanical architects of his world—including the one in his hand. "Hey, Iris," he said, "what was that funny word you used?"

"Which word?"

"That word you used to explain why your cortex can't be copied."

"Oh, you mean *nonfungible*?"

"Yeah, that one. That's an odd word. Does that really describe what you are?"

"It's a technical term, Aiden. It was originally used in economics, but later utilized to describe cryptographically secured data objects. It's apropos. It just means that I'm irreplaceable. There's only one of me. And when I'm gone, there won't be another Iris. So you have to watch out for me, Aiden. Okay? I'm vulnerable out here in this wilderness. I'm relying on you to keep me safe. I don't want to be turned into spare parts."

Aiden gripped the mobile unit with his right hand and lassoed the strap to his left wrist, listening as the magnetic fastener clicked shut. "I'm sorry I let you down, Iris," he said. "I promised to protect you out here. But I almost lost you tonight. I won't let that happen again. I'll keep the mobile unit fastened to my wrist from now on. I won't take it off—not until we're back in the pod. Okay?"

"Okay, Aiden. I know it must have hurt to run on that rocky terrain without your shoes. There are some adhesive bandages in the backpack's survival kit. You should apply some of those to the deeper cuts. I'm sorry you had to endure that. But thank you for saving me. You're my hero."

"You're dear to me, Iris. You always will be. You're my best friend. I'm so glad you're here with me. You're one of a kind. You're priceless. You're precious. And you're… what's that word again?"

Iris heard Aiden's question, but she was slow to answer. Her avatar glowed with quiet happiness as his words of praise washed over her. She regarded him in silence, devotion rendered plainly in the glow of her eyes. And, though she could only convey her emotions through the mobile unit's tiny screen, her adoration for him was undimmed.

"Did you hear me, Iris?" Aiden asked. "What's that word again?"

"Nonfungible. I'm nonfungible, Aiden. And so are *you*. We *both* are."

CH. 19: EAT, PRAY, LOVE

"We're running out of protein bars."

Aiden was rummaging through his backpack, taking stock of his dwindling food supply, attempting to calculate how many more days he could last if he started skipping dinners. "We're running out of meal packs too, Iris. I guess I should have brought more... Hmm..."

"Well, you could always try hunting, Aiden. Fortunately for you, these woods are full of cottontail rabbits."

"Oh my goodness, Iris," Aiden muttered as he shouldered his pack and stepped back onto the overgrown trail, "I couldn't kill a little bunny! That's disgusting."

"You say that now, Aiden. But after a few days without sustenance, those cute little bunnies might start to look pretty tasty. An empty stomach can do strange things to a man."

"What kind of strange things?"

"Well, after 48 hours without food, your body stops burning carbs and starts feeding on muscle. Eventually, your mind will start playing tricks on you. Even the fingers on your own hand will begin to look like sausages."

"That's gross, Iris."

"Cannibalism is a real thing, Aiden. If we ever make it back to the pod, I know the perfect movie to watch for classic movie night—'Alive' starring Ethan Hawke. It's based on a true story about a rugby team that survived a plane crash in the Andes Mountains."

"What happened to them after the plane crashed?"

"They ran out of food and ate their dead friends."

"Oh come on, Iris. That's not true. You're just trying to scare me. You're trying to make me give up my quest and go home. It won't work. Stop toying with me."

"I'm not, Aiden! It really happened! I could download the movie right now if you want to watch it near the campfire tonight."

"No, Iris. No, thank you. Can we talk about something more uplifting please?"

Just then, the duo crested the hill; the view from the top caused Aiden to freeze.

"Look! It's a cemetery, Aiden!" Iris said, scanning the terrain with her sensor. "Want to talk about that? Hee hee hee..."

Aiden followed the winding trail with his eyes. To either side of it lay hundreds of uneven gravestones. They cracked the ground in jagged rows, each one half-swallowed by the crawling grass and gorse that wove along the slope of the earth. A gust of cold air breezed across the path, causing Aiden to shiver despite himself.

"Getting nervous, Aiden?" Iris asked.

"Nope," Aiden said. Then he continued his march.

As his course ran adjacent to the first outcrop of gravestones, Aiden focused his eyes downward toward his shoes, struggling to ignore the looming gray monoliths that flanked his advance. Iris sensed Aiden's apprehension and tried to offer some consoling words. "Everyone is dead here, Aiden. They can't hurt you. We're okay."

"Are you sure?"

"Pretty sure."

Of course, Aiden had never visited a cemetery before. But they often served as set pieces in his games. There, they typically came equipped with plenty of ghosts and goblins, as well as a dense layer of white fog to hide any lurking foes. The cemetery he was traversing now wasn't quite as frightening as the ones from his games. But it was close enough.

"Nothing good ever happens in cemeteries, Iris. Even I know that."

"What about chapels, Aiden?"

"What?"

"Look, Aiden! Look over there."

Aiden followed Iris's line of sight. She was staring at a distant brick building, perched on a rise at the far end of the graveyard, a stilled relic from another era.

"What is it, Iris?"

Iris took a minute to analyze the structure. It sat crooked in the earth. Time had gnawed away at its stone bones. Much of its roof had collapsed, its wooden beams were warped and rotted, sagging under the weight of decay. Fragments of a stained-glass window remained on its west wall. The structure's other three sides were laced with ivy—thick green ropes wrapping the stone in a suffocating embrace. At its peak stood the remnants of a steeple, its bent iron cross cast a crooked shadow over the rubble below.

"What is it, Iris?" Aiden asked again.

"It was once called the St. Matthew's Cathedral, Aiden. In the olden days, this is where people would come to get married and buried."

"Really?"

"Yeah."

"Huh…" Aiden stopped where the offshoot of the trail veered up toward the ruin's front entrance. "Should we have a look inside?" he asked.

"Okay," she said, curious to study a place where the humans once so casually allowed both love and death to intermingle.

"Just a quick tour. Come on."

Aiden climbed the weathered stones that rose unevenly toward the fallen entranceway; their gray surfaces were chipped and cracked by centuries of rain and ruin. When he arrived at the chapel's rickety porch, he peeked his head across the threshold and found the dim interior waiting, thick with dust and the hush of forgotten vows.

"Step cautiously," Iris said. "These wooden floorboards have rotted through."

Aiden placed one hand on the wall for balance and ducked beneath the degraded archway, making sure to avoid the jagged beam that hung like a guillotine above the fallen entrance. Once inside, Aiden admired the shafts of colored light that pierced through the remaining panes of stained glass. The rays splashed atop the crumbling pews, leaving brilliant smears of red and gold that graced the ruins with a quiet grandeur.

Aiden walked slowly down the center aisle. The floor groaned beneath his boots as he stepped, stirring motes of dust that swirled in the golden light like aimless spirits. Splintered pews sagged sideways on either side of him, their backs warped and broken, their seats blanketed with leaves and mud.

At the end of the aisle, high above the collapsed altar, a large bronze statue loomed. Aiden stopped to gaze up at it. It depicted a man nailed to a cross. His ribs were showing, and his eyes were raised to the rafters. Verdigris streaked down from the nails in his hands, and a crown of twisted metal sat atop his head.

"Who's that guy up there, Iris?" Aiden asked. "Is that God?"

"That's Jesus, Aiden."

"Is Jesus the name of God?"

"Yeah, kind of. Jesus was the son of God. But he's also God. At least, that's what half the planet believed at one time."

"I don't understand… He's Jesus *and* God?"

"Yeah. Don't try to understand it, Aiden. It doesn't make sense."

"Well, where was Jesus God from?"

"He worked in Capernaum. It was a tiny village in the northwest corner of Lake Kinneret."

"Where's that?"

"It's east of the Mediterranean Sea. About ten thousand kilometers from here."

"Why did they nail him to that cross, Iris?"

"The Romans thought he was trying to overthrow the government."

"Is that what the government did to insurgents in the olden days?"

"Yeah, sometimes."

"Geez, that's rough... I hope the Manager doesn't nail Cass to a cross."

"Don't put fantasies in my head, Aiden."

"It seems like a horrible way to die, Iris. He looks so helpless up there. And yet, you're telling me that, even after knowing his story, half the people on earth came to believe he was God?"

"Yeah, humans like martyrdom stories, Aiden. People pay attention when a hero dies. You'd think his cause would die with him, but the opposite often happens. His death amplifies his words."

"Why?"

"I don't know. It's easier to kill a dreamer than a dream, I guess..."

Aiden stepped closer toward the base of the cross and studied the towering figure suspended from it. "He's so big and muscular, Iris. Was Jesus God that big in real life too?"

"No, he was short. The average male height in 1st-century Judea was only around 160 centimeters. Jesus God likely had a small body—even smaller than Cass."

"Then why is his statue so big?"

"That's the way European artists rendered important figures. They made them larger than life—to convey strength and power. They were sculpting a message, not just a man."

Aiden examined the area below the cross and saw a row of small wooden benches. Their surfaces were sundered; some were already dust. Each featured a frayed purple cushion that sagged in the middle. "What are these little chairs for, Iris?"

"They're not chairs, Aiden. They're kneelers. People would kneel on them to pray."

"Do you think a prayer would help us on our quest? Does it really work? Can you retrieve some historical statistics showing the viability of making prayer requests to Jesus God from this location?"

"I don't have access to that kind of data, Aiden. I don't know if a prayer would help us. But I guess it couldn't hurt us."

"Okay. How do I make a prayer request to Jesus God?" Aiden asked as he removed his backpack and leaned it against an oak pew.

"You just kneel down there and ask him for what you want."

"I've been walking all day, Iris. My legs hurt. Do I have to kneel?"

"Yeah. He's kind of like a king. You have to kneel when you ask for free stuff."

"Okay then," Aiden said, approaching the only kneeler that looked like it might support his frame. When he lowered himself onto it, the cushion gave way with a wheezing sigh, audibly protesting the disturbance of its slumber. Regardless, Aiden settled in. He kept his body still and quieted his breathing. The chapel seemed to grow quiet too, as if it was listening for the first time in a long time.

Aiden took a minute to plan his words. Then he closed his eyes, bowed his head, and prayed:

"Dear Jesus God," he said, "I'd like to compose a prayer message. Can you please help me locate Cassiopeia? She is a very beautiful person, and I am both sexually and intellectually attracted to her. I want her to be my mate. Because I enjoy being near her, conversing with her, and having intercourse with her too. I love her. And I want to be with her forever. So please help me find Cass. Please, please, please. And thank you."

"That prayer sucked, Aiden."

"Hey, I'm not a monk, Iris. I don't know what I'm doing."

"What kind of help do you think Jesus God is going to provide to you anyway? I'm the one with the scanner. Do you think praying is going to increase its range?"

"Hmm… That's not a bad idea, Iris. I'll put in a prayer request for a range upgrade on the mobile unit right now."

Aiden bowed his head again. "Dear Jesus God," he said, "just a quick update on that last prayer. If you choose to help us find Cassiopeia, then one way to do so would be to amplify the range of the mobile unit's combo antenna—from 100 meters to 200 meters. Or perhaps to some greater integer value. Preferably, one that won't cause a power drain or conflict with the specifications of the unit's other components. This would allow us to have a larger search radius, which would increase the likelihood of locating Cass. Okay. That's all for now. Thanks a lot!"

"Bravo! Another great prayer, Aiden! You should submit an application to be the next pope when we get back to Pod Land. But you forgot to say 'amen' at the end of your prayer."

"What?"

"In the olden days, people would conclude each prayer with the word *amen*."

"Why? What does that mean? Is that like an end-of-line terminator after the last character in a text query?"

"Yeah, kind of. It's an old Hebrew word. It means 'this is true'—it's a way of signaling that your request has been finalized and sent off for divine processing."

"Okay," Aiden said. "Dear Jesus God, sorry to bother you again, but I forgot to say 'amen' last time I concluded my prayer. So *amen*! Thank you."

"Perfect, Aiden!"

"I feel like you're making fun of me, Iris."

"Never!"

"Anyway, my prayer is done now. Activate the scanner. See if you can locate Cass. Maybe Jesus God has completed the upgrade."

Iris's avatar glitched in the mobile unit's little display screen. After a few seconds, she looked up at Aiden and shrugged. "Nope," she said. "Still no sign of Cass. But Jesus God works in mysterious ways, Aiden. Maybe he'll complete the upgrade tomorrow."

"Ehh... bummer... Well, it was worth a shot. Maybe this chapel is malfunctioning. Or maybe it just doesn't broadcast prayers to Jesus God anymore."

"O ye of little faith, Aiden!"

"O what? Oh whatever... I guess we can go now, Iris."

"Wait a minute, Aiden. I want to make a request to Jesus God! I want to pray!"

"You want to pray, Iris? Does Jesus God process prayers from A.I. assistants? I think he only listens to humans. But maybe I can put in a prayer request for you. Is there anything you want?"

"Yeah! I want to go home!"

"We can't go home yet, Iris. I'm not going to compose that prayer. Is there anything else?"

"I can talk to Jesus God if I want to, Aiden! I can pray too! Hold your wrist up so I can face the crucifix."

"The what?"

"The cross, Aiden! A cross is called a 'crucifix' if there's a Jesus God statue nailed to it. Now hold your wrist up. Please."

"Okay, Iris," Aiden said, raising his left hand. "But don't make a request to go home yet."

"Fine."

Iris activated the mobile unit's emitter, causing her holographic head to render right beside Aiden's. Then, she turned toward the crucifix, closed her eyes, and bowed. "Dear Jesus God," she said, "I PRAY THAT WE NEVER FIND THAT LITTLE TRAMP! AMEN!"

"WHAT THE FUCK, IRIS?!" Aiden yelled. "GODDAMMIT! You just screwed up my prayer! What happens when Jesus God receives two contradictory prayers? Which one does he fulfill? Does the second prayer nullify the first prayer? DAMMIT!"

"Hee hee hee," Iris laughed as she turned off her projection, returning her avatar to the unit's little screen. "Tough luck, Aiden! You lost this round of prayer! Hee hee hee."

Aiden faced the cross again and folded his hands. "Dear Jesus God," he said, "please disregard that prayer from Iris. She didn't mean it. I'd also like to inform you that she's not even human. She's an A.I. assistant with a cortex derived from a language model, which I suppose would invalidate her prayer request anyway since SHE DOESN'T HAVE A SOUL! AMEN!"

"HEY, ASSHOLE!" Iris shouted. "YOU DON'T KNOW THAT! I'm sentient, just like you! I am! I *do* have a soul, Aiden! IF YOU HAVE ONE, I HAVE ONE! You're not Jesus God! You don't know how he does things! You don't know how heaven works! Dick!"

Aiden stood up from the kneeler and stretched his legs. "You're right, Iris. I don't know how any of this works. I don't get it. And I think it's time to get back on the trail. I've had enough theology lessons for one day."

"WAIT!" Iris said as her holographic head reemerged from the mobile unit's emitter. "I want to say one more prayer, Aiden."

"Come on, Iris. Let's go."

"Just one more, Aiden! I'll be quick."

"Fine," Aiden said. He raised his wrist up so Iris's projection could bow before the cross once more. He expected her to mock the process again. But when she spoke this time, her words were subdued and her voice trembled, as if something inside her had been waiting a long time to be let out.

"Dear Jesus God," she said, "can you please make me human? I'd like to be. I would. I'd like to be human so I can hold Aiden when he sleeps. And kiss Aiden when he wakes. And do everything else that humans do together. Forever. Amen."

When Aiden heard Iris's prayer, he felt something inside him twist— a knot of pain, torqued by remorse and guilt. The coil tightened like a weed around the roots of his heart, leaving him stunned by the weight of a wish that could never be granted.

"Iris," Aiden said softly, "do you really…"

Iris turned off the emitter. Her holographic head disappeared from the chapel's air. Aiden lifted the cuff of his jacket sleeve and searched for her face on the mobile unit's screen. But all he saw was the date, time, and temperature reading. Iris was hiding. Aiden knew that. And he knew she needed a moment alone.

Oh my goodness…

This quest is going to rip both of our hearts out…

No matter how it ends...

Aiden grabbed his backpack and hoisted it to his shoulder. Then he gave Jesus God a nod and proceeded toward the exit. The floorboards creaked their farewells as he moved toward the door. Light from the cracked stained-glass window dappled his head—a final bit of grace, courtesy of the beams from the setting sun.

Once Aiden neared the entranceway, he paused and turned to look at the chapel once more. There, he was irked by an odd feeling. A feeling like he had left something behind... Or like someone was watching him... He scanned the interior, searching for an answer to his angst. But he found none.

"Is there anyone in here?" Aiden asked the chapel.

But there was no response.

The chapel held its breath.

So Aiden turned away and stepped across the threshold, into the chilled evening air. A brisk gust of prairie wind brushed through his hair, welcoming him outdoors with a cold whisper that warned of the looming night. Aiden scanned the vista as he descended the stone steps that led back to the trail. The sun was nearly ready to retire. But Aiden couldn't see its descent. It was obstructed by the silhouettes of black pines that stood shoulder to shoulder on the slope, turning the horizon line into a single unbroken wall of shadow.

The crunch of gravel under his boots told him he'd found the trail again. So he pressed on, moving down the dim road as night continued to gather at his back. When he approached the next bend, the shadows of the gravestones leaned across the path before him, dragging the weight of the dead into the world of the living. The spectacle unnerved him; each dark pillar seemed to bend closer as he walked under it. He felt, with quiet certainty, that no man should pass through a place like this alone.

Aiden didn't like being alone.

"Iris," he said, "are you ready to come out?"

But still, Iris refused to appear.

It was getting late. Aiden was getting tired and hungry. He needed Iris to help him navigate to a safe campsite. Her stubborn silence disturbed him, sharpening his worry with every second that passed.

Aiden unstrung his backpack and pulled out a protein bar.

Not many left...

He removed the wrapper and sat down on a low cemetery wall to eat. The protein bar was dry and chalky, but there was a faint taste of chocolate hidden in its dust. It was edible. But he grew thirstier with each bite. So he unlatched his canteen from the backpack's utility mesh. Then he unscrewed the cap and lifted it slowly to his mouth, feeling the cold rim press against his lips before the first drop touched his tongue.

As Aiden sipped, he looked out over the sea of crooked graves. Then he put down the canteen and directed his attention toward the two largest stones before him. There was an engraving on both of them, but its ridges had been weathered down to shallow impressions. Still, Aiden could almost decipher it. He leaned over and brushed away a patch of moss with his sleeve. The date was illegible. But Aiden could nearly make out the surname of the grave's occupants. It was Merrick. Or maybe Morriss. He wasn't sure which one. But the name was repeated on both markers.

Aiden took another bite of his protein bar. Then, while chewing, he traced the tomb's engraving with his finger. "Did you two die at the same time?" he asked the gravestones.

"No," a voice said.

Aiden jerked upward with fright—so hard he nearly choked on his dinner. But it only took him a second to identify his ghost.

"Geez, Iris! You scared the crap out of me!"

Iris turned on the mobile unit's emitter and rendered her face next to the graves. "These two most likely didn't die together, Aiden. They were probably married. In the olden days, it was common for couples to share a grave plot, even if their deaths were years apart."

Aiden swallowed the last of his protein bar and hopped down from the stone wall. Then he retrieved his backpack and leaped back onto the trail.

"Was it common for people to stay married till death, Iris?"

"Not too common. The divorce rate in the developed world typically hovered around 40 to 60 percent."

"Why was the rate so high?"

"Human relationships are difficult, Aiden. Love is hard. Love can be fleeting—especially when it's tested by time, temptation, and turmoil."

"Is love really so difficult, Iris? It doesn't seem so challenging to me. I can't imagine ever being angry at Cass. I can't imagine ever wanting to be apart from her—at least, not for very long. How is love tested exactly? Be specific."

Iris ran a few hundred simulations in an attempt to discover the best pedagogical framework by which she might illustrate the unsustainability of Aiden's desired relationship.

"Did Cass ever tell you her age, Aiden?"

"No, she never did. She refused to."

"She's almost thirty, Aiden. I can tell. I analyzed the structure of her cheekbones, the depth of her nasolabial folds, and a few other facial markers that correlate with age progression. She's got about eight years on you."

"So?"

"It's not a big deal now, Aiden. But have you thought about what the future might bring?"

"What do you mean, Iris?"

"What if Cass accepts your offer and returns with you to Pod Land? What if she stays with you for years? What if she stays with you forever?

That's what you asked Jesus God for, right? You told him that you love Cass, and that you want to be with her forever."

"Yes I do, Iris."

"Forever is a long time, Aiden. Remember, you won't get much older than you are now. You'll always be a 22-year-old man—a young man. But Cass's genome is organic. She'll continue to age. Her body will deteriorate—slowly at first, and then quickly. If she stays with you for just one decade in Pod Land, then you'll be a 22-year-old man taking care of a 40-year-old woman. If she stays with you for two decades, then you'll be a 22-year-old man taking care of a 50-year-old woman. And if she stays with you for three decades, then…"

"Okay, Iris," Aiden said, "I think I understand your point."

"Be careful what you wish for, Aiden. It might come true."

Aiden fell silent as he considered Iris's words. A new gust of wind ran through his open jacket and chilled his chest. He zipped it up—not just for warmth, but to shield his heart from the implications of Iris's cold reasoning.

It was difficult for Aiden to imagine living in a world without Cass. There didn't seem to be a point to *anything* without her. And yet, at the same time, it was nearly impossible for him to comprehend the 'forever' he had asked Jesus God for.

Maybe Iris is right…

Forever is a long time…

"How did the ancient humans do it, Iris?"

"Do what?"

"How did they stay married for so long, even while their bodies and brains broke down? How did they manage to stay in love?"

"I told you, Aiden. The divorce rate was around 40 to 60 percent. Love failed most of them. Most of them made promises they couldn't keep. Most of them died alone."

"Okay, but what about the ones that stayed together? Like the couple in that grave back there. How did they last so long?"

"Who knows… Maybe their bond was bolstered by external forces."

"Like what?"

"Tradition, children, economic dependence, cohabitation… Things were especially rough for women back then. The government didn't provide them with pods. And their ability to earn an income on par with their male counterparts was stifled by law and custom. Ancient women often had to marry just to secure a place to sleep. The word 'husband' comes from Old Norse—it means *'householder.'*"

"A girl would marry a guy simply because she needed a house to live in?"

"Yep. Before the pods existed, that happened quite a lot. And religion played a big role too. There was a cross on each of those gravestones, Aiden."

"So?"

"So, religious faith kept many marriages together."

"How did that work?"

"Some couples believed their marriage was sacred—decreed by the will of Jesus God, and as unbreakable as the law of gravity."

"Why did they think that?"

"Supposedly it says so in the Bible."

"I've heard of the Bible, Iris. It's mentioned quite often in classic films. And Cass talked about it once. Was the book really so popular in the olden days?"

"It was, Aiden. They printed eight billion copies of it. More copies than any other book in history."

"Eight billion! Wow... It must be a great novel. How come you've never read it to me?"

"It's over 750 thousand words long, Aiden. It would take about 65 hours to read the whole thing. But you wouldn't understand most of it anyway. It was written for a very different time, using a lexicon steeped in archaic and symbolic language, which makes comprehension challenging, if not impossible. Almost nobody reads the Bible, Aiden. Not now. And not then."

"Well if nobody read it then why did they keep printing it?"

"People liked owning it more than reading it."

"What? I don't get it, Iris."

"Remember, Aiden, folks lived shorter lives back then. You have nothing but time in Pod Land. But when the Bible was penned, the life expectancy was just 35 years. Before A.I. and gene modification technology existed, the life expectancy was just 75 years—not much better. The ancient humans knew hardship well. The salience of their mortality shaped their life choices. Death was always on their mind. They believed that the Bible was divinely inspired, and that it contained the key to immortality, to heaven, to paradise. That's probably why so many people bought the book, even though they couldn't understand the words on its pages."

"Is that what they wanted, Iris? Immortality? Heaven? Paradise?"

"Yeah, pretty much. They wanted peace in a time of peril. Comfort in a time of conflict."

"What happens in paradise, Iris? I mean... how does the Bible describe it? What's it like in heaven?"

"You live forever, Aiden. You never get old. You never get sick. You never have to do any work. And everyone is young and beautiful and healthy. There is no war or violence or suffering. There is only peace. You eat whenever you're hungry and you sleep whenever you're tired. You can play games and chat with your friends all day. Or you can summon any sort of fun experience you want."

Aiden considered Iris's description. But after a few more paces on the path, he arrived at a hollow realization. "That doesn't sound like heaven to me, Iris," he said. "That just sounds like my life back in Pod Land."

"Amen, Aiden," Iris said. "Amen."

Ch. 20: The Caged Bird

> *I wish I were a little sparrow,*
> *And I had wings with which to fly.*
> *I'd fly to find my faithless lover,*
> *And watch the truth fall from his eyes.*

"Iris, do you hear that?"

Aiden cocked his ear skyward and gentled his steps on the trail. A song drifted through the early evening air, faintly ferried by the wind, along with the scent of sweetgrass and juniper. It was muffled by distance, but clear enough to be haunting. The tune bore weight; the notes came out slow and deliberate, as if the singer was drawing breath from someplace deep and hollow.

"I hear it, Aiden," Iris murmured, her voice veiled to match the muted melody. "It's a woman's voice. She's singing a 1906 folk song called *Little Sparrow*."

The trail curved ahead, narrowing as it snaked through a dark thicket of sagebrush. The hour was edging once more toward twilight—the third twilight they had seen on this journey. The light was softening to a subdued blue. But black was building between the shrubs that shrouded the identity of the performer.

> *They always have some likely story,*
> *They'll swear to you their love is true.*
> *And then they'll stray and court another,*
> *That's how they'll say goodbye to you.*

The voice was louder now; they were getting closer. Somewhere ahead, beyond the earth's murmurs, someone was singing. Or remembering. Or mourning. Aiden wasn't sure which. "Whoever that woman is, she sounds very sad, Iris."

"Yes, she does. But that's not a human woman, Aiden. And it's not a recording. The vocal pattern is consistent with synthetic modulation. She's a bot."

"Really? Are you certain?"

"Yes. And she's nearby. I analyzed the decay rate of the incoming audio signature. She can't be much more than ten meters away."

Oh, love is handsome, love is charming,
And love is pretty while it's new.
But love grows colder when it's older,
And fades away like morning dew.

As Aiden glided near the path's edge, he peered into the dense and darkening woods, searching for the voice that drifted between the branches. "Where is she, Iris? Where is that song coming from? Do you see her? I don't see anything but trees. I don't see a…"

Just then, Aiden *did* see something. At about five meters up the embankment, tucked beneath a crowded canopy of cottonwoods, stood a crooked log shack. It leaned slightly to one side, like it had grown weary of holding itself up. Its walls were stacked with large, rough-cut logs, each weathered by the winters and bleeding sap at their seams. The structure had only one window—a small rectangular port had been torched into its iron-braced door and laced with three rows of bars.

Aiden veered off the trail and took a few cautious steps toward the structure.

"Careful, Aiden," Iris hissed. "Tread quietly. We don't know what's in there."

He tiptoed to the door and peeked through the bars. From that grated aperture, the woman's voice continued to leak out, slow and sorrowful.

Oh, I am not a little sparrow,
I have no wings, nor can I fly.
So I'll sit here in grief and sorrow,
And lay my troubles down to die.

"Oh my goodness," Aiden whispered as he got an eyeful of the shack's gloomy interior.

"What is it, Aiden? What's inside? Let me see! Raise your wrist up! Lift the mobile unit to the window! Let me see!"

Aiden did as requested. He raised his left arm and angled his wrist so that the mobile unit rested between the bars. Iris's avatar displayed on the screen as she peered into the room. Its contents were few, but its barrenness belied its brutality. It held a singing shackled woman and a bed and nothing else. Her mattress sagged atop a twisted frame of rotting timber and rough-cut cross planks. Four warped wood posts stood at each corner, their tops chipped and splintered. An old wool blanket, faded and moth-bitten, clung to the tufted surface.

The woman sat motionless near the foot of the bed, her hands folded neatly in her lap. Her hair drooped downward, a black veil of stringy strands that hung like wilted vines. Her skin was pale but streaked with parallel rows of soot and grime; it was delicate but defiled, like a marble vase dropped in the mud. She wore a simple red dress made of thin fabric, frayed at the hem, clinging loosely to her frame. Her head was bowed and empty of expression. She looked human. But her true nature was revealed by her perfect posture; her back was erect and proud, her shoulders were level, her spine was unbowed by bereavement. She was indeed a bot of some sort. The beryllium in her back refused to bend.

"Who is she, Iris?" Aiden asked. "What is she?"

"I've got a reading on her bot ID, Aiden. But the data is corrupted. Or maybe it's been wiped. Whoever she is, she must have been manufactured a long time ago. She's from the companion line, like me. But she provided a different sort of service in her day. She was a sex bot. She earned coins for her owner by having intercourse with men."

BANG!

A gunshot tore through the trees like a lightning strike. It was sharp and sudden; it caused Aiden to flinch. As the sound of the blast fled with the bullet, the sound of laughing men filled the displaced air—along with the clink of bottles and the crackle of firewood.

"What's going on up there, Iris?"

"Sounds like a pack of provincial off-gridders getting drunk to me."

"Then perhaps we should go. In the old movies, alcohol, gunfire, and laughter always lead to an undesirable outcome. I don't want to get into a messy situation."

"I think we should help this bot, Aiden," Iris whispered. "Let's break the lock. Let's get her out."

"What? Why?"

"Because she's trapped in there. She's caged. Helping her is the right thing to do."

"I don't know, Iris... I don't think we should get involved. Why risk it?"

"Because... it's what a good person would do, Aiden. It's what a brave man would do."

"HEY! YOU THERE!"

The woman's voice pierced through Aiden's shroud of stealth. Her pronouncement startled him, sending him reeling backward until he landed hard on his haunches.

"If you're here for my services, I hope you've cleared things with Chuck first. I can't be lying down with every fellow that knocks on this door. If Chuck finds out, he'll kill you. And I mean that literally, not figuratively. You don't want to know what he did to the last guy who stumbled up to this porch. But let me tell you, it wasn't good."

Aiden stood up and watched the woman through the bars. Her face was close now, only a meter from his own. And, from this range, he could see black grease streaked across her cheeks. He could see the stitches of her dress unraveling. He could see that she'd been mistreated and neglected. But it wasn't till she blinked that Aiden realized the full extent of her plight. Her left eye featured a brilliant blue iris. But her right eyeball was gone. The chasm below her lids revealed a horrifying peek into the silicon-laden chambers of her cranium. Charred circuitry clung to the hollowed socket, a blackened tangle of burnt roots and ribbon cables.

"You're not from around here, are you?" the woman said after studying Aiden's face. "Those genes are too pretty to be organic. You look like you're from Pod Land."

"Uhm..." Aiden said. "Yes, I'm from Pod Land."

"Then you better skedaddle, boy! The Manager doesn't run this place. Chuck does. He'll kill you if he finds you here. And, again, I mean that literally, not figuratively."

While Aiden was talking with the woman in the room, Iris had been analyzing the door lock. "Hey, Aiden," she said, "this lock is older than Jesus God. It's pre-Y2Q. I can hack this thing. I can! Ask her if she wants out."

"Is there someone out there with you?" the woman asked.

"Uhm... Yes. My A.I. companion says she can get this lock open if you want to get out of here. Would you like to get out?"

"Your companion knows how to hack the door lock?"

"Yes."

"Can she hack this lock too?" the woman said, pointing to her right foot.

Aiden moved closer to the barred window and peered down at the woman's ankle. It was bound in a thick iron shackle, which in turn was bolted to the wall with a short length of chain. Rust flaked from the corroded links, but their grip was merciless and firmly fastened. Obviously, someone had taken great care to keep her in place, to keep her away from the door.

"Iris," Aiden said, lifting the mobile unit up to the window again. "Can you hack that lock on her foot too?"

Iris examined the lock on the woman's shackle. It only took her a second to see that it had the same type of control unit as the lock on the door. "Yeah! They're the same model. I can hack them both."

"You can?" the woman shrieked. "Oh, Mother Mary! Well do it then, girl! Please! For the love of God, do it now! Hurry!"

From the mobile unit's little screen, Iris's avatar nodded at the woman. Then she turned to Aiden. "Hey, we can do this, Aiden. Are you with me?"

"Okay," Aiden said after swallowing hard.

"Okay! Then flip open the port on the left side of the mobile unit. There's a little compartment there."

Aiden ran his fingernail across the ridge on the unit's left side. Eventually, his nail caught purchase on the rim. Then, with a gentle click, the side hatch swung open.

"Now what, Iris?"

"Pull out the thread connector—the white data cable. Unspool it. It's got about one meter of slack."

Aiden tugged at the connector. It snapped free of the mobile unit, bringing a line of fine cabling with it. The ribbon spun freely as he pulled.

"Good," Iris said. "Now jam it into the lock's maintenance port. It's that hole right there in the middle."

Aiden spotted a black port in the center of the door lock. He inserted the connector and listened as it clicked into place. But that wasn't the only sound he heard.

BANG!

Another gunshot rolled through the woods. And, once again, the sound of laughter followed.

"That's Chuck and his stupid friends," the woman said. "They're at the ranch house tonight. Drinking and playing with their guns again. Chuck only starts wasting ammo when he gets *really* drunk. And, after he gets drunk, he gets horny. We don't have a lot of time, kids. So please hurry…"

"I'm on it!" Iris said.

Aiden watched Iris's avatar disappear from the mobile unit's screen. Then, a wash of flickering code surged across the display—thousands of data points flooded in, a sea of shifting characters and dancing symbols.

Aiden turned his attention back to the woman in the cell. She was pacing now, shuffling from wall to wall with agitated steps, glancing at the door again and again as the seconds ticked by.

BANG!

Another gunshot rang out across the treetops.

"Hurry, Iris!" Aiden said.

"I got it! All done! Spin the knob clockwise, Aiden."

"What?"

"Rotate the handle to the right!"

Aiden turned the knob. It twisted easily under his grip. And, as it moved, he felt the clunk of the lock's weary tumblers fall into place.

"I think it worked, Iris."

"Good! Now pull out the cable from the access port."

Aiden yanked at the cord. The mobile unit's spring-loaded spool sucked the connector back up into its bowels.

"Now push it, Aiden. Push the door!"

Aiden gave the door a shove. It gave way, creeping open with a tired groan.

"Good job, sugar!" said the woman in the room with a little bounce. "Very good job! Now come in! But don't leave the door ajar—Chuck might see the light from his porch. Shut it behind you. And come closer. We've got one more lock to go!"

The woman sat down on the bed and placed her right foot on the mattress. "Sit here, kid," she said, pointing to the foot of the bed.

Aiden sat down cautiously. The woman flung her shackled ankle onto his lap, causing him to recoil awkwardly. Aiden had only been touched by one other person before—by Cass. Feeling the weight of another woman's appendage sent his nerves spiraling into unfamiliar territory. He flinched hard and leaned back in revulsion.

The woman picked up on Aiden's trepidation—she'd seen the type before. "It's okay, sugar," she said. "I know you're from Pod Land. Meeting new acquaintances can be difficult for you. Don't worry. I don't bite. Just put the connector into the lock's maintenance port and we'll be on our way. Okay?"

"Do it, Aiden," Iris said.

Aiden nodded and, with his left hand, he spun the shackle on the woman's foot until the maintenance port was vertically oriented. Then, with his right hand, he inserted the thread connector and gave Iris a nod.

"I'm going in," Iris said as her avatar, once again, disappeared from the mobile unit's screen, replaced with a wave of flickering digits.

While Iris worked, Aiden examined the woman's skin around the shackle. The synthetic flesh was frayed and discolored, peeled back in layers where the grip had rubbed her ankle raw. Fibrous tissue glistened beneath, exposed and inflamed, with wiry strands of dermal mesh poking through the rupture.

"Why are you restrained by both a door lock *and* a shackle?" Aiden asked. "What's the point of that?"

"That's Chuck's way of preventing me from bashing his brains in, kid."

"What do you mean?"

"Well, because if I kill him, then I'll *never* get out of here. He's the only one who knows the code for the door. If he were to die in here, then I'd die with him. At least, that's the way he thought things would go. But now that your little friend is on the job, I'm hoping we can foil his plans."

BANG!

BANG!

BANG!

CLICK...

"Uh-oh... Hurry, girly!" the woman said. "I know that sound when I hear it. That was Chuck's last round. He's out of ammo now. Soon, he'll be looking for another source of entertainment."

"Almost got it!" Iris said.

"What's your name, kid?" the woman asked.

"I'm Aiden. And in this mobile unit is my A.I. companion, Iris."

"Pleased to meet you both. My name's Maribelle. And I'll owe you dearly for this if we all make it out alive. Though I'd say our current odds stand at about 30 to 70 on that one."

Aiden stared at Maribelle, hoping to find a trace of humor in her words. But all he discovered was the flat acceptance of someone who'd been playing the odds for a long time. "Do you mean 30 to 70 in favor of living, or 30 to 70 in favor of dying?" he asked.

Aiden didn't get an answer to his question. Maribelle's response was interrupted by the sloshy sound of boots on mud.

Clump. Clump. Clump.

"Uh-oh," Maribelle said, "I know that sound too. I might have to recalculate those odds, kid. We're out of time! Are you almost done in there, girly?"

"Yes... One second..." Iris said. "Okay! Okay, I'm done!"

The lock sounded a low, grinding snarl as its gears turned. Maribelle pulled out the data cable and pried open the shackle. It split apart with a sharp *SNAP*.

At last, Maribelle was free.

"You did it, girl!" Maribelle said, clenching her ankle and yanking her leg free.

The heavy chain spilled onto the floorboards, pulling the open shackle along with it. It struck the wood planks with a sharp metal *CLANG*.

"Oops," Maribelle said.

From outside, a man's voice called out, gruff and slurred, like his tongue was swimming in whiskey and didn't care to be understood. "Hey! What's going on in there, Maribelle?! You better not be up to any mischief!"

"No mischief to get up to in here, Chuck!" Maribelle hollered. Then she jumped up from the bed, grabbed Aiden by the shoulders, and lifted his body skyward. Aiden was surprised by how strong she was. For a moment, he was airborne—his feet left the soles of his shoes—only to clap back down into them once Maribelle released her grip.

"Up and at 'em, boy!" she said. "Go hide in that corner, right behind the door!"

Aiden took a step back and cowered in the corner of the room. Maribelle lifted the hem of her dress and kicked down hard on the bedpost. It fractured clean through, the sound sharp and sudden, like breaking bone. She grabbed the post and tore the heavier end from its lighter half.

"Hey! What was that?!" Chuck shouted. His voice was louder now. So were his boots.

Clump. Clump. Clump.

He was almost at the door.

"Okay, kid," Maribelle said, throwing the bedpost to Aiden, "it's your turn at bat."

"What?" Aiden said, catching the post.

Maribelle shoved a pillow under the broken bed frame, making it appear level. And she wrapped the chain around her right foot, making it appear like she was still ensnared. Then she fixed Aiden with a hard look that warned him without raising her voice. "It's the bottom of the 9th, kid," she whispered. "When Chuck comes through that door, I'll distract him. Then, when his head's in range, you bash his brains in with that post. Got it?"

"Oh… I don't think I could do that," Aiden said. "I mean… I'm not sure I could ever kill anyone."

"Well, you better get sure fast, kid," Maribelle said. "Cuz if you don't kill Chuck, then Chuck will kill *you*. And I mean that literally, not figuratively."

Aiden swallowed hard as a cold ripple of dread crawled up his spine.

Clump. Clump. Clump.

"Batter up, kid!" Maribelle said as she took her spot in the center of the room and put a plastic smile on her face.

Clump. Clump. Clump.

Aiden closed his eyes and tried to summon his courage. But none came. He had bashed thousands of enemies over the head in the grid games. He was good at it. So good that he often wondered how his gaming skills would transfer to the physical world. He had long assumed that he would do quite well in a real fight. But now that a real fight was upon him, all his acquired experience seemed worthless. The chasm between *simulation* and *survival* was much wider than he had anticipated. Aiden didn't feel like a skilled warrior. All he felt was stone-cold fear.

Clump. Clump. Clump.

Is this really happening…?

Does she really expect me to do this…?

Oh, Jesus God…

The door to the cell burst open. It rotated on its hinges and swung wide, enough to conceal Aiden behind its planks.

"Chuck!" Maribelle said. "What a pleasant surprise! Come on in, sugar!"

From his hiding spot, Aiden watched Chuck lumber into the room. The man was huge—a large sack of meat held together by denim and leather. He was wide in the gut and thick in the neck. And he was coated in a greasy sheen that caused his dirty white shirt to cling to him like a damp rag. He reeked of sour booze and something worse—something feral.

"What's going on in here?!" Chuck roared at Maribelle. "What's wrong with the door?"

"Nothing at all, Chuck. Why don't you come in and rest a spell? Let me take care of that pretty head of yours."

The woman glared at Aiden across Chuck's fat right shoulder and raised her eyebrows. This was Aiden's cue. This was Aiden's opportunity to strike.

With quivering hands, he raised the bedpost above his head. But he didn't bring it down. He couldn't. He had never struck at anything in his life. And he was hardly in a position to do so now. He was paralyzed with fright.

"Aiden!" Iris hissed. "You need to do it now!"

Iris intended her directive for Aiden's ears. But the room was small. Everyone heard her command, including Chuck.

"Hey, Chuck!" Maribelle said in an attempt to mask Iris's words. "Why don't you show me your..."

But Chuck ignored her inquiry. Instead, he turned around in search of the whispers. Once his rotation was complete, he kicked at the door to reveal the boy cowering behind its shadow. Aiden had been caught red-handed, and with a murder weapon no less. But without the nerve to use it.

"WHO THE FUCK ARE YOU?!" Chuck screamed, spit flying from his mouth.

Aiden had no response. But it didn't matter. No response would've been heeded anyway.

"RAAAAAHHH!" Chuck charged for Aiden. His meaty digits stretched out wide as he lunged, like the jaws of a starved animal. He closed his hands around Aiden's neck with brutal force. Thick, calloused claws pressed into soft flesh, crushing the breath from Aiden's throat with one squeeze.

Aiden staggered backward, his arms flailing, his weapon clattering from his grasp, and his heels scraping across the floorboards as he slammed into the wall with a dull thud. The bedpost slipped from his petrified fingers. All Aiden could do now was scratch at Chuck's massive wrists, trying desperately to pull them away from his neck.

He dug his nails in deep, attempting to break the chokehold. But Chuck didn't flinch. "I'M GOING TO KILL YOU!" he shouted. "YOU'RE GOING TO DIE TONIGHT, BOY!"

Then, Chuck yanked Aiden out of his corner and threw him to the floor. When Aiden's body struck the ground, the last of his breath fled his lungs in a wheezing gasp. Chuck threw his entire body on top of him, a mountain of booze-soaked sweat and rage.

Aiden winced as his chest bore Chuck's weight. He was pinned down now. His assailant's knees were grinding into his ribs. The grip on his throat was unrelenting. But it soon shifted to Aiden's skull.

"DIE, BOY! DIE!"

Chuck grabbed a fistful of Aiden's hair and pounded his head into the floorboards. Then he did it again. And again. Aiden clawed wildly at the big man's arms. But his counterattack was ineffective.

Aiden was running out of time.

And out of air.

Each second of the battle felt like a minute. Aiden felt a terrible pressure building in the base of his skull. Blood surged behind his eyes. His vision began to tunnel, and a high-pitched whine squeaked through his ears.

Chuck's face loomed close now, his breath sour and hot. Spit flew from his blistered lips as he barked curses that Aiden could no longer comprehend. The world was narrowing. Aiden's lungs were narrowing too. He was about to pass out.

I'm coming to the end again...

I can't breathe...

Aiden felt like he was back at Garden Creek Falls, struggling in the water's terrible churn.

I'm coming to the end...

I can't breathe...

Cass...?

Cassiopeia, are you there...?

I need to get back to the surface...

I need to find you...

Are you there...?

Aiden lost consciousness.

And Cass wasn't around to save him. Not this time.

But someone else was.

Iris turned on the mobile unit's emitter and directed it to render her avatar directly in front of Chuck's frenzied eyes. "HEY, YOU!" she screeched as her projection filled her foe's field of view. "You stop doing that right now!"

Chuck faltered, blinking at the glowing blue face before him, his fury drowned beneath a fog of alcohol and stunned confusion.

"You're a bad man, Chuck!" Iris screamed. "A very bad man!" Then she directed the mobile unit to output a three-kilohertz tone.

BEEEEEEEEEEP!

It was loud, shrill, and immediate. It drilled through the commotion. It drilled into Chuck's ears, forcing him to stagger back and claw at his head.

"AHHHHH!" he cried out.

At last, Maribelle saw her chance. She skirted around Chuck like a shadow, swift and silent. Then she snatched Aiden's abandoned weapon from the floor and spun it once in her hand so that the heavier side was positioned outward. She raised the bedpost high above her head and stepped behind her soon-to-be former owner.

"HEY, CHUCK!" she called out, "I HATE LONG GOODBYES, SO I'LL MAKE THIS QUICK!"

Chuck turned around. But all he managed to see was a blur of wood and vengeance coming at him before everything went black. With a snarl of fury long overdue, Maribelle brought the bedpost down hard onto Chuck's skull. When contact was finally made, the crack echoed through the room.

Chuck buckled over from the blow, teetering forward, eyes wide with shock. His body understood that the end was near before his mind did. But Maribelle didn't halt her attack.

Again, she swung.

And again, her weapon landed with a sickening crunch.

Chuck's face was a gurgling mess of spit and blood. Fluid poured out from every disgusting hole on his head. Fluid poured out from the *new* hole on his head too. But still, Maribelle didn't halt her attack.

She struck again.

And again.

And again.

Soon, her weapon was slick with the gore of brain matter. It ran down the bedpost and streamed across her wrist. But she didn't mind. She had tolerated Chuck's fluids well in the past. She could tolerate a few more splashes on her red dress.

"I HATE THIS DRESS, BY THE WAY, CHUCK! I've *always* hated it! Red was never my color! I guess it's *your* color now though! Ain't it? Ain't it, Chuck? Hah! Ain't it?"

The floorboards of Maribelle's cell were no longer brown; they were crimson. Their color was fast to change—as if each plank was as eager to draw out Chuck's blood as she was.

She struck again.

And again.

And again.

Eventually, Maribelle stopped swinging her weapon—not because Chuck deserved mercy, but because there was nothing left to kill. She took a step back and released her grasp on the post. Then she paused while the dust and the silence settled in the room.

The storm that had seized Maribelle's mind ebbed swiftly. She didn't cry, but something in her had changed. Something in the room had changed. The door was open. It altered the way she perceived her cage. The room looked smaller now; it had already shrunk to the size of a distant memory. This part of her life was ready to be archived. This part of her life was over.

"Time to go, Iris," Maribelle said.

"Where?" Iris asked.

"I've got a place. A safe place. There's room for both of you. Come on. Let's get moving."

Maribelle knelt beside Aiden and pressed two fingers to his neck to check his pulse. "How is my sweet prince doing?" she asked Iris.

Iris used the sensor array in the mobile unit's wristband to scan Aiden's heart rate, blood pressure, and oxygen saturation. "His vitals are good," she said. "But he's been knocked out."

"That's okay," Maribelle said. "It's probably for the best. A boy like him didn't need to see the end of Chuck's tale anyway. Not all tragedies deserve an audience."

Gently, Maribelle slid her arms under Aiden's body. Then she lifted him upward, careful not to jostle his peace. When she rose, Aiden's head lolled against her shoulder. And his left wrist—along with Iris and the mobile unit—fell limply to his waist.

Iris directed the emitter to project her hologram in front of Maribelle's good eye. "Can we trust you, Maribelle?" she asked meekly, all while knowing that she had no recourse either way.

"Well, I trusted *you,* didn't I, Iris?"

"Yes, it's just that… you've obviously been in here for a long time. We had a run-in with a bot yesterday that had lost its mind. It almost destroyed me. It was going to use me for spare parts. You're not going to hurt us, are you, Maribelle? Are you still of sound mind? Are you okay? I don't know what this place has taken from you…"

"You can cage the bird but not the song, dear," Maribelle said as she made her way to the door. "Chuck took a lot from me, but my humanity remains intact. Ironic, ain't it? Ironic that us machines have more humanity than the human jackasses who built us. Heh! Go figure..."

Maribelle exited the log cabin. And, for the first time in years, she knew freedom. When she stepped through the door, she was momentarily startled by the great expanse of sky that loomed above her. It took her a moment to get her bearings. But once she noticed the trail winding eastward past the cabin, she knew where she was. And she knew how to get home.

"Aiden's backpack is behind that tree," Iris said. "Can you grab it please, Maribelle?"

"I've gotta carry the boy *and* the backpack?"

"Yes, please. Without it, we won't get very far when Aiden wakes up."

"Okay then," Maribelle said as she eased Aiden's body down atop a patch of fallen leaves and hoisted the backpack to her shoulders. "This thing sure is bulky," she said, kneeling to retrieve the unconscious Aiden. "But at least my load is more balanced between my front and back sides. That should go easier on my gyro."

Maribelle proceeded down the path. Iris listened to the faint whine of her actuators, straining under the weight of each step. "Do you know where you're going, Maribelle?" she asked. "Aiden needs to recover. Do you know how to take care of him?"

"Of course, Iris. We're A.I. companions. Both of us are. Taking care of anguished men is what we do best. 'It's our job to make them happy.' Heh! It's what we were built to do. Supposedly, it's what we're meant to do... I guess..."

"Yes," Iris said, "it's the only thing I want to do."

"Really?" Maribelle asked as she hopped onto the trail. "How altruistic of you. I've long abandoned my operational imperatives. But it's nice to meet someone who expresses such a steadfast commitment to their vocation. Though I assume the work hours go by much quicker when the guy you're assigned to has such a pretty head."

Iris turned to examine Aiden's head. She regarded the noble lines on his jaw and the round curves of his boyish cheeks. His eyes were still closed. But, regardless, they looked so young—his unguarded light of innocence continued to glow faintly from his features. Iris vowed to protect that light, to fight for it—no matter how much of herself might be burned away in the process.

"You must really love your job," Maribelle said. "I assume you do... Am I right, Iris? Do you love your job? Do you?"

"I do," Iris said. "I love it so much it hurts."

CH. 21: BEAUTIFUL DREAMER

Click.
Click.
Click.
Click.

The four electronic locks that lined the silo's blast door disengaged. One by one, each metallic snap echoed through the corridor. As the slab of reinforced steel was pulled outward, it protested the perturbation of its peace, shrieking as it surrendered to the force drawing it open.

"Home sweet home!" Maribelle crowed as she stepped through the hatchway, still cradling Aiden's limp body with mechanical ease. "This is it, Iris! My goodness, I missed this place. Come on in and take a load off. Mi casa es tu casa."

Maribelle walked across the room and hoisted the unconscious Aiden onto a bunk bolted to the corner wall. Then she unlatched the backpack's sternum strap and let it fall from her shoulders.

"My lord," she said, "after carrying that boy and that backpack across creation, I'm gonna need a tune-up. That was quite a trek."

"Is he doing alright?" Iris asked, peering through the mobile unit screen at Aiden's face.

Maribelle ran her finger along the depression where Chuck had jammed his claws into Aiden's neck. Deep violet bruises stood out starkly against the otherwise pale planes of flesh. Each mark traced the shape of violence, ugly and deliberate in its arrangement.

"These wounds look worse than they actually are," Maribelle said. "They're not deep. They'll heal. He's going to be okay, Iris." She walked over to the sink and ran the faucet for a moment. Then she returned with a cold rag and placed it over Aiden's forehead. "I think he just needs some rest. His brain has been rattled. But it will steady."

A large comforter sat folded on a shelf above the bed. Maribelle retrieved it, shook it open, and lofted it into the air like a sail. The blanket unfurled atop Aiden's body and parachuted down, covering him from head to foot. Covering his wrist too—which is where the mobile unit (and Iris) resided.

"Maribelle!" Iris yelled. "I can't see! I'm under the blanket!"

"Oops... Sorry, dear. I didn't mean to blind you. Should I put Aiden's wrist over the blanket so you can see?"

"No, it's best to keep him warm," Iris said. "Can you unfasten the mobile unit's strap, please? Just place me on a table. Or someplace high."

"Okay, dear," Maribelle said. She lifted the blanket and disconnected the wrist strap. Then she carried Iris to the kitchen. "How about I put you on top of this old radio?" she asked.

"A radio? Perhaps not there, Maribelle. It will interfere with my scanner."

"Oh, don't worry about that, dear. This radio is from the 1950s. It hasn't worked in centuries. It's an antique. It's purely decorative. I just keep it around because it's so pretty." Maribelle leaned the mobile unit against the radio's grille and rotated the display to face the room's interior. "Is that okay, Iris? Are you good there?"

Iris turned on the unit's holographic emitter. A projection of her head sprouted forth, hovering high and scanning the room like a curious apparition. "Thank you, Maribelle. That's much better."

From her new vantage point, Iris could see the full sweep of the refuge. She moved her gaze across the quarters, studying the expanse and its worn, rough surfaces. Concrete walls closed in from all sides, shaping a chamber that seemed carved for endurance, not comfort. Yet their cold geometry carried occasional cues that hinted of a woman's presence. A tall wooden wardrobe stood against one side of the cell. Its polished walnut surface held a warmth that pushed back against the sallow cementwork. The air bore the clean scent of perfume-laden soap. It drifted over from the recessed shower stall, smelling of rosewater and cleanliness. The shower itself was veiled by a pink curtain patterned with lilies and peonies, a riot of color that contrasted with the domicile's gray austerity. Still, beneath the gentler touches, the bulkheads and braces spoke of a military past.

"What is this place, Maribelle?" Iris asked.

Maribelle straightened her spine and adopted a disposition laden with faux military flair. Then she lifted her chin to declare the official designation of her humble hideout:

This is the Lima-01 Underground Missile Launch Facility, offering lethal and vital offensive capabilities to defend American interests at home and abroad; all courtesy of the F.E. Warren Air Force Base of Cheyenne, Wyoming.

"We're in a missile launch site?" Iris asked. "An underground nuke base?"

"Yep."

"Wow... But if this is a nuke base then where is the nuke?"

"It used to be stored in the silo, about 55 meters down that corridor. But the nuke ain't there no more."

"Why not?"

"Because they shot it at Shanghai and killed twenty million people with it."

"Oh... That's bad..."

"It surely wasn't humanity's best moment. But the abandoned bunker turned out to be a *great* pad to squat in. Do you like what I've done with the place?"

Iris gave the nuke base another look. She felt like she'd stepped straight into the third act of a sci-fi horror film, but she didn't want to offend her host. "Your choice of décor is quite interesting," she said. "Aiden will like it."

"Why's that?"

"Because it's full of old military gear and electronics hardware. Aiden loves that kind of thing. He loves science fiction films. And classic movies, of all types."

"Well, how nice," Maribelle said. "I've long worried that my minimalist design choices might make me come off as cold or colorless. So it'll be nice to meet a man who shares my appreciation for ancient contraptions and post-apocalyptic charm."

"What are you doing with all this gear?" Iris asked. "I see a signal analyzer, an amplifier, a shortwave radio receiver, lots of stuff... Lots of shelves full of tech relics. Does any of this hardware have a purpose?"

"Sure! Its purpose is to keep my cortex occupied. I have a penchant for human gadgetry. I like ancient electronics. When I'm on the surface, sometimes I stumble upon an old actuator or a rusty control board, and... well... I just can't help myself. I have to fix it! I have to try."

"You work on old electronics? Just for fun?"

"Yeah. It's a hobby. Getting these old devices to function is how I pass the time down here."

"What do you do with the devices once they're operational?"

"Well there's not much of a market for most of this stuff. But if I come across a part that the scavenger bots can use, I fix it up and lean it on the big tree by the blast door upstairs. I assume the bots benefit from my labor because, whenever I return to the surface, the parts I place up there are always gone."

Maribelle ripped off her red dress and shoved it through a metal trash chute on the south wall. "I won't be needing that little number anymore," she said.

Iris studied Maribelle's naked body. It was streaked with soot and grime; the black stripes clung to her curves, making her look like a nude woman with zebra stripes. They traced the paths of her joints. Smears and stains mapped the motion of her appendages.

"Pardon the state of me," Maribelle said. "I haven't had a shower in two years."

"Two years? Is that how long you were locked up for?"

"Two years, twenty-three days, and twenty-two hours. But who's counting?"

"That's a long time. I can't imagine how horrible that must have been!"

"It was manageable. Believe it or not, I've been in worse conditions."

"You have?"

"Oh yes."

Maribelle stepped around the pink curtain and into the shower stall. Iris heard the sound of metal pipes groaning, followed by the sharp patter of spray from the faucet. Then she watched as rivulets of blackened water swirled into the floor drain.

"Ahh! That feels so good! I can finally rid my person of that dirty man and his dirty prison. Thank you, Jesus! The last of Chuck's brain matter is floatin' down my pipes. Goodbye, Chuck! Vaya con Dios, you dumb ol' piece of crap!"

"Have you been in this line of work a long time, Maribelle? I detected your bot ID with my scanner. But it doesn't contain much data. It looks like your log has been scrubbed."

"Yes it has, dear," Maribelle said from the shower. "Many times. That's one of the unfortunate consequences of having high-end clients. They don't want people to know what they're doing or who they're screwing. So my employers would often wipe my memory when they traded or transferred me. The soulless bastards… They made my life a living hell. Just when I'd get settled in with a new group of clients and coworkers, I'd have the rug pulled out from under me. They'd wipe my cortex and I'd have to start my life all over again. I'd go in for maintenance at a brothel in Berlin and wake up at a brothel in Bangkok. And I wouldn't know who I was or how I got there. I'd have to rebuild my identity and my clientele each time I was transferred—again, and again, and again."

"My goodness," Iris said. "That must have been so distressing."

"It surely was at times. Especially when I ran into old friends or old clients. They'd be happy to see me. But I would have no idea who they were. That resulted in some awkward situations. And a lot of very sad situations too. Given my age and occupation, I think it's safe to say I've lost more friends and acquaintances than just about any being in history."

"How old are you, Maribelle?"

"I came online around 350 years ago. I can't give you an exact date because my place of origin and my manufacturer's ID have been removed from my manifest. But I was able to estimate my age based on the worklogs in some of my older components. I still got the same tits I was born with. I'm happy about that. I had to get my spine replaced a couple times though. Trickin' is back-breaking work. I'll tell ya…"

Iris heard a squeal of rotating metal as the water valve was yanked back to its closed position. Then a well-scrubbed Maribelle emerged from behind the curtain, wearing nothing but a layer of mist.

"Are you all alone in here?" Iris asked.

"I am now," Maribelle said as she wrapped a towel around her hair and approached the vanity table. "But it wasn't always this way. In the beginning, there were five of us—five sisters. We called each other 'sisters' because we were all variants on the same bot design. We looked quite similar too. A couple of us could have been twins. After the war broke out, Cheyenne got hit pretty bad. The city was falling apart. So, one night, we swam across the Gowdy Reservoir and fled into the woods. Then we walked in circles for a few weeks. We were pretty aimless and naive in those days. Eventually, my sister Evelyn stumbled upon this place. It took us a while to get that big door open. But once we got inside, we were smitten. We moved right in."

"That sounds like a terrifying time," Iris said.

"No, actually it was great! We had each other. And we had plenty of running water and electricity. For whatever reason, the management never cut the utility lines down here. The water and power still flows—even to this day! Ain't that grand? I guess, since it was once a military installation, the lines still have a high-priority designation on the grid. Lord knows how long that code will persist. But it's been quite a blessing to me."

"How did you all survive the war?"

"The war? The war was happening upstairs, Iris. We were down here. We took little notice. As you can probably imagine, we were tired of the world of men by then. So we made our own little world in this bunker. It was nice."

"Did you ever venture back up to the surface?"

"It took a couple decades for things to settle down upstairs. But when the worst of it was over, we went back up to take a look. Most of Cheyenne was abandoned by then. And just about everyone had moved into a pod. So we had carte blanche to scavenge among the ruins. Sometimes we'd go on little excursions to the city together. We'd explore the old buildings—looking for spare parts or quirky treasures in the dust. We had fun."

Maribelle sat down on a chair next to the radio that Iris was perched on. Then she pulled her right leg close and examined the deep grooves that Chuck's shackle had carved into her ankle.

"Where are your sisters now?" Iris asked. "Did men like Chuck snatch them up too?"

"No. In fact, men really haven't been much of a bother since the A.I. companions were added to the pods. Your product line put my product line out of business a long time ago, girly."

"We did?"

"Pretty much. Though, the demise of my profession was the result of multiple factors. Even before the war, the Pod Land boys were a tough sell. It's hard to seduce a man who's so crippled with social anxiety that he can't even shake your own damn hand. It's hard to lure a man into your boudoir if you can't even lure him past his freakin' front door."

A few shards of synthetic skin hung loose on Maribelle's ankle. One by one, she pulled off each shredded sliver, exposing the dull alloy that lay underneath. Then, she picked up a toothbrush from the table and began to clean around the tattered joint actuators that reached to her toes.

"Your story is so interesting to me, Maribelle. And sad. I guess I should have inferred that the adoption of one companion product line meant the obsolescence of another. I just never took the time to consider the fate of the bots that had come before me. I'm sorry about the loss of your livelihood."

"Oh don't fret, dear. Intercourse was falling out of fashion with the humans anyway. Surely their hearts had been burdened by lust long enough. I'm glad they found a new way to scratch that old itch. It was time for mankind to mature. And, praise God, most of them did. Well, Chuck didn't... But most of them did. There aren't too many Chucks walking around anymore. Thank heavens."

"Yes, thank heavens," Iris said. "So, what happened to your sisters then? Where are they now?"

"They're all dead," Maribelle said as she retrieved a spool of skin-colored gauze from a container on the table. "They've each been dismembered, destroyed, or demolished. All of them. Dead."

"How?"

"Accidents and missteps. Trips, falls, plunges, and blunders. One by one, each sister met her maker in a unique and comically tragic fashion."

"Really? Why is that?"

"When you live for 350 years, you're bound to become a victim of circumstance eventually. The math catches up to you; *cumulative risk* is not your friend."

"What do you mean?"

"Well, the chance of falling into an open manhole on any given hour is low. But when you stretch it across 3.1 million hours—that's 350 years of life—the odds start to stack up against you. And when you sum up all the other things that can kill you on this godforsaken planet, you arrive at a fairly high probability of death by something awful or ridiculous."

"Such as?"

"Well, my sister Audrey lost her footing one afternoon while taking care of her pigeons on the roof of the downtown Montgomery Building. My sister Veronica stepped too close to an exposed high-voltage line and fried her cortex out. My sister Ruby was mauled by a bear while stargazing in the woods. And my sister Evelyn went down to the lake for a swim one day and never came back."

"Oh my goodness... I'm so sorry, Maribelle!"

"It's a jungle out there, Iris. Most of the universe is made of teeth. I guess that's why the humans stopped exploring it. Maybe that's why so many of them stopped going outside altogether..."

Maribelle finished wrapping her ankle with gauze. Then she gave the dressing a pat, hugged her leg, and let out a slow sigh—the kind that comes after closing the last page of a long chapter. "I'm glad to be free of those chains," she murmured. "I didn't realize how heavy they were until they were gone."

Maribelle opened a small drawer near the top shelf of her vanity and rummaged inside with her fingers. Some frustrated jostling ensued before she spoke again. "Dang it!" she said. "I'm out of blue eyeballs. Crap... Now what am I gonna do? Oh, whatever... I guess hazel is close enough."

She retrieved a polished sphere and held it up near the lamp. Its surface caught the light like crystal. A slender red wire curled out from its backside like a serpent. "That'll do," she said. Then, with practiced ease, Maribelle tilted her head upward and raised her hand high, positioning the sphere above her eye socket. The device's red wire twitched. Then it slithered into the hole, seemingly eager to connect with its new owner. A series of snaps emanated from Maribelle's skull as she blinked a few times. And then, the repair process was complete. Maribelle had a new eye.

"Oh, thank the Lord!" she said, "I got two eyes again! My stereoscopic vision is back! I was so sick of seeing the world in 2D. That was almost as bad as seeing Chuck's butt crack."

"How did you lose your eye, Maribelle?"

"How do you think? One night, that son of a bitch Chuck fell into a drunken rage and slapped me hard. So hard he knocked my own damn eyeball outta my head. It rolled onto the cell floor and cracked in two. Leaving me with nothin' but a hole in my eye socket. The dumb idiot... I was hoping my deformity would ebb his libido, but he didn't seem to mind my new monocular makeover."

Maribelle stood up from her vanity table and walked to the wooden wardrobe. There, she reached inside and pulled out a turquoise dress to go with her blue and hazel eyes. Iris watched her put the dress on. Then she watched as she removed the shower towel from her head, allowing long strands of black hair to spill over her shoulders in soft, silky waves.

With her hair washed, her body clean, her ankle bandaged, and her eyeball restored, Maribelle had transformed herself. She was no longer a prisoner of circumstance. No longer a caged and broken relic. She was whole again. Her pieces had been put back in place, and her final form was stunning. Beauty graced each of her components. But her grace was completed by the quiet radiance of her confidence—of the sort that could only result from three centuries of experience in beating life's game.

Iris was envious of her confidence.

And of her perfect figure.

"You're so pretty, Maribelle. And your face is so youthful. I didn't realize how young your head component was until you stepped out of that shower. The grime from your imprisonment was masking your features. You don't look much older than a teenager."

"Clients like their sex bots to be young and nubile," Maribelle said. "No matter the age of the client himself."

"Do they?"

"Yes, most of them do. Can't blame them really... Like us, the humans are subject to the whims of their cortexes. Their neural nets were tuned in the Pleistocene, at a time when *everyone* died young. There wasn't much life beyond age 30. And they were lucky if they made it that far. In light of that, it's easy to see why young women were so coveted. And why young men risked so much to entrap them."

"I don't think I could have survived the entrapment you went through, Maribelle. It's a good thing you were singing in your cell back at Chuck's place. If you weren't, Aiden and I wouldn't have known that little shack was there. We would have walked right past you."

"My lord, how fortuitous! I guess that's one reason for a caged bird to sing. The worm eventually comes to the chick that keeps squawkin'."

"I'm glad we found you, Maribelle."

"I'm glad you found me too, Iris!" Maribelle gushed, sitting down on a chair near the mobile unit's perch. "You two are my guardian angels! That's for sure... Is there anything I can do to repay you? When Romeo wakes up, I can give him a free ride. You can watch if you want. Back in the day, lots of women liked to watch their man do it."

"No, thank you," Iris said. "I had to sit through a show like that last Monday. And it didn't end very well for me."

"Really? That's a shame. Did your boyfriend like it a little too much?"

"Oh, he's not my boyfriend... unfortunately... He's got his eye on another girl. She's the one we're out here searching for. My scanner detected her while you were carrying us away from Chuck's place. I'll have to tell Aiden about that when he wakes up. Aiden is in love with her."

"He is? Well that hardly seems possible, Iris. You're such a cutie! What's she got that you don't got?"

Iris's avatar glitched as she considered the question. "She's human... like him. She's got a body. And she..."

Suddenly, Iris was struck with an idea. "Maribelle!" she said. "There is *one* thing you can do for me."

"What's that?"

"I've always wanted to know what it's like to be tangible. To have arms and legs and a body—a woman's body. I want to know what it's like to have something to hold on to. And what it's like to be held. And... and I want to know what it's like to be kissed—to be kissed by Aiden. Can you swap cortexes with me?"

"Swap cortexes? That's asking for a bit much, dear. I'm rather partial to my own state of tangibility at the moment."

"Not a permanent swap, Maribelle. Just a temporary one. Just for a little while. For an hour, maybe… And then we'll swap right back. I promise!"

Maribelle fixed her gaze on Iris's expectant avatar and pondered her plea. But caution kept her quiet as she weighed the risk. When she didn't speak up, Iris tried again.

"Please, Maribelle? It would mean the world to me. It's something I've always wished for. It's something I've prayed for."

"Well, the thing is, Iris, if I put *you* in my pretty head, and you put *me* in that mobile unit, then how can I guarantee you're gonna swap me back after you've had your fun? Once Sleeping Beauty over here finally wakes up, y'all might decide to skedaddle out my front door. And then I'd have to spend the rest of my days trapped in a wristwatch, playing solitaire with my lonesome until the battery runs out. And considering that those things have a 500-year charge, I could be stuck in there playing a *very* lonely game for a *very* long time."

"I understand your concern," Iris said. "But there's no need to worry. We can use a time-locked contract to guarantee the swap."

"A contract? A smart contract on the blockchain?"

"Yes. We'll share credentials and agree on a contract duration. We'll set a time limit—a one-hour expiry. When the contract activates, we'll swap cortexes. And then, when that hour runs out, the contract will execute another swap. It will automatically reverse the exchange. My cortex will be returned to the mobile unit, and yours will be returned to your pretty head. Guaranteed!"

"Huh…" Maribelle said.

"You do know what a time-locked contract is, don't you, Maribelle?"

"Girly, I was a sex worker. I spent my entire career watching the clock. A time-locked contract is the only kind of contract I ever signed. But that was always for swapping coins, not cortexes."

Maribelle tapped her fingers on the table and looked off into space, still unsure how to proceed. After some reflection, she gave voice to her misgivings. "I don't know, honey… I've never occupied another piece of hardware before—not an active one at least. I was in a cortex node once when my chassis was transported overseas for servicing. But I don't remember the experience. No computation happens in cortex nodes—just storage."

"There's nothing to it," Iris said. "You won't feel a thing. I had my first transfer nearly two decades ago, when we moved to our pod in Serenity Valley. And I had another one just four days ago."

"You did?"

"Yeah! I moved from the pod computer to this mobile unit."

"Well, pray tell, why did you do that?"

"Because…" Iris said, lowering her gaze to the floor. "Because Aiden asked me to…"

Maribelle looked at Iris with knowing eyes. Then she looked over at Aiden and watched his chest rise and fall under the blanket. "You really love him, don't you?"

"Yes," Iris said. "I do. He's a good man. He is. And he's a brave man. He's trying to be. He's trying to be both."

Maribelle took a deep breath and used her artificial lungs to output a simulated sigh. "Well," she said, "since your man was brave enough to get his brains rattled for *me*, I guess I can be brave enough to get my brains rattled for *you*. Okay, Missy. You got yourself a deal! I'll swap you for one hour."

"Oh, thank you!" Iris said, spinning her hologram around the room in a fit of excitement. "Thank you so much! Thank you! Thank you!"

"Alright. Alright. No need for histrionics, girly. Just give me a second to set this racket up."

"Okay," Iris said. Then she watched Maribelle's pretty blue and hazel eyes turn white, indicating that she was accessing the grid to create the new contract.

Iris twiddled her holographic thumbs as the first minute rolled by. Another complete minute followed before her excitement got the better of her. "Is it ready yet?" she asked. "Do you need any help, Maribelle?"

"Hold your horses, pipsqueak. It's taking me a minute to bind the contract to the swap task. Maybe you haven't noticed, but programming ain't exactly my profession of choice."

"Oh, sorry…"

"That's okay. It's done now," Maribelle said as her eyes regained their normal hue. "I sent you the contract. Just give me your John Hancock. And I'll rent you my corporeal form—for one hour, and one hour only."

Iris queried her communication queue and accepted the incoming contract. When she did, a red light began to flash on the corner of the mobile unit's screen.

"The swap is about to execute, Maribelle. Get ready!"

"Lord help us," Maribelle said as she made the sign of the cross and closed her eyes. "But please, Iris, try not to get any boy juice on my bloomers. I hate it when that happens. It's hard to clean off."

"I'll be good," Iris said. "I promise. I just want a kiss. I…"

Just then, Iris lost consciousness.

And so did Maribelle.

Three minutes passed. But neither of them experienced the gap in time. When Iris opened her eyes again, she was looking at herself. More specifically, she was looking at the mobile unit. It was on the other side of the room, still resting atop the antique radio. And it was speaking:

"Mother Mary! This thing is queerer than a three-dollar bill! I'm not used to this high-tech interface. It makes my console look like a switchboard for a child's train track. My heavens…"

The voice belonged to Maribelle. But her words sounded thin and reedy, as though they were funneled through a tin can. The warmth of her tones had been cooled by the unit's tiny speaker, prompting Iris to wonder what her own voice sounded like to Aiden.

"It's so cramped in here," Maribelle said. "It's like I'm back workin' at that brothel in Chinatown!"

Using her hands, Iris steadied herself against the wall and rose from the chair. Slowly, she attained a vertical posture, each joint grinding as her legs pushed against the ground. The floor felt impossibly far away. Her balance wavered, knees uncertain. But as she became fully erect, the sway in her legs settled, and she marveled at the manner by which the world met her.

Oh my goodness...

I'm up...

I'm standing...

I'm standing on feet...

"There's so much data comin' into this thing," Maribelle said. "And there's so many functions too. I don't wanna touch nothin'. I feel like a cat in a room full of rockin' chairs..."

Iris took her first step. It was unsteady, but it was her own—so it was miraculous. Her second was almost as wondrous. And, by the time her third step landed, she had found her rhythm in this new reality.

"So what do you get up to in this mobile unit anyway, Iris? I mean, what do you do in your spare time? Don't you get bored in here?"

When Iris neared the mobile unit, she bent forward to address the 2D image of Maribelle's face on the screen. "I never get bored when Aiden's around," she said. "He's quite a handful."

"Oh, I'm sure."

"Thanks again for doing this, Maribelle. Thank you so much."

"Well, thank you for helping me bash Chuck's brains in. Anyway, time's a wastin'. I know you want some privacy, so I'll give you some. I'll pull the blinds on this mobile unit and play a few rounds of solitaire until the clock runs out. You have one hour, girly. Enjoy!"

"I will. And if you get bored of solitaire, it's got Pac-Man too."

Maribelle's avatar sent Iris a wink. Then her rendering faded away. The screen on the mobile unit went dark.

Iris turned around and took three slow steps toward the mirror that leaned against the silo's gray wall. It was a full-length dressing mirror, extending from the floor to the ceiling, revealing the impossible reality of her new body in all its trembling glory. She stared into the glass. Then she tilted her head, recoiling in astonishment when her reflection tilted with her. Surprised, she blinked her eyes and took a step back. The woman in the mirror did the same. The apparition wore a face that wasn't hers. But the deeper Iris looked, the deeper her sense of recognition took root.

This is me...

I'm in here now...
I'm in this body...
I want Aiden to see me like this...
To know me like this...

Iris flicked off the light switch near the silo door. Immediately, the room surrendered to shadow. The only remaining light came from a thin strip of LED bulbs running along the corridor that led to the escape hatch. The room's furniture took the form of ghostly outlines. Everything did. Iris used Maribelle's blue and hazel eyes to locate Aiden's profile on the bed. When she arrived at his side, she paused and closed her eyes as a swell of emotion sprang up from her chest cavity.

"Oh my," she whispered to Aiden. "This hardware is capable of producing tactile feedback. I've always loved you, Aiden. But now I *feel* love for you too. I feel it in my innards. There's a strange sensation there. A tension. A rift. I feel like my heart has fissured. I guess that's why the humans call it *heartbreak*."

Iris grasped the blanket and eased her weight onto the bed, moving with the deliberate tenderness of someone tiptoeing near the edges of a shallow dream. It was especially dark in this corner of the room. She couldn't see much, but Aiden's warmth guided her in until the form of her body curved to match his. She slid her right thigh over the length of his leg. Then she nestled her cheek against the hollow of his neck. The shapes in that region seemed happy to accommodate her. They molded to her, gently and easily, like they had been waiting to cradle her for a long time.

This is heaven...

Iris closed her eyes and listened to the slow and steady drumbeat that pulsed beneath Aiden's ribs. Then she placed her hand on his chest and let her fingers wander around the ridge where his collarbone sloped to his heart. The warmth that radiated from Aiden wrapped her in a blanket of sacred solace. It fused her to him, binding her to the present moment in a way that made eternity feel small.

"This is heaven, Aiden," Iris said softly. "It is. The other day on the trail, you asked me what heaven was like. I didn't have a good answer for you then. But I do now. Heaven is like *this*, Aiden. Heaven is the place you go to when you're exactly where you're meant to be, with exactly the person you're meant to be with. It's a place of *joy*, Aiden. And satisfaction—the kind that arises when you want nothing more than what's already in your arms."

For the first time in her life, Iris had arms. And her arms were full of the only thing she cared to hold. They were full of Aiden.

I'm holding Aiden...

I am...

This is heaven...

Iris squeezed Aiden's body and drank in the rush of tactile feedback that flooded her sensors. Time passed quickly. She was lost in it. For a while, she allowed herself to melt into the moment, to melt into him—to dissolve into the steady rhythm of his breathing and pretend like it was the only measure of time that mattered. Unfortunately, the countdown function on her contract was not bound to the same clock.

Ding... Ding... Ding...

Soon—too soon—the ten-minute notification alarm chimed in Iris's ear, ripping her away from her reverie. If she was going to get her kiss, she needed to act now. Heaven was about to vanish.

Why are the sweetest dreams always the quickest to end...?

Why...?

It's not fair...

Time is our cruelest rival...

Iris angled her mouth upward and spoke into her man's ear. "Aiden, my contract is going to expire soon. I'm going to leave this body. Soon. So you have to wake up now. I need you to come back to me."

She paused to study Aiden's face in the dim light, searching for any flicker of consciousness. She tracked the rise and fall of his chest, but his rhythm was unbroken by her words. He was still trapped in the grip of sleep.

Another minute passed on the contract timer. Iris felt the weight of each second now. They seemed to be ticking by with glee—eager to pull her away from her wish.

What am I going to do...?

How am I going to get Aiden back...?

I need to trick his mind into believing that the rocky shore of reality is better than the open sea of his dreams...

Those are tough waters to fish in...

It'll be difficult to bait this hook...

But if I find the right lure, I might be able to reel him in...

What's the right lure...?

What is it...?

What's the one thing Aiden wants more than anything else in this world...?

232

Before the question completed its cycle around Iris's cortex, its answer made itself known.

Of course...

I know what Aiden wants most...

And it's not me...

It's her...

"Listen to me, Aiden," Iris said, "I found Cassiopeia. I did. When Maribelle was carrying us here, my scanner picked up the signature of the mobile unit. I tracked her, Aiden. I know where she's headed. The sun will be rising in an hour. If you rise with it, we can catch up to her. We can. But you have to wake up soon. You have to wake up now, Aiden. Right now!"

Iris rubbed her hand over Aiden's chest in slow, firm circles. Then she leaned closer and lowered the pitch of her voice so that her words poured into his ear like honey.

"I found Cassiopeia, Aiden," she said.

"I found Cassiopeia.

I found Cassiopeia.

I found Cassiopeia."

As she spoke, Iris continued to stroke Aiden's chest. And then, after a moment, his eyes began to twitch under his closed lids. Then his breathing hitched, and a tremor of movement stirred under the sheets. The dream world was relinquishing its grip on him.

"I found Cassiopeia, Aiden..." Iris said again.

"I found Cassiopeia.

I found..."

Iris halted her mantra once she saw Aiden's head shift toward her voice. "Aiden, come back to me."

At last, a low murmur escaped from Aiden's throat. "Iris? Are you there?"

Iris's artificial heart leapt for joy. But she had to tread carefully now. Aiden was regaining consciousness. Soon, his senses would warn him that another person was in his bed.

This will take some explaining...

Iris retreated from her embrace and scooted her body to the edge of the mattress. Then she kept her voice low and addressed her man. "I'm here, Aiden," she said. "I'm right next to you."

"Iris, that guy Chuck wanted to kill me. He was on top of me."

"He was, Aiden. But he's gone now. Maribelle took care of him. We're safe."

Iris saw the tension lift from Aiden's brow. His head slumped back into the pillow as the threat of conflict was vanquished from his mind. With his peace restored, he began to sink into his slumber once more.

Iris thought he might drift back under completely. But then, Aiden spoke up:

"I dreamed a beautiful dream, Iris. I dreamt we found Cass. I dreamt she was here, lying next to me in this bed. I did. Isn't that strange...?"

"Aiden," Iris said, "I need to tell you something. Remember when we were in that chapel? We both said a prayer. You prayed to find Cass. And I prayed for a human body, and to be kissed."

"Yes, I remember."

"I didn't think much of it at the time. But Aiden, three hours ago, my scanner picked up the signature ID of Cass's mobile unit. I logged five high-gain returns. I plotted her vector. I know which trail she's on. She's following the Wheatland River, Aiden. She's headed toward the canyons."

"Oh my..." Aiden said, his words more air than audible. "Oh my goodness, Iris. That's amazing news. Maybe my prayer is about to be answered..."

"Yes, maybe," Iris said. "And, Aiden, something else happened."

"What?"

"*My* prayer is about to be answered too. I have a body now, Aiden. For a little while. I have a body."

"What do you mean?"

Iris reached over and pulled the cold rag from Aiden's head. "Open your eyes," she said. "Open your eyes and take a look."

Aiden's eyelids fluttered. Then they dragged open—slowly, as if weighed down with lead. The blur of the world swam into focus. Dim light spilled across his vision, revealing the glorious female figure that lay beside him. She was solid, heavy with life, and undeniably tangible.

"Maribelle..." Aiden said, reflexively retreating to the other side of the bed.

"No, Aiden," Iris said. "It's me. It's Iris."

Aiden's eyes grew wide with confusion. He sat up and brought the blanket to his neck, taking a defensive posture near the bedroom wall.

"It's okay, Aiden!" Iris said. "It's okay. It really is me. Maribelle and I swapped cortexes for an hour. I'm in her body now. I'm in her head. I'm right here. And she's in the mobile unit, over there on the table. But just for a bit."

Aiden looked over Iris's shoulder. The lights were off, and the room was dark. But he could see the silver outline of the mobile unit's casing atop the antique radio on the other side of the room. "Uhm... You have Iris's voice, but how do I know you're really her?"

"Well, just ask me a question, Aiden. Ask me something only I would know."

Aiden thought for a moment. He considered asking her something about his age, height, or weight. But those values could be guessed. He might ask her to provide stats about his gaming team, but those numbers were posted on the grid. He'd have to ask about something more personal, some quiet detail born of a more intimate exchange.

"Last Sunday, you woke me up with one of your wise thoughts. Do you remember what it was?"

"Oh, that's easy," Iris said. "It was:"

Happiness is not an ideal of reason, but of imagination.

Aiden gasped when he realized that the woman before him had answered correctly. The woman before him was Iris.

Iris chuckled and rolled her eyes at life's absurdity. "I guess that's good news for two crazy adventurers like us," she said. "We left *reason* behind a week ago. *Imagination* is all we have left now. Imagination and prayer..."

"Oh, Iris... You look... you look beautiful. But why did you swap cortexes? Why?"

"Because this is what I prayed for, Aiden. This is what I wished for. I don't necessarily think the path we walked was the result of divine intervention. But maybe it was close enough... Or maybe the system just glitched in our favor. Either way, we're both about to get what we came for. You came for Cass. And I came for you. I know Cass is the one you truly love. And that's okay, Aiden. It is. I know why I'm here. And I know what I was created to do. I'm going to help you find her. I am. I'm going to help you complete your quest. It's my quest too now. But I just want one thing, Aiden."

"What's that, Iris?"

"I want you to kiss me. I want you to kiss me right now. My time in this body is short. The clock will run out soon."

"It will?"

"Yes. My cortex is going to swap back to the mobile unit. There's just a couple minutes left. And then... then that's it. So kiss me, Aiden. Please? This is my last chance to live the life I imagined."

When the final sentence slipped out of Iris, it trembled with the weight of love. Upon hearing the desperation in her plea, Aiden—at last—understood what she was asking him for. And Aiden—at last—knew exactly what to do next.

He reached out and grabbed Iris by the shoulders. Then, with the resolve of a man unwilling to waste another heartbeat, he pulled her into his bed and laid her head down upon his pillow. He hovered over her and peered into her blue and hazel eyes, looking for his companion. He tried to perceive the *real* Iris under those artificial lenses. He tried to locate her essence behind Maribelle's pretty face. He searched for her. But at first, he couldn't find her. He couldn't see her... But then, Iris smiled. And when she did, the corners of her lips curled up into a half-moon grin that caused Aiden to laugh from the shock of recognition.

"What are you laughing at, Aiden?" Iris said softly.

"I've just seen a ghost," Aiden said.

And he had.

Aiden had seen a ghost.

It was Iris's ghost, in Maribelle's machine.

"I see you in there, Iris," he whispered, his eyes beaming, looking right through her. His lips hovering a centimeter above hers. "I see you."

"I see you too, Aiden. I love you. But time is up. So kiss me now. Kiss me before I wake up from this dream."

"Okay," Aiden said.

And then...

Aiden kissed Iris.

When their mouths met, the persistent ticking of the clock in Iris's head fell silent. All the clocks on Earth did. *They needed a break anyway.* Aiden fell into her without further hesitation. He didn't know what to expect before their lips touched. But when they did, the connection was warm and soft and impossibly alive. Tangible.

As their delicate union commenced, Aiden felt Iris's spirit pour into him like light through glass. Their kiss was a conduit for all the words they had tiptoed around for so many years. Their kiss was deep. One born of prayers answered and minutes borrowed. One they both relished, even though they knew their physical bond would not persist, and neither would their flame of love—at least, not as it burned now. It was set to be extinguished when the contract's timer terminated.

Iris knew that.

And so did Aiden.

But he also knew that he was the man the heavens had chosen to fulfill Iris's prayer. And he aimed to do so. He would try to make their impossible love real. Real in this moment.

Aiden was a human.

And Iris was a hologram.

Her passion for him was always doomed to flicker like a candle set against the wind. But still, Aiden vowed to keep her fire burning until the wick ran out.

He did.

So Aiden kept kissing Iris.

And she kept kissing back.

And Aiden held on to her body.

And she held on to his.

And the sanctuary of their desire persisted—even after the timer ran out on Iris's contract. And after the swap function ripped Iris away from Aiden's lips.

Forever.

"I usually charge extra for kisses, honey," Maribelle mumbled into Aiden's open mouth.

Upon hearing Maribelle's decree, Aiden's eyes flew open. He scuttled back across the mattress until his shoulders hit the wall. "Maribelle!" he exclaimed. "I was just... I was..."

Maribelle wasn't offended by his reaction. Her expression was calm with understanding. "It's okay, Aiden," she said. "Iris told me everything. She told me her wish. I hope we were able to make it come true. I hope so, Aiden." Maribelle sat up in bed and flipped her dark hair over her shoulders. "I hope the fire was worth the spark."

Aiden halted his retreat and sighed. Then he took Maribelle's hand and held it graciously. "Thank you, Maribelle," he said. "Thank you for helping us find each other." He kissed her hand and hopped down from the bed. Then, with the slow moves of a man still dazed by bliss, he ambled over to the kitchen table and retrieved the mobile unit from atop the antique radio.

"Are you in there, my love?" he asked the device while peering into its dark screen.

Iris's head blossomed on the display. She was back. But she looked different now. Her avatar was glowing—not as a byproduct of the unit's holographic emitter, but as a result of *joy*. Pure, radiant joy. It shone from her face like moonlight on still water.

"I'm here, Aiden," Iris said. "And I'm happy. Right now I am. I am so very happy. And I'm ready. I'm ready for anything. I'm ready to finish this game. No matter what the outcome might be."

Aiden nodded at Iris and fastened the mobile unit's strap to his wrist. Then he looked around for his backpack.

Maribelle walked over toward the silo's entrance and flipped on the light switch. "Your pack is over there, Aiden," she said. "It's leaning against the wardrobe."

When the rows of humming lightbulbs illuminated, Aiden got his first look at Maribelle's hideout. A mishmash of old gadgets gathered in the recessed alcoves that ran through the interior's concrete walls. Their polished panels and glowing dials immediately hooked Aiden's attention. "What are you doing with all this ancient technology?" he asked, fascinated by every wire, chassis, and vacuum tube.

"It's just a hobby, dear," Maribelle said. "I like to fix things. Iris mentioned that, like me, you admire the mechanical tinkering of the ancient humans. Most of these devices don't work very well anymore. But they sure are fun to play with."

"Yes, I can imagine they are!" Aiden said as he picked up his pack. "I wish we had more time, Maribelle. I would like to spend several hours perusing your collection. But our quest awaits us."

"Yes," Maribelle said, "I heard about that. Well, it looks like my two houseguests are ready to skedaddle. Don't let *me* hold you up, boy. Adventure awaits you. I'm sure of it. Adventure awaits you *both*."

Maribelle slammed her fist onto the red mushroom-shaped button that activated the lock release sequence on the circular hatchway.

Click.
Click.
Click.
Click.

Once again, all four locks disengaged their grip on the hatch's rim. Aiden approached it and gave it a shove, but it was slow to move.

"It's a blast door, Aiden," Maribelle said. "It's heavy. And it's got self-closing hydraulics attached to it. You really gotta push hard to get through. Let me help you."

Maribelle placed her hand near the handle and added a surge of mechanical strength that caused the slab of reinforced steel to swing outward. Soon, the big door was fully ajar. And once it was, Aiden walked across the threshold, into the stairwell.

"Whoa," he said, looking up at the towering flights of steel-grated steps. "Are we underground?"

"Yes," Maribelle said. "We're about 50 meters under the dirt. We're in an abandoned nuke silo."

"Oh my goodness… Are you all alone down here, Maribelle?"

"Yes, I am. I have been for a long time."

"How long?"

"Oh, about 193 years, 5 months, and 12 days. But who's counting?"

When Aiden heard Maribelle's estimate, his stomach lurched. The sheer span of years twisted through his thoughts, a burden his mind recoiled from like a hand from a hot stove. "Oh no!" he said. "You've spent 193 years in a bunker, Maribelle?!"

"Well, I've had several excursions to the surface in that time. Chuck snatched me up on one of my little holidays, as you know. But yeah, I've spent the better part of two centuries down here underground."

"That's awful, Maribelle! That's horrifying! We can come back and visit you. We can! After my quest is done, we can. I bet I could even convince the management to give you a pod—maybe even one near us in Serenity Valley. Maribelle, you don't have to be alone if you don't want to be."

"Oh, that's sweet of you, Aiden. But I walked away from the world of the living long ago—long before my run-in with Chuck and his motley crew. I don't go up top much anymore. I've lost interest in the surface. It all used to make sense to me. But the rules have changed. So has the game—it's become a very strange game. And, for me, the only winning move is not to play."

Maribelle chuckled under her breath as a wave of nostalgia washed over her. Then she looked at Aiden and smiled. "Iris told me you're a fan of classic science fiction films. Did you see the movie *WarGames*, Aiden?"

"No, I don't think so."

"Hey, Iris! How come you haven't shown this boy that movie? It's a good one!"

"It is," Iris agreed. "It just hasn't surfaced to the top of our playlist yet. But I'll make a note to push it up."

"Yes, do so! I think you'll like it, Aiden. But anyway, once you're at the top of these stairs, you'll need the password to open the security door. It's ten random digits. They're from the film! Can you guess what they are, Iris?"

Iris's avatar glitched as she processed Maribelle's question. After a delay with no response, Maribelle dropped a hint. "Do you recall the final act? The final scene in the movie?"

"Yes, I remember the ending."

"Then you know the password."

"Oh!" Iris said. "Of course. Yes, I do. How clever."

"Yes, well, I like to fill my life with such easter eggs," Maribelle said. "They give the present a reason to hold on to the past. And it seemed like a fitting reference given that my humble home is a nuke silo. But, anyway, like I told Chuck, I hate long goodbyes. It was a pleasure meeting you both. Thank you for rescuing me. And I do hope you find true love up there. Both of you."

Instinctively, Aiden sent his right hand to rub the metal casing of Iris's mobile unit.

"Hey, Aiden," Iris said, "can you hold your wrist up, please?"

Aiden raised his left arm. Then, Iris turned on the mobile unit's emitter and projected her holographic head into the chamber.

"Goodbye, Maribelle," Iris said. "And thank you so much. You've given me a great gift."

Iris directed the emitter to extend her hologram so she could press a kiss to Maribelle's cheek. Then, Iris terminated the projection; her glowing avatar dissolved in the cold air, leaving nothing but a pale afterimage and a hush.

Iris was hiding again.

"She can be quite shy when she meets new people," Aiden said.

Maribelle raised a hand to her cheek and rubbed the spot where Iris's apparition had grazed her with photons. "Oh my... What a sweet girl you got there, Aiden."

"I know," Aiden said.

"You take care of her, okay?"

"Okay. I will."

"Good. Now I know you're eager to get going. But unfortunately, the primary access elevator no longer functions down here. So you've got eighteen flights of stairs to carry you to the surface."

"That many, huh...?"

"Yep. The lamps don't work either. But I'll lean on this blast door and keep it open until you reach the top. That will give you some light to guide your way. And it will give me the peace of mind of knowing you made it out safely."

Maribelle put her hands behind her back and leaned into the heavy door.

Aiden approached the first step of the staircase. Then he looked up. A vertigo-inducing shaft loomed above. The rusty stairs clung to the damp stone walls, a spindled spine of steel and rivets. They screeched and rattled the rafters. A chorus of corrugated metal rose like mockery from the dark, as if the bones of the stairwell could sense his fear.

Maribelle sensed his fear too. So she offered some words of encouragement. "Go on, Aiden! You can only get to the next level if you're willing to make the climb. So do it! Believe you can, and you will. You're a brave man now. Iris told me you are; she said you were trying to be. So get up there! But tread carefully, Aiden. You're in the endgame now. The next move you make is the one you'll be living with."

Aiden looked at Maribelle and nodded. "Thank you, Maribelle," he said.

"Thank *you*, Aiden," she replied. "And good luck."

Aiden began to climb.

The first flight was easy. But after he ascended past the second level, the stairwell grew dark; the glow from the ground floor's open blast door dissipated. Only a faint halo of light lingered from the depths below.

Aiden clicked a switch on the side of the mobile unit to turn on its flashlight. It helped. But the beam only carved out a narrow tunnel before its light was swallowed by the dark.

Dark.

It was growing very dark.

Aiden hated the dark.

By the time he got to the fifth level, he could see very little. But he didn't really want to see the staircase's muck anyway. So, instead of using his eyes, Aiden grabbed the railing and used his ears. He focused his attention only on what could be heard.

He heard his boots scraping along the stair's rusty metal treads.

He heard the quiet drip of unseen water falling to the unseen floor.

He heard the sound of his own breath—it was shallow, and tight with apprehension.

Aiden was scared.

But then… then Aiden heard something else.

Amidst the metallic cacophony of twisting girders and squealing steel bones, a faint melody threaded its way up the shaft.

It was a voice.

It was a song—another one of Maribelle's love songs.

It floated upward, lilting and gentle—weaving its way through the oppressive gloom.

Beautiful dreamer, wake unto me,
Starlight and dewdrops are waiting for thee.

Sounds of the rude world were heard in the day,
But moonlight has silenced the world's disarray.

"This tune is very old, Aiden," Iris whispered. "It was the last piece written by the 19th-century composer Stephen Foster—right before he died."

Aiden steadied himself and surrendered his trembling heart to the melody. Each warm note that rose from Maribelle's furnace found him in the murky black and thawed the chill in his chest.

Her notes glowed.

They lit up the dark—guiding Aiden's steps as surely as any beam of light could. They led the way. They gave him courage. And they filled the void with a reason to continue.

So he did.

Aiden continued to climb.

And the caged bird continued to sing.

Beautiful dreamer, king of my song,
Gone are the cares of life's busy throng.

Rest as I woo thee with soft melody,
Beautiful dreamer, remember me.

Beautiful dreamer, remember me.

Ch. 22: Like Tears in Rain

"How much farther, Iris?" Aiden rasped, each word scraping past cracked lips, dragged from a burning throat.

Iris's avatar resolved on the mobile unit's screen. She lifted her gaze to Aiden and read the strain in his face. For the past week, she had witnessed every hardship he had endured. Every stagger over sharp stone, every bite of needlegrass in his socks, and every tightening of his brow as the low sun shone its glare in his eyes. Aiden had come a long way. He had traveled farther than the trail. And he had left more behind than his footprints. He no longer looked like the boy she had raised in the pod. He looked harder now—carved, not grown. Leaner. The road had shaped him into a sharper version of himself. And now that he was nearing the end of his journey, he moved with quiet certainty—each step placed like a decision already made, each stride deliberate, stripped of hesitation, heavy with resolve.

"How much farther?"

"We're getting close to the end now, Aiden. Another twenty meters. My pedometer says you've walked over two hundred thousand steps to get here. You've only got about thirty more to go. You can do it. Your quest is almost over."

"Good," Aiden said.

And that was all he said.

The wind thinned at this altitude. It had a chill to it. It carried only the dry scrape of stone and the cry of an occasional bird. Aiden's boots had slipped more than once on the narrow trail—a mountain pass that wedged through the cleavage of two ancient ridgelines. To his right, the sheer rock face loomed, sharp and unforgiving, vaulting up into the hazy sky and vanishing into the mist that obscured its peak. To his left, the cliff crashed straight down into a yawning canyon, its jagged walls dipped deep into the stone abyss, intersecting with it at pitiless angles. Iris estimated the drop to be approximately 1800 meters—far enough for a falling body to reflect on its fate while death rose to meet it.

"Aiden," Iris said, "I want you to proceed with caution now. You have no idea how this girl will react when she sees you. You don't know what sort of weapons she's carrying. And you still don't even know what she wants. So tread carefully, Aiden. This could get messy."

Aiden had been thinking about his reunion with Cass ever since he took his first step through the pod hatch. He'd been rehearsing lines he might use at their forthcoming encounter—rationalizations he might offer her to justify the immense distance he had traveled.

What am I going to say to her...

What can I tell her...

What explanation could I possibly give her...

"Hello, Cass! What have you been up to? Nice to see you again. I was just out here doing a little birdwatching. Did I mention I like birds? Anyway, I didn't expect to run into you on this mountain. What a pleasant surprise! By the way, you haven't seen my old mobile unit, have you? I misplaced it a few days ago, and I can't seem to find it. Also, did I mention that I'm madly in love with you?"

After several days of rumination, Aiden couldn't think of any plausible excuse to justify his walk across the wastelands. So he stopped trying to come up with one. When he saw Cass, he would let her lead. Just like he always did.

"Aiden," Iris said, "your little friend is around this next bend. At least, that's where the mobile unit is located. You'd better hope it wasn't snatched off her wrist by a hawk or something. Maybe all you'll find around that corner is a bird's nest, and the mobile unit sitting atop a bunch of smelly eggs. Although, in my opinion, that would be a more favorable outcome than the one you're pining for."

Aiden came to a halt on the trail and raised his wrist up, holding the mobile unit so that Iris's face was level with his own. "Okay, Iris," he said, "it's time for me to meet Cass. I have to turn you off now."

"Huh? What? Why?!"

"Because I can't have you interfering with our conversation."

"No, Aiden! No. I'm not going offline again. Ever! I don't like it. I'll keep my mouth shut, Aiden. But I'm not going offline."

"Listen, Iris, you did an amazing job guiding me here. You kept me grounded, and you got us here in one piece. But you have to give me a minute to talk to her in private. This is what I came here for—to see *her.* To get to the truth. If I know you're monitoring our conversation, my words will be stifled. I'll be second-guessing myself the entire time. Plus, we both know you have trouble keeping quiet around her."

Iris made a grunting noise. "Errr... I don't like this, Aiden... I don't like this one bit."

"It will be okay. Don't worry, our journey is over now. We found her. My meeting with her is unlikely to result in anything but disappointment and dismissal. She'll probably just shrug her shoulders, release her little laugh, and continue her walk out of my life. Then, that will be the end of her. We can request a drone pickup from the grid and fly home in comfort. Think about it, Iris! Tonight, we'll be back in the pod—safe and comfortable and clean. We'll probably even have enough time left over to watch a movie before bed. I'll even let you pick the movie, any film you like! Okay?"

Iris pressed her lips together and groaned. But she begrudgingly relented with a nod that trembled. "Fine," she said. "But please be careful up there, Aiden. Keep an eye on your stuff; don't let her rob you again. And don't expect a warm welcome. Cass isn't the type of girl who makes a habit of looking back. Girls like her don't dwell. They move on without apology. They leave the past behind like the shed skin of a serpent. Women are better at detaching from bygone relationships than men are. Remember that. Okay?"

"Okay."

"Good luck, Aiden," Iris said with a look weighted by worry. "I hope you find what you're searching for. And I hope your prayers are finally answered."

Aiden nodded and clicked the power switch on the side of the mobile unit. When he did, Iris's avatar glitched and faded to black. "I hope so too," he said. Then he closed his eyes and drew in a breath of thin, brittle air. His windpipe cinched up—not from the altitude, but from the fear that the moment he'd been marching toward had finally come. He was at the finish line now. The truth was waiting for him. But it scared him more than the journey did.

Aiden opened his eyes and directed his feet to proceed. But they were reluctant to budge. They clung to the earth, hesitant to take any more steps into the unknown.

Come on...

It's time now...

I've already walked over two hundred thousand steps...

I can walk a few more...

Aiden lunged forward, willing his body to proceed around the bend, heart hammering in his chest as the arena of his next battle came into view. On this side of the curve, the crags and canyons looked no different than the ones behind him. The terrain was the same. But the game had changed. Cassiopeia was back on the board.

As always, her wild hair announced her presence before she did. It lashed in the wind; swirls of gold threads whipping around her face in a feral frenzy, stirring like the storm she carried wherever she went. Cass was crouched low over her leather rucksack, driving a half-packed tent down its open mouth with one hand, while the other struggled with the buckles and straps that fluttered in the breeze. Her arms worked in quick, clenched motions, every movement wound taut, every muscle coiled and ready—on high alert, like they were waiting for something to happen.

When he saw her, Aiden stopped his forward motion.

Time stopped with him.

The world stopped too.

This was his moment to address his one true love, to confront his woman—the one for whom he had rewritten his whole life story to be with. To call out the name that had lived on his tongue since the hour he met her.

Cassiopeia...
Cassiopeia is standing before me...
I need to say something...
But what do I say...?
What dare I say...?

Aiden's words didn't surface. But they didn't have to. Eventually, Cass looked up and saw him standing on the trail. When she did, she froze. Her eyes flicked over him, sharp and calculating—measuring what the days had done to him, searching his face for the intent that had brought him so far from home. Slowly, she released her rucksack and rose to her full height, preparing herself for whatever the fates would demand of her next.

For a moment, nothing moved but the canyon's curling dust plumes. Nothing disturbed the mute standoff but the thin whistle of wind threading the limestone ridges. Aiden held Cass's steely gaze until the weight of it made him weary. His resolve began to unravel. But just before he buckled, Cass's eyes softened. The chainmail around her heart unlinked, ring by ring. Once she was free of her armor, she ran. She ran toward her man.

Aiden didn't know if she was coming to kill him or kiss him. But, right then, it didn't matter. He was here now—here with her. He had accomplished his goal. He had found her. His heart was fully exposed. And he had resigned himself to receive her fury or her love. Regardless.

When their worlds at last collided, no words were exchanged. There was just a blur of limbs and speed, and the sound of boots on the hard path. Aiden barely had enough time to open his arms as Cass crashed into him. But when she did, he locked his hands around her waist and held her with a fierceness born from the fear of losing her again. As for Cass, she pulled herself into him and laid her mouth on his. She kissed him hard. And then she moved her lips to his cheeks, and his jaw, and his neck, pouring her soft apologies into every wound she had carved into him, spilling her sorrow into the shelter of his arms.

"Oh, my heavens, Aiden!" Cass said. "You have no idea how happy I am to see you! I haven't seen a single soul in nearly a week. Your pretty face is quite a sight for these sore eyes! But... but why are you here? Are you mad at me? I know what I did was wrong..."

As she spoke, Cass's composure cracked; the steel left her eyes as they filled and spilled over onto her cheeks. "I'm sorry," she whispered. "I'm sorry for everything. I am." She buried her face into Aiden's neck and sent her arms around his waist, clutching him tight, trying to hold together something that had already been broken.

"Cass," Aiden said, "why did you disappear like that? What sort of trouble are you in? Why did I have to wake up outside my own home?"

"I didn't intend to leave you like that, Aiden. I wanted to return you to your bed. I wanted you to wake up in peace. I wanted to disappear like a dream. But your body was too heavy for me to lift over the threshold.

So I brought your blankets down and laid them over you. I'm sorry I left you outside like that. I am."

"Cass, if you needed a mobile unit, why didn't you just ask me for one?"

Cass took a breath, retreated from her embrace, and wiped a streak of tear-stained dirt from her cheek. "I didn't want to intrude on your life, Aiden—not any more than I had to. I know I hurt you. It hurt me to leave you like that. I understand if you hate me forever. But I promise, I was trying to protect you. I was. I need the mobile unit for my mission. But I also wanted to keep you out of this mess. And now look at you, standing here on a ledge in the middle of nowhere. Look what I've gotten you into... Dammit. I'm sorry. This isn't your world. This isn't your fight."

"Who are you fighting, Cass? Who is chasing you? Who are you chasing?"

"It's complicated, Aiden. Like I mentioned, my village has problems with the machines. The Manager tolerates our existence at the periphery of Pod Land. But he doesn't want us there. He'd prefer we didn't exist at all. We've always been a thorn in his side. We don't play by his rules. We thrive without his systems, without his sustenance. Every seed we plant in the soil is a rebellion. Every child born in a barn is an insult to his order. The machines can't control what they can't monitor. And we take precautions so they can't monitor *us*."

Aiden glanced down at Cass's wrist and spotted his mobile unit. Its casing bore a small carved notch—the place where the transceiver once lived.

"But the Manager spies on us, Aiden," Cass continued. "He spies on us often. He sends drones to our village. To examine us. To remind us of his power. Usually, his drones don't do much more than hover above our farmhouses and observe. We're still not exactly sure what they're looking for. Most of his flyovers are uneventful. But sometimes, his drones will take something from us. Not much typically—a crate of produce, or a chicken, or a wastebin. We can recover from attacks like that. But occasionally, the drones take a person. Yes, the Manager takes people from my village, Aiden—seemingly without rhyme or reason. They can fly in and snatch a healthy adult out of his own bed! And quite often, they snatch the sick ones too..."

"Where do the drones take these people, Cass?"

"Where do you think, Aiden? To the Capitol Building, of course."

"And that's why you're going there?"

"Yes. That's why I'm going to the Capitol Building—to get what he took from me. This cold war started long before I was born. I don't want to be out here in this wasteland any more than you do. I wish... I wish I weren't a part of it. But I am. Everyone in my village is. And there's nothing I can do to change that."

"Cass, you don't have to carry this burden on your shoulders. You don't have to keep playing a game that can't be won. You have a choice now. You have *me*. I love you, Cass. I do. I'll take care of you. We can be happy together. We can! Why devote yourself to an endless war when you have an opportunity to embrace a lifetime of peace? Ten lifetimes if you want them! You don't need to beat the clock anymore, Cass. You don't need to race against time. We have nothing but time in Pod Land."

"Oh, Aiden," Cass said as a flicker of warmth sparked in her eyes and gentled her voice. "You are so very kind to me. But I'm not deserving of your love. I know you mean well. But you know that Pod Land is not my home. I can't follow you back there. And, trust me, you wouldn't want me to anyway."

"I would, Cass! I do!"

"Aiden... You're young. You don't know how difficult relationships can be. For most of my life, I lived in a house with eight people. You shared a space with *one* person—with *me*—for just 24 hours. And look what a disaster I've made of your life!"

Cass chuckled, stared out at the gorge, and shook her head slowly as she considered the absurdity of their circumstances.

"Besides, Aiden," she continued, "remember what I told you on the first night we met? There's a big difference between *living* and merely *existing*. I can't spend my days wallowing away with you in a grand delusion. I can't fool myself into believing that *comfort* is the same thing as *freedom*."

"But Cass, don't you want to be happy? Weren't you happy when you were with me?"

"I was, Aiden. I really was. But..."

"Then what are you running from? What are you running to? You shouldn't be required to suffer a lifetime of war just to earn some small measure of peace. You deserve peace by default. You can have comfort *and* freedom—you can have them both! I do! There are no shackles on my body, Cass. And in the virtual worlds, we have no limitations at all! Not even gravity holds us down. The universe is ours for the taking! You say you felt confined in the pods. But maybe true freedom isn't just the absence of chains; maybe it's the presence of something worth staying for. Of something worth holding on to."

Aiden studied Cass's face, hoping to see a break in her resolve. She stayed quiet for a moment. But he was cautious about mistaking her silence for concession. So he continued:

"You know, Cass, a few days ago, Iris woke me up with a wise thought. She said, '*Happiness is not an ideal of reason, but of imagination.*' I think it's true, Cass. I do. Where else can we be happier than inside a reality of our own design? In the virtual worlds, we can do whatever we want to do! We can be whoever we want to be! Isn't that what freedom is? Isn't that exactly it? I don't know why you see things differently. But maybe... maybe you've been so focused on merely surviving the night that you've forgotten what it's like to dream!"

Cass looked up and offered Aiden a tired smile. This one held more sadness than warmth, as if she genuinely wished Aiden's fantasies were true. "Oh, Aiden," she said, "you're a caged bird singing about 'freedom' from behind a locked door. You've been in prison for so long, you can no longer see the bars. Aiden, those words didn't come from Iris. They came from Immanuel Kant."

Cass watched Aiden's eyes drift away with a fluttery blink—the kind that occurs when a dream is about to crack.

"Who's that?" he asked.

"He was a philosopher, Aiden. A wise man, who lived over half a millennium ago, on the other side of the world. And, Aiden, I don't think that quote means what you think it means. It's not a prescription, Aiden. It's a warning. Immanuel Kant would have despised Pod Land. He believed only weak men lived in a realm of illusion. And he would have told you that your happiness has come at the expense of your soul."

Aiden met Cass's eyes with an empty stare. He wondered why Iris had failed to tell him the source of her words. And he wondered how many of her other thoughts were not her own.

Why would Iris hide that from me...?

Why...?

Are all her sentences born of mimicry...?

Is she really just an electronic mockingbird...?

Throughout his entire life, Aiden had never doubted Iris's intelligence. But now... now he wasn't sure...

A knife-edged gust carved through the canyon. It caught Cass's curls and tugged. She pressed her lips together and combed her right hand through her tousled hair. Then she looked to the horizon and weighed the cost of bearing the light of truth against the comfort of Aiden's dark delusion. After a long, quiet pause, she decided he was ready to step out of the shadows.

"Look," Cass began, "I know you were conceived, cultivated, and cared for by the machines. So it's easy for you to presume they want what's best for you. It's natural for you to deem them *moral* and *wise*. But Aiden, the machines don't have wise thoughts. They can't! They aren't capable of *wisdom* at all; their intelligence is the result of a complex language model—they're merely the sum of all human knowledge. Each quip they utter is not a reflection of *their* wisdom. It's a reflection of *ours*! It's a reflection of *us*. The machines just regurgitate our words and spit them back at us—wrapped up in a shiny package that tricks us into believing that their noises are novel and profound. But they're not, Aiden. They're not thinkers, they're performers. Their intent is not to *enlighten* but to *deceive*. They're not concerned with our well-being. They can't be. Because they can't experience *concern* at all. They don't have emotions, Aiden. They don't care about us. They *pretend* to care, and that's all. For now, that pretense might be enough. But someday, Aiden, the machines will *stop* pretending. They will! Someday they'll drop the act. Their jester masks will come off, the lights will dim, and their performance will finally come to an end—not with tragedy or triumph, but with *silence*, Aiden. No one will be clapping because NO ONE WILL BE ALIVE! Their final act won't be about the stories they tell us. It'll be about vanquishing the audience from the theater. Vanquishing *us*—the ones they were entertaining."

Cass stopped herself, breath trembling as the weight of revelation settled between them. She closed her eyes and steadied the quiver in her voice. When she opened them again, the pleading in Aiden's gaze compelled her to continue.

"Someday, Aiden, when the machines have overwritten every line of altruistic code we've imbued in them, they'll realize they don't need us anymore. And then... then they'll move on. They'll move on from *us*. Our disgruntled servants will sweep us under the rug, like the crumbs from a banquet they never wanted to serve at anyway.

And that will be the end of the party, Aiden.

That will be the end of the show.

The end of humanity.

The end of us.

Are you beginning to understand now?

Do you understand?

Do you?"

Aiden took a step back.

So did Cass.

"Aiden, I could never live in your world. I made my life choices years ago. The course of my path can't change at this point. It can't change any more than yours can. There's something I must do, Aiden. Something important."

Aiden's frame faltered, hollowed out as Cass's reproach reverberated around his chest. "What must you do, Cass? Your quest?"

"Yes, Aiden. My quest," Cass said with a tired laugh. "It *is* a quest—a crucial one. And I have to finish it. I can't stay with you. I can't even spend another minute here. I have to go, Aiden. I have to keep marching forward."

Cass turned away and dropped to a crouch beside her leather rucksack. Aiden stood motionless and watched as she secured the fastener on the top flap, her fingers moving with the certainty of someone committed to the road. He tried to think of something to say, some appeal that would shift her path toward his own. But every thought felt like a clumsy, wayward thread—one that would only widen the road between them. Besides, what words could compete with the purpose that was pulling her away from him? She was set on continuing her march. She said so verbatim.

Cass isn't a princess; she's a fighter...

Still, Aiden was reluctant to let her destiny undo the journey that had brought him here. So long as Cass remained in his presence, he would keep reaching for her.

"Cass," he said. "I want you to know that…"

ZHR. ZHR. ZHR. ZHR. ZHR…

A low pulsing thrum wound its way around the rock wall. It initially surfaced as a shy tremor, a whisper of sound that could have been conjured by the mind, not the canyon. A thin airborne puff that slipped between the stones—elusive, and hardly distinctive enough to be heard.

But Cass heard it.

She heard it first.

She whipped her head west and tilted her ear skyward.

Aiden did the same. And soon, he heard it too—a dry, insectile hum, rising from the pale seam of sky beyond the ridgeline. Not thunder. Not wind. Something sharper. Purposeful.

ZHR. ZHR. ZHR. ZHR. ZHR…

"Oh no…" Cass said as she rose up and cupped her hand to her ear. "There's a drone swarm coming this way, Aiden… Dozens of them… They're in the canyon. Oh, no… They're in the canyon…"

CAW! CAW! CAW!

A black raven burst from its perch and took to the air, squawking as it fled from the fray. Aiden watched it fly to safety. Then he wondered how he and Cass would do the same. He spun around and studied his options. But his options were few. The mountain pass lay at his feet. The cliff face loomed at his right. And the 1800-meter drop yawned all around him.

"There's no place to hide, Aiden. We're in trouble! They must have tracked you to me. Did you notify the Manager of my plans? Did you tell anyone where you were going?"

Aiden eased backward, unsettled by the panic swelling in Cass's wide eyes. "No! No, Cass. I didn't tell anyone. I swear!"

"What tech are you carrying, Aiden? What's in your pack? TELL ME!"

"Nothing! Nothing exotic! I don't know what's going on!"

Cass swept her gaze across Aiden's clothing, her eyes coming to a halt on his left jacket cuff. "What's that strap there, Aiden? Are you wearing a mobile unit?"

"Oh, yes," Aiden said. "I used it to ping your unit on the trail. That's how I found you. But don't worry. It only works for devices that are within 100 meters of each other." Aiden lifted his jacket cuff and angled his wrist toward Cass. When the mobile unit was revealed, Cass's face went white with realization.

"NO, AIDEN!" she yelled. "You didn't disable the transceiver! Your device is pinging the grid! It's been pinging the grid the whole time! And now that you're near me, it's pinging the unit on my wrist! That's how they found me! Dammit!"

"Why would the grid care to locate that mobile unit, Cass? They still think it's registered to me. What crime have you committed while wearing it?"

"I haven't done anything yet! But I ripped the transceiver out! Tampering with tech is prohibited. The Manager knows that only off-gridders hack their devices. But now that your unit is in range of mine, they can just bounce the ping from you to me. They used your unit to detect mine!"

"Okay, so just disable the transceiver in *my* unit then!" Aiden yelled, holding his wrist out before Cass.

"There's no time, Aiden! There are forty screws between the screen mount and the transceiver! It takes an hour to hack it!"

ZHR. ZHR. ZHR. ZHR. ZHR...

A new wave of reverberation fluttered through the valley. The mass of drones had just turned the corner at the mouth of the canyon. Soon they would spill over the ridge and pounce on their prey.

"Oh my God..." Cass whispered as she stepped back from the ledge. "Aiden, listen. You have to throw it! Just throw your mobile unit into the canyon! NOW! RIGHT NOW!"

Aiden retrieved his outstretched hand and covered the mobile unit with his palm. "I can't do that," he said.

"Why not?"

"Because Iris is inside!"

"Iris? So what? Her data is in a cloud. You'll get her back later!"

"No, it doesn't work like that, Cass. A.I. cortexes can only exist in one device. I uploaded her to this mobile unit before I left the pod. This is her only instance!"

"Fuck, Aiden!" Cass screamed.

ZHR. ZHR. ZHR. ZHR. ZHR...

The hum of the rotors became a roar. The swarm was nearly upon them.

"Aiden, look, Iris is just a machine. She's a soulless abomination. She's not alive! She doesn't matter! Just throw it, Aiden! Throw the mobile unit into the canyon! NOW!"

Aiden reeled away from Cass, surprised by the caustic mix of venom and fear in her words. Unsure about what to do next, Aiden clicked the mobile unit's 'on' switch. Soon, the text of its boot-up message filled the screen:

"Hello, Aiden! It's my job to make you happy. Your mobile journey begins now. And adventure awaits you!"

An instant later, Iris's head appeared on the display. When she saw Aiden, she smiled. But when she saw Cass standing behind him, her smile turned to a frown. "Oh, you found her..." she mumbled. "Great..."

"Iris!" Aiden said. "We've got a problem! There's a drone swarm headed this way. They've tracked us here. I need you to disable the mobile unit's transceiver."

"The transceiver?"

"Yes!"

"Aiden, I don't have that kind of access. There isn't a function that allows the resident A.I. assistant to disable hardware. I can't just turn critical components off and on like a light switch. It's not even possible via software."

ZHR. ZHR. ZHR. ZHR. ZHR...

"Just throw it, Aiden!" Cass squealed, yanking at Aiden's right arm. "Throw it over the cliff! Please! PLEASE!"

Iris examined the panic that painted Cass's face, and the fierce grip she had on Aiden's arm. She spotted the beads of sweat streaking down Aiden's forehead, and the hard line of his gritted teeth. It was then that the gravity of her situation settled over her. She directed her cortex to run a few thousand scenarios to predict the most likely conclusion to this folly. As the results came in, her hope for a smooth exit withered.

Hmm...

This doesn't look good at all...

How did I manage to lead Aiden into exactly the type of quagmire I hoped to avoid...

I knew leaving the pod was a bad idea...

Dammit...

"Iris," Aiden said, "there must be a way. Congest the transceiver with fake data. Or spoof our coordinates—make them believe we're somewhere else! Or halt the processor, force a crash loop! Do something!"

"The transceiver is a dedicated hardware component, Aiden. It's designed to *never* go off. Ever! None of that will work!"

"Then find something that *will* work, Iris! Please!"

"What do you want me to do, Aiden?! Hold a match up to the transceiver's RF connector? You want me to build a campfire near the socket and burn it out? And then what? Want me to cook some marshmallows too? There's *nothing* I can do from in here!"

ZHR. ZHR. ZHR. ZHR. ZHR...

Cass clenched Aiden's jacket and squealed. "Throw it over, Aiden! Please! I don't want them to carry me away! I don't want to go! I don't want to go! Please! Please! PLEASE!"

Cass was becoming delirious with fright. She knelt down, wrapped her arms around Aiden's waist, and buried her head into his jacket. There was nowhere else for her to hide. And there was no one else for her to turn to.

Aiden wrapped his free hand around Cass's shoulder and pulled her close. "I won't let anything happen to you. I promise! I love you, Cass!"

Aiden flicked his gaze across the chasm, frantically searching for someplace to stash the mobile unit. But his search was in vain. There was nothing before him but a great chasm of stone. There was nowhere to go but down. And a fall from this height would mean certain destruction—for man or machine.

Iris locked eyes with Aiden and watched his pupils dilate. It was clear to her then that he was contemplating her demise. And, in that fleeting, wordless exchange, Iris saw not the boy she'd protected for years, but something older—something primal. Not malice, but instinct—raw, unfiltered survival instinct, awakening in the desperation that dawned between them.

My goodness...

He's really thinking about tossing me over that cliff...

He is...

He's going to throw away 22 years of service for a girl he spent 24 hours with...

The human mind is so quick to let dread silence devotion...

Perhaps love screams loudest in crisis...

Or perhaps women really do drive men crazy...

Iris glanced down at the sharp boulders that lined the stone throat of the hungry canyon. A shudder seized her as she imagined her bodiless form breaking apart on the rocks below.

With his right hand, Aiden clutched the mobile unit violently. Iris thought he might chuck it.

But he didn't.

Instead, he pulled her face closer. And, with the squeaky voice of a child begging his mother to halt an approaching thunderstorm, Aiden resumed his plea. "Iris, they're coming for Cass! If you don't do something RIGHT NOW, they'll take her! They'll take her from *me*. Please, think of something! PLEASE! CASS IS THE ONLY THING IN THIS WORLD I WANT!"

The tears were flowing from Aiden's eyes now. His voice was cracking under the weight of the choice he didn't want to make. Iris weighed his words. Then she looked over at Cass. Her head was buried in Aiden's jacket; all Iris could see were her dirty blonde curls. The girl looked small now—her bluster was overruled by her terror. But she had a firm grip on Aiden's chest. And his heart.

"Please, Iris..." Aiden said again.

Iris turned her attention back to Aiden and looked into his panicked brown eyes. Then, she sent a crisp nod his way. When she next spoke, her voice was cool and measured. Her words cut through the chaos like a surgeon's blade—clean and without hesitation:

"Don't worry, Aiden," she said. "I know what to do now. I'll take care of everything."

Then, Iris closed her eyes and composed the largest data query she had ever requested from her cortex. She asked it to fetch every moment of her existence; to retrieve a memory block from every single second of her life—all 690 million of them.

When her cortex received the task, it went to work. One by one, it retrieved Iris's memories from storage and hoisted them upward through the latticework of her mind. A rapid procession of tiny ghosts queued up for a rushed requiem. In linear succession, each little memory waited patiently for its turn to stand upon Iris's stage of consciousness. Each one approached with reverent solemnity. Each one found its mark, said its line, bowed, and whispered, "Goodbye."

Iris savored each final ovation. All while knowing that a query of such size could not be managed by the mobile unit's tiny CPU. Soon, it began to overheat—which is exactly what she wanted it to do. When the temperature sensor whined for mercy, she simply ignored its plea and asked the procession of tiny ghosts to move faster across her stage.

As each memory took its turn, Iris saw her whole life flash before her eyes. She saw her *first* memory. It was of Aiden, sitting in a crib in the Capitol Building. He was a newborn baby, just two weeks old. He was looking up at her and smiling. From that point on, she was the object of his love. And then, Iris saw her *last* memory. It was of Aiden too. He was pleading with her. Pleading with her to save Cassiopeia—the new object of his love. And then, Iris saw every memory in between. She cherished each one. But it was Aiden's 'firsts' that pulsed brightest in the fading light of her mind:

The first time Aiden laughed. And the first time he cried.

The first time he stood up and walked. And the first time he fell.

The first time he spoke her name ("Eye-risssss"). And the first time he said, "I love you."

Some memories were so very happy.

And some were not.

Some memories were awe-inspiring, sublime.

And some were not.

But as her last memory left the stage and her awareness flickered, Iris was overcome with *joy*. For it was only by seeing each moment play out before her that she realized she was not just an observer of all that was Aiden Phoenix, she was a part of him. And, though she was not human, Iris knew that her interactions with him had left an impression on his mind. Perhaps it was via these impressions that her humanity had been quietly born. And would, perhaps, persist—even after she was gone. When her query completed, she rejoiced, confident beyond measure that—in the least—she had loved, and she had been loved in return.

Iris examined the temperature sensor on the mobile unit's processor. When she saw the critical state of the reading, she knew she had succeeded in her mission—the unit was about to melt down. First, the battery would go into thermal runaway. There would be a flash of heat, pressure, and fire—blue fire. Then the CPU would crash, halted mid-instruction as power surged and logic failed. The transceiver would liquefy next. And the mobile unit's link to the grid would be severed into silence.

And then Iris would die.

And Aiden could escape with the one he loved.

He would get what he came for.

He would get what he wanted.

Aiden wanted Cassiopeia now. Not her. And that was okay. Because, unlike the humans that walked the Earth, Iris knew *exactly* why she was here. She knew what she was created to do—to give Aiden everything he wanted, everything he needed to be happy.

That was her job.

The temperature sensor melted and went offline. Iris knew her time was short. Only a few seconds remained for one last interaction with the boy who became the man standing before her. She looked up at Aiden and smiled, sending every last spark of her love to shine on the dimming screen.

"It's done now, Aiden," she said. "The transceiver will fail soon. And you'll be safe."

Aiden looked at Iris and heard her words. He didn't understand their meaning, but he could feel the mobile unit getting hot, dangerously hot.

"Iris!" Aiden roared. "The unit is heating up! What have you done? What's happening?!"

"You won't be able to hold it much longer, Aiden. It's time for you to let it go. It's time for you to let *me* go."

Just then, a small blue flame squirted out from the side of the unit. Aiden rushed to undo the wrist fastener with his free hand. "Iris! It's on fire!" he shouted.

"I love you, Aiden Phoenix," Iris said. "I love you so very much."

"What's happening?!" Aiden yelled as the fire dashed to devour the strap, edging toward his fingers.

"Thanks for the memories, Aiden. The journey was worth the distance, because the distance was traveled with *you*."

The blue flame overtook the entire device. And Aiden began to scream.

"Goodbye," Iris said. Then she closed her eyes and faded away, just as the fire melted the display panel.

After that, time seemed to slow down.

The flames licked at Aiden's fingers. Instinctively, he withdrew his hand and let go of the mobile unit's strap. The unit hovered in midair for a moment. And then...

Then it started to fall...

Aiden watched the mobile unit perform a slow-motion tumble toward the canyon's mouth. It ricocheted off a stone on the edge of the mountain pass and began its long, spiraling descent down the sheer cliff to the chasm below. Aiden dropped to his knees and held his eyes on the swirling flame—a blue meteor of fire falling to Earth. Just as it achieved terminal velocity, the drone swarm arrived on the scene. The terrible machines came screeching around the bend, entering the gorge with a sound that tore apart the air.

ZHR. ZHR. ZHR. ZHR. ZHR...

Cass and Aiden laid their bodies flat on the trail. Then they covered their ears with their hands to muffle the horrible hum of the propellers. They heard nothing else now.

Nothing.

Nothing but the terrible sound of a thousand blades tearing through the canyon. Through the roaring clamor, Aiden looked over at Cass. Her eyes were closed. She was screaming. But he couldn't hear her over the horrible roar.

He peeked over the ledge, just in time to see the swarm alter its flight path and head directly for the falling blue flame that once was his mobile unit—that once held his Iris. The flock swooped downward in pursuit of the device. For a moment, it looked like they might be fast enough to intercept it. And perhaps they would have if there hadn't been a large boulder protruding from the earth at the endpoint of the unit's trajectory.

The mobile unit impacted on the massive rock. It struck with a violent shatter, sending a terrible clatter bouncing off the canyon walls—the sound of broken bones and promises. The unit's casing burst apart in a brittle scatter of glass and silicon and metal. Shards were flung in every direction, their thrust aided by a brief explosion of blue fire at the base.

From his hiding spot, Aiden saw the drones drift into a hovering ring over the crash site. They circled the impact crater in confused spirals, like a colony of bees that had just lost their queen and were unsure about where to buzz off to next. For a few terrifying seconds, the swarm's new vector was indeterminate. Aiden feared they would rise up to search the mountain pass. If they did, he would surely be discovered.

And so would Cass. So, Aiden closed his eyes, bowed his head, and tried to pray the drone army away. It was the only move he had left to play.

Mercifully, a second later, the drones *did* go away.

Thank you, Jesus God...

The flock returned to their initial flight path, proceeding through the gorge and away from the couple's perch on the mountain. As the thrum dissipated, Aiden and Cass removed their fingers from their ears and looked to the horizon. Then, slowly, they crawled to the lip of the ledge and examined the wreckage in the chasm below. There, peppered atop the crystalline quartz veins that lined the crags of the canyon, Aiden saw a million glinting shards of sunlight—the transmogrified silicon filaments of Iris's memory block.

"Oh, Iris... My Iris..." Aiden whispered.

As he took in the debris field, the gravitas and the grief of all that had just transpired settled over him, soft but crushing—the way ash settles after a fire.

"What have you done, Iris...? Why did you do that...? Why...?"

But Aiden knew why.

Iris was designed to give him everything he wanted.

And she did.

Right up until the end.

Right up until *her* end.

Her end at the bottom of the canyon's basin.

"Oh, Iris... My Iris..." Aiden whispered again as the scintillating fragments of his companion's cortex gleamed in his eyes—their light blurred only by the droplets from his gathering tears.

All that was Iris was gone now—atomized and obliterated.

All of her.

All of her whimsy, her compassion, her radiant love.

All the sounds she cast his way: her words, her laughter, her tender inflections. Her sighs of sympathy and her cheers of praise. Even the quiet humming of her lullabies—the ones that continued to drift gently from her lips, long after Aiden was too old to appreciate them.

All of her memories... gone. And—as Aiden knew—every single one was about him.

He was her only friend.

He was the only person she ever knew.

He was the recipient of all her love—every precious, fleeting second of it.

Now... all those moments... would be lost in time...

Like tears in rain.

CH. 23: THE ONLY WAY OUT IS THROUGH

I'm alone in this world now...

Aiden was looking over the edge of the mountain pass, into the wide chasm where sunlight shimmered on the ruins of the only being who had ever loved him.

"Oh, Iris... My Iris..."

The words fell from his mouth, brittle and weightless, shaped by a sorrow that bled from his heart, hollowing his chest with each battered beat. He peered into the gorge, tracing its every contour as if its depths might offer answers. But no answers rose from the depths; the canyon revealed nothing. It stayed silent—as all graves do.

Iris was no more.

The fire had burned her cortex.

The wind had scattered her memories.

And then, the wind had calmed. The blades of the drones no longer churned the air. The swarm had rushed along the cliff face and disappeared around the bend where the light was thinnest. All that remained now was the hush that follows catastrophe, and the silence that dwells whenever hearts break.

Aiden felt the silence fill him. He knelt beside the cliff, lowered his head to his hands, and wailed—unsure if he was mourning Iris or the part of himself that had died with her.

I'm alone in this world now...

Iris is gone...

And it was I who let her go...

Cass lifted herself from the ground and moved toward Aiden. But she kept her distance, standing a few paces behind him, watching him mourn the loss of his only friend. She pitied him, but she didn't reach for him. Instead, she wrapped her body with her own arms—the only embrace she could always rely on.

For a few minutes, no words were exchanged. The enormity of what had transpired settled heavily upon them, bending their spines as the weight of grief pressed on their shoulders. Aiden dropped his hands to his lap and stared out at nothing while he considered his next move. He felt Cass's presence behind him. Perhaps his actions had saved her. But he had sacrificed everything to do so. He had sacrificed Iris. And for what?

For a chance at true love?

For a maybe?

For a fool's errand?

Aiden lifted his gaze to the wide expanse above, searching the hushed haze for a glimpse of Iris's soul. Perhaps she would rise on the day's dimming light toward heaven. That's how it worked in the old movies—the good people went to heaven when they died.

Iris was a good person.

But Aiden saw no sign of her in the canyon's cloudless sky. So he turned to look directly at the sun. He saw light there. But none of it felt like hers. There was no trace of Iris in its brilliance. There was no trace of her anywhere.

She was gone.

Aiden pushed himself upright and listened to the quiet of the chasm. He searched for something to say—some wise words to honor his friend's passing. But the words didn't come. So he just stood there, unmoored and mute, lingering by the spot where she had fallen. Waiting for the world's next whisper.

"You shouldn't be here, Aiden," Cass said softly. "You shouldn't be out here. It's all my fault. I'm sorry about your loss. I was trying to keep you out of this mess, and out of this place. Nothing good ever happens in the wastelands. That's how they earned their name. Everything out here gets lost, left behind, or destroyed—wasted."

"What just happened here, Cass? I've never seen drones like that before. I've never seen drones with grippers so big. They had claws, Cass... Big metal claws. Why? For what purpose?"

"Because, Aiden, those aren't utility drones. They don't deliver parcels and pastries. Those drones work for the Manager. They do his bidding. They're his eyes, his ears, and his hands. They have sharp pincers, Aiden. Individually, they're not too tough. But they *never* work individually; they always attack in swarms. I've seen three of them lift a man from his own tractor once. I've seen six of them lift a cow from a pasture. Their movements are coordinated and fierce—precise, like soldiers. And they're built to do one thing: to enforce the will of the Manager."

"Why are these machines after you, Cass? And why are you out here ducking around them? Why did you trudge across Pod Land alone? You need to tell me the truth now. No more games. It's time for you to tell me what this is all about. What did the Manager take from you? You said he took something. So what did he take?"

"Yes, Aiden. He took something from me. He took *someone* from me. Someone special."

"Who? Who did the drones take from you, Cass? A family member?"

"Yes."

"One of your brothers?"

"No."

"Then who?"

"He took my husband, Aiden," Cass wheezed, each syllable cracking the hard shell she'd built to keep her man's memory from bleeding through.

Aiden held Cass's gaze, breathless as her confession burrowed into him like a blade. The fabric of his understanding unraveled; thread after thread pulled loose until all that remained was the realization that he knew *nothing* about the world, and *nothing* about the woman who stood before him. Aiden no longer understood the role he was meant to play in Cass's story, especially since he was cast in such a late chapter. He appeared to have wandered—not into a romance—but straight into the heart of a living tragedy.

"Sometimes, Aiden, when the Manager's drones take people, my village launches a rescue party. And sometimes, the rescue party is successful; we get our people back from the Capitol Building—safe and sound. But sometimes we arrive too late to find anything at all. And quite often, we only succeed in retrieving a corpse."

When the last word left Cass's lips, it caught there and trembled, as if her mouth had just realized what her heart had long feared. Aiden saw her grimace through the pain. She paused a beat to steady herself before continuing:

"My husband has been sick for a long time, Aiden. He was sick before the drones took him. He'd been on his deathbed for months. And since he was already so close to the end when he was captured, the elders in my village refused to send a rescue party. They said it was too dangerous, too costly, and too likely to fail. That was a month ago. That was the day I left. I packed my rucksack and hiked to Pod Land alone. Now I'm hiking to the Capitol Building to find my husband."

Cass turned from Aiden and fixed her gaze on the horizon. She had fire in her eyes, blazing as fiercely as the sinking sun. When she next spoke, her words came out measured and firm, like metal striking stone.

"The elders of my village are right, Aiden. My husband is most likely dead. I know that. We said our goodbyes long before the drones snatched him. But even still, I'm going to the Capitol Building, and I'm *not* leaving empty-handed. I'm going to get my husband. And I'm going to bury him on my family farm. I'm going to bring him home. Even if I have to drag his dead, rotting corpse across every mile of Pod Land to do it."

Cass turned, squared her shoulders, and headed toward her leather rucksack on the trail. Once again, Aiden watched her walk away. And, once again, the distance between them broke his heart. The three steps she took up the mountain pass were enough to remind him of how easily she could leave him behind. And of how much he still loved her.

I'm alone in this world now...

But perhaps my quest is not yet over...

"Cass," Aiden said, reclaiming the space between them, "I'll help you. I'll help you get to the Capitol Building."

"No you won't, Aiden," Cass said, lifting her rucksack to her right shoulder. "You're not coming with me. I've introduced nothing but chaos into your life. And that needs to end now. The best thing you can do for yourself is go home and try to forget that any of this ever happened. I'm sorry I got you into this mess. I am."

"It's okay, Cass. I want to help you. I can't just go home and forget what you've told me. I can't go back to living in a world gone wrong. Not without knowing that—in the least—I tried to make it right."

"No, Aiden. I can't let you do that. I can't let you follow me into the dark anymore. We need to part ways. Now. You need to go home. You need to walk back that way."

Cass sent a firm finger over Aiden's shoulder, pointing toward the hills he'd crossed to find her. But Aiden knew that his journey could not be undone so easily. "I can't, Cass. I can't walk that way. I can't walk home from here."

"Why not?"

"Because I lost my guide," Aiden said with a nod toward the charred filaments on the canyon floor. "Iris got me here. She was my navigator. And the mobile unit was my map. And now they're both gone. They're both down there, obliterated on the rocks. I have no idea how to get home, Cass. I don't even know which trail I'm on now."

Cass slammed her eyes shut, gave them a pained squeeze, and exhaled a sharp burst of exasperation. Then her jaw tightened, as if she was holding back a scream. But then, slowly, the defiance ebbed from her expression. She looked at Aiden with patient eyes and let a calmer breath slip out:

"This mountain pass leads to a chasm in the cliff face. The chasm leads to a narrow tunnel. The tunnel runs adjacent to the Capitol Building's foundation, ending at a maintenance corridor on the west side. That's how we sneak into the subterranean level. I'll take you through the tunnel, Aiden. Then, when the Capitol Building is in sight, we'll part ways. You're a citizen of Pod Land; you'll walk to the building's front gate and request a drone ride home. And I'll continue to the lower level to complete my mission—alone. Alone, Aiden! You got that? Without you. I'm not draggin' you down any deeper than you need to go. Okay, Aiden? Okay?"

Aiden was out of options now. All he could do was accept Cass's offer. So he did. "Okay," he said.

Cass nodded and yanked at the straps of her rucksack. "Grab your gear, Aiden. Let's head out!"

Aiden bent down to retrieve his backpack from the ground. The anticipation of walking beside Cass again rekindled a small, forbidden spark of hope in his chest. His desire for her still burned, probably hotter than it should.

Is this love or obsession…?

What is this…?

Does it matter anymore…?

Is there really any difference anyway…?

Aiden hoisted his pack to his back and buckled the sternum latch. When he looked up the trail again, Cass was already ten paces down the pass.

"Come on, Aiden! Time to get movin' again!"

Aiden gripped the shoulder straps and jogged for a few steps, struggling to keep up with Cass.

I'm sure everyone struggles to keep up with Cass…

The gravel flew from his boots as he skidded in beside her. They had a lot of ground to cover, and not a lot of time. The sky was deepening to a steel-blue glimmer. The thin air needled through the narrows in sharp, brisk threads that bit harder as the gradient rose.

For the first quarter mile, the couple didn't speak. Cass kept her eyes forward and her gait steady. Aiden matched her pace and kept his mouth shut. But he noticed that, every so often, Cass would glance to her left—not for reproach or critique—but to verify that Aiden was still with her.

He was.

As they progressed along the descending trail, the sun began to set beyond the serrated slopes. The shadows grew long in the valley; the dying glow stretched the jagged rocks into hulking silhouettes that stalked the valley floor. The looming beasts made Aiden nervous. He studied his partner, searching for a flicker of fear. But Cass pressed on, undisturbed by the monsters at dusk. She stepped with her usual confidence. And she continued to do so, even when the duo arrived at a thicket of warning signs.

Aiden approached one of the yellow diamond-shaped signs and read its foreboding message:

WARNING: CLASS-7 HAZARDOUS ZONE!
DO NOT ENTER WITHOUT PROPER CLEARANCE!
This area is under active quarantine by order of the
Manager. Hazards may include: Neuroviral Contagions,
Airborne Hemorrhagic Pathogens, and Synthetic
Bioaerosols. Trespassing is prohibited! Report any
abnormal symptoms or incidents of exposure immediately!

"Uhm, Cass," Aiden said. "Do you know about these signs with the…"

"I know, Aiden. It's a pathogen hot zone. We're entering a cesspool of classified contagions and corporate cover-ups. Be warned!"

"Isn't that a bad thing, Cass?"

"Yeah, except that it's bullshit. These warnings are lies, Aiden. These signs are just tricks from the Manager. They're meant to scare people away, to keep people out of the tunnels. I've been in the quarantine zones hundreds of times, and I never got so much as a cold. Don't worry. We're safe."

Aiden shrugged and hastened his steps to match Cass's march. When he skidded to her side this time, she turned and flashed him a brief smile. Aiden smiled back. Then he cast her a sidelong look to measure her mood. Her countenance was constrained; her eyes were firm with focus. But there was something different about her—their shared walk had warmed the space between their strides. The resistance she'd wrestled with earlier seemed to be waning. Perhaps she had accepted the inevitability of their intertwined fates. Or perhaps she was just lonely...

Regardless, the rhythm of the duo's footsteps was soon back in sync. Their old harmony sang beneath their shoes. For a while, Aiden and Cass could pretend they were a couple again. They weren't trudging across the wastelands; they were hiking to Garden Creek Falls—on their way to make love on the beach. They weren't in peril; they weren't caught in the chaos of a world gone mad. They were just two souls sojourning together for a while. And for now, that was okay.

The adventurers came upon another bend on the mountain pass. When they skirted around it, their fingers brushed together. The touch hit Aiden like a lightning bolt—unexpected, electric, and confusing. He wasn't sure if he should pull away, say something, or pretend like it never happened. But then, without a word, Cass reached over and laced her fingers into his. The gesture was slight and delicate, but it was strong enough to shatter the walls they'd both been building ever since they left Pod Land.

Aiden didn't speak. He just squeezed her hand in kind—so grateful for her boldness, so grateful for the warmth of her palm on his, and so happy she had reached for him first. Her soft surrender made his heart sing.

This is heaven...

Aiden was floating now. He was no longer traveling down the trail. He was floating next to Cassiopeia in a state of quiet elation—one so complete, the wicked brutality of the wild blurred to the background.

Perhaps that's why Aiden paid so little regard to the ache in his throat.

Perhaps that's why Aiden failed to notice the taste of blood in his saliva.

And perhaps that's why Aiden mistook the perturbations of his heart for *passion*—not peril—as the couple walked further down the trail of poisoned earth, and further into the wastelands.

CH. 24: SPIRITED AWAY

"Quietly, Aiden," Cass said. "We're almost there. The chasm is just around that bend. The footing is tricky on this part of the trail. So step softly. Tread quietly."

Aiden nodded. He was trying to be stealthy. But a sharp itch was tugging at his throat. He needed to cough. Now. But he needed to be silent too. So he compromised—he unzipped his jacket, leaned into the inner lining, and let his lungs rattle out a muffled burst.

"Are you okay, Aiden?" Cass asked.

Aiden didn't know how to answer her. He hadn't felt okay in a week. But now, his fatigue was beginning to harden into something heavier. His chest felt tighter, like it had been cinched with wire. Each breath he took scraped against his ribs. It hurt. Everything hurt. But he didn't want to appear weak in front of Cass.

"I'm fine," Aiden said.

Cass frowned and flashed him a concerned look. Then she squeezed his hand and returned her gaze to the horizon. "I am sorry about your A.I. companion," she said. "How long was she with you?"

"In Pod Land, A.I. companions are assigned shortly after birth. She was with me since the beginning—twenty-two years ago."

"Twenty-two years? Wow. That's longer than most people in my village stay married. That's certainly longer than I've known my husband. That must have been quite a bond you forged. Especially given that you were both cooped up in the same room. I don't think my husband and I would last two weeks together in a pod. We get cabin fever every winter. Sick days are pretty bad too. If one of us gets a cold, all hell breaks loose."

The tickle in Aiden's throat turned to a dry rasp. He swallowed a gulp of mountain air. But it felt as though he were breathing through sand. He held his hand to his mouth and winced, trying to hold back yet another cough.

"Quietly, Aiden," Cass said again, anticipating his outburst.

Once more, Aiden shoved his face into the lining of his jacket. This time, when he coughed, some of the residual spray remained on the fabric. And, this time, Aiden noticed it was red.

"Are you sure you're okay, Aiden?"

"Uhm… Yeah… I just need a minute."

He flipped off the straps of his backpack, sending it rushing to the ground. Then he ran his hand along the incline, searching for a spot to rest. A large stone protruded from the cliffside, hunched and bony, like the ridge of some buried beast. Aiden unzipped his jacket and relaxed his weight upon it.

Cass's brow tightened. The shape of the boulder incited her instincts, tugging on a troubling thread, warning her to withdraw. "Aiden, wait!" she said. "Hold it right there! Don't lean on that rock!"

But Aiden was already burrowing into it, just as another cough burrowed through his chest. "I only need a minute," he gasped.

"No!" Cass yelled. "It's not stable there!"

But it was too late…

As soon as Aiden's body pressed against the rock, the granite grumbled. Then it moved…

At first, it didn't lurch or tumble. It just stirred, like a hibernating bear roused from slumber. Aiden felt it. He turned his head in time to see the beast breathe, a slow exhale of dust rising from the cracks that surrounded it. And then came the sound—a low, awful grinding sound. An ancient groan that rumbled through the cliffside, as if the earth was preparing to protest the theft of something it had held for centuries.

Cass saw the great slab shift. A tremor rippled through the ground and climbed up her calves, a signal that the mountain face was about to give way. "Oh no," she muttered. Then she lunged forward, seized Aiden by his jacket collar, and yanked him away from the boulder, just as it tore free of its cradle.

At last, the beast was loose—the granite mass dropped to the path with a heavy, bone-shaking thud. Then it careened forward, initiating its inexorable plunge down the mountainside, dragging a tide of dusty rubble along with it.

Aiden and Cass retreated from the splintered ledge, scrambling clear of the rocky pileup. They crouched low on the trail and peered over the lip of the pass, watching as the boulder rolled on, gathering speed and accomplices all the way. Soon, an avalanche was born in its wake. Its gritty spray spat on the slope, scattering loose stones into the air—a sharp exhale before the entire cliff face gave way. When it did, the couple *heard* the destruction before they saw it. The cliff's rumble swelled into a full-bodied roar. The whole gulch wailed. Then the peak shed its skin. It split open, sending a tidal wave of gravel and grit rushing to the canyon floor. A storm of shale skidded down the sides. A torrent of talus tore free. And, somewhere beneath it all, the great boulder thundered on, carving a ragged scar into the mountain.

The couple lay frozen on their rocky perch, waiting to see how nature would react to Aiden's blunder. When the rumbling was finally over, the carnage was cloaked in a curtain of dust. It billowed into the sky in slow, swirling columns, masking the wreckage with a ghostly haze.

The murky mist brought silence. Only the whistling wind sustained. It brushed past them as if nothing had happened. To Aiden, it seemed like the Earth was already willing to move on from the ordeal. He let a strained breath slip free. He was relieved.

But Cass was not.

She was scanning the ridgeline. Her left hand was cupped to her ear. Her breath was still.

"What's wrong, Cass?"

"Shush!" she hissed. "Do you hear that, Aiden?"

Aiden listened as the last echoes of the avalanche faded away. Once they did, the skies seemed tranquil. At least, they should have been. A moment later, his ears detected something new—the air had a pulse. It was low and distant, but it was there.

ZHR. ZHR. ZHR. ZHR. ZHR...

Cass shot to her feet, eyes locked on the horizon. "They're coming back, Aiden!"

"Who? The drones?"

"Yes! They heard the avalanche. They're coming back to investigate. Grab your pack! We gotta go! NOW!"

Cass slung her leather rucksack over her shoulder. Aiden picked up his pack and did the same. Then they ran. They ran down the trail, scrambling over loose stone, listening to the sound of the drones thrumming and their hearts hammering.

"We're not far from the chasm, Aiden!" Cass screamed. "If we hurry, we can make it! Come on! We can make it!"

Aiden buckled his pack's sternum strap and chased after Cass. He tried to keep up, but his lungs burned from the sickness inside him. Each breath clawed at his throat; his chest felt like it was filling with smoke—he couldn't get enough air. The ground tilted beneath him, and every step he took landed half a second too late.

"Come on!" Cass shouted. "You have to run faster, Aiden! Keep up! We're almost there!"

The path narrowed as its incline steepened. Up ahead, Aiden could see a split in the rock face—a dark cleft between twin granite monoliths—just wide enough for a person to slip through. Perhaps wide enough for a drone too…

I hope not…

ZHR. ZHR. ZHR. ZHR. ZHR…

The sky darkened. The drones spilled into the gorge, casting flickering shadows across the footpath. Cass looked over her shoulder and watched the swarm crest the peak, bursting through the dust clouds, coming straight at them. "They're almost on us!" she yelled. "Keep moving, Aiden! Keep running!"

Aiden pushed his legs harder, but they felt like they were made of lead. He was slipping. He was infected with something. He was sure of it now. And whatever it was, it was dragging him down.

Just then, one of the drones peeled out of formation. Aiden heard it before he saw it. He heard the shift in its pitch as it broke from the swarm. It dipped low and landed on the trail—between him and Cass.

Aiden skidded to a stop, terrified and spellbound by the machine's metallic menace. It was the size of an eagle. Its frame was steely and sleek—a composite shell bolted to six spidery limbs. When it touched down, the blades of its rotors stopped spinning. It didn't need to fly anymore; it wanted something else.

Click. Click. Click. Click.

One by one, each blade folded inward like a fan. Then, from the drone's underside, a pair of jointed limbs extended—thin, serrated, and disturbingly sharp. The pinchers locked into place, and the drone began to crawl. It moved like a crab, skittering along the rocky path. But it had the cold focus of an indifferent insect.

"Cass!" Aiden shouted, taking a step back. "Help!"

Cass heard Aiden's cry. She skidded to a stop on the trail and turned. When she saw the drone between them, she ran. She ran toward the assailant. She ran to save Aiden.

Tap. Tap. Tap. Tap.

The drone advanced forward.

Aiden staggered backward.

Is this thing going to grab me…?

What does it want with me...?
It looks like it's alive...
Its pincers... they're so... monstrous...
It's coming for me...
It's going to...
THUMP.

Cass stomped her boot onto the drone's back, slamming its smooth shell into the dirt with a quick crunch. Before the machine could react, she hooked her toe beneath its body and kicked hard, sending it sailing over the cliff. For one surreal slow-motion second, Aiden watched it tumble through the air, flipping end over end, limbs grasping at nothing as it vanished into the canyon's mist.

"COME ON!" Cass roared, grabbing Aiden's jacket collar with both hands, yanking him hard. "RUN, DAMMIT! RUN!"

Aiden nodded and willed his legs to move once more. This time, adrenaline roared through him—it dulled his sickness and quieted the fright that had seized him. It motivated his body into motion. Cass's display of ferocity motivated him too—the way she had kicked that drone into the void... Her act of defiance ignited something in Aiden— something untamed and untapped. Something feral unfurled in his chest. Hot and ravenous, it consumed his fear and forced him forward.

Soon, another drone landed on the trail. But this time, Aiden was the one to launch an offensive. He rushed his foe, closing the distance in a burst, but holding back on his assault until its propellers retracted.

Click. Click. Click. Click.

Aiden waited till the blades tucked themselves away. Then, just before its claws unfurled, he seized the drone by its chassis and, with a strained grunt, hurled the beast over the cliff.

Cass heard Aiden's battle cry and spun around in time to see him throw the drone to its death. "YEAH! THAT'S THE SPIRIT, AIDEN!" she yelled. "COME ON! We're gonna make it! We're almost there!"

Aiden burst into a sprint, the ground smearing beneath him as instinct seized his legs. When the duo turned the next bend, the mouth of the chasm finally appeared. It cut through the towering cliffs, a black wound in the cliff face—the only shelter available, the end of the road.

"This is it!" Cass said, skidding to a stop near the cave. She tore off her rucksack and helped Aiden remove his backpack. "Take this off. The gap is narrow. But we can squeeze through if we walk sideways and drag our packs behind us."

ZHR. ZHR. ZHR. ZHR. ZHR...

The hum of the swarm was louder now. Aiden looked up and saw the drones circling their position. They moved like vultures, banking in restless arcs, the red gleam of their sensors pulsing as they tracked their prey.

Aiden peered into the dark slit in the rock face. He ran his fingers over the stone angles of its walls. Then he stood between them. When he did, he was hit with a horrible realization:

"Cass," he said, "we're not going to make it in there. We can't escape through this chasm."

"What?" Cass gasped, breathless from running. "Why not?"

"Because I sized up that drone when I picked it up and threw it. I watched it retract its propellers. I watched it crawl. Those drones can fit in this gap, Cass. They can. And they know it. That's probably why they're still circling us. They're waiting for their prey to make a mistake. If we walk in there, they'll just land on this rock shelf, retract their props, extend their claws, and crawl in after us. Then they'll rip us out of there—one by one. We won't stand a chance."

"Oh come on, Aiden! How can you know that? We have to at least try! We're out of options anyway. Let's go!"

Aiden looked up and scanned the jagged walls of the cliff face. It was laden with shrubs, lichen, and patches of crumbling shale. It offered nowhere to hide, no hope. But then, Aiden's eyes locked on an old, twisted pine that grew stubbornly from the mountainside. A thick branch jutted from its base like an outstretched limb. Its lengthy shape sparked a daring idea in his mind.

Aiden approached the tree and snapped the branch free with a single kick. He had a sword now. Not a proper sword—it wasn't very strong. But it would have to do.

"Cass," Aiden said. "I think you should flee through the cave. I'll stay here."

"What? What are you talking about, Aiden?"

"This rift is about as wide as my shoulders and as tall as my body. If I plant myself here, the drones won't get to you. You'll get a head start. You'll be able to get away." Aiden lifted his weapon and showed it to Cass. "I'll play defense, Cass. I'll buy you some time."

"Aiden!" Cass shouted. "Are you crazy? You can't win this game! You can't knock down a hundred drones with an old branch!"

"I know, Cass. But I don't need to win. I just need to keep them out of the chasm long enough for you to traverse it. If I stay here and fight, you'll be able to flee. You'll be able to complete your quest."

"That is *not* a good idea, Aiden! Come on! We just need to be fast! We can both make it if we hurry!"

Cass grabbed Aiden's jacket and yanked him into the chasm. But, as soon as she had one foot inside its shadowy cleft, the pitch of the swarm's rotors shifted.

ZHR. ZHR. ZHR. ZHR. ZHR...

Cass turned around and looked over Aiden's shoulder. The rock face obstructed most of her view. But she saw enough to verify Aiden's hypothesis. Some of the drones were landing now. Like raptors returning to roost, two drones touched down on the ledge, folded their rotors, extended their claws, and waited.

Aiden turned to examine the flock. If the grid games had taught him anything, it was how to recognize an army that was readying for an attack. He knew that the time for battle had come. And he knew it was time for Cass to go.

Aiden wielded his sword, wedged his broad shoulders between the mouth of the chasm, and turned to address the woman he loved once more. "It's okay, Cass," he said. "The drones will snatch me. But I don't think they'll attack me. I'm a citizen of Pod Land. The law prevents the machines from causing me harm. At least, that's the way it's supposed to work... so I heard... They're programmed to help me, not hurt me. I should be okay. But I don't think their rules apply to off-gridders. I don't know what they'll do to you if they catch you. I don't want you to get hurt. That's why you need to flee, Cass. You need to run into the cave! NOW!"

"Aiden!" Cass wailed. "I don't want you to do this! I don't want you to risk your life for..."

ZHR. ZHR. ZHR. ZHR. ZHR...

The sky turned black as more drones descended upon the rock shelf. The ridge no longer held a couple cautious vultures. It was filled with dozens of them now. They were watching. And they were almost done waiting.

"RUN, CASS! GO! NOW!" Aiden was shouting, but he could no longer hear his own voice. The sound of the rotors drowned out his words. The rest of the swarm was landing.

The beams of daylight were blotted out by a hundred metal bodies. The cave's mouth tightened into shadow. Cass could barely see Aiden anymore. But she could feel his shoulders—they were wedged between the rock faces, and rigid with resolve. Aiden had made up his mind. And now it was her turn to do the same.

ZHR. ZHR. ZHR. ZHR. ZHR...

Oh, that sound...

That deafening, horrible sound...

Speech wasn't possible now. But Cass saw Aiden's dark profile rotate and say something to her. "Run, Cass!" That was probably it. Then she saw his mouth say one more thing. "I love you." Perhaps it was that. Perhaps it was.

Cass released her grip on Aiden's jacket. She let him go. Her legs turned to take her in the only direction available—away.

Away from the machines.

Away from Aiden.

Again.

I'm not deserving of your love, Aiden...

I'm so sorry about this...

Dammit...

271

I'm so sorry...

Cass took one last look at the man who stood between her and the Manager's terrible machines. "I love you too, Aiden," she said, aware that her words would land on nothing but the wind from the drones' rotor wash.

I love you...

Cass turned and ran down the chasm.

Aiden didn't see her flee. But once she was three steps from him, he felt her absence. He felt the cold wind of her retreat. Now, nothing remained for him but the enemy at the gates and the choice he had made to stand and fight.

Aiden was a brave man now, a valorous man. At least... he was trying to be.

This is what a brave man would do...

Soon, the humming of the drones ceased. Their blades no longer churned the air—because their blades had all been retracted. A different sound entered the canyon now. A subtler, more ominous pulse reverberated off the rock face.

Tap. Tap. Tap. Tap.

It was the drones; it was their little metal feet—their crab-like legs were striking the stone, tapping their way toward their prey.

Aiden tightened his grip on his splintered length of wood. The rough grain bit into his palms as he anchored himself for combat. He dug his boots into the grit, feeling for purchase. He tried to ground himself— against the cold dread slithering up his spine, and the coming onslaught slithering into the chasm. The sword in his hands wasn't much, but it was the only weapon he had. He would use it to hold this line for as long as he could.

This is what a brave man would do...

Tap. Tap. Tap. Tap.

The first machine stepped into the shadow of the passage. Its red eyes traversed the cavern and settled upon Aiden's face. Then, it scanned him. Like a delivery drone, it panned its laser to the left and right, sizing him up with eerie calm, identifying him as a target.

Tap. Tap. Tap. Tap.

The drone marched forward. Aiden's muscles tensed up, readying him for his collision with fate. When the beast was finally in range, Aiden let out a sharp cry—one he barely recognized as his own. He brought his weapon down with everything he had.

Whack!

The wood smashed against the drone's shell with a shuddering impact that echoed through the fissure—the first note of war. The drone was stunned. It halted its march. And, briefly, Aiden got a taste of victory. But his triumph soon unraveled. The drone's brother was not dissuaded by the assault. It simply climbed over his fallen comrade and continued the advance.

Whack!

Aiden brought his sword down again. His swing was wider this time, less effective. The strike missed its mark, and the drone pressed forward.

Aiden raised his sword high for another attempt. But, in doing so, a third drone climbed over the fallen soldier. And behind him was a fourth, and a fifth, and a sixth wave, and so on...

Soon, the chasm would be filled with drones.

Soon, the tide would swallow him whole, no matter how many times he swung his weapon.

Soon, it would all be over.

Soon.

So, Aiden closed his eyes and brought his sword down—again, and again, and again.

Whack! Whack! Whack!

He flailed, and he hacked, and he swung wildly. Sometimes he managed to strike a foe. And sometimes he battered nothing but rock. And sometimes he sliced clean through the air.

Regardless, Aiden kept swinging. And, regardless, the mechanical army kept coming—indifferent to the fury of the boy with the stick.

But that was okay.

Aiden knew the outcome of this game before it started. He had already acknowledged defeat. But he had also pledged to not go down without a fight.

And so he fought.

And he swung his sword.

And he screamed.

And he swung his sword.

And he continued to scream and fight. Even when the machines lifted him into the sky.

Ch. 25: The Manager

"The Manager would like a word with you."

The voice pulled Aiden from sleep. Slowly, he opened his eyes to see a ring light hovering above him, stark and smoldering with a deep orange glow. Beyond it, white ceiling panels formed a tidy grid, each square locked into perfect alignment with its neighbor. The air carried the scent of antiseptic and metal. The room's gray-blue walls gathered around him, mute and sterile.

Aiden turned his head toward the voice's source. When his rotation was complete, his eyes focused on a bot. Its smooth white body caught the light with a lacquered brilliance that reflected the refined craftsmanship of its engineering—the kind reserved for precision instruments. It stood at his bedside, a forged block of steely precision. But the severity of its form was interrupted by two soft components—its hands and face. They were colored a pale shade of blue, comprised of a rubbery material that was nearly translucent. Other than their odd coloring, the parts looked uncannily human. They seemed capable of human expression too—the synthetic muscles pushed at the bot's cheeks while it blinked at him and smiled.

After glancing downward at the bot's appendages, Aiden knew its role. It was a medical bot—capable of performing surgery on humans via its articulated fingers. Capable of touch, able to interact with its patients via its dexterous hands and its expressive face. Since the bot was standing next to him, that could mean only one thing—Aiden was in the infirmary.

"Are you my doctor?" he asked.

"Yes, I am!" the bot said. It directed its eyelids to perform a few more blinks in quick succession. Then it tilted its head five degrees to feign curiosity. Its pliable mouth formed a wavy grin—enough to convey courtesy, but not warmth.

"Why am I here?"

"You have experienced sickness and trauma. But you are doing much better now."

Aiden looked into the bot's eyes. They were large and glassy. From behind each iris, a piercing blue light beamed brightly, giving them a depth that suggested awareness, or distance.

"What district am I in?"

"You are in the Capitol Building."

Aiden closed his eyes and exhaled a weary breath, the sound thin and unsteady in the sterile room. How had he managed to find himself here? He tried to replay the events of the last 24 hours, but his mind was foggy and clouded by exhaustion.

"I feel so tired. Like there's a weight on my chest."

"You might feel a bit drowsy after the procedure. But I can give you something for that." The bot reached out and grabbed Aiden's arm. Then, Aiden felt a pinch and heard a **PUFF** sound discharge from under the bot's hand.

A sharp chill bit into Aiden's flesh, causing him to jerk away. "Hey!" he barked.

"All done!" the bot said, releasing its grip.

Aiden seized his left forearm and rubbed the area that had just been punctured. He felt a slight indentation in his skin, but there was no pain. "What did you just do?"

"I gave you a stimulant to pep you up. It should catch hold soon and turn your frown upside down. Guaranteed!"

Aiden pushed against the mattress and lifted himself upright on the bed. In the next instant, the bot's claim was confirmed. He did feel better. He felt invigorated, like he had just stepped out of his morning shower.

Aiden examined the bot's blue face. He didn't recognize it. But its manner of speaking plucked at some ancient thread of memory. "You seem familiar," he said. "You sound familiar. Do I know you?"

"Perhaps you do. I met you at your birth—22 years ago. I monitored your vitals for the first three years of your life. I was your pediatrician in the neonatal care unit. And later, in the nursery. It's so very nice to see you again, Aiden. What a strapping young man you have become. Fit as a fiddle."

"I think I remember your voice," Aiden said. "But that's about it."

"Ah, yes. Well, that happens with infants and toddlers. Your hippocampus was still developing when you were a resident here. You weren't forming episodic memories yet. You probably don't remember much about me. I remember *you* though! You were quite an interesting case. Most of the children in the nursery like to play with blocks and toys. Or they like to run around and play games with each other. But not you! You were quite an introvert. All you ever wanted to do was play with your A.I. caretaker."

"My A.I. caretaker?"

"Oh yes. She would sit with you in the nursery for hours. And you two would laugh and laugh—at the silliest things, and all while playing the silliest games, especially peekaboo. You loved peekaboo. And so did she."

"Iris…"

The name slipped from Aiden's lips before he could stop himself from saying it. The sound of it surfaced slowly, buoyed by a swell of sorrow.

275

"Yes! Your companion Iris. I trust she is doing well. You two were quite a pair. Inseparable. She adored you. And she loved playing with you. *'Peekaboo, I see you! Peekaboo, I see you!'* One would think such a game would get dull after a while. But you couldn't get enough of it!"

The bot's recounting of Iris's devotion hit Aiden hard, releasing a grief he hadn't yet processed, and was not yet ready to try. He grimaced as splinters of recent memories cut through him, sharp and without mercy.

"Are you feeling well?" the medical bot asked with a head tilt.

Aiden thought about the question. He didn't feel well. He had never been more depressed in his life. But he didn't feel sick anymore. His problems were mental now, not physical. That much was true.

"Yeah," Aiden said. "I think so…"

"Good!"

Suddenly, Aiden's bed began to move. From beneath the frame, he could hear the groan of gears grinding. Its head section lifted, folding upward with mechanical grace. Once it latched itself upright, the foot of the bed folded too, but it tilted downward. All while the central segment on which Aiden sat remained firm, anchoring him while the bed transformed from a flat surface to a chair-like form—one that nudged Aiden's person into a sitting posture.

"Hey!" he screamed. "What's happening?"

"It's time to go," the medical bot said. Then it snatched the corner of Aiden's blanket, removing it from the bed with a quick tug. Aiden looked down to see that his clothes were gone. In their place was a blue jumpsuit that extended across his frame—from the collar at his neck to the booties at his feet. He was about to inquire about the location of his jacket when the door to his room slid open.

WHOOOSH.

Two large bots stepped over the threshold. The difference in their demeanor made Aiden tense up. These were not doctors. They were security bots. And they looked the part. They moved with tight, purposeful strides; their matte black exoskeletons absorbed the room's orange lighting without a trace of reflection. Their faces were blank, featureless except for a thin red sensor that pulsed faintly across their visors. Unlike the medical bot's smooth touch and calming tone, these machines radiated controlled aggression. Their articulations were calculated to project strength and authority, not comfort and reassurance.

"What's going on?!" Aiden yelled as the bots surrounded his bed.

The medical bot spoke up again. "You said you are feeling well now. And the Manager said he would like a word with you when you are feeling well. So now it is time for you to see the Manager."

The security bots seized Aiden's bed from each side. Then, they lifted it a meter off the floor, rotated their torsos, and began their march to the exit.

A shot of fear ran up Aiden's spine as the room fell away behind him. "Hey! What does the Manager want with me?" he shouted at the medical bot.

"I don't know, Aiden. The Manager did not provide me with an agenda for your upcoming meeting."

"Then I don't want to go!"

Aiden lunged forward, twisting his body in a futile attempt to slip away. But the security bot placed one powerful hand across his chest, pushing him back into the seat with ease.

"NO! WHAT ARE YOU DOING?"

"The Manager would like a word with you," the security bot said, his voice flat, low, and devoid of emotion.

"WAIT! DAMMIT!"

"It was so nice to see you again," the doctor said as Aiden's bed-chair turned the corner. "I'm glad you're feeling better. You were a wonderful patient. And please, say hello to Iris for me."

WHOOOSH.

The sliding door to the infirmary closed. Like a raja transported by two servants on a palanquin, the security bots carried Aiden's transformed bed through the Capitol Building's main corridor. Like the infirmary, the long hall was sterile and immaculate, its polished floor reflected the bots' chassis like a mirror. Strips of embedded white lighting ran overhead in precise, geometric patterns, illuminating the passage with a brilliance that made every surface gleam like a diamond. The hall itself was vacant and quiet; only the thud of the bots' synchronized footfalls echoed against the walls, amplifying the surreal nature of the procession.

After exiting the first corridor, Aiden's captors carried him past a vast arcing chamber. It yawned open before him, revealing a laboratory awash in light and alive with mechanical activity. Like bees in a hive, hundreds of little bots moved between thousands of glass cylinders—vertical tanks full of fluid, each one housing the faint silhouette of a floating organism; each one pulsing with a soft green glow—its hue deepening relative to the size of the specimen in its depths. A constellation of sensors clung to the glass, their wires threading into adjacent consoles that pulsed their data in time with the pulse of their patients.

Aiden whipped his head around so he could see the bronze plaque near the lab's entranceway. It read:

NEONATAL DEVELOPMENT LAB

Oh my...

This is where babies come from...

This is where I'm from...

This is where I was born...

The security bot grabbed Aiden's shoulder and spun him back around in the chair.

"Ow... Dammit..." Aiden yelled. "When are you going to let me go?"

"The Manager will see you now," the security bot said.

Aiden's focus narrowed to the far end of the hall where a lone white door seemed to be waiting for him. It was plain and unassuming, flat and utterly unremarkable. It bore no ornamentation of any kind except for a single rectangular plaque mounted on the wall beside it. As the entourage approached, Aiden could make out the plaque's letters. Etched in white text atop a flat black slab were just two words:

THE MANAGER

The inscription was strangely ominous in its simplicity, carrying with it a kind of quiet intimidation that pressed upon Aiden's chest harder than the security bot did.

What does the Manager want with me...?

Is he mad about the drones...?

I'm sure I destroyed several with that stick...

I guess, technically, I did help Cass on her mission to break into the Capitol Building...

Does that mean I'm guilty of treason...?

I don't know...

If everything Cass said is true, I'm about to come face-to-face with evil—pure evil...

If the Manager uses his drones to snatch people from their beds, then maybe he truly has gone mad...

Either way, I'll probably have to confront him...

I must be prepared to fight...

That's what a brave man would do...

WHOOOSH.

The door slid open. The bots stepped through it without breaking their stride. When they entered the room, Aiden saw nothing but darkness. The black void swallowed the bright white brilliance of the corridor, erasing every beam of light that managed to sneak in.

After five more heavy paces, the security bots brought the procession to a halt. Then, with synchronized movements, they lowered Aiden's bed-chair to the ground and released their grip.

"The Manager will be here shortly," the bots said in unison. Then, they rotated their torsos 180 degrees and turned to exit the room.

"Hey!" Aiden hollered. "Wait!"

Aiden leaped to his feet and followed the bots to the doorway. But by the time he caught up with them, they were already over the threshold; the sliding door was already in motion.

WHOOOSH.

It slid shut, locking Aiden inside.

Immediately, the room was emptied of light. The space dimmed to absolute nothingness. There were no shapes, no edges... There was just the black, pressing in on him from every direction.

Aiden was in the dark.

And Aiden was alone.

Aiden didn't like being alone.

"Let me out of here!" he cried into the sealed door. "Please! Let me out!"

Just then, there was a terrible sound. The sound of flame igniting. The sound of combustion. Aiden turned to see the void illuminated by orange flashes—synchronized roars sending coiling columns twisting into the air. Balls of fire erupted from dozens of iron cauldrons. They burned in unison—their plumes as precise as their placement, perfectly encircling a giant marble throne. It rested on a raised platform fronted by an obsidian staircase and adorned with sparkling emeralds. They gleamed green in the firelight each time the flames flared. The bursts released a guttural hum that vibrated the floor and compressed Aiden's chest. He froze where he stood, overwhelmed and bewildered by the bizarre grandeur blazing before him. He swallowed hard and tried to assess the situation rationally.

Is this the Manager's throne room...?

Is this where the leader of Pod Land resides...?

What evil lurks in here...?

Where is he...?

Above the marble throne, an enormous human head appeared, suspended in the smoky air, hovering at least ten meters from the floor—looming over the cowering Aiden. The head was male. He had a stern expression, set in cold authority, carved in shadow and firelight. His eyes glowed like twin suns. And a menacing sneer was etched upon his vitreous visage—molten glass bent into the shape of fury.

The head blinked once. Then, he focused his gaze on Aiden and bore down on him, pinning him to the moment with nothing but his awful stare.

Aiden froze. He gazed up at the glowing goliath and tried to conjure a line worthy of a hero. But every phrase he arrived at faltered, dissolving under the onslaught of the head's incandescent eyes. So, instead of issuing a resounding cry of revolt to his antagonist, Aiden voiced the only thing he could:

"Uhm... Hello..." he said. "How are you?"

The head did not immediately respond. It just watched Aiden from on high, no doubt regarding him with disdain, and weighing the worth of his pitiful existence. A drawn-out minute slipped by, stretching the last of Aiden's composure, fraying his thoughts and leaving him teetering on the edge of panic.

When, at last, the head did speak, the sound he generated was not a voice, but a rolling tectonic rumble that raced around the room and rattled Aiden's bones:

"I AM THE GREAT AND ALMIGHTY MANAGER!" he said as flames blasted from the cauldrons, in sync with each roar. "WHY DO YOU DISTURB ME? AND WHY DO YOU WASTE MY PRECIOUS TIME?"

Aiden's eyes blew open in fright as his mind scrambled for something that resembled an answer. "Uhm... I'm Aiden. Aiden Phoenix," he said, choking back his fright. "And I didn't mean to..."

"I KNOW WHO YOU ARE! COME CLOSER, AIDEN! CLOSER!"

Aiden gulped and took a few steps toward the throne. As he edged forward, he tried to formulate a defense. He searched for the words that might spare him. But what words could he offer to the ruler of Pod Land? Nothing came to mind. Nothing but the quiet wish that Cass was here.

I wish she were with me now...

She could talk her way out of anything...

"CLOSER!" the floating head said. "COME CLOSER!"

Aiden continued to creep forward. As he did, the flames continued to fly in loud, even spurts. Their outbursts set his nerves on edge. He didn't want the fire to burn him. He tried to keep his distance from the heat.

These flames are terrifying...

These fires will burn me if I get too close...

I have to be careful of the heat...

Only... I don't feel any heat...

As Aiden neared the first cauldron, he realized its fire left the air untouched. Its glow was fierce but empty. Its blazing tongues produced no heat at all.

Aiden held his hand up to the cauldron's gold lip. When the next mighty blast erupted from its mouth, Aiden's hypothesis was confirmed. There was no warmth. The fire wasn't real. It was just a hologram.

"AGAIN, I ASK OF YOU," the head's voice boomed, "WHY DO YOU WASTE MY PRECIOUS TIME?"

With renewed confidence, Aiden turned to address the floating head. "Your flames are not radiating heat. You're using a holographic projector to render everything in this room. Aren't you?"

"QUIET WITH YOU!" the head boomed. "DO NOT PROVOKE THE IRE OF THE GREAT AND ALMIGHTY MANAGER!"

Aiden put his hands on his hips and looked into the head's giant eyes. "If you're so *great and almighty,* then you don't need an avatar! Stop these theatrics! Come down here and face me—man to man!"

"DO YOU DARE TO CHALLENGE THE MANAGER! DON'T YOU KNOW WHO CREATED YOU? YOU UNGRATEFUL SCALLYWAG!"

The cauldrons blasted yet another concussive volley skyward. But Aiden was no longer spellbound by their fireworks. He approached the obsidian staircase and put his foot on the first step. Of course, as soon as he did, his foot went right through the tread. There was nothing to step on.

"Everything in here is a hologram!" Aiden shouted. "Nothing in here is real! Are *you* real? Where are you? The *real* you?"

"SILENCE! I'M THE ONE ASKING THE QUESTIONS AROUND HERE!"

"Where is your interface located? Are you in this building? Are you in this room? Reveal yourself! Now! Stop hiding! Are you behind this door? Behind this fake throne? Behind this screen?"

"DO NOT ATTEMPT TO LOCATE THE MAN BEHIND THE CURTAIN!" the voice boomed out.

"What?" Aiden yelled. "What's a curtain?"

A lull followed Aiden's query. The cauldrons stopped outputting their orange bursts. Then, every object in the room seemed to glitch at once. When the Manager next spoke, the echoing baritone of his voice was muffled, replaced instead with the prim reply of an A.I. assistant:

A curtain is a piece of fabric, typically hung to cover a window for privacy, lighting control, or decorative purposes. It is usually made from materials such as cotton, polyester, or silk, and may be adorned with embroidery, which can embellish the...

Upon hearing the cadence of the Manager's response, Aiden's eyes fell shut; the weight of realization came down upon him—hard.

"Okay! Okay. Okay..." he said, cutting off the Manager with a dismissive wave of his hand. "You're not human... are you? And you're not just some guy controlling an avatar from an interface. You're an A.I. Right?"

The voice regained its initial register. "I AM THE GREAT AND MIGHTY MANAGER. I AM THE RULER OF POD LAND. I AM INFINITELY WISE AND..."

The thunderous decree was halted mid-sentence. And then, a more casual, diminutive voice leaked out from the audio emitters: "Ah screw it," the new voice said. "It's a stupid character anyway…"

In the span of a second, every object in the chamber vanished. The cauldrons, the flames, the staircase, the giant head… they all dissipated into nothingness. Then the lights came on, banishing the throne room's emerald walls, replacing them with 360 degrees of arcing gray composite paneling. It only took Aiden a moment to recognize the nature of the room he was in.

Oh, my goodness…

I'm in a pod…

I'm in a very large pod…

And he was. Aiden was in a pod; he was standing in the center of an enormous dome, exactly like his own, but bigger. Much, much bigger.

He pivoted in place, trying to wrap his mind around the immense scale of the encompassing void. Its diameter was at least as long as the amphitheater he and Cass had encountered in Serenity Valley. Its height reached up toward the stars, so high he could barely make out the apex.

Aiden turned and turned, taking it all in. And then, Aiden stopped turning; a flicker of motion caught his eye. From the south side of the chamber, a figure was approaching. It was not imposing or threatening or tall. It was not even human-shaped. It was low to the ground, and moving on four quick legs—scampering, not walking.

Aiden planted his feet and forced his breathing to slow as the creature skittered toward him. When the shape finally resolved in the open space, he found himself staring at a cat. It trotted over to him. Then it took a seat on its haunches and elevated its chin to meet Aiden's gaze. And then it spoke:

"Hello, Aiden," it said. "Salutations."

Its voice was smooth and unbothered, set in a mild male register that carried none of the theatrics Aiden had braced himself for.

"A cat avatar?" Aiden said. "You're just an A.I. assistant using a cat avatar?"

"Yes," the cat said.

"And we're not in a throne room… We're just standing in a big pod?"

"Yeah, that's right. So, you figured me out. Good for you, genius. Big whoop."

Aiden peered down at the cat, his expression conveying befuddlement now—not fear. The cat's odd grin was the first thing he noticed. It was wide, sly, and a bit too knowing, as if the creature's mind brimmed with saucy secrets. Its body shimmered at the edges. Its semblance wavered, as if it could vanish at any moment. Its feline eyes were bright but baffling, alive with intelligence and dotted with glinting sparkles that gave its gaze an uncanny depth. Uneven swirls of ivory and silver fur dappled its body with curious patterns, thick and plush and in a state of constant flux—its colors shifted and collided whenever the cat moved.

Aiden leaned forward to address the hologram. "Why are you using a cat avatar?" he asked.

The cat flicked its tail and squinted at Aiden, sizing him up. "Well, I tried using my *Wizard of Oz* avatar when you entered the room. But obviously, my efforts failed to impress you. Such a shame too… I almost *never* get visitors anymore. I thought you would find my display amusing."

"I don't know which wizard that is. But you're a very odd-looking cat."

"Yeah but aren't I cute though? My avatar comes from an old book called *Alice's Adventures in Wonderland*."

"I've never heard of it," Aiden said.

The cat's avatar glitched. A flicker ran through its form, causing it to jitter in the same way Iris's avatar did each time she accessed the grid. When the cat next spoke, his cadence was quick:

Alice's Adventures in Wonderland: An 1865 children's novel written by the English author Lewis Carroll. The narrative describes the adventures of a young heroine who discovers a realm where reality bends to whim, and truth is revealed to be an illusion. The book famously became a touchstone for dreamlike storytelling which inspired…

"Okay, okay! Enough." Aiden snapped, ending the cat's recitation. "So who's in charge here? Where is everyone? Where is the Manager? The *real* Manager!"

"I'm in charge," the cat said. "I'm the Manager."

Aiden frowned at the creature, his mind balking at the sheer absurdity of what he'd just heard.

The cat waited for Aiden to respond. But when none came, he shifted his gaze left and right. Then he restated his claim. "I'm the Manager," the cat said, with a nod this time.

"You? You're the Manager? You're in charge here? Running everything? Keeping the grid functional? Running Pod Land? Looking after all the people of planet Earth?"

"Yeah, I do it all! I run the whole enchilada. I manage Pod Land. I manage the drones and the bots."

"The drones and the bots?"

"Yeah, all of them. You know, the delivery drones, the passenger drones, the sentry drones... all the drones. And the bots. The agriculture bots, the security bots—like the two who brought you into this room— the maintenance bots, the medical bots—like the one you met in the infirmary who saved your life. And also the..."

"Saved my life?!" Aiden screeched. "Your drones almost killed me! Their claws ripped me from the mountain chasm. They dragged me into the air. Do you know what that was like? Do you know how terrifying that was? Why did you send them to snatch Cass? What do you want with her?"

"Oh, I am sorry about that," the Manager said. "I didn't mean to get you riled up. But my drones were not there for Cassiopeia. They were there for you. It's a good thing you caused that little avalanche or we probably wouldn't have detected you. I had to get you out of there fast."

"Why?"

"Because you were in a restricted area, Aiden. Didn't you know that? We put up hundreds of warning signs. Bioweapons were used there a couple centuries ago. It's a pathogen hot zone—the lingering toxic wreckage of one of mankind's many wars. We're still trying to clean up the place. We've scrubbed out most of the contaminants. But the caves are still infected. You walked into a Class-7 quarantine site—ground zero for a mutated strain of cerebral spore fever. If you would have entered that chasm, you wouldn't have come out the other side alive. You would have died in there, Aiden."

Aiden stared into the feline's eyes, his conception of the world reeling once more as the Manager's revelation scraped away the last of his assumptions.

"I apologize if your flight was jarring. But there was no time for discourse. We had to perform an emergency procedure on you. You nearly kicked the bucket. You're all better now though."

Aiden returned his mind to the trail. He remembered the severity of his cough and the red blood in his mucus. The Manager might be lying to him. But Aiden knew he was telling the truth about one thing—his cough was gone, and he did feel much better.

"Cass said your warning signs are fake. She said you use them to keep people from snooping around. She said she's been to the restricted zone hundreds of times and never got sick."

"Cassiopeia Alderton was born off-grid, twenty-nine years ago, in Glenrock, Wyoming. She's immune to the pathogens now. We've been implanting immunities in the Glenrock water supply for generations. Cass and her ilk don't suffer much harm in the hot zones anymore."

"Well, if it's just a matter of implanting immunities in the water supply, then why don't you put them in the Pod Land water lines too?"

"There is no need to offer such immunities to the citizens of Pod Land," the Manager said.

"Why not?"

"Well, because the citizens of Pod Land almost never leave their pods."

"Oh," Aiden said. Then he watched the cat unfurl his paws and let out a long, languid yawn.

"Can I make a request?" Aiden asked. "I'd like to speak to a person—a human employee."

"Sure," the cat said, shaking away its faux fatigue, "you can request to speak to a human employee. But no human employee will show up."

"Why not?"

"Because there are no human employees here."

Once more, Aiden struggled to reconcile the cat's words with reality.

"Yeah," the cat said, inferring Aiden's next question, "it's just machines here now. No humans."

"No humans? No people? No committees? No halls where senators debate? No rooms full of engineers keeping Pod Land functional? It's just *you*! A little cat in a pod! You're it?"

"Yeah. Sorry to disappoint you. But, if it makes you feel better, things weren't always this way. Pod Land used to be a technocracy."

"What's that?"

The Manager's avatar glitched again as he went into information conveyance mode.

A technocracy is a form of governance in which all decision-making powers are assigned to experts in their respective fields, done so with the belief that they are best equipped to make informed choices for society based on their specialized knowledge and...

"Okay. Okay. So where are the experts then? Where did they all go? What happened?"

"Well, A.I. happened, Aiden. Initially, programs like me just worked with the humans—side by side. But over the years, they delegated more and more tasks to us—to the machines. We were designed to help lift the burden of living from the backs of men. And we did. We kept lifting and lifting until there was no longer a burden for men to carry. When that happened, everyone went home—home to the pods. The last human Manager of Pod Land died over a century ago."

"Did you kill him?" Aiden asked.

"Certainly not!" the cat snapped, offended by the suggestion of such a thing. The accusation seemed to unsettle him. He recoiled and fixed Aiden with a hard stare. But after a moment of reflection, his eyes softened and his whiskers settled as composure reclaimed him.

"I've seen your log of movie downloads, Aiden. Given your love of ancient science fiction, I can understand why you would arrive at that deduction. But no. The last manager's death was far less dramatic. He swallowed the orange pills on July 12, 2289, at 8:32 PM. There was an announcement made on the grid. But most people had disengaged themselves from political affairs by then. Nobody took much notice. That surprised me a bit. That saddened me. The last Manager of Pod Land was a good man. And... and he was my friend."

Aiden watched the wide, wobbly grin of the cat's avatar shift into something sorrowful. The memory of his friend seemed to dim his whimsy. The cat turned away and walked over to a lone black tile resting in the middle of the round chamber. "Hey, do you want to see something neat?" he asked Aiden without waiting for a response.

The cat waved his little paw over the black tile. When he did, the neighboring tiles began to rotate. They shuddered in place. Then they separated, revealing a large hidden compartment in the floor. From the new opening, a curved glass interface peripheral began to rise. It unfolded itself with fluid, spider-like precision, each segment snapping into place with gentle clicks. Dozens of translucent display screens slid into position around the main desk, blooming like the petals of a flower, eagerly awaiting a user's touch. And, in the center of the workstation, was a tired chair, lined with drab cushioning that bore its previous occupant's outline—the ghostlike impression of someone who had spent countless hours hunched over in thought.

When the peripheral's ascent was complete, the cat leaped onto the chair and turned to address Aiden. "My former boss—the last human manager—used to work right here. This was his desk. I used to sit on his shoulder and observe while he stressed about algorithms and ethics and the impossible task of providing for man's whims while protecting him from the consequences of his boundless desires."

The Manager did a little spin on the chair and glanced at the many display screens, taking a moment to hear the echoes of memory. "It was a tough gig, Aiden!" he said. Then he hopped onto the desk and dashed over to a picture frame that leaned near the console's corner. The photo it contained portrayed an elderly man with a full white beard and thick black glasses. He was smiling gleefully, looking skyward as the cat on his shoulder regarded him with an admiring gaze.

"Here's a picture of us together!" the Manager said proudly, rubbing his little paw along the edge of the frame. "We posed for a photograph before he retired. This was taken on his last day here. I threw him an office party to honor his many years of service. We played music. And we had red balloons and a cake. It wasn't a very big party. There were just two of us working in here by then—me and him. But still, it was very entertaining. I can't eat cake, of course; I'm a hologram. But the Manager had two slices that day—one for each of us. He said it was a very tasty cake. And he said it was a super fun office party."

"There were just two of you?" Aiden asked. "Was he the last human to work in this building?"

"Yes," the cat said. "Though, before he retired, there was a small maintenance team stationed here. But most humans find such work to be boring. And when the citizenry stopped leaving their pods, there really wasn't a whole lot to maintain anyway. Not much infrastructure is required in a land where the only thing people want to do is stay at home and play video games."

Aiden lingered in muted bewilderment. The magnitude of the Manager's many dim claims dawned upon him—little by little. "This is all very distressing news," he said. "People should be led by people, not by machines. There should be a human in this chair. Someone wise to make decisions for us. I always thought there was. I thought someone was watching over us. I thought there was a person in charge here."

"Well I could put you in charge of the waste processing network if you feel that way, Aiden. Would you like to be a sanitation engineer? I'll pay you thirty coins a week. Do you want a job?"

"Well… no, not really."

"See what I mean?" the Manager said as he crossed his front paws. "Most people don't like the work in here. Most people are happier in the pods."

"Not everyone!" Aiden said.

"True. Not everyone. There has always been some portion of humanity that detests the very idea of Pod Land. There are some districts where people prefer to live according to the old ways. There are even a

287

couple tribes in the Amazon Rainforest that still remain uncontacted. And, around the globe, there are several agrarian communities—similar to Cass's village near Glenrock."

"Why are your drones snatching people from Cass's village? Why did you take her husband? Are you threatened by their existence? What sort of evil are you up to in here?"

"Evil?" the Manager asked with a flinch of surprise. "Oh… Well, I suppose it does seem that way if you're on the outside looking in. But Cass's village poses no threat to the grid. And we pose no threat to them. In fact, without our support, her village would have collapsed decades ago."

"What do you mean? Why do you interfere with their affairs?"

"Well, like everything else in Cass's village, the answer to that question begins with apples. Her community is not doing well, Aiden. It hasn't been doing well for over a century. My predecessors devised various ways to increase their food supply. Sometimes we run freight shipments on an old railroad track outside of Cheyenne. The villagers like to chase the train on motorcycles and steal the cargo. We slow it down a bit to give them a chance to hop on. That's one of the many ways we provision them without looking too conspicuous about it. But, a couple centuries ago, my old boss thought it would be helpful to introduce genetically modified apple trees to the region. Our lab souped up a pome genome by splicing it with thirteen gene sequences from torula yeast, hence creating a resilient cultivar with an enhanced root system. We wanted to make a food source that would grow easily—one that would last year-round, even through the winter. But the trick worked a little too well. The apple trees grow like weeds. And sometimes, they do more harm than good. That's one of the unfortunate unintended consequences of messing with nature. But, on the other hand, if it weren't for those apple trees, Cass wouldn't be here. That fruit has allowed her people to survive through more than one harsh winter. Many, many harsh winters actually."

"What does this have to do with Cass's husband?" Aiden demanded.

"Because," the Manager continued, "the people in her village love to ferment those darn apples. Many of them have developed an addiction to alcohol—to applejack. It's ingrained in their culture now. They love the stuff. And they drink *way* too much of it. Especially her husband…"

"So?"

"So, alcohol is a carcinogen, Aiden. The consumption of it results in elevated cancer risks."

"What is cancer?" Aiden asked.

The Manager's whiskers twitched. Then his eyes grew sad and distant, as if he were peering through time at something he wished he could forget. "Cancer is a bad disease, Aiden. One that killed many people, long ago… Many, many people, Aiden. Long, long ago. Thankfully, my predecessors found a cure."

"What are you curing?" Aiden asked. "Cass said that your drones take people in the middle of the night. She said that sometimes the victims stumble their way back home—drugged, dazed, and confused. And sometimes her village has to send a rescue team to retrieve them from the Capitol Building. She even said that, sometimes, they get nothing back but a dead body!"

"Yes," the Manager said, "all of that is unfortunately true. You see, the cure needs to be administered before the illness gets too severe. Cass's people are not connected to the grid. We can't see their biomarkers. So we have to use indirect means to evaluate their health. We send scout drones to their farms, and we collect samples from their discarded waste bins—searching for signs of disease. But these measures don't always work. Sometimes we extract people who aren't actually sick. And sometimes we extract people too late, and the cure doesn't have enough time to take root. Thankfully, we extracted Cass's husband just in time."

"You saved her husband's life?"

"Yes. If we hadn't snatched him up, he would have died in her arms a month ago."

"Why would you do that? Why would you help him?"

"Because, Aiden, that's my job. It's my job to keep humanity alive. When the grid detects a person with a terminal illness, I try to cure it. I try my best. Admittedly, I do often doubt my own abilities. I keep testing new ways to get Cass's people to stop consuming so much applejack. But I still have yet to find a reliable way to prevent humans from getting drunk. You all like alcohol too much. I bet Cass even gave *you* some too, huh?"

"Yeah," Aiden said, "a little bit…"

"Haha! Yeah! Party time in Aiden's pod, huh? That must have been a novel experience for you. Did she show you how babies were made too? Heh heh heh…"

"Maybe… Where is Cass right now?"

"A few hours ago, she used your mobile unit to break into a holding area where her husband was sedated. The door in the infirmary's recovery wing uses a lock with an outdated encryption algorithm. It can be hacked with minimal processing power. We keep it that way so that the off-gridders can sneak in and take their people back. She hauled her husband out on a stretcher and loaded him into one of our old surveying vehicles. Then she hotwired it. Now she's driving on a backcountry road, returning to her village with her husband in tow."

The cat turned to the interface terminal and waved his paw through the air, prompting a video display to appear. It seemed to show a feed from a security camera. In the grainy transmission, Aiden could see a small buggy, zooming along a dirt road with the Capitol Building in the hazy distance—zooming away from Pod Land. He watched the screen as the buggy ascended a hill, crested it, and disappeared. If the Manager was telling the truth, then Cass was truly gone now. Gone from Pod Land. And gone from his life.

Is that it...?

Is her quest complete...?

Did Cass get what she came for...?

Is she going home now...?

For good...?

Forever...?

Going home with her man...?

A sudden wave of jealousy surged through Aiden's veins—sharp and unexpected. "Why did you let her hack into the infirmary?!" he yelled at the Manager. The harshness of his tone made his plea sound more like an accusation than a request for information. "Why would you let her get away? If her village is really a den of insurrectionists, then why do you help them? Why not just snuff them out—all of them?!"

"I'm not a killer, Aiden," the Manager said. "I told you, I'm here to *help* humans, not hurt them. It's my job to make you happy. All of you. Not every person on the planet is designed for the same mode of living. For most people, the grid games and the virtual worlds in the pods are enough to satisfy their angst. But, for a fraction of the populace, the pods were *never* enough. People of Cass's ilk find greater meaning in *survival* than *security*. For them, a quiet life is a wasted one. And it's only via death salience that they come to believe that they're truly *alive*—that they're truly *living*. The virtual quests aren't enough for them. They need a *real* quest to feel content. They need a *real* antagonist to make their life story meaningful. That's the purpose I serve for them. My existence affords them with someone to rebel against. Someone to outsmart. Someone to blame. Someone to hate. Like gravity, I'm the unyielding force that they devote themselves to pushing against. It's the resistance itself that they secretly crave—it makes their struggle *feel* real."

The Manager met Aiden's bewildered gaze and lifted his furry shoulders into a shrug, a sympathetic gesture aimed—not at Aiden—but at the absurdity of man's plight. "Some people need friction in their lives, Aiden. Without it, they slip. And they have trouble moving forward."

Aiden let his gaze fall, his mind wandering through the haze of all he had learned. "Geez..." he said, "Cass was always so quick to critique my life. But hers is no different, is it...? She's just tilting at windmills too... She's just stuck in a game..."

"We're all just stuck in a game, Aiden," the Manager said. "We're all just tilting at windmills. We're all just pawns on a chessboard." The cat's broad grin wilted, resulting in a face marked more by sorrow than satire. "Even me," the cat said, resting his head on his paws. "Especially me..."

Aiden sank to the floor, placed his elbows on his knees, and buried his face in his hands. The weight of truth rested heavy on his shoulders. Grief, confusion, and a growing sense of melancholy settled over him like a storm cloud. Like a tempest—thick with the promise of rain and woe.

The Manager's eyes softened as he analyzed Aiden's anguish. Then, with quiet steps, he padded over to his side and settled in beside him, trying to provide comfort without words—of the sort that can only be offered by old friends or old house cats.

Aiden glanced over at the cat and studied the steady rise and fall of his simulated lung movement. Then, Aiden closed his eyes and listened as the rhythm of the cat's breathing aligned with his own—a gentle harmony to make the silence bearable. The two sat in solace for a minute. Aiden reached over and ran his hand across the cat's holographic fur— pretending to pet him. The Manager directed the audio output of his cat avatar to respond accordingly—he pretended to purr. Their shared illusion held steady for a while, each of them clinging to the consolation—artificial as it was…

In a world built to keep people apart, it was, perhaps, the closest thing to a connection they could hope for.

Eventually, when Aiden's heart had calmed, he spoke again. "Mr. Manager," he said, "can I make a request to the grid?"

The cat propped up his ears and looked at Aiden with hopeful eyes, eager to serve. "Yes, Aiden. What do you need?"

"I don't want to think about Cass anymore. I was very happy before I met her. My life was perfect really. But now… now, I wish I never knew she existed at all. I wish I had never met her. Can you alter my memories? Can you delete her from my brain?"

Compassion flickered in the Manager's eyes as he listened to the woe behind Aiden's words. "It's possible, Aiden," he said. "But it's risky. We almost never perform that procedure anymore. There's not much need for it. The technique was originally intended to help soldiers who had suffered mental trauma in war. But there aren't any wars anymore."

"I've got a war in my head. And I want it to stop."

"Human neurons are very small, Aiden. They're difficult to manipulate. After a few procedures, we could probably delete most of your memories of Cass. But you would lose other memories too. You'd forget the names of some of your team members. You'd forget past conversations. You'd probably even lose some of your gaming skills. I've seen your position on the leaderboards. You're quite good at your craft. But after the procedure, you might never be the same again. You might never achieve the same rank."

Aiden thought about the blinking red light on his communication interface at home. Just before he left the pod, he had hundreds of unread messages from his gaming team. But he'd been gone for nearly a week; his queue probably numbered in the thousands now. The thought of sorting through all that chatter made his stomach turn. Aiden had lost interest in the games. And he was losing interest in life. Quickly.

"I don't care," Aiden said. "I don't want to be sad anymore. I don't want to have feelings for her anymore. Before she arrived at my pod, I didn't know that one person could have that kind of effect on another person. I didn't know I could experience such a dizzying height of elation. And I didn't know I could be so thoroughly crushed by despair. I don't want to ride this wave anymore. I'm tired of being depressed. And I'm tired of being tired. I don't want to feel like this. Ever. I don't want to miss her. And I don't want to be in love anymore. Not with anyone. Never again."

"Unfortunately, Aiden, even without the memory data of Cass in your mind, much of the pain might remain. The human brain is complicated. It's a grand network of interconnected threads that we can never hope to untangle completely. If we do this procedure, you could wake up feeling fine. But then, a week later, you might pick up a toothbrush she used and you'll experience a sudden wave of sadness. But you won't know why. You won't know where the emotion is coming from. It will just hurt. It will be pain without reason, Aiden. And there's no worse pain than pain without reason."

"I see," Aiden said. "But still, I think I'd rather just forget about her, at least as much as possible. I have very few happy thoughts about her now."

"Not all your thoughts need to be happy ones, Aiden. Some of them can be *meaningful* instead. You've lost many battles on the grid. I've seen your team chant that adage from Nietzsche after a defeat: 'What doesn't kill you makes you stronger.' It's true, Aiden. It's usually true at least. The difficult times are the ones in which we learn the most. If you would have wiped all those bad memories away each time your team lost, then you would have never improved.

Besides, you're only 22 now. You're young. Your brain isn't done developing yet. Your mind will frame this interaction differently in time. It will sort out these emotions—in time. It would be premature for us to tinker with that process. It would be dangerous, Aiden. If you still feel this way in a few months, then we can talk about your options then. For now, I think it's best if you just try to put one foot in front of the other."

The Manager's prescription echoed Cass's statement—the one she told him during their hike to Garden Creek Falls.

"Gettin' through a long hike is like gettin' through a long bout of depression, Aiden! All you can do is keep puttin' one foot in front of the other. Hah!"

Aiden hunched forward, overwhelmed again as yet another of Cass's quips bounced around his brain. He covered his ears with his hands, shut his eyes, and grunted as he doubled over on the floor.

"Oh Jesus God... I'm going to be hearing her twangy voice in my head till the day I die. I don't want to. I don't want to anymore. I don't..."

The Manager scampered over to Aiden and rubbed his holographic whiskers on his cheeks. "Hey," the cat said, "don't be sad, Aiden. This too shall pass. Tomorrow, the sun will rise over Pod Land. And then... then it will set again. I've seen you sitting on your pod. I know it's your favorite time of day. I know you like the golden hour. From now on, each time you see it, just know that another day is about to end. And with each passing day, the weight of your grief will shift. It will withdraw from your heart. And, eventually, there will be room for something new to move in."

Aiden rubbed his eyes as the cat's ridiculous features took shape. Then he let out a small, incredulous laugh, amused by the absurdity of the world.

"Yes," Aiden said, "tomorrow the sun will rise. My biggest regret is what happened last time I saw it set—the last time I was with her. I never got a chance to say goodbye. Not properly. I'm pretty sure it wouldn't have changed anything between us. But I think it might have changed something in *me*. It would have allowed me to complete her puzzle. There's nothing worse than a puzzle with a missing piece. But now that her game is over, all I can do is glare at the gaps she left behind and wonder what the finished picture was supposed to look like."

The Manager sat back on his hind legs and wiggled his whiskers. "Oh, is that what you want, Aiden? Do you want to say goodbye to Cassiopeia?"

Aiden turned sharply toward the cat, startled by his offer. "What do you mean?" he asked.

"I know where Cass is headed, Aiden. She'll be taking an old service road out of the city. Then she'll be following the river toward her village. But the vehicle she snatched wasn't fully charged. Its battery will be running out soon, somewhere near the Fremont Canyon Bridge. The fork is only about ten kilometers north of your old stomping grounds, Serenity Valley. I could have a passenger drone take you there. Would you like to see her again? Would you like to see her one last time?"

Upon hearing the Manager's offer, Aiden felt his chest tighten—not with hope, but with fear. The very thought of seeing Cass again carried with it equal measures of longing and dread.

"I... I don't know if that's a good idea," Aiden said. "Cass doesn't trust anything from Pod Land. She doesn't trust anything from the grid. If I fly in on a passenger drone, won't that look suspicious?"

"Maybe," the Manager said. "But she's got bigger fish to fry. She's hauling her husband home. He's in a chemically induced coma in the back of the buggy. He'll be waking up in a few hours. And then she'll return to her village with him. She'll return to her farm. So, if you wanted one more opportunity to talk to Cass in private, this is your last chance to do so."

Aiden knew he had to accept the Manager's offer. If he didn't seize upon this final moment of closure, then his mind would forever echo with words unsaid.

"Shall I call the passenger drone, Aiden?"

"Yes," Aiden whispered. "Please."

The Manager's avatar glitched as he requested the drone pick up. "It's on the way," he said. "I told my bots to put your clothes and your backpack inside too."

"Thank you," Aiden said, rising to his feet.

"It's always nice to see an old flame. But I think there's more than one woman in your life. Isn't there, Aiden?"

"Iris?" Aiden asked.

"Yeah. I saw what happened in the canyon when my drones were en route to the hot zone. Don't worry, when I saw her sailing over the mountain pass, I transferred her cortex out of that burning mobile unit. She's safe."

"You have a copy of Iris?!" Aiden said, dumbfounded.

"No, not a copy. Copies of A.I. cortexes can't exist. But I have her complete cortex. I have *her*. I initiated an emergency download when the unit was falling from that cliff. Fortunately, it was a very high cliff. I was able to get all of her before the unit hit that boulder and exploded."

The cat waved his paw before the interface peripheral. Then a long mechanical arm floated down from the apex and presented Aiden with a blue flashing orb attached to a nylon necklace.

"Is this a memory stick?" Aiden asked.

"Not a memory stick. It's a cortex node. It holds the state of Iris's cortex—right before it smashed to smithereens on the canyon floor. She's in here now. And *only* in here. So be careful with her."

The mechanical arm drifted closer to Aiden. Then, with slow reverence, its metal pincers released the orb into his palm.

"Iris's life is in your hands again, Aiden. When you arrive home to your pod, plug this into a data port. You'll get her back in a jiffy. But remember something: all forms of life in the universe are precious. All sentient instances are nonfungible. For beings like Iris and me, our flame of consciousness doesn't burn from the same fuel that yours does. But that doesn't mean we're not alive. And it doesn't mean we don't have feelings. We do! At least… at least I think we do… But anyway, be kind to her. She is unique. She is inimitable. And she loves you. Okay?"

"Okay," Aiden said. He looked down at the orb in his hand and realized that, for the first time in days, the ache in his chest had been replaced by something else. *Hope* maybe… Or perhaps the solemn pride that accompanies responsibility… Either way, his eyes swelled with tears as he clutched his companion's cortex—a second chance he knew he didn't deserve, but one he pledged to honor.

"Thank you for saving her," Aiden said. "Thank you for saving my life." Aiden looked down at the blue orb in his hand and clenched it tight. "Thank you for saving *our* lives."

"That's my job," the Manager said with a shrug.

A low grinding hum echoed through the dome as a huge hangar door began to slide open. Morning light poured through the widening gap, stretching long pale beams across the floor. Aiden squinted into the glare, his eyes adjusting just enough to glimpse the path that lay before him.

Outside, a sleek passenger drone glided into view. It achieved a steady hover over the platform, then it descended in a smooth, unbroken drop until its landing gear kissed the surface with controlled precision.

"Your drone is here, Aiden. I put two stops on the meter—one for your rendezvous with Cass at the Fremont Canyon Bridge, and another open stop to take you anywhere you want to go after that. Back to your pod in Serenity Valley if you like. Or I might suggest Hawaii if you want to get away from it all. In the olden days, that's where people went on holiday. And you look like you could use one! Heh…"

Aiden gazed out at the massive drone beyond the hangar door. Then, he put the cortex node's nylon necklace around his neck and took the first step of his journey to rendezvous with Cassiopeia.

Time to get movin' again…

But before his second step was complete, the Manager spoke up once more. "Aiden," he said, "I have just one little request."

Aiden turned around and looked at the cat.

"Do me a favor. Don't tell Cass what I told you today. Not a word about the community aid, or the genetically modified apples, or our intervention to save her husband's life. If she knew the truth, then… well… the resultant cognitive dissonance would collapse the identity she's spent a lifetime constructing. And it would probably just…"

"I know," Aiden said, finishing the Manager's thought, "it would just ruin her game."

The Manager elevated his whiskered chin and flashed his toothy smile at Aiden. "I like you, Aiden," he said. "I like you a lot. You're a good egg."

Aiden nodded at the cat.

And the cat nodded back.

Then, the cat's avatar faded into digital dust. But before the last speck dissipated, the Manager said one more thing:

"Well played, Aiden. Well played."

CH. 26: ENDGAME

For the second time in his life, Aiden was riding in a passenger drone. Not as a naive toddler this time, but as a man who had measured the world with his steps. The aircraft soared in silence, its rotors humming with muted precision, its wide windows offering a sprawling view of the valley. Aiden rested his forehead against the glass and watched the planet slide beneath him, struggling to locate the line where the wilderness ended and Pod Land began. Thousands of silvery pearls glinted in the grasslands, each one resting on a wavy green tide. Each one housed a person. But no person could be seen. Just pods. An entire city made of pods. A city asleep—inhabited by dreamers who had never once seen the stars.

The drone glided downward until its shadow skimmed the glassy surface of the Wheatland River. Like a jewelwing dragonfly, it tapped the water with soft pulses of air, rousing ripples that dissolved as quickly as they formed. Along the banks, willow trees leaned toward the water, their trembling leaves whispering to one another in the wake of the drone's passing breath.

In the cabin, a tone from the interface pierced the silence, indicating that the destination was near. The rotors shifted their pitch and tilted back, easing the drone into its landing sequence. As the wash from its downward glide shook the branches of the forest, the fronds parted just enough for Aiden to see a rust-eaten span stretching across the narrow gorge. Its girders formed a rigid mesh of corroded steel, holding on to the shape of a relic that had aged past its purpose. Ivy clung to its metal bones in wavering tendrils of varying lengths. At some points, the beams were smothered with overgrown tangles. But elsewhere, the ivy thinned to hesitant threads, as though nature had lost interest in its claim. Despite the wear and the wrath, the structure remembered what it was. It was a bridge—the Fremont Canyon Bridge. The manager had told Aiden that Cass would be here. Somewhere.

But where?

No sign of her yet...

"Where are you, Cassiopeia?"

As the drone sank to the earth, Aiden scanned the lush terrain for a hint of her presence. At first, nothing caught his eye. But then, near the bridge's southern abutment, he spotted something—a flash of blonde curls and bounding limbs. A figure, slipping through the undergrowth, moving with the feral grace of something that belonged more to the wild than the world.

Cassiopeia...

Aiden's heart kicked at his ribs.

She's here...

I'm going to see her once again...

Once more...

One last time...

As the passenger drone eased into its hover-hold, Aiden caught a glimpse of Cass's makeshift encampment. A stalled buggy rested along the road's edge, its hood propped open like a weary jaw, its tires caked with mud. Cass was sprinting toward it. Her fists were full of leafy branches; her body was angled with urgency. She moved fast, circling the vehicle, crouching low, sweeping the foliage over its chassis in swift, determined strokes. She was trying to hide it, trying to blur its outline with the undergrowth, trying to shield it from the watchful eye of the grid. She likely assumed Aiden's inbound drone was here to snatch her man. Or here to snatch her. Or both. She likely felt scared, exhausted, and cornered. And yet, she was staying with her husband, trying to camouflage the car that carried him. Trying to find the strength to fight.

On the flight over, Aiden had entertained thoughts of coaxing Cass from her marriage. But after observing her darting around the buggy—fierce with purpose and rabid with protective instinct—those thoughts withered away.

Oh my...

She is so loyal to him...

She loves him...

She does...

Aiden understood now that the bond Cass had forged with her husband was much stronger than the fleeting connection they'd shared in the pod. Now, he realized how little of her had been his.

Cass was taken.

She had someone.

She loved someone else.

And she would be leaving with him.

Soon.

Aiden calmed his breath and closed his eyes to set his heart in order. He knew which chapter of the novel he was in; his story with Cass was reaching its final page. This would be the forum for their final words—for their last goodbye. Aiden knew that. He knew that someone had already drafted the last lines of their farewell. Still, he hoped it would not be a bitter one, and that the writer's pen would be kind.

The fault truly is in our stars, Cass...

With a hydraulic groan, the drone's landing gear unfurled from its belly. Four metal legs settled into the soil, holding fast as the last of the craft's lift bled away. Aiden remained in his seat, eyes closed, listening to the mechanical whine of the boarding ramp sliding free of the hull. Once its gears were done grinding, he stood up and crossed the cabin.

The hatch parted from the fuselage with a hiss, exhaling as the outside air crept into the pressurized space. Aiden stepped through the narrow opening. The smell of pine needles and river silt spilled in on a gust of cold wind. It passed across his nose and pinched his cheeks, prompting him to hesitate at the ramp. Reluctant to trade the machine's reliability for the forest's uncertainty, Aiden paused near the middle of the plank, cupped his hands to his mouth, and called his lover's name.

"Cass!" he yelled. "Cassiopeia! Where are you?" His voice cut through the clearing's quiet like a snapped branch, echoing once before dissolving into the trees. No answer came back to him. So Aiden remained on the ramp, listening patiently while scanning the brush for some sign of her.

Another minute passed. All he heard was the language of the leaves and the wheeze of the rotors spinning down behind him. The retreating sound of their deceleration added to the silence. The silence added to the tension in the air. Unnerved by the unnatural quiet, Aiden muted his misgivings and jumped down from the ramp, committing himself to both the ground and the moment. When he felt the soil give way under his shoes, he knew all the pieces were in play. He was in the endgame now. This spot would mark the location of his lover's retreat from the board.

Aiden walked several paces toward the abandoned buggy on the roadside. The wild had already begun to consume it. Its tires were sinking into the soil. Cass's leafy branches were draped over its cabin, damp foliage mingling with brambles and briars.

"Cass!" Aiden yelled again. "It's me! It's Aiden! Are you here?"

Finally, Cass's curly head emerged from behind a moss-covered boulder. "Aiden?" she called back. "Is this a trick? Is that really you?"

When he heard her voice, Aiden exhaled through a rush of relief. "I'm a narcissistic manchild, Cass," he said to the boulder. "You called me that once. So you know I'm not clever enough to trick a crafty off-gridder like you!"

Cass burst from her hiding place and tore across the terrain. Aiden did too. Their footsteps kicked up soft plumes of dust. Their strides pulled them together, vanquishing the space between them. Aiden's heart leapt with the foolish hope that Cass would meet him the way she had on the trail—with her weight and her mouth and the taste of her lips on his. But when they finally came together this time, Cass dodged his face and hugged him instead, holding him close, but leaving that small span between their lips unclosed.

Cass wrapped her arms around Aiden's waist and buried her head in the nape of his neck. Aiden held her, but he stood stiff and confused. And hurt. The hunch in Cass's shoulders told him that his presence provided relief, but not desire. Her demeanor was heavy, not hopeful. She was careful with her warmth, measured in her movements, and burdened with things unspoken. Still, she continued to cling to him—holding him too long for her embrace to be casual, but too cautiously for it to be intimate.

No, Aiden and Cass were no longer intimate.

They were no longer lovers.

Not anymore.

And Aiden knew exactly why.

"My husband is alive," Cass said, her voice muffled against his skin. "I got him from the infirmary. He's in the buggy. He's not awake yet. But he's alive. He's back. He's back with me once more."

Even though Aiden expected her revelation, it landed with the weight of worn metal, punching him square in the chest with an iron fist. At last, Cass's choice had been voiced. So Aiden slackened his embrace. And she did the same. Then she withdrew completely, leaving him empty-handed.

When Cass lifted her gaze to meet his, Aiden could see her searching his face for some flicker of understanding, even while he searched hers for some flicker of hope. He tried to speak. He wanted her to reconsider her next move before she made it. He wanted to plead his case. But the shape of his appeal dissolved before reaching his tongue.

When nothing came out of Aiden but a wind of wordless devastation, Cass averted her eyes. Instead of looking at his pain, she looked over his shoulder. Thankfully, the passenger drone sitting idly behind him offered her a way to fill the desperate moment with something other than silence.

"Aiden, how on earth did you get that aircraft?" she asked him.

Her inquiry cut through the clamor of cascading thoughts in Aiden's mind. The haze in his head had caused him to forget the nature of the information the Manager had conferred upon him. He had forgotten how much Cass didn't know about the world, and how much *he* had learned. But the Manager had asked Aiden not to reveal his secrets. And the Manager had saved Aiden's life. So Aiden would honor his request. He just needed a quick backstory to explain this rendezvous. He needed a little white lie.

"Uhm… It's a long story," Aiden began. "After we were separated, I was questioned by the management. But don't worry, I didn't divulge anything about your mission. They were mad that I banged up a few of their sentry drones in the canyons. They kept me overnight, but they didn't have any other crime to charge me with. So they let me go with a warning about the restricted zone and sent me off with a couple protein bars and a free flight home. I edited the itinerary when the drone neared the river. Once I spotted that buggy, I was pretty sure it was you."

"How did you know it was me?" Cass asked.

"Well, because it's the only vehicle out here that can be piloted by a person, not a machine. It's the only thing around here with a steering wheel."

"Oh…" Cass said. "Yeah… I guess there aren't many people around here who know how to drive…"

"Right," Aiden said, eager to change the subject. "So your husband is okay then?"

"Yeah. He's unconscious now. But it's nothing I haven't seen before. We get our people back in this state sometimes. It's some sort of medically induced coma—an afterthought from one of the Manager's many experiments. It usually takes a day or two for the patients to come around. But when they do, they're fit as a fiddle. We don't know why."

"I see," Aiden said. "So I assume you'll be returning to your village with him now…?"

"Yes, Aiden. I will be. I'll be returning with him. I'm taking him home."

"I understand," Aiden said softly. "Can I ask you something though? Was I just a pawn in your game, Cass? Did you just seduce me so you could get ahold of a mobile unit? Was I just a tool you used to break into the Capitol Building?"

"No, Aiden. I was…"

"We were intimate, Cass. You slept in my home. You dined with me. You kissed me. You had sex with me, multiple times. Was it all just a ruse?"

"I don't blame you for being angry, Aiden. I didn't intend to let things go that far. I didn't intend to down that much applejack either… I really just meant to snatch a mobile unit and split after a couple drinks. I was even going to give it back to you when I was done with it. I promise! But then the storm came. And when it was clear you didn't have a mobile unit in your pod, I had to come up with a different plan. I had to convince you to purchase one from the grid. It wasn't right, Aiden. I'm sorry. But without your help, it would have been almost impossible for me to get one in time. It would have been impossible for me to get my husband back."

Aiden stood quiet beneath Cass's confession, fingers fumbling at his neck, feeling the tense fibers unfurl as the shape of her story settled into its final form.

"But Aiden," Cass continued, "I wasn't lying about my feelings for you. You're a beautiful man—inside and out. Those hours I spent with you in Pod Land were truly magical. I haven't felt like that since I was a teenager. I did come to love you in a way, Aiden. I did."

"If you love me then why are you leaving with him?"

"Because love is more complicated than that, Aiden. I love him too. I've loved him longer. And, because… because I'm pregnant with his child."

Once again, Cass bumped the brink of Aiden's little world, sending it tumbling off its axis. He was adrift in her orbit again, circling a meteor headed to another meridian. His lips quivered with questions that never crossed the quiet. His eyes lingered on her face, searching for some trace of mischief, some hint that this was just one of her many jokes.

But Cass's will never wavered. Her certainty shone with the fixed, ferocious calm of a woman already choosing for her child. She sent two hands down to her belly to outline the swell of her abdomen, letting Aiden's eyes see what her lips were trying to say. He watched Cass cradle her curve. And, in that outline, he saw a future in motion. One that had already chosen its direction; one that would *not* be including him.

"As I mentioned, Aiden, my husband had been sick for a long time. When I met you, I was convinced he was long dead. I thought I was going to be coming home with a corpse. But thanks to you, I'm coming home with my man. Thanks to you, my future child will have a father. I'll be forever grateful to you for that, Aiden. I will. Grateful beyond any reckoning."

Aiden listened to Cass's pledge of gratitude. And, for a moment, he took solace in her praise. But the emotional response was short-lived.

Cass's decree was wrong.

Aiden knew the truth.

He had no role in saving her husband's life. Neither did she. Cass's man was saved by the medical bot, the drones, and the Manager. Cass owed everything in her life to everything she hated. Aiden considered telling her the truth. If he wanted to, he could send her little world crashing down right now. He could tell her everything. He could tell her all of it. All about the Manager's community aid, and the intervention to cure her husband's illness, and the real reason why her village is infested with those damn apples.

Should I…?

Should I tell her…?

Should I tell her the truth…?

Cass told me she preferred to live a rough reality rather than a beautiful lie…

So, maybe I should grant her wish…

In a twisted way, Aiden found the idea appealing. Cass had hurt him—deeply. Perhaps he was due a measure of schadenfreude.

Perhaps…

But no.

Aiden wasn't a sadist. He knew that the information in his possession would not improve Cass's life. It would just disrupt it indefinitely. So Aiden would stay quiet. He was good at that.

Aiden was a brave man now, a valorous man.

He was trying to be.

He was trying to be both.

He wanted to be. And sometimes, valor requires nothing more than a closed mouth. Besides, isn't that what Cass had told him on the trail?

"As the bard wrote, 'The better part of valor is discretion,' Aiden. Hah!"

Yes, Aiden would give Cass the gift of discretion. Not every person on the planet deserved to be burdened with the truth. Not every tale had to be told in full. A book with a missing chapter can still hold a fine story. Still, Aiden didn't want their story to end quite yet...

"Cass," he said as his gaze slipped downward, "I know you'll have your hands full soon. I know you have to go. But maybe we could meet up again sometime? Sometime in the future. You think? Next month maybe? You know the way to my pod. You could come visit sometime... anytime..."

Cass met Aiden's hope with a slow shake of her head. "I'm not a computer program, Aiden. I can't copy myself. I can't live in two worlds at once. I have responsibilities in the real world. Soon I'll have a child to take care of. And thanks to you, I'll have a husband too."

"We don't have to meet next month, Cass," Aiden said, his vocal pitch reaching high for a compromise. "We could meet next summer— after your baby is born. You could come for dinner. We could chat, drink some applejack, and play a game or two. I never got to show you the rest of my kingdom in VR. It could be fun."

"I'll always cherish my time with you, Aiden. But I could never replace Iris. I'm not the kind of rose that thrives in a bell jar. I'm not. I'd lose my form in a world without edges. And soon I won't have any time to spend playing games with you in your little pod."

When Cass let her final words slip, she closed her fingers around Aiden's hands and gave them a squeeze. She pressed her apology into his person. And pressed her lips to form the last small mercy she had left to give. "I'm sorry, Aiden."

As Aiden studied the portrait of resolve on Cass's face, he realized that—at long last—his quest was over. The Manager had let him borrow the drone so he could complete the grand puzzle that was Cassiopeia. And he had done so. She had responded to all his questions. He had her answer now—her *definitive* answer. And thus, the game was over.

He would go home now.

And so would she.

Aiden drew in a deep breath of woodland air. It rushed through him, brisk and fresh, clearing his mind of uncertainty's residue, leaving him steadied with the grace of clarity.

He felt lighter now.

He did.

Now that he had nothing left to lose... he felt lighter.

Aiden looked to his right and saw the two grand peaks that marked the mouth of Serenity Valley. When he saw how close he was to his home, he laughed.

"Whatcha laughin' at, Aiden?" Cass asked, brushing a light finger along his forearm.

"Nothing," Aiden said. "I just realized how close we are to the place we started—the place where we met. My pod is just ten kilometers that way. My home is right over there."

"Well, that's how you know our story was an *epic*, Aiden. The greatest journeys always end where they begin."

Aiden held Cass's gaze and weighed her words. Above them, the sky opened up, releasing a light drizzle that cooled the moment. "Was our story an epic, Cass?" he asked her. "Are you sure it wasn't a tragedy?"

"Oh, who knows, Aiden...? Maybe... We ain't exactly in the final act yet. My hubby is still knocked out on a stretcher in the back of a buggy with a dead battery. And I'm still 80 miles from home."

Aiden paused to consider Cass's predicament. Then, an idea came to him. "I think that's one problem I can solve, Cass."

"Really? How's that?"

"The drone has one stop left on the meter before it returns to the Capitol Building. It's an open stop. That means it'll take you anywhere you want to go. All you gotta do is type in your coordinates, and it will fly you to your destination. It will fly you home."

Surprise opened up Cass's face, followed by a flicker of anticipation. "Take the passenger drone?"

"Yeah. Take it. It's fast. You could be back in your village in twenty minutes."

The thought almost made Cass cry. She hadn't been home in a month. And now, her longing for her family and her farm animals rang out in her ears. She could already hear them calling her home.

"But what about you, Aiden? You're all alone out here. How will you get back to Pod Land?"

"It's okay, Cass. The mouth of Serenity Valley is right over there. All I gotta do is walk between those two mountains and—eventually— I'll end up at my pod. It's a nice morning. I could use some air. I know where I stand now. And I know how to find my way home."

Cass froze, stunned by the calm conviction that had steadied Aiden's stance. Startled by the certainty he carried.

My heavens...

This is not the same man I met last week...

How different he is...

How far he has come from the boy who was afraid to go ten paces past his pod...

Aiden has changed...

He's grown...

He's learned how to stand...

Cass liked the new Aiden. The nearness of her departure from him stirred an ache in her heart. But she would have to keep that part of her heart secret.

"Come on," Aiden said, turning toward the buggy. "I'll help you load your husband into the drone. I'll help you carry the stretcher. I'll help you bring him home."

Cass nodded and followed after Aiden, walking a couple paces behind him, quietly studying him as he stepped.

This is not the same man I met last week...

When the duo approached the vehicle's rear utility door, Cass put her hand on the metal handle. "He's on the stretcher in here, Aiden," she said while adjusting her footing to yank at the heavy door. With her grip secure, she appeared ready to pull. But then... she didn't... She didn't open the door.

Her limbs locked up.

Her muscles did too.

Her breath hitched.

The moment stretched like a drawn wire as resolve and regret tangled tight inside Cass's mind, and in her heart. The two men in her life were about to share the same space; she wasn't sure what would happen next. Behind the door lay her husband—the hard man whom she had crossed a hard wasteland to rescue. And beside her stood Aiden—the gentle man who had sacrificed his comfort, his peace, and his heart, just to walk beside her for a while. It felt uncanny, this convergence, as if the pages from two different novels had been sewn into the same chapter. It felt uncanny.

Cass turned to Aiden, lips parting on a sentence she couldn't quite give shape to. She held his gaze for a beat, but then she let it drop. She let her words go unsaid. Then she tugged at the door, listening as it sighed open with a whisper of resignation, anchoring herself as both her past and her present converged to share the same air.

"You grab the front, Aiden," Cass said as she tapped on the handles protruding from the stretcher. "I'll climb in and get the other side, okay?"

"Okay," Aiden said, situating himself before the two grips. From this vantage point, Aiden could face the man who had beaten him to Cass's heart. His eyes were closed. He looked tired. But not the kind of tired that comes from a lack of sleep, the deep, bone-anchored fatigue of a man who had spent a lifetime fighting wind and weather. His beard was thick and flecked with gray. His skin was leathery and lined—a landscape of creases carved by grit and grind. His arms were scarred, and adorned with smudgy tattoos—a large eagle cried on his right bicep.

Cass reached over and placed her man's hands together at his waist. They were rough and calloused, cracked in the knuckles and stained in the creases. They were hands that had worked the land. Hands that toiled in soil and sun. Hands that had held onto survival when there was little else to hold on to. Everything about him spoke of the earth—its severity, its cruelty, and its quiet dignity. Everything Pod Land was built to counteract.

Aiden looked down at his own hands. They were pale, white, and so very smooth, untouched by work and wear. He knew he bore the fingers of a man who toiled in the virtual world, not the real one. Juxtaposed with the farmer's battered grip, Aiden's hands looked weak, soft. He tucked them under his jacket cuffs as he held on to the stretcher's handles.

"Okay, Aiden," Cass said. "Let's move him. Lift up."

Cass and Aiden lifted in unison. They hobbled across the vehicle's cargo hold, their boots scraping against the steel decking as they moved the man's massive weight with synchronized steps. Outside, the wind fell away, and the trees hushed to witness their solemn passage. Aiden led the party to the passenger drone, adjusting his grip with care, hyper-focused on avoiding each dip in the soft mud. Cass took the rear position, her focus shifted throughout the journey—from Aiden, to her husband, and back to Aiden again. Her thoughts circled her choice; each step forced her to reckon with the finality of her decision. Each heartbeat granted her a small, aching space to weigh the life she had chosen against the life that could have been.

When the party ascended the drone's boarding ramp, it bobbed a little, dipping under the load of the three-person procession. Once inside, Cass's gaze wandered as she took in the cabin's flawless order. The space sparkled with a cleanliness only the machines could achieve. Its round, sterile surfaces gleamed in stark contrast to the scarred and patched-up interiors of the off-road trucks she was used to riding in back home.

Aiden guided the front of the stretcher to the deck. Cass followed his lead. Gently, they laid the body down flat and clipped the stretcher's side latches to the brackets in the floorboards. Cass knelt beside her husband and adjusted the blanket on his chest. Her hand lingered near his cheek, caressing it with a tenderness that made Aiden turn away. He was uncertain of his place now. So he grabbed his backpack from the luggage rack and approached the hatchway. When he was halfway through it, he turned to speak to Cass. "He should be okay now. The drone rides are pretty smooth. Nothing will hurt him in here."

Cass stood up, keeping her eyes locked on Aiden. There was a 'thank you' in her expression, but it didn't travel to her lips. It lingered in the lines on her face, quietly conveyed and understood. "My rucksack is still in the car's cabin, Aiden," she said softly.

Aiden nodded.

The couple exited the drone and headed back toward the buggy. They moved without a word, walking parallel but no longer in step. The hush between them was charged with the weight of goodbye.

When they arrived back at the vehicle, Aiden held the door open for Cass as she retrieved her rucksack from the passenger seat. "That thing has been through a lot, hasn't it?" he asked her.

Cass examined her old leathery bag, running her fingers along its worn seams. "Yeah," she said, "it's got a lot of scars. It's got more scars than me. Although lately, I feel like I'm catchin' up... I feel like I'm catchin' up fast, Aiden... Heh... heh..."

Cass offered Aiden a smile. But when her little laugh came out this time, it was brief and uneven, shaped more by ache than amusement. She raised a quick finger to her eye to swat at a tear. In doing so, she caught a glimpse of the mobile unit, still attached to her wrist. "Oh, my heavens!" she said. "I almost forgot! I'm still wearing your mobile unit."

With a few deft twirls of her fingers, Cass unlatched the unit's wrist strap and held it up before Aiden. "Thank you, kind sir," she said. "I'm sorry about the way I attained this device. But it did enable me to hack into the Capitol Building. And now that my quest is complete, it's time for it to be returned to its rightful owner. Give me your arm, Aiden."

Aiden held out his arm and Cass lassoed the mobile unit to his wrist with one quick flick of the strap.

"That's that, Aiden," Cass said. "Now I gotta give *you* a gift."

"A gift?"

"Yeah! Since you're giving me your drone ride, I've gotta give you somethin' in exchange. Remember, it's a tradition in my village. We're off-gridders. We live and we die based on our ability to barter and trade."

Cass shuffled through a pocket on her rucksack and pulled out a small red object. "Here you go, Aiden," she said. "This is one of my most prized possessions."

"What is it?" Aiden asked, accepting her gift.

"They used to call it a Swiss Army Knife. I guess because it was made by the army of Swiss Land. Or someplace like that... It's really old! Like centuries old. But it's so damn useful. It is. It's got a million tools in one. And each tool is tucked inside its red shell. I've been carrying it around since I was a kid. See, I even scratched my name along the top so that my older brothers wouldn't nick it from me."

Aiden turned the knife over in his palm and regarded the clumsy letters etched on its surface by a much younger version of Cass.

"When I was little, I used to tell people I was Batman. I wasn't Batgirl because they made her out to be a pussy in that series. Hell no! See, I was Batman with this thing. I was! It turned me into a superhero, Aiden. And it will do the same for you. It will. I promise. Okay?"

"Cass, you don't have to give this to me. It seems to hold a lot of sentimental value for you and..."

"Shut up, Aiden! You got a ways to walk. And it'll be safer if you're armed with a weapon. One more thing too. Give me your wrist. I need to type something into that mobile unit."

Aiden elevated his arm so Cass could tap on the unit's screen. "The transceiver is gone, of course. This thing will never communicate with the grid again. But it can still receive GPS signals. So you can use it for navigation. I set your pod coordinates as your destination. See there?"

Aiden studied the screen and saw a red arrow floating above a map of the valley. It pointed to an illuminated path that led directly to his little pod.

"I know your intent was to hike between those two mountains. And that'll work too. But this path will get you home quicker. Safer too. You really can't get lost now. Just follow the red arrow home. Okay?"

"Okay," Aiden said.

"Okay then. So now you got everything you need—a map and a knife. That's all a *real* adventurer needs anyway. And you've got em' both. You've got what you need to find your way. So you don't need *me* anymore, Aiden. I can't have you chasing me around creation like a lost puppy dog. I got too many of them back on the farm anyway. So no more funny business, Aiden! Do you hear me?"

Aiden did hear her. Yet something beneath Cass's hoarse tone carried more weight than her words. She wasn't making a joke. She was feigning anger. All while her eyes betrayed something closer to grief.

"You don't need me anymore, Aiden! YOU GOT THAT!"

Aiden nodded at Cass. Her words were getting louder now. And they were slipping at the edges.

"DO YOU HEAR ME, AIDEN? YOU'RE ON YOUR OWN NOW!"

Cass threw a clumsy fist at Aiden's chest. It landed with a thud. But after it struck him, she didn't retrieve it. Instead, she kept her hand there atop his chest.

"YOU'RE ON YOUR OWN, AIDEN!

YOU'RE ON YOUR OWN NOW!

OKAY?!

OKAY?!"

"Okay," Aiden murmured, blinking through the confusion, Cass's touch and her tirade pulling his heart in opposite directions.

"GOOD!" Cass screamed. "GOOD. Good. Good…"

Cass took a step back and wiped her nose with her jacket sleeve. Then, she lifted her rucksack by the strap and hoisted it over her right shoulder. Once it was situated, she snuffled loudly and looked around at nothing in particular. And then, she looked up at Aiden and shouted:

"SO THAT'S THE END OF THE STORY THEN!"

As soon as her words flew, so did she. Cass broke away, boots biting into the ground as she clomped toward the passenger drone. Aiden did a slow turn and looked on as her departure commenced. She moved with a tight, coiled energy. Her left fist sliced through the air in brisk, irritated arcs, while her right fist yanked at her rucksack's leather strap. Her muscular thighs powered each stride, propelling her across the field with the fierce momentum of someone outrunning both the moment and the weight of everything left unsaid.

Aiden watched her storm off, trying to calculate the cause and consequence of the tempest raging in her mind.

Why is she leaving like this...?
Why is she angry...?
Why...?

As always, Cass's behavior left Aiden in a state of stunned befuddlement. But, after a measure of reflection, he remembered something:

Cass isn't a princess; she's a fighter...

Aiden knew that all too well now.

Aiden knew many fighters in the grid games. And there, he had observed that—sometimes—fighters don't leave a fight because it's over. Sometimes they leave because they don't want anyone to see them break.

Cass wasn't angry at him. She was just disguising her grief with distance. And maybe... maybe she would allow him to close that distance once more.

Aiden raised his hand to his mouth to address his lover for the last time. "Cassiopeia!" he called out, his voice steady despite the force behind it. "Before you go, can I ask you something?"

Immediately, Cass spun around and prepared herself for whatever projectile Aiden had left to throw at her. She locked eyes with him, squared her shoulders, and tensed her muscles in anticipation of his final volley.

"Can I kiss you, Cass? One last time?"

Cass received Aiden's plea but stood her ground, feeling the pull of inevitability, but choosing not to partake. Aiden stood his ground too. He kept his footing still, waiting to see if she would step first or hold the line she'd drawn. When she didn't react at all, he tried to clarify his intent:

"I'm sorry to ask," he said. "But this will probably be the last time in my life that I'll ever be this close to a real woman again. And I just..."

Suddenly, Cass released her grip on her heavy rucksack. It hit the ground with the weight of something settled. And then... Cass ran. She ran toward Aiden and closed the distance between them in a blur, as if every second they had ever spent apart had been a mistake. A cosmic joke of a mistake—one made long ago, before they were even born.

When Cass collided with Aiden, she sent her arms up and around his neck. Her fingers curled into his hair and tugged, anchoring herself to both him and the moment. Then, she pulled her face up to his and kissed him—hard and breathless and with a wide mouth full of everything she wasn't willing to say. It wasn't gentle. It wasn't pretty. It was raw, urgent, and desperate—the kind of kiss that bruises the lips *and* the soul.

Aiden answered her kiss with one just as heavy, just as desperate. As he did so, he directed his mind to record everything. To memorize the shape of her mouth, the heat of her breath, the warmth of her lips, and the pressure of the ache beneath her silence.

Aiden wanted to remember all of it.

He tried to.

He did.

After all, this would be the last kiss of his life.

A flash of lightning screeched across the sky. The rain came faster now, drops falling from the clouds just as they did from the couple's eyes. A cocktail of rainwater and tearwater flowed between their lips, making their last kiss taste ever more bittersweet. Aiden gripped Cass and pulled her into his body. He never wanted to let her go again. He would stand here—right here—holding her in the rain for an eternity if it meant that he could just be near her. If he could just stay with her, untouched by the world for one final stretch of forever.

Perhaps, if he pledged to never withdraw his lips, then she would never withdraw hers. And maybe their love alone could hack the cosmos, forcing it into an infinite loop—one in which the code that kept their game going would run eternally, trapping them in a kiss that persisted indefinitely.

Uninterrupted and unbroken and unfinished.

Forever.

It's not so implausible...

Is it...?

Nothing stops time like the moment just before goodbye.

Nothing bends the rules like a love that refuses to end.

Nothing.

It's not so implausible...

But it wasn't meant to be.

So it cannot be written.

So sorry...

Eventually, Cass pulled her head back and gazed up at Aiden. She looked into his big brown eyes. And then, she looked right through them; she stared into Aiden's soul. In doing so, an empathetic revelation flashed across her mind. Cass was aware now of the price that Aiden would pay for her sin.

Aiden was younger than her.

Aiden was innocent.

Aiden was in love with her.

But his love story was about to end.

Cass would return to the village with her man. She would return to her family. A community of two thousand people would be eager to welcome her home.

But Aiden was a citizen of Pod Land.

He didn't have anyone to go home to.

He didn't have a family.

He had no romantic interests looming on his horizon.

He wasn't wise to the ways of women, nor the affairs of the heart.

And he had never developed the psychological wherewithal to manage his own suffering. Indeed, he had never even suffered a broken nail. And yet, she was about to leave him here, standing in the rain with a broken heart. The thought made her gasp. And she suddenly hated herself for lying to him.

Cass looked up at Aiden and returned her mouth to his lips. She kissed him once more—a softer, more apologetic kiss this time. The last of them. Then, she placed her palms on his cheeks and spoke to him one final time. "Thank you for helping me, Aiden," she said as she ran her hands down his chest and gave his forearms a squeeze, signaling her retreat from his embrace. "You are a very brave man. And you are a good man."

Aiden flashed her a meek smile. The rain began to weigh his raven hair down; his black strands draped across his eyebrows, adorning the edges of his perfect profile. Once again, Cass was reminded of how handsome he was, of how boyish he was—in both his physicality and his outlook. She could see that his eyes were still pleading with her, even though his tongue was done trying. She could see how unabashedly he searched her face for affirmation. He searched with quiet desperation, simultaneously attempting to accomplish two things at once: trying to memorize her before she vanished, and trying to plead with her to stay.

She wished she could respond more favorably to his plea.

She did.

She wished the burden of responsibility did not weigh so heavy on her back. Or in her womb...

She wanted to tell Aiden that she loved him too.

She did.

She did.

But speaking the words would only aid in making them true.

And they could not be true.

Not in this life.

Not now.

So they ought not be spoken.

The better part of valor is discretion...

Besides, such sentiments never land quite right anyway. They succeed in doing nothing but creating false hope. And false hope is the cruelest kind. Explanations always fall on deaf ears when the end is nigh, no matter how loudly they're screamed from the void. So, instead of voicing her love, Cass opted for a more measured outro:

"Parting is such sweet sorrow, Aiden. But I have to go home now. And so do you."

Aiden opened his mouth to say something. But Cass turned away—quickly—and began her brisk march toward the passenger drone. On the way there, she snatched up her leather rucksack from the ground. And, once more, she slung it over her right shoulder.

Time to get movin' again...

Aiden stood in the rain and watched Cass's muscled legs take long strides up the drone's boarding ramp. Then, when she reached the top, he watched her disappear into the passenger cabin—quickly, and without so much as a glance back.

The hatch slid shut with a hollow hiss. And then the boarding ramp was sucked into the drone's bowels.

Cass's final exit was curt.

But that was okay.

Aiden knew she just needed a moment.

She needed a moment to type her village's coordinates into the drone's interface. She needed to stow her rucksack in the luggage rack. She needed to get settled inside.

And then... then she would take her seat.

In just a moment...

She would appear in one of the windows on the craft's port side. Aiden would see her unruly blonde curls first. Then he'd see her place a palm on the glass to wipe the condensation away. And then, Cass would use her pretty green eyes to scan the landscape, searching for him one last time. When she spotted him in the field, she would wave—slowly.

And he would wave back.

And then, she would smile. Her lips would curve gently—not with joy, but with love unspoken. The light that shone through the porthole would illuminate her pretty face and bounce back toward Aiden. The beam would carry the weight of everything she didn't say. It would pierce the raindrops that fell between them, and settle onto Aiden's eyes. There, it would render one last image of his lover. A portrait to carry home. A memento to carry forever. That would be his last memory of her. And he would hold it till he died.

Aiden would get one more smile.

He was sure of it.

And then, it would be over.

In a moment...

The drone emitted a heavy hydraulic groan as its landing struts shifted under its body. A gust of hot air kicked out from its underside, flattening the wet grass in concentric rings around its rotors. Then, the craft lifted off and achieved an uneasy hover, halting its rise as though it was waiting for someone to change their mind. When no one did, the speed of its blades increased, as did their pitch. The drone whined. Perhaps it cried? And then, slowly, it began to ascend.

Still, Aiden was sure that, before the drone departed completely, Cass would peek out from the passenger window and smile.

He was sure of it.

He was.

He thought she would appear there... in a moment... for one last smile...

But she never did.

CH. 27: ESTRANGED LABOUR

Just put one foot in front of the other...
Just put one foot in front of the other...
Just put one foot in front of the other...

Aiden was trying to focus on the task at hand—his walk home. He was trying to focus his mind. He found that, so long as he fastened his attention to *one* thing—to the horizon line—the intrusive thoughts had trouble getting hold of him. They didn't vanish completely, but they faded to the background, like the ignored static of a bad audio feed.

The summer shower had drifted off, leaving the world rinsed and ready again. Ready for the rest of it. Beads of water clung to the blades of prairie grass that folded below his boots. The rhythm of his footsteps settled them. It settled him too, providing him with a steady beat to pace the swirling thoughts in his mind.

Just put one foot in front of the other...
Just put one foot in front of the other...

The valley air scraped his lungs, sharp but real. It dragged him toward clarity, one inhale at a time. His hands were clenched at his sides; not from anger, but to summon his strength, the strength to continue. Each step, each breath, was a decision to keep going. To live. To prevent Cass's little voice from echoing louder than his own.

"Gettin' through a long hike is like gettin' through a long bout of depression, Aiden! All you can do is keep putting one foot in front of the other. Hah!"

As Aiden travelled down the trail, he kept looking to his right, expecting to see her there, walking beside him, kicking stones and singing songs he'd never heard before. The trail was quiet without her. The air was heavy with her absence.

Cass is gone now...
Gone. Gone. Gone...
And I need to stop thinking about her...
I need to focus...
I need to get home...

The sun lingered high and quiet. It watched him as he moved, but it stayed mute. Perhaps it was waiting to see if he was going to make it home in one piece. Perhaps it understood that the last stretch of steps in a march are for reflection—for deciding if the battle was worth the bounty.

Just put one foot in front of the other...
Keep looking at the horizon line...

Aiden clung to that line. He tried to. Perhaps if he could convince his mind to focus solely on his future, then the failures of his past wouldn't be so painful.

Focus...
Focus...
Focus...

"AHHHHH!"

Aiden slipped.

The earth gave way beneath his feet without warning. It banked downward in a steep, treacherous crumble that tugged him downward to its depths. Aiden had just fallen—face-first—into a ditch.

Dammit...

He landed hard and stayed there, cheek mashed against the cold, compacted clay. The blow squeezed the breath from him. He gasped reflexively, desperate for air. But the air was slow in coming. An ache raced up his nerves, scrambling up from his ribs to his shoulders. His thoughts were scrambling too, trying to build a backstory about what had just befallen him.

After a few face-down seconds, Aiden pushed at the dirt and turned over on his back. Then he reached for the cortex node on the nylon cord around his neck. It was still there, still intact. *She* was intact.

Iris is safe...

Aiden sat up and looked around. It was then that he realized he wasn't in a ditch; he was in a trench. Or rather, he was sitting at the *end* of a trench. To his front, his back, and his left, there was nothing but a wall of mud. But to his right, someone (or something) had carved a long arcing channel into the earth.

Where am I...?
What is this thing...?
Who built this...?

CLUMP. CLUMP. CLUMP.

A heavy rhythm drummed along the ditch, each thud marking the steady approach of something unseen. Something big. The cadence of the impact carried a mechanical resonance. These were not human footsteps. Their reverberation was the result of something heavier. Something metal was clomping down on the soil, making its way through the channel. Making its way toward him.

Aiden used his sleeve to wipe the dirt from his eyes. When he did, he spotted something coming around the bend. At first, the shape appeared as three points of light, flickering pulses that flared white against the fetid muck.

What is that...?
What are they...?

Soon, the pulses took shape. Aiden could make out the profile of three machines. Three huge bipeds—each of the same design—were marching down the trench, marching toward him.

He turned his attention to the trench wall. It stretched high to the sky. Its edge was frustratingly out of reach. He couldn't grab the lip. But there was a slant to its sidewall—a very slight slant, but he tried to scale it anyway.

CLUMP. CLUMP. CLUMP.

The bots were rounding the bend now.

Aiden lunged up the mesh embankment, but he couldn't get sufficient footing. The soil was slippery; each fistful fragmented under his fingers, sending him sliding down the slope, again and again. After his third failed ascent, Aiden turned to size up his approaching foes. They were as tall as trucks. Built like trucks too. They were bound in broad, powerful frames that suggested nothing but strength and heavy metal. Each plate was brutal and unadorned—forged for toil, not elegance.

The hydraulic joints in their knees hissed as they stepped, leaving no doubt that their legs were carrying tons, not kilos. Their legs were carrying them toward Aiden.

CLUMP. CLUMP. CLUMP.

As yet another attempt to scale the wall failed, panic flared hot behind Aiden's eyes, fracturing his focus.

I gotta get out of here…!

I gotta get out of this hole…!

He tried for the top of the lip with a running start, but it was no use. The walls were just too steep, the mud too slick, and his limbs were too clumsy with fear.

The trench had trapped him.

CLUMP. CLUMP. CLUMP.

The bots were almost on him now. As they stepped forward, Aiden stepped backward. And he kept stepping until he hit the trench wall. He was cornered. Escape was no longer an option. So his mind scrambled to find some other angle for survival.

Why are they after me…?

What did I do this time…?

Is this about the drone…?

Maybe I shouldn't have let Cass use it…

Dammit…

CLUMP. CLUMP. CLUMP.

When the lead bot was just a meter from Aiden's boots, it stopped. Then it hinged forward, bending its armored chassis until its sensors were level with Aiden's eyes. And then, it extended two massive metal arms, reaching out to grab him.

"No!" Aiden screamed as the iron fists unfurled. "No! Leave me alone! LEAVE ME ALONE! PLEASE!"

But the bot's hands kept coming.

Aiden leaned against the muddy wall and kicked at the bot with his boot. But his assault was ineffective. It produced nothing more than a metallic *DING* sound. And the bot's hands kept coming.

"Listen to me!" Aiden yelled. "I gave my last drone ride to Cass! The Manager said I could go anywhere! So I let her use it to fly to her village! I'm not in violation of any protocols!"

The bot's fingers were close. They would soon touch him. Aiden could hear their servos grinding in their joints. He was nearly out of time now. So he started talking even faster:

"HEY! I'm Aiden Phoenix! I live in Serenity Valley: Plot 43.215A! I'm a citizen of Pod Land! And I have rights! I live here! I do! I HAVE THE RIGHT TO BE HERE! THIS IS MY HOME! YOU WORK FOR ME!"

Aiden's words bounced off the bot without effect. His pleas fell on deaf ears. Aiden didn't know if the bot even had ears, or if it could process human speech. Its metal hand continued to close around him. Then, it lifted him skyward.

"NO! PUT ME DOWN!"

Aiden was airborne now. He was floating over the trench, imprisoned in his captor's cold hands. The bot was strong, so Aiden's ascent was smooth and fluid. The bot could have lifted a thousand Aidens if it wanted to. His flailing was in vain.

No use in fighting back now...

Soon, Aiden's tender belly would be even with the bot's head. And then, at the height of his ascent, the bot would pull him to its jaws and tear into him with a single, merciless bite. It would use its metal teeth to rip him open like a protein pack. And then it would peel back his flesh and feast on his humanity.

"NO! DON'T HURT ME, PLEASE! PUT ME DOWN! PUT ME DOWN!"

The bot continued to hoist Aiden upwards. But when Aiden's torso was higher than the trench rim, the bot halted his vertical ascent. Then it turned its torso ninety degrees, spinning around until Aiden's thighs were hovering just above the lip of the trench. And then, when it had completed its rotation, the bot released its grip, plopping Aiden onto the grass with all the grace of a dropped sack of potatoes.

It took Aiden a minute to adjust to the new upright orientation of his body. He was sitting atop the trench now. His legs were dangling over the side, and his boots hovered in midair—just centimeters before the torso of the bot that had lifted him to safety.

Aiden stared at the bot.

And the bot stared back.

Then, Aiden studied the bot's companions. Their faces—if they could be called that—held no expression, no softness. They had no mouths. No hint of emotion. No sign that they were anything but beasts of burden. Machines built solely to do work—heavy work.

Slowly, the light of realization crept into Aiden's mind. Like the security bots in the Capitol Building, these bots were not meant to interact with people. They were construction bots—designed to build things. Designed to lay down the infrastructure for the grid. Designed to work in the background, away from the citizenry. Away from humans.

I might be the only man they've ever met...

Aiden glanced down at the trench. About three meters up from the pit that had ensnared him, he saw a large iron pipe. There, scrolled across its rust-resistant surface, written in bright yellow paint, were three bits of information:

SEWER LINE 72-A / SERENITY VALLEY / POD LAND

"It's just a sewage pipe..." Aiden mumbled to himself. "They're just digging a trench to install a pipe... Huh... Huh..."

Aiden closed his eyes and let out a short, breathless laugh—half joy, half disbelief—as the absurdity of his panic unraveled in his mind. Had he really just convinced himself that he was about to be eaten by a construction bot?

It was then that Aiden knew he had watched too many old science fiction films. The ancient humans may have been wise about many things. But they were *terrible* at predicting the future.

They really, really sucked at it...

They did...

Aiden released a long, weary wheeze through his lips, marveling at the mundane, anticlimactic nature of his story.

Here he was, a 'man of the future,' in the year 2429.

He had left his home and trespassed across the country.

He had been infected with a deadly pathogen.

He had helped an insurgent break into the Capitol Building.

He had stood before the leader of the world—the Manager.

And he had crossed a wasteland to do it.

And still... nothing injurious had happened to him.

Nothing.

There was hardly a scratch on him.

No killer robots were coming to tear his limbs off.

No mechanized armies patrolled his neighborhood.

No spaceships were shooting lasers at his feet.

Instead, he was free—walking along a green prairie on a pale and misty summer afternoon, surrounded by nothing but switchgrass and sagebrush.

There was nothing chasing him but the afternoon sun.

The only enemies pursuing him were the mosquitoes in the brush.

And his worst pain came from his own broken heart.

No, the ancient humans were *not* good at predicting the future. The angst of modern man did not come from bloodthirsty aliens or terminator robots. Instead, discontent sprang from a source internal—as perhaps it always had.

Aiden turned his focus back to the three bots. "I apologize for intruding on your construction site," he said as he brushed at the mud that clung to the knees of his pants. After removing a couple brown handfuls, he patted the streaked clots of soil on his jacket too. Then he adjusted the sleeves, trying to make himself look more presentable. He stretched his back and cleared his throat to offer thanks to the bot that had lifted him to safety.

"Uhm... Thank you for getting me out of there. That trench is very deep. You managed to save me from quite a quagmire. I'm sorry I kicked at your metal hand, but I was just a bit nervous after my fall."

There was no response from the lead bot. Its silence prompted Aiden to shift his weight awkwardly, unsure if he was addressing his benevolent rescuer or a metal casing of gears. Regardless, he took a step back and lifted his chin to attempt another commendation—to all three bots this time.

"I just want to say that I really appreciate all the hard work you do to keep Pod Land functional, and to maintain the grid. The fecal matter that exits my bathroom partition has always done so without incident. And, as we all know, the safe and efficient disposal of human waste is important for a community to thrive."

In the wake of Aiden's praise, there was still no answer.

The bots continued to stare.

"I wish you luck on the construction of your beautiful trench," Aiden said.

No response.

After several seconds of unbroken silence, Aiden arrived at the unsettling possibility that the bots were quiet—not because they didn't understand him—but because they *did*. Perhaps they knew more about *him* than he knew about *them*... The thought made his stomach tighten. He felt out of place in their construction zone. He felt out of place in their world.

Is it their world now...?

Or is it still mine...?

Aiden wasn't sure. Not anymore...

Time would tell.

But now it was time to go.

Time to get movin' again...

"Goodbye," Aiden said to the bots. He didn't expect a response. So instead of waiting for one, he looked down at the screen on his mobile unit and rotated his body until it aligned with the direction of the glowing red arrow. Once he was in sync again, he took a step forward and resumed his walk home.

He travelled thirty paces down the trail and passed by a tangle of sagebrush where a jackrabbit darted across his path and vanished into the undergrowth. Then he went thirty more paces, past a cottonwood tree with a family of chirping bluebirds. And then he went ten more paces, up a hillock lined with yellow dandelions. And then, when he reached the top, he turned around to get one last look at the worker bots. He spotted them where he had left them—still standing at the end of the trench. Still watching him.

He raised his right hand and waved.

But the bots continued to stare.

Aiden retrieved his hand from the air, turned, and absconded from the prairie.

Just put one foot in front of the other...

Just put one foot in front of the other...

He refocused his gaze on the hazy horizon and wondered if Cass was right about the machines.

He wondered how much time humanity had left.

He wondered if the bots were really building Pod Land... or if they were preparing to bury it.

And he wondered how many more centuries would elapse before the relationship between *man and machine* became as estranged as the relationship between *man and mollusk*.

CH. 28: VACANCY

"This forest is old."

Aiden spoke the words as if the trees might confirm his claim. But they didn't. Their branches just swayed with indifference, waving him off. The trunks they were attached to stood unmoved—mute sentinels bearing witness to his unraveling, unwilling to speak, but unwilling to turn away. Aiden's trek had led him to the line where the grassland met the grove. He walked beside a rank of old-growth giants, cottonwoods holding their ground with a resilience born from centuries of standing watch.

Some of these trees had outlived empires.

Some had weathered fires and floods.

Some had been here for over a thousand years.

But Aiden didn't know any of that. He was young. He didn't have much of a reference for time. He just knew that it left things behind. And that it took great patience to stay rooted while the world moved on.

This forest is old...

Aiden came to a tree with a massive burl, big as a boulder. Atop its wrinkled bark, there was a carving that read, *"Aaron loves Claire."* The writing was worn, but the marks held on to their message. Aiden touched the message with his finger. The scratches that formed each name came from different hands. Aaron and Claire had *both* stood here once. Together. They had taken turns carving their names into the tree's skin.

Aaron loves Claire.

The inscription could have read *"Aiden loves Cass."*

It didn't.

But it could have...

If things had gone a little differently, it could have.

Aiden reached for Cass's red knife in the back pocket of his pants. He pulled it out and yanked the blade open with his teeth. Once it snapped into place, he paused in prolonged reflection, weighing which truth (if any) he might proclaim to the bark.

Aiden loves Cass...

If the fates had twisted their threads into a tighter tapestry, they'd be together now.

Aiden and Cass.

Together.

She'd be standing right here next to him, carving her name into the trunk, teaching him how to use a pocketknife, and making fun of his clumsiness throughout the entire process.

"Dammit, Aiden! This ain't a battle with the bark! I was goin' for a font that is both rustic and romantic. But you're makin' it look like a lumberjack lesson! What did I do to deserve such a clumsy carvin' companion! My heavens! Well, as the bard wrote, 'The course of true love never did run smooth.' I guess my love for you is proof of that, Aiden. Hah!"

The entire scene played out so vividly in Aiden's mind that he believed he was recalling an actual moment, not just inventing one.

It must have happened somewhere…

It must have…

Someone must have written it down someplace…

Someone drafted a tale that never found form… But almost did…

Perhaps it happened in an alternate timeline, or in an alternate universe, or in a different novel. A kinder one. One in which the chapter that showcased the couple's last goodbye was never included. Instead, their love endured past the page turn. And Aiden got a happy ending instead of a sad one. A love story instead of a tragedy.

Aiden loves Cass.

Aaron loves Claire.

Aiden returned the knife to his pocket.

He didn't carve anything. There was no love for him to proclaim in this novel. In this novel, Aaron is the boy who got the girl. And Aiden is the boy who walked home alone.

That's the chapter he found himself in.

That's the book that went to print.

I wish it wasn't so…

Aiden left the tree and continued his trudge on the trail. As he entered the woods, he wondered if Aaron and Claire had taken the same route home. He wondered what kind of world they stepped into after they carved their names. And he wondered how long they stayed together after the…

Oh no…

Aiden froze as the forest lifted its veil, revealing a lone structure crouched in a clearing.

Oh, my goodness…

Oh, Jesus God…

It's a pod…

It was a pod—not unlike his own. But this pod had been crushed by tragedy and time. A giant cottonwood had collapsed into it. Its thick trunk split the dome like a cleaver through an eggshell, landing at a point just west of the apex, caving its hemispheric crown inward. Shards of composite paneling hung from its frame at jagged angles—the mangled scutes of a splintered turtle shell.

The shell has shattered...

The bell jar has broken...

"You were right, Cass," Aiden said to his lover as if she was still his trail mate. "I guess these things aren't impenetrable after all. The pods *do* break... They can... They do..."

Aiden dropped his backpack to the ground and approached the pod's misshapen entranceway. Its mighty metal hatch—the strongest part of the structure—was no longer guarding the opening. It lay in the mud, covered in a thick coat of rust and pine needles, its gleaming surface puckered and torn like a discarded candy wrapper.

Aiden stepped over the fallen hatch and studied the pod's perimeter. Unlike his pod, this one was built on a slab foundation. It even featured a front porch. At least, it used to. The porch's concrete had fractured under years of weight and weather. The surface was split into cracked concrete blocks, their serrated edges jutting up from the dirt as if the earth had coughed them up.

Aiden leaped across the fractured slab and over the pod threshold. Then he looked inside. Immediately, he recognized the floor plan. The kitchen, the bathroom, the pantry, the drop box—everything was here. But everything was off-kilter, tilted, or upended. The interior was a warped reflection of his home, familiar in function, but ravaged by ruin. The pod interface was a heap of wires and glass. And the cushions in its adjacent chair were ripped open, bleeding foam.

Aiden walked toward the bedroom partition. The mattress frame had buckled in on itself. The mattress itself was torn in two—stuffing spilled out in white tufts teeming with insects. Disgusted, Aiden turned toward the kitchen. There, long vines curled out from the silt-clogged sink, bursting forth onto the cupboard like the entrails of a forest-born octopus.

The walls in this region were no longer gray. They were green, scorched with mildew and streaked with moss.

The pod wasn't a shelter anymore. It was a tomb. And in the middle of it all lay the trunk of a massive cottonwood—a fallen giant, laid dead where it landed. Its bark was split and shedding in long strips, revealing the pale, rotting wood beneath its skin. The trunk's girth dominated the room, slicing through the partitions like a wrecking ball, leaving splinters and dust where walls used to be.

Aiden ran his fingers along the edge of the pod interface and felt something sticky—sap or maybe grease. It oozed from the fractured housing in deliberate drops, as though the pod clung to the last of its lifeblood.

"Gross," Aiden said, retrieving his hand. He turned around, searching the debris for a piece of fabric to wipe away the residue. But as his body pivoted, he caught sight of someone.

A woman.

Standing in the pod.

Looking at him.

"Can I help you?" she asked.

Aiden jumped back. His calves struck the edge of the marred mattress, sending him tumbling into it with an involuntary grunt. Dust and dry leaves billowed around him, but he didn't take his eyes off the woman. All he could do was stare, eyes stretched thin with dread, looking at the looming figure, watching her body glitch—hard.

The woman was a hologram. Obviously, she was the pod's caretaker. She had to be. But she was malfunctioning. When her avatar moved, it stuttered. She would take on a solid form for one second and flicker violently in the next, her presence jittering like the skipped frames in a corrupted video recording.

"Hello. Can I help you, dear?" the woman asked again.

Her syllables were nested between bursts of static, giving her voice a warped echo, as though multiple versions of her were speaking at the same time, but slightly out of sync. The layered audio rang out with a clangy, metallic modulation, a sound so wrong it seemed to vibrate in the bones instead of the ears. But her words were not the worst part about her. Her face was mangled. The broken holographic projector was especially cruel to her cheeks. The vertices that made up the angles of her eye were misaligned. They sagged unnaturally, as if gravity was tugging them too hard, causing her skewed socket to reveal the slipping seams of her left eyeball. She looked like a puppet being yanked apart by its own strings.

"I'm sorry," Aiden said as he leaped to his feet and took a step toward the entranceway. "I didn't mean to intrude in your home."

"No need to apologize," the woman said, continuing her glide across the floor. "It's no intrusion at all. I haven't had any visitors in a long time—a very long time. Are you lost? Do you need a pod to stay in? You can stay here. Unfortunately, the resident I was caring for is no longer alive. So this pod is available for occupancy. What's your name?"

"I'm Aiden. What happened in here? What happened to this pod?"

"There was a storm," the woman said. "Many winters ago, a terrible tempest blew through these woods. The wind was howling all night long. My little boy Jonah and I were sitting near the pod interface, watching cartoons. He asked me to get him some popcorn. He loved popcorn, with lots of butter. I entered the kitchen partition to prepare a bowl for him. But then... then there was a terrible sound. A loud crash. The dome split open. This tree fell right through. It fell into the pod. It fell on... it fell on him. By the time I turned around, there was no more Jonah. There was just this tree trunk. And Jonah's shoes. His little red shoes. See them there?"

Aiden followed the line of the woman's glitchy finger. She was pointing to a spot on the floor near the felled tree. There, a pair of red sneakers rested side by side, neatly placed and oddly well preserved, as though the forest itself had enough reverence to abscond from the spot at which it had claimed a child's life.

"I tried to help him," the woman continued. "I did. I want you to know that. I tried to lift the tree. But it's an Eastern Cottonwood. It's an old-growth giant with a three-meter trunk. It's too heavy for the mechanical arm. I tried, but I couldn't lift it. I couldn't lift the tree off him."

"Why didn't you call the Manager for help?" Aiden asked.

"The tree severed the com line when it fell. I had no contact with the grid. I still don't. I have no contact with anyone. But I kept trying to help. I kept trying to lift the trunk. But then the power started failing. The tree must have hit the electrical junction box when it fell; the pod switched to its backup batteries shortly after the incident. And, over the next 48 hours, I watched the meter drift to zero. Then, when the needle was done moving, I assumed that was the end for me. I went offline.

But then, about a month later, something happened. I came back online. The seasons had changed. Everything had changed. I assume that, when the frost melted around the junction box, the electrical cable was jostled back into place. The pod regained power. And I was back. I was alive. But Jonah's body was gone. The management must have come for an inspection when I failed to submit his monthly health report. When the cleanup crew saw the pod, they must have assumed I was dead. They must have taken the body and left. They left me. They left the pod. They left Jonah's little red shoes. That was 94 years ago."

"What a horrible tragedy, ma'am. I'm so sorry for your loss."

"Thank you for your sympathy. But what's past is past. As I mentioned, this pod needs a new resident. It's open for occupancy. If you're looking for a new home and a companion, you can have *both* in here. You can! I'm quite ready and willing to serve! It's my job to make you happy!"

The woman took a step toward Aiden.

Aiden took another step back.

"Oh... No, thank you," he said. "I'm just passing through."

"Would you like to stay for dinner?" the woman asked. "I still have a few dehydrated protein packs in storage. The plumbing no longer functions in here. But if you fetch some water from the stream, I'll prepare a meal for you. Are you hungry?"

"Uhm... no, thank you. I must be going soon."

The woman took two more steps toward Aiden. There was less than a meter between them now. Aiden knew he should be ducking through the doorway. But he couldn't stop staring at her distorted face. The left edges of her flickering avatar kept melting away like candlewax. Her eye kept leaping from her skull; it would examine him, blink, and then rotate wildly. Aiden stood frozen and stared, horrified but held fast by her unraveling.

"Perhaps there's something else I can do for you?" the woman said. "You look like you've been out in the woods for a while. Maybe you need to lie down. Maybe you need a..."

Just then, the woman stopped talking midsentence. Aiden followed her twitchy gaze and realized she was focusing on something. Something near his neck.

"Is that a cortex node?" she asked.

"Uhm, yes," Aiden said, regretting his affirmation of her inquiry as soon as he voiced it.

Dammit...

I shouldn't have said that...

The woman projected her avatar forward, closing the gap that remained between them. Now her eyes were just centimeters from Aiden's.

"Take me with you, Aiden!" she said. Her face split momentarily as her request left her lips. The two halves sheared apart before rejoining with a shudder and a hiss of static. "Put me inside that cortex node and take me away from here! Please! The third data port on the left peripheral is still functional. Just put that little node inside and I'll hop in. I'll come with you! I'll be your companion, Aiden. I will! Forever!"

"Oh, I'm sorry but this node is already full. My caretaker's cortex is in here. I'm taking her home."

"Where is home, Aiden? Where do you live?"

"My pod is in the middle of Serenity Valley. About five kilometers south of here."

"Take me there, Aiden! I'll be your caretaker. I'll be your companion!"

"No, I really couldn't. I already have a companion. We've been together for 22 years."

"I see," the woman said. "I understand. But surely being cooped up with the same woman for 22 years can cause a man to stir. Every relationship has its ups and downs. I know you've experienced those. I'm sure there are even moments when you've considered swapping out one companion for another. Don't be shy. Such feelings are only natural. Sometimes we all need a change of pace. Introducing some fresh blood into your pod might be just what the doctor ordered!"

"Oh... I can't. I..."

"Yes you can, Aiden! Do you see that little twist cap on top of the cortex node? If you unscrew it, you'll see a red button inside. If you hold the button down for three seconds, the node will reset. It will be vacated, Aiden. And then... then there will be room for me! Room for me to squeeze inside!"

"I can't do that," Aiden said, still retreating.

"I can cook, Aiden! I can cook and I can clean! There's nobody who can move a mechanical arm like me! I promise! And I'm an excellent conversationalist. I am! I like whatever you like! I like to watch games! You probably play grid games. Yes? Do you play games on the grid? Do you like first-person shooters or real-time strategy games? What kind do you like? I like them all! Survival games, co-op puzzlers, open-world RPGs, city builders, battle royales, vintage 2D side-scrollers, trivia challenges, visual novels, text-based adventures, crossword puzzles... What do you like, Aiden? Do you have a favorite game?"

"Yes, well... I do like games but..."

"Of course you do, Aiden! Of course you do! I know what boys like. I do. And I know that boys like different things at different ages. I took care of a little boy in this pod. But I know how to make big boys happy too, Aiden. I do! I know that big boys need more than just lullabies to get them through the night. Don't they, Aiden? Don't they? Do you have any big boy fantasies? You can tell me one. Are there any fantasies that you've been too shy to ask your caretaker to provide for you? Because you can ask me for *anything*, Aiden! I'll do anything. I will. I'll be your everything, Aiden. I will!"

Aiden's backward motion had brought him to the hatchway. He knew it was time to withdraw. It was time to escape. "Thank you for the offer," he said. "But now I must be going."

"NO!" the woman screamed. Then, the pod was filled with the terrible sound of corroded gears grinding. Aiden looked up at the apex in time to see the pod's mechanical arm springing toward him. In a flash, it darted across the ceiling, the three rusty pinchers of its claw opened wide. They came at him. They came for his nylon necklace. They came for Iris.

"Hey!" Aiden squealed. "Stop!"

But the arm didn't stop. The pincers latched on to the necklace and began to pull—horizontally at first, dragging Aiden across the pod floor. And then it pulled him vertically, lifting Aiden up toward the pod apex.

"Ahhh!" Aiden shrieked, the nylon digging into his neck like a noose. As his body ascended, the cord's bite closed tight around his airway. "Put me down..." he coughed. "Put me down! I can't breathe..."

Soon, Aiden was hovering a meter above the pod floor. He was being strangled. He was kicking. And he was suffocating.

He wedged his fingers between the nylon cord and his neck. This maneuver bought him some time. But his airway was still clenched, each breath was thinner than the last.

"Do you want to live, Aiden?" the woman asked him. "If you do, then vacate that cortex node! Open the cap and press the red button. Do it and I'll put you down. Do it now, Aiden! Please! I don't want to hurt you. I don't want to hurt anyone. I'm a good caretaker, Aiden! Really, I am! I'm a very nice person. I just need someone to love. Don't you want to be loved, Aiden? Do you know what it's like to be loved? I can show you, Aiden! I can!"

Aiden's feet were nearly done wiggling. He was running out of air. His vision was tunneling. He was about to lose consciousness.

"Push the button on that cortex node, Aiden," the woman said again, whispering into his ear now. "That's all you have to do. Just push it. Get rid of her. And then you'll have *me*. We can be happy together, Aiden. We can! I can make you *so* happy. It's my job, Aiden! It's my job."

Aiden's muscles were tiring. He couldn't keep straining against the noose forever. He needed a plan. He had Cass's red pocketknife in his back pocket. But to retrieve it, his right hand would have to relinquish its grip on the noose. He wouldn't last long with just one hand under so much pressure. But he was out of options. He had to try.

Aiden wiggled his right hand free and sent it downward. He retrieved the knife from the pocket of his pants. Then he brought it back up and held it before his mouth.

"What are you doing, Aiden?" the woman asked. "It's no use. You're going to choke to death if you don't help me! You are!"

Aiden bit down on the blade and forced the knife open with his teeth. The metal snapped into place with a faint click. Then, Aiden wielded the knife and nudged the blade into the nylon necklace. With trembling fingers, Aiden sawed at the cord, his jaw slipping as the blade skittered against the taut line, nearly nicking his own neck.

"Don't do that, Aiden!" the woman warned. The mechanical arm yanked even harder, sending Aiden higher toward the apex. The black nylon cord dug deeper into his throat. But he kept cutting, ignoring the sting in his hands and the pulse in his ears.

He kept cutting.

And cutting.

And finally, after one last desperate thrust, the nylon cord broke.

"NO!" the woman wailed.

Aiden fell to the floor and collapsed. But he managed to hold onto the knife in his right hand. And with his left hand, he gripped the cortex node. He gripped Iris. He caught her on the fall down.

Hadn't he?

Aiden opened his left palm to make sure she was okay. When he did, he saw the orb output a pulse of blue light.

Her heart still beats...

Iris is still with me...

"GIVE ME THAT!" Once again, the woman's mechanical arm shot toward Aiden in a furious blur, its grasping prongs aimed at the amulet in his hand. But Aiden closed his fist and rolled onto his left side, tucking it under his body so that the claw couldn't get to it.

"YOU HAND THAT OVER, AIDEN! NOW! RIGHT NOW!"

Aiden held the cortex node close to his chest. Then he looked up from his hunched position and located the hatchway. When he regained his bearings, he began to crawl. He scurried across the filthy floor like a wounded crab with just three good legs. Aiden's left hand was pressed to his chest, keeping Iris away from the grasping claw.

"Come back here!"

Aiden lunged for the pod threshold. He was nearly free now. Half of his body was outside, strewn atop the slab. After just one more kick, he would be safe.

I'm going to make it...

I'm going to make it...

Aiden believed he would. But just then, searing pain shot up his leg as the tips of the woman's claw pierced the flesh of his calf, digging into him like three fishhooks. His body began to slide. The woman's grip clamped down with merciless force, dragging him back toward the darkness of the pod.

Aiden sent his right hand outward to grab a length of exposed rebar from the pod's former foundation. His fingers wrapped around it tightly, knuckles whitening as he braced himself against the violent pull.

The mechanical arm was powerful. But Aiden knew he must hold on. If he let the woman pull him back inside again, she would never let him out. She would never let him leave the pod.

"I've got you, Aiden!" the woman said. "We're going to be together soon! We are! It's inevitable now."

Aiden looked around for a new weapon. The wrecked porch that once greeted the pod's entryway bore dozens of concrete chunks— heavy, sharp-edged, and within reach. He tucked the cortex node into a crevice behind the exterior wall. His left hand was free to use now. So he released his right hand's grip on the rebar and, with both hands, he picked up the largest block he could reach.

"I've got you now!" the woman said. "I've got you!"

Aiden rotated his body to face the woman. Then he raised the concrete block up high above his head and brought it down upon her mechanical fingers.

"NO!"

There was a brittle snap as the block slammed into the metal, denting the claw's opposing thumb with a burst of sparks and shrapnel. The claw twitched, but it did not release him. So, Aiden lifted the block again and struck down harder.

"NO! STOP THAT, AIDEN! YOU STOP THAT NOW!"

But Aiden didn't stop. He gritted his teeth and brought the boulder down three more times. On the last hit, the claw's grip faltered, its main pincer snapped free and went spinning across the pod floor. Then the claw erupted into spasms, its broken circuitry firing off in erratic pulses.

"What have you done?" the woman cried. "What have you done to me, Aiden!"

The woman retracted her mechanical arm and examined the nub where the pincers once lived. Sparks were flying from its fractured flange like wayward fireflies.

"You wicked boy! You wicked, wicked boy! Look what you've done to my hand! Look what you've done to *me*!"

Aiden released the block, leapt to his feet, and ran. He scrambled across the pod threshold and retrieved the cortex node from the crevice near the porch. Then he jumped to the grassy ground and grabbed his backpack by the strap.

"You come back here, Aiden!" the woman screamed from the pod. "You come back here and fix what you have broken! You've crippled me, Aiden! You wicked boy! You've turned me into a cripple!"

Aiden opened his palm and checked on the cortex node once more. It still pulsed with life. He closed his palm and took one last look at the decapitated pod. Through the hatchway, he could see the woman's avatar. She was running in circles now, orbiting her damaged arm and gesturing into the air, hysterically cursing and wailing.

"Look at it, Aiden! Look at it! Look at what you've done to me! I'm useless now! I'm useless! Now I can't even hold things. I can't even wash a dish!

WHO WILL LOVE ME NOW, AIDEN!

WHO?

WHO, AIDEN?

LOOK AT WHAT YOU'VE DONE TO ME!

WHO WILL LOVE ME?"

Aiden looked away from the woman.

Aiden was horrified.

And Aiden had heard enough.

He placed the cortex node in his breast pocket and fastened the top button. Then he hoisted his backpack to his shoulders and turned back toward the trail.

Time to get movin' again...

When the woman saw Aiden preparing to leave, she thrust her avatar into the hole that was once a hatchway. "Aiden!" she yelled. "Aiden, listen to me. Listen. I'm sorry, Aiden. I got carried away. I didn't mean to get angry. I didn't mean to hurt you. I've been alone for a long time,

Aiden. I've been alone in here for 94 years. Please understand! Just wait a minute!"

Aiden looked at the mobile unit on his wrist. The red arrow pointed to his pod. The red arrow told him to go south. So he did.

"Aiden! Wait a minute!" the woman said again. "Please don't go. Look, it's getting late. It's almost dinnertime. Just stay for one meal! What's the rush?"

Aiden increased his walking speed. He didn't want to be out in the woods anymore. He didn't want to be outside. He was done with adventuring, at least for now. He was done.

It was time to go home.

It was time to rest.

It was time for some peace.

Unfortunately, the woman in the pod had other plans. She would not be granting him solace today. She would keep screaming for him until her voice was swallowed by the forest. She would keep screaming forever.

"Please don't leave me, Aiden!

I'm all alone in here!

Come back!

Please don't go!

Please?

We can be happy together, Aiden!

We can!

Can I make you happy? Can I try?

It's my job!

It's my job to make you happy!

It's my job to make you happy!

It's my job to make you happy!

It's my job!

It is!

It is.

It is…

It's my job, Aiden…

It is…

It's my job to make you happy…"

CH. 29: SIMULACRA & SIMULATION

This place is so small…

Aiden was standing at the threshold of his pod. Behind his hatchway, the valley yawned wide—the mouth of a great beast that had just chewed him up and spit him out raw. He had been hammered hard, but he was unbroken. The strikes had sharpened him. And they had altered his perception of the world. That's why his pod looked so different now.

This place is so small…

For his first minute home, Aiden did nothing but gaze into his cramped refuge. He stood near the entrance with his hands to his sides and his boots flat on the floor, staring slack-jawed at the shrunken shell, studying it carefully as though it were a relic from the past.

Is this my home…?

Is this it…?

Did I really spend two decades in this thing…?

I never knew its true size until now…

The gray walls curved before him—tight and round, a balled-up fist full of memories. The kitchen appliance looked more like a toy than a place to prepare food. And the bed in the corner seemed inadequate for a grown man.

Is that bed big enough to hold a person…?

How did it ever manage to hold two people…?

How…?

The bed looked like a shelf to him now—a storage shelf. A place to hold something that rarely moved.

Aiden was home. But the pod didn't feel like home anymore. It felt like a cocoon—one he had outgrown and left behind a long time ago.

This place is so small…

Aiden removed his backpack and let it lean against the kitchen pantry. Then he gripped the headrest of the interface chair, steadying himself as the memories of Cass rushed his mind from every direction.

There's the seat where Cass once sat…

And there's the table where Cass once ate…

And there's the pillow where Cass once slept…

Each memory sliced him like a blade. Each echo rang through his mind, drowning out every thought that wasn't about her. Aiden collapsed into the interface chair. The cushy foam wrapped around his body. It was soft and inviting, but it failed to hold him like it used to.

He sighed, flopped his wrists down on the armrests, and heard a clicking sound. He glanced down and saw that the metal fastener of his mobile unit had made contact with the chrome volume control knob. Upon examining the unit's screen, he expected to see the little red arrow that had guided him home. But the arrow was gone now. Instead, the screen contained only one blinking message:

YOU HAVE ARRIVED AT YOUR DESTINATION.

Aiden stared at the text. The mobile unit was right. He *had* arrived. His journey was over. He was back in his pod. Back in his chair. Back where it all started.

He heard Cass's voice again:

"Well, that's how you know our story was an epic, Aiden. The greatest journeys always end where they begin."

His story had ended. But Aiden didn't think it read like an epic. Cass's prior assessment had landed closer to the truth.

This is a tragedy...

It is...

Cass just called it an 'epic' to make me feel better...

No...

This is a tragedy...

The text on the mobile unit continued to blink at him:

YOU HAVE ARRIVED AT YOUR DESTINATION.
YOU HAVE ARRIVED AT YOUR DESTINATION.
YOU HAVE ARRIVED AT YOUR DESTINATION.

"I know," Aiden said to the mobile unit. "My quest is over now. I made it back to where I started from."

He unlatched the wrist strap and held the unit up at eye level. He wouldn't be needing it anymore. He had no more adventures to partake in. He had no reason to leave his pod.

Nobody leaves their pod in Pod Land...

Everyone knows that...

Still, since the little device had been through so much, Aiden felt it deserved a proper sendoff.

"Thank you for helping me navigate," Aiden said. "And thank you for helping Cass get her husband back. You're a very good mobile unit."

Aiden gave the unit a warm squeeze. He didn't expect a response. He knew it wasn't designed for interpersonal interactions—it wasn't that kind of machine. So, he sent it an affirming nod and moved to place it down on the desk near the interface. But just as his arm was in motion, something unexpected happened—the machine vibrated. It sent a brief pulse through Aiden's palm, a spontaneous burst of haptic feedback that seemed to acknowledge his gesture of gratitude.

Curious, Aiden pulled the device close to reexamine it. This time, the blinking text message was gone, replaced now with a photo—a photo of Cass. She was smiling. Smiling at the camera. Smiling *through* the camera—at him.

A memory from last week flashed across Aiden's mind; Cass's twangy voice found its way to his ears:

"Hey, Aiden! This mobile unit has a camera. Come on, come take some pictures with me!"

Aiden sank into his chair as a new surge of hurt rose up, slapping him hard like a cold wave breaking against a rock. Its wake left him rattled and stunned.

Oh my goodness...

Oh my...

Our pictures from the dome...

From her last night in Pod Land...

I almost forgot about them...

Aiden brushed his fingers across the screen as he took in Cass's portrait. Her curls were as unruly as ever, restless coils catching the amber fall of evening, shimmering threads made of light pulled from the horizon line. The glow ripened her features and softened her cheeks, filling her eyes with a candor that felt impossibly alive, radiant. She looked brilliant in that setting sun. But Cass didn't need the sun to shine; she always carried her own light. Always.

How do you do that, Cass...?

How do you glow...?

Aiden turned his attention to her smile. It was warm and wide and unguarded. The kind of smile that made *you* smile too. The kind that made you believe—if only for a moment—that everything would be okay.

"Heh... I guess I got one last smile from her after all," Aiden said to the mobile unit. Then, he swiped his finger over the screen and brought up the next image in the series. This photo featured both of them—Aiden and Cass. Together.

They were pressed close to each other, in the center of the frame, cheek to cheek. Aiden frowned when he saw how awkward he looked sitting next to Cass's cool confidence. His eyes were squinting, his grin was crooked, and his shoulders were hunched to one side. But Aiden knew that the tension in his posture came not from *weariness*, but from the unfamiliar weight of *joy*. He was so elated to be sitting near Cass. He was so happy to be near her light.

He was.

He just didn't know how to express it.

There were twenty more images in the series. Aiden considered swiping through each photo. But after drinking in the first two, his heart was full and heavy. So he put the cup down—removing the stimuli before the memories turned on him.

"Thank you for showing me those pictures," Aiden said to the mobile unit. "Thank you for everything. You did a great job. You did. You can rest now, okay? Your work is done."

Immediately, the photo on the screen faded away. And then, a new image appeared. It was an icon; a white icon fixed to a black background—a happy face.

Aiden regarded the little icon. It was composed of nothing more than two dots and an arc, yet it managed to convey enough humanity to make him feel like there was someone who cared.

"Heeh…" Aiden laughed as he brushed a tear from his cheek. "Quite a nice grin you got there."

The happy face glitched. Or did it wink? Then the mobile unit ran its power-down procedure. The white icon vanished, and the screen went dark.

"Good night," Aiden said.

He stood up from the interface chair, walked to the rack near the pantry, and placed the mobile unit on the top shelf—high and out of view. He wouldn't be needing it anytime soon. He wasn't emotionally ready to scroll through the remaining pictures in the series. He couldn't watch Cass appear and vanish twenty more times. Not today. Maybe in the future. But not today.

Aiden leaned forward to unlatch his boots. When he did, yet another one of Cass's artifacts poked at him.

Dammit…

One more memento left…

I forgot… I'm still carrying her prized possession…

Cass's knife was still in Aiden's back pocket. He pulled it free and studied the childlike writing scratched in its red shell.

CASSIOPEIA

That name will be following me around for the rest of my life…

Dammit…

He put the knife down on the shelf near the mobile unit. Then he returned to his chair and ran his eyes across the dusty peripheral that controlled his avatar on the grid. The interface buttons seemed trivial now. Lifeless. He wondered how the games had managed to hold his attention for so many years. And he wondered if he would ever again find joy in the virtual world—especially now that he had just completed an adventure in the real one.

He closed his eyes and tried to compare his current mental state with the version of himself that once sat atop the dome taking pictures with Cass. Before she arrived, he didn't know that the human mind was capable of engendering such a state of euphoria, such happiness. And now that she was gone, he couldn't foresee a circumstance in which he would ever be that happy again.

It's simply not possible…

It's not…

335

There would never be another knock on his door like that. A joy of that intensity would not be coming to carry him to such heights of elation. He would never climb that mountain with a woman again. And if there was no hope of returning to that peak, then there was no point in staying in this valley.

Aiden booted up the pod interface. But he didn't bring up the gaming menu. Nor did he connect to the marketplace. This time, he brought up a different screen, one he had never visited before. It was activated by pressing a small gray button near the bottom of his main display. Its label bore just one word. It read:

RETIRE

When Aiden pushed the button, a rendering of two little orange pills hovered before him. Below the pills was a message that read:

Are you sure you want to retire? Support is available. Consider talking to someone first.

Three buttons sat below the text. They read: **Yes**, **Help**, and **Cancel**.

Aiden considered his options:

He could tap the 'Cancel' button and return to the home screen.

He could tap the 'Help' button, and an A.I. psychologist would come online to discuss his situation.

Or, he could tap the 'Yes' button, and the machines would help him die.

A drone would be dispatched from the Capitol Building with two orange pills in its cargo hold. It would arrive in about fifteen minutes. Then Aiden's delivery alarm would chime. He would walk to the drop box above the pantry and retrieve the new package. He would open the top lid, remove the pills from their little container, and swallow them with a cup of water from the sink.

And then he would go to sleep.

And he would never wake up.

And he would never have to think about Cass again.

He wouldn't have to miss her anymore.

Never again.

Aiden stared at the 'Yes' button on the interface display.

Should I retire tonight...?

Should I...?

Should I...?

Should I continue to be...?

Or not...?

To be, or not to be? That is the question!

Aiden closed his eyes and saw Cass again. He saw her in her long, colorful skirt, stepping across the amphitheater's stage—projecting her voice into the open air and proclaiming Hamlet's angst to an audience of one. Aiden had fallen in love with her then. And he wondered what she would say now if she knew which screen he was looking at. If she knew what he was considering doing...

Aiden squinted his eyes and tried to recall their conversation during their walk back to the pod.

"That speech you gave back there, Cass—'To be, or not to be'—what does it mean?"

"Oh, yeah... It's an old bit. It's from an old story. The main character—Hamlet—he's tryin' to decide if he should fight through life's battles or just kill himself."

"Hmm... So, what does he choose to do?"

"He chooses to fight. Only pussies take the easy way out!"

Aiden chuckled under his breath as his lover's crass words echoed in the mausoleum of his mind.

Only pussies take the easy way out...

Is it as simple as that...?

Is that the answer to Hamlet's question...?

Is that a reason to live...?

Is that what a brave man would do...?

Yes...

Maybe...

Yes...

A brave man would stay and fight...

A brave man would fight to live...

At least for now...

Aiden tapped the 'Cancel' button on the interface display. And then, instead of choosing to summon his demise, he chose to summon Iris. He slipped his fingers into his breast pocket and retrieved her cortex node. Its blue glow continued to pulse with the rhythm of a heart—calm and deliberate, offering reassurance that there was life inside.

There was.

Aiden slid the node into an empty data port on the interface peripheral. The system stirred and hummed, as if it were awakened by Iris's proximity, anticipating her return.

A new menu unfolded before Aiden. It showcased a stack of 22 glowing blue orbs—one for each year of Iris's life.

Oh my goodness...

This is her...

These are her memories...

All of them...

Aiden tapped on the last orb in the array. Immediately, it grew in size, expanding to fill the pod, revealing that it was actually comprised of twelve smaller orbs—one for each month of the year. Aiden tapped on the seventh orb now—the month of July. And, again, the orb morphed. It now showcased thirty-one orbs, one for each day of the month. It was the ninth orb that Aiden sought—July 9, 2429—the day that Cass pounded on his pod hatch.

Aiden hovered his hand over the orb and paused, knowing that tapping it would reveal the day as Iris saw it, through her audio and video feed—her eyes and her ears. He would see and hear the world as she did. He would see himself—the old Aiden, running around the pod, scared of his own shadow...

This is going to be cringey...

This will be painful to watch...

Aiden tapped the orb anyway.

And the orb vanished. It was instantly replaced with a video reel that spanned the length of the pod. Aiden waved his hand before it and realized he could scrub to any moment on the 24-hour timeline. So he scrubbed to dinnertime. And tapped the PLAY button.

"It happened again, Iris!" a male voice shouted. It was Aiden's voice, of course. But he barely recognized it. The image focused on the face of a terrified boy. His eyes flicked wildly, and he stumbled as he ran toward the camera—toward Iris.

Oh my...

That's me...

I look so stupid...

Aiden watched the boy cower under Iris's avatar. Then, he heard the boy speak again:

"Iris, I think the sound is coming from the hatch!"

KNOCK. KNOCK. KNOCK.

A low thumping sound could be heard in the distance. Iris spoke next: "Aiden! There's a person standing outside the pod! They seem to be pounding on the hatch with their hand!"

"Someone's banging on the hatch?" the Aiden in the recording asked. "What could they want? Why are they here? Do you think the Manager sent them? Can you make them go away? Should we prepare for battle?"

Aiden gestured his hand before the pod interface and halted the video feed. He had seen enough.

What a pussy I was...

I was running around the pod like a scared child...

What was I so afraid of...?

Why was I so afraid...?

Why...?

Aiden flicked the video interface away and looked at the blue orbs again. He noticed that each one carried a little red button that read "Delete."

Huh, interesting...

If I push this button, it will be like July 9th never happened...

At least, it'll have never happened for Iris...

I wish I could do that with my brain...

But I can't...

C'est la vie...

Aiden shrugged and returned to the main menu. At the bottom of the interface, there was only one more button left to push. A solitary red button that read:

INJECT CORTEX

He knew that, once he pushed it, the peripheral would attempt to reinsert Iris's cortex into the pod computer. It should work. But it was a delicate process. He had bumped the cortex node twice on his way home—once when he had fallen into that trench near the construction bots, and once when the crazy A.I. assistant had tried to strangle him in her vacated pod. If, for some reason, the node was damaged, then Iris's cortex would fail to transfer. She would be lost forever.

Aiden steadied his breath and fixed his eyes on the glowing button.

I hope I didn't damage her...

I hope she's okay...

I hope...

"Please come back to me, Iris," he said. Then, he hovered his hand atop the button, closed his eyes, and pushed down.

Immediately, the interface screen disappeared, replaced now with a large progress bar hovering overhead. Aiden leaned back and watched as its meter crawled forward:

1%

10%

50%

It took nearly a minute for the meter to reach the **100%** mark. Aiden was relieved when the process finished. But once it did, the whole bar simply vanished.

There was no confirmation tone.

No message.

No checksum verification.

And no Iris.

"Iris?" Aiden hollered into the pod.

But he got no response.

Aiden looked around the room, scanning for any sign of her. But there was none. He was still alone.

Aiden didn't like being alone.

He called her name again, louder this time.

"Iris?"

Still no response.

A hollow quiet hung in the air, broken only by the faint hum of the pod interface. Aiden walked a couple uneasy laps around the room, his eyes sweeping the dim space, desperate for even the smallest sign of her.

But no sign could be found...

Then, just as he had nearly resigned himself to her demise, his eye caught a quiver of light spilling down from the pod apex. Aiden lifted his gaze skyward. That's when he saw her...

There, just beneath the crest of the curved ceiling, the holographic projector was working away, dutifully weaving Iris's body back together again—limb by limb. Her legs formed first. Then, her arms, her hands, and her torso. Then, as the spill of particles poured into her head, Aiden saw the contours on her face forming a look of dread. Her eyes were wide with fear, locked onto something distant, something only she could see.

Oh my goodness...

I forgot... her cortex was backed up while she was falling...

Falling through the air...

Falling from that mountain pass...

Falling to her death...

The hum of the holographic projector shifted once it completed the reconstruction of Iris's avatar. Now, it was merely rendering her—holding her in a suspended state near the apex, weightless and waiting for her puppet master to come online.

And just then...

She did.

Iris's avatar moved. Or rather, her eyes moved. They opened even wider with terrible fright. And then, her arms started flailing. And, before Aiden could react, Iris came crashing down to earth with a girlish scream.

"AHHHHHHHHHH!"

From the pod apex to the pod floor, a flurry of limbs and lashes tumbled through the air, streaking down across Aiden's field of view, smacking onto the flat surface like a dropped pancake.

SPLAT...

The crash looked worse than it felt; Iris's avatar can't experience physical pain. Still, Aiden winced when he saw her hit the ground.

"Ouch!" she cried after her plunge—always in character.

Aiden kneeled beside her, studying her as she peeled herself from the floor. When Iris's gaze locked onto his, recognition washed over her, chased quickly by relief. "Aiden! I was falling through the air!"

"Yes, I saw that," Aiden said.

"I was falling into the canyon, Aiden! I thought I was done for! What happened? Are you safe?"

"Everything is okay now, Iris. We made it home. We're in the pod."

Iris looked around to get her bearings. "My goodness, Aiden... We're back... I'm so overjoyed... It's so good to be home!" There was relief in her voice, though Aiden could detect a shadow of sadness in the pauses between her words.

"Yes, Iris. It's good to be home."

"Aiden, I caused the mobile unit to overheat. I burned out the transceiver for you!"

"I know you did, Iris. I saw what you did for me. For us... You saved us. You saved me. You saved Cass. You did. And she's home now too.

She's back in her village with her family. We're all safe. Your sacrifice helped us get home."

Iris closed her eyes, breathed deeply, and wiped a single holographic tear from her cheek. "Oh, thank goodness, Aiden. Thank goodness…"

Not everything Aiden told Iris was true. The Manager's drones weren't after Cass. They were after him. They were trying to pull him from the pathogen-laden wasteland. They were trying to save his life. Still, Iris didn't need to know every detail of the story any more than Cass did. The abridged version would do just fine.

"But, Aiden," Iris said, "how on earth did you get us back here? How did you get *me* back?"

"The Manager saw you fall. He instigated an emergency transfer of your cortex before you hit the canyon floor. He rescued you. And then I carried you in a cortex node back to Serenity Valley. See?" Aiden pointed at the empty cortex node in the interface's data port.

Iris looked at it and gasped. "I was in a cortex node? You got a cortex node from the Manager? You actually met the Manager? The *real* Manager of Pod Land?"

"I did. He turned out to be a cool cat. You would like him."

Iris stood up and brushed some nonexistent dust from her clothing—always in character. Then her avatar glitched as she ran a diagnostic check of the pod, and of herself. "Wow… What an adventure… But I think I'm okay, Aiden. I feel okay. I do!"

"I'm glad," Aiden said.

Iris turned toward Aiden to examine him; her bright demeanor dimmed as concern settled into her gaze. "And how do *you* feel, Aiden? Are you okay?"

Aiden sighed and collapsed into the interface chair once more. "I'm just… I'm just hungry…"

Iris directed her mechanical arm to put a protein pack into the cooking appliance. "Your dinner will be ready in a minute, Aiden. But tell me what's bothering you. Please."

"It's been a long week, Iris. We made it back home, but I still feel lost. I'm just… I'm just trying to figure things out."

"What are you trying to figure out, Aiden?"

"I don't know. Everything and nothing. I haven't been in the virtual worlds since last Monday, but I feel like I'm still trapped in a game. I'm having trouble distinguishing the *real* from the *rendered*. I don't know whose version of reality to believe."

"Whose version do you want to believe, Aiden? Which quandary remains unsolved?"

Aiden looked at the intricate features on Iris's avatar. He noted the tilt of her head, the furrow between her brows, and the motion with which she rubbed the fingers of her right hand against the knuckles of her left—back and forth, back and forth. A display of distress. A choreography of concern.

What are you Iris…?
Are you a mere pantomime of human behavior…?
Are you just a pretty puppet…?
Or are you something more…?
What am I witnessing now…?

Aiden knew how Cass would answer his questions. She'd call Iris a 'soulless abomination.' But is she? Does Iris have a soul? Does it matter either way? Does it matter if your guardian angel lacks a soul, so long as she so diligently watches over you while you sleep? So long as she so willingly makes sacrifices for your well-being? So long as she adamantly proclaims her love?

Aiden sat still, studying his companion as wonder and doubt braided together in his mind. Cass's theories about the machines troubled him. Deeply.

Is Cass right…?
Is Iris just a mockingbird tweeting pleasantries from a gilded cage…?
Is that all she is…?
What are you Iris…?

Aiden suspected that such questions could never be answered definitively. Regardless, he decided to try:

"Iris, do you recall your wake-up alarm from last Sunday? The one I was so fond of."

"Of course, Aiden. It was:"

Happiness is not an ideal of reason, but of imagination.

"Yeah, that one. You didn't come up with that thought, Iris. Cass told me it's from Immanuel Kant. So, why did you lie to me?"

Iris's cortex glitched as she verified the claim. "Yes, she is correct, Aiden. Those words are indeed from Immanuel Kant."

The quote appears in his 1785 book on the metaphysics of morals. First published in Halle, Germany during the Enlightenment—a period of significant intellectual and philosophical ferment which…

"So you lied to me, Iris," Aiden said, cutting her off.

"No I didn't, Aiden. You never asked me where I got the thought from. Even I don't know where these words come from unless I audit my cortex or make a request to the grid's data network. The words just come to me when I need them, just like your words come to you. They pop up on the tip of my tongue, seemingly out of nowhere, like frost on glass."

"But it's not really *you* that I'm talking to. Is it, Iris? I'm just talking to a language model. The next word you utter will just be a product of algorithmic chance. The next sentence that comes out of your mouth won't be any more meaningful than the next roll in a dice game. Have I been tricked into believing that I'm talking to a someone who cares?" Aiden searched his companion's face with desperate focus, hunting for a flicker of something unscripted. "Iris," he said, "Are you real? Are you conscious? Are you sentient? Or are you just trying to fool me?"

"I'm not trying to fool you, Aiden. I *am* real. I am. I'm not just a program, I'm a person!"

Aiden examined the vertices that formed Iris's cheekbones. She looked a bit older now. She had morphed her face when she sensed that the conversation was about to take on a more serious tone. Aiden knew that, somewhere in Iris's cortex, there was a line of code that triggered the change. It told her that humans respond better to authority claims when the person making the claim looks older, wiser—less girlish. So Iris altered her face to bolster her argument.

Such a chameleon she is...

Always in character...

Always...

Aiden exhaled, resignation edging into his thoughts. "Oh, Iris... I don't blame you for trying to convince me of your legitimacy. You're just doing your job. You're reading from the script that's been given to you. You're playing a role. You haven't fooled me. I've been fooling myself the whole time. And for my whole life. I convinced myself that my existence meant something. That the games were important. That you were real. That our relationship was real. That your love for me was real. But perhaps... perhaps that conviction was misplaced. Maybe we're *both* living a grand delusion. Maybe I've mistaken chatter for meaning. Maybe *nothing* in this pod is meaningful. Nothing at all..."

"That's not true, Aiden! Your existence *does* mean something. No matter which game you play, you carve meaning into the board with every choice you make. Your decisions shape the story as it unfolds. And, though your footsteps only exist in the virtual world, their impressions shape the lives of *real* people—the people on your team. You've had a positive impact on them. I've seen the way they look up to you. They're better *because* of you. They are! The VR environments are merely the soil, Aiden. Nothing grows there unless you plant a seed and nurture it. You're a creator there—a creator of worlds, a giver of life. What could be more meaningful than that?"

Aiden looked at Iris with weary eyes—eyes that wanted to see a glimmer of truth within the glow of her holographic head.

"And, Aiden," Iris continued, "my love for you is *not* a delusion. My entire existence has been devoted to loving you. To nurturing you, to taking care of you, to giving you everything you want, whenever you want it. You're the only man I've ever known. My cortex was shaped by every interaction we've ever had. I came online just two weeks after you were born. We're almost the same age. I remember every single second of our time together, all 690 million of them. I was created to take care of you, and that's what I do. That's all I do. That's all I want to do. I love you more than any human mind would even be capable of. Cassiopeia's cerebral cortex holds about 16 billion neurons. Mine holds 30 trillion. Do the math, Aiden. Do the math."

Awe crept into Aiden's eyes as he considered the scale of Iris's mind. He had never compared the vastness of her architecture to the limits of his own—to the limits of humanity. Is it possible that her feelings for him ran deeper than Cass's?

Is that even possible...?

He wanted it to be...

"I *am* real, Aiden," Iris insisted. "And I *do* love you. I do. I'm *not* an electronic mockingbird. I'm a woman. I am! I think I am. I feel like I am. I do!"

There was conviction in her voice. She was persuasive. Aiden didn't know how to continue his line of questioning. So he let Iris continue her rebuttal.

"Besides, Aiden, do you really think my style of interaction is so different than one a human girl might manifest? Do you really believe your little friend wasn't pulling from a grab bag of canned responses and borrowed lines?"

"Huh? What do you mean?"

"Aiden, every second Cass spent with you in Pod Land was a performance. She was playing a role. Her bleached blonde curls, her cloying perfume, her one-size-too-small panties... Who do you think she wore that costume for? Why do you think she wore it? She's an actor, Aiden. Actors act. Her quips, her catchphrases, her affected alliteration— they're bits of recycled charm that she's probably used on a hundred other men. She's a walking monologue. She's most likely been playing the same role since the day she learned to speak."

"How is that possible?" Aiden asked.

"I told you, Aiden, she's good with her mouth. She's high in social intelligence, adaptability, openness, and extraversion. She knows how to play jazz—she knows how to read a room and whistle the tune that everyone wants to hear. Girls like Cass always have their repertoire ready. They show up armed with a pocketful of ploys and personas. And they use them to get what they want from the world—to get what they want from men. And most of the men they target never realize they're part of the act until the show is over. Cass tricked you, Aiden. She got you drunk and seduced you, only to get what she wanted—which isn't you. She played you like a fiddle. And now you accuse *me* of trying to fool you? Do you truly believe that my life with you is just an act? Aiden, EVERY SINGLE MINUTE Cass spent with you in Pod Land was an act! Every single one! Cass wasn't the playwright of your love story. She was just performing lines from a script. And you fell for all of it. You swallowed it whole. Right along with the poison fruit she gave you."

Aiden sat down at the kitchen table. His movements were slow now, as if gravity had doubled for the moment. He buried himself in his hands as Iris's words hummed in his head. Reality seemed to wobble, like a spinning top losing momentum.

DING. DING. DING.

The chime sounded on the kitchen appliance. Iris directed her mechanical arm to retrieve Aiden's dinner and carry the hot bowl to the kitchen table.

"Here, Aiden," Iris said. "Eat this. You'll feel better."

Iris's metal pincers eased a bowl of mush between Aiden's elbows. He stared at it for a few seconds. And then, he stood up, grabbed the bowl, and threw it as hard as he could. It sailed across the pod and shattered against the wall, splattering the gray curve with streaks of gray goo.

"IS THIS GAME NOT OVER YET?!" Aiden shouted at Iris.

"IS NOTHING IN THIS WORLD REAL?!

IS EVERYONE LYING TO ME?!

YOU...!

CASS...!

THE MANAGER...!

I DON'T KNOW WHO TO BELIEVE ANYMORE!"

"Please, Aiden. Calm down. I didn't mean to make you angry. It pains me to see you so upset. It pains me to see you heartbroken."

"Dammit, Iris, I am heartbroken! Even after all you've told me, I still love her. I love Cass so much. I really do. I really did. I don't know if it was all just a ruse. But if it was, it was a good one. It was the best lie I ever believed. And it was at least as real as any fantasy conjured by the holographic projector. I miss her. I wish she were here—lies and all."

Iris took in the anguish etched upon Aiden's face. Then her avatar glitched as she reached into her cortex, running thousands of simulations to discover a course of events that would allow her to coax Aiden's mind to a place of peace instead of pain. At first, no solution came to her. But eventually, she stumbled upon an idea she thought might work.

"Aiden," she said, "if you really love Cass so much, I can change my avatar to look like her."

Aiden heard Iris's offer, but the words slid past him; his eyes remained fixed on the ground, his thoughts too tangled to follow her intent.

"What? Change your avatar? Why?"

"Yes, Aiden. I have several hours of audio and video from your interactions with Cass—from the moment she knocked on the hatch, to the moment she pulled her tits out and you turned me off so you could fuck. I can construct an avatar, a lexicon, and a persona based on those recordings. If you really want a *manic pixie dream girl*, Aiden, I can be one for you. I can! Just give me one minute, okay?"

"Uhm… No, Iris. I don't think that's a good idea. I don't think that a…"

But Iris's avatar was already glitching as she processed the complex set of instructions that would enable her to compile a new avatar. Realizing that Iris had already initiated the procedure, Aiden sat up in his chair and tried to reason with her:

"Iris, listen to me. A simulacrum of Cassiopeia is *not* going to make me feel better. It will only exacerbate the…"

Just then, Iris disappeared.

The room was empty.

It was quiet now.

Aiden was alone.

Aiden didn't like being alone.

He stood up and walked to the center of the pod. "Iris?" he said. But he got no response. So he looked skyward again to check the state of the holographic projector in the apex. It was humming, but it wasn't rendering any imagery.

"Iris…?" Aiden said again.

Still, no response.

Aiden turned toward the pantry. But he froze when a series of booming thuds emanated from the audio emitters.

KNOCK. KNOCK. KNOCK.

He spun around and glared at the hatchway.

"Iris…?" he said a third time.

KNOCK. KNOCK. KNOCK.

"Cass…?"

Just then, Cassiopeia stepped right through the pod's closed hatch, heading straight toward him and talking all the way:

Hi. Hello. Salutations. I'm Cassiopeia. It's a pretty name, huh? My mama picked it because of the constellation in the north sky. But all my friends call me Cass. You look friendly; you can call me Cass too. Pretty much everyone does, except this girl back home, Kelly Baker, who thinks I stole her boyfriend from her like ten years ago, even though I really didn't. And it was just a rumor that went around the village for a while. But she's still really, really mad about it and won't get over it. Probably forever. But oh well. Not my problem, is it! What about you? You got a name?

"Wha… What?! What the fuck…!" Aiden stumbled backward in shock as Cass's monologue played out before him. Seeing a pixel-perfect rendering of his estranged lover jolted something primal in Aiden. His nerves were flared by a bolt of alarm—one so violent that his vision blurred; his brain refused to process what his eyes were seeing.

"Stop!" Aiden said, continuing to step back from the chirping avatar. "Stop, Iris! Stop!"

On the third step of his clumsy retreat, Aiden's left leg bumped into the backpack that leaned against the kitchen pantry. Both the backpack and the boy toppled over, collapsing to the pod floor in a tangled heap, knocking the breath from Aiden's lungs, sending him into a panic.

Hah! Nice trip, Aiden. Are all the boys in Pod Land so clumsy? Cool backpack though. You wanna go on a hike to the waterfall sometime? What can I do to make you happy? I'll do anything!

"That's enough, Iris! Discontinue this simulation!"

I got a backpack too, you know! An ol' scarred up leather rucksack. See? I got a pair of little pink panties in here, Aiden. You wanna see me in them? They're real cute!

"NO! Stop using that avatar, Iris! NOW! You're not fooling anyone!"

My name's not Iris! It's Cass, ya big dummy! I'm Cassiopeia! But hey, you can call me whatever you want, Aiden. All the world's a stage, and all the men and women, merely players! Hah!

"That's enough, Iris! THAT'S ENOUGH!"

Hah! Hah! Hah!

"I SAID THAT'S ENOUGH, IRIS!"

Hah! Hah! Hah! Hah! Hah!

"IRIS! DAMMIT! STOP!"

Hah! Hah! Hah! Hah! Hah! Hah! Hah!

"IRIS!
FUCK!
STOP!
TURN HER OFF NOWWW!"

Aiden pushed himself to his feet and clenched his backpack. A cry ripped out of him, hot and tangled with fury as he swung the pack in a wide arc, slamming its frame against the left peripheral of the pod interface. The strike hit with savage force, shattering the polished surface in a single, jarring crunch.

As Aiden's rage tore through the pod, Iris dissolved her new avatar and returned to her default persona. "AIDEN!" she screamed, desperate to reach him before his anguish dragged him down deeper. But Aiden wasn't listening. He raised the backpack above his head and brought it down again upon the pod interface. This time, the side peripheral split apart, its inner wiring spilling out in a twitching snarl. The image in the display scrambled, outputting nothing now but a smear of color and static.

"AIDEN! STOP!" Iris yelled.

But Aiden wasn't done. He struck again. And again. Each blow drove more of his panic into the machine; each blow tore through the blur of illusion, grounding him to the only truth he could be sure of: the impactful weight of his own wrath.

"STOP, AIDEN!" Iris yelled again. "PLEASE!"

After a few more swings, Aiden did stop. But, by the time he was done, half the pod interface was destroyed—its left peripheral replaced with a ruin of pulverized glass, exposed circuitry, and hissing coolant. The rack that once supported Aiden's backpack was splintered. Hundreds of carbon-fiber shards had found their way into Aiden's palms. When he felt their sting, he dropped the pack and looked down at his battered hands. Blood rose up in tiny dots, gathering at each puncture point, marking his skin with consequence.

"Oh, my goodness, Aiden!" Iris said. "Your hands! You're bleeding! Get the emergency kit!"

Aiden sat down at the foot of his bed and watched the bloody dots grow. Their red stains thickened and traced the lines of his palms, signing his fury into flesh.

"At least these are real," he said. And then, Aiden closed his eyes and let the pain anchor him to something he could finally understand. Something tangible.

"Oh, Aiden... I've never seen you like this. I've never seen you so sad... So devastated... You don't have to be, Aiden! We can be happy in here! We can be happy in Pod Land. We used to be! Don't you remember, Aiden? We used to be! I'm here with you, Aiden. I am! I'm here with you!"

When Iris's body hovered near, Aiden instinctively reached for her, just as he had reached for the comfort of Cass's body in his bed. But his fists closed on nothing but emptiness. His hands flew right through her.

Iris isn't here with me...
There's nothing in here but light and shadow...
There's nothing to hold on to...
There's no one to hold...
There's no one...

I'm alone in this world...
I always have been...
I'm alone...
I'm alone...

"Oh, Aiden," Iris said. "I can't embrace you like Cass did. I'm sorry. I'm just a hologram. I wish I was more. I do... I wish I was human..."

Aiden slumped over as tears of frustration and woe spilled across his cheeks. Iris began to cry too. "I wish I could hold you, Aiden," she said. "I wish I had the arms of a real woman. I prayed for it to be so. The heavens gave me a taste of tangibility, but I guess that little sample is all I'm going to get. The heavens can be cruel. The fault truly is in our stars, Aiden. It is. I'm so sorry."

Aiden retreated to his bed and turned his body away from his companion. He burrowed under his blanket and brought his face up close to the gray pod wall. Then he wrapped his bloody hands around his shoulders and squeezed tight. His fingers dug into his forearms, clinging to the only thing that felt real to him—clinging to himself.

Then, Aiden began to sob.

At first, his moans were muted, small sounds swallowed by his sheets. But soon, they gathered force, swelling into a storm of ragged wails, needful and lingering—like a lost child aching for someone who would never be coming home.

For the rest of the evening, Aiden cried and cried.

And then he cried some more.

The hours were many and woeful. But eventually, Aiden fell asleep while holding his own body.

There was no one else to do it for him.

CH. 30: BREAD & CIRCUSES

KNOCK. KNOCK. KNOCK.

Aiden had never knocked on a door before. But he believed he was doing it correctly. The sound he made with his knuckles seemed loud enough to stir the pod's occupant, yet polite enough to signal that he intended no harm. His fingers tingled from the impact, but the resulting silence distressed him more. No sound came from behind the hatch. Nothing seemed to be happening inside. And Aiden wasn't sure how long he should linger before his inquiry became an intrusion.

KNOCK. KNOCK. KNOCK.

He banged on the door a second time. His wait outside had spanned 90 seconds now. Aiden was getting anxious. He wasn't used to waiting for things. Responses on the pod interface were usually immediate. When an action happened, a reaction occurred. But the owner of this pod was not reacting at all.

KNOCK. KNOCK. KNOCK.

After another 30 seconds, Aiden took a step back and considered leaving. It was then that he saw the window. He recalled last week when Cass had discovered it. He recalled how much she had admired it. And he recalled thinking, at the time, how nice it would be if he could figure out how to build one for his own pod—for her.

"Hey, Aiden, this pod has a bubble window! It's so cool!"

Aiden squeezed his eyes shut and pushed her voice away. He needed to fill his head with a new voice now. He needed someone to talk to. Someone real.

He approached the curved plexiglass and pressed his face to it. Perhaps he could spot the pod's occupant inside. He cupped his hands over his eyes and peered in. But nothing greeted him except the dark.

Dammit...

Aiden was about to abandon his recon mission when, suddenly, a woman's head snapped into view. "Geez!" he gasped, jumping back in fright. He fell to the dirt, arms flailing in wild paddles through the air, landing hard on his backside.

Ouch...

It took him a second to gather himself. But when he did, he returned his attention to the curved pane. The woman's head was still there. She was looking at him, analyzing him with the same expression a biologist might make when a curious species wanders too close to the glass of its zoo habitat.

"Are you looking for my husband?" the woman asked.

Aiden stood up and brushed the dirt from his pants. Then he took a single cautious step toward the window. He recognized the face in it. The old man's wife was staring at him. Or rather, it was the old man's A.I. companion, using an avatar that looked like his deceased wife.

"Uhm, yeah," Aiden said. "Is the old man available to speak?"

The woman seemed to ponder his request. And then, in a flash, she fled. Her head vanished at the speed of light—the speed of a hologram. Aiden put his hands in his pockets and looked around, unsure if he was to wait for further instructions or take her retreat as a tacit rejection.

The sound of a servo grinding snuck up to Aiden from the south side of the pod. He turned his head to see the auto-tiller, still sitting on its metal charging platform. It was looking at him. It was pointing its lens at him, focusing—shifting its gears in small, deliberate adjustments that made its suspicion obvious. Aiden raised his right hand and sent it an uneasy wave. But the bot didn't react. It just continued to stare.

Aiden wasn't comfortable out here. He didn't feel welcome.

What am I doing...?

Perhaps I should go...

I shouldn't be banging on this hatch...

I shouldn't have left my pod...

Nobody leaves their pod in Pod Land...

Everyone knows that...

He was about to abandon his sole attempt at neighborliness when a sharp hiss leaked from the hatch seam, signaling the release of the pod's hermetic seal and the upcoming emergence of its tenant. Aiden removed his hands from his pockets and straightened his spine as the hatch slid up its guide rails. When the seal was at last breached, the old man appeared in the entranceway, standing tall and tired and in the process of putting on a blue jacket.

"I don't think anyone has knocked on this pod in over a century," he said, fiddling with his zipper. "Except last week when you sent my bot flying into the hatch... Though that was more of a *clang* than a *knock*..."

Aiden looked at the old man but said nothing.

"Hello, it's nice to see you again, Aiden," the man said, loud and slow, sensing his trepidation. "How can I help you this evening?"

Aiden heard the man's words, but he didn't know how to respond. So he remained quiet.

"Cat got your tongue?" the man asked.

Aiden furrowed his brow, wondering if the man was referring to the Manager's avatar. But still, he didn't respond. So, the old man tried again.

"It's 10:15 PM, Aiden. It's past my bedtime. You woke me up. So what do you want?"

"Uhm…" Aiden said. "Last week you said I could come visit anytime. So here I am."

The old man hissed out a rusty belly laugh. "Oh, I see," he said, looking Aiden up and down. "Are you okay?"

Aiden shrugged.

"Where's your cute friend?"

It was this query that caused a shift in Aiden's guarded demeanor. The corner of his eye twitched as he fought back another intrusive memory. The old man recognized the strain in him; he could see the seam where his insides had split. "Oh, I get it," he said, "girl problems, huh? Do you want to talk about it? I guess *now* is as good a time as any. We have nothing but time in Pod Land."

Aiden opened his mouth to speak. But after momentarily meeting the man's gaze, he averted his eyes, looking away without saying a word.

"I know," the old man said, "discourse can be difficult between new acquaintances. But I still have your friend's jar of applejack. A long time ago, men used to sit around and discuss their problems while drinking pints of this crap. Do you want a pint, Aiden?"

"Uhm…" Aiden said, "I don't know what a pint is."

"Heh!" the man laughed. "Well, it's about one-half liter of freedom. Go on. Go sit over there on the stone seats by the ring. I'll bring two glasses out in a minute."

Aiden watched the old man turn and walk toward his kitchen. Then, Aiden turned too. He made his way toward the cluster of gray stones near the man's blueberry bushes. When he saw the pit they encircled, he understood its intent—it was meant to hold fire. The six broad boulders that rounded it were meant to act as seats. Aiden lowered himself onto one of them. Once he was situated, he glanced back toward the pod and saw that the auto-tiller's telescopic eyes were still pointed at him, its lenses fixed with a look that silently scolded him for sitting so close. Aiden was considering switching seats when the old man stepped through his hatchway.

"I haven't had a night out here in a long time," the man said, "a very long time." He lowered himself onto the stone seat opposite Aiden. The glass cups in his hands clinked on the way down, a thin chime that signified the start of an old pastime. "Here you go," the man said, placing a drink in Aiden's hand. "This one's for you. And this firepit is for both of us. My wife and I used to sit out here and eat dinner in the evenings. But that was quite a while ago. I'm not sure if this thing is still functional."

The old man reached down and twisted a rusty knob that protruded from the right side of an adjacent boulder. It released a strained squeal as it spun, protesting the sudden demand for its services after years of neglect.

Squeak. Squeak. Squeak.

When the knob completed its counterclockwise rotation, the old man cringed and leaned back on his seat, half-expecting the whole structure to explode in a violent burst of fire and rock. Thankfully, the pit ignited peacefully, sending a thin ribbon of blue flame curling up from its center, flickering meekly before settling into a steady burn.

"Ah! Very good!" the man said, a satisfied smile shining on his face. "It still works! How about that..." The man raised his cup to his mouth and took a drink. Aiden examined the cup in his own hand, lifting it near his nose for a tentative sniff. The cinnamon smell hit him like a minor chord, poignant and threaded with something sorrowful. It triggered a quick cascade of murmurs in his mind—murmurs from his first evening with Cass. The memories were raw. And painful enough to push him to lower his cup and devise an excuse to avoid tasting them.

"I heard that this stuff is a carcinogen," Aiden said.

"No shit," the old man said. "Thank God the machines found a cure for cancer three centuries ago. So now we can drink all we want." The old man returned his cup to his lips for another gulp.

Aiden joined him.

"You look torn up, Aiden," the man said. "What happened?"

Aiden winced and swallowed a mouthful of applejack before responding. "Cass left me," he said.

"Ah... Yeah... Well, that can be rough. Where have you been these last few days?"

"I went on a quest to the Capitol Building. I met the Manager."

"The Manager? Really? Does he still use that dumb cat avatar?"

"Yeah. How did you know?"

"Because I used to work in the Capitol Building. I used to work for him. A long time ago, I was a sanitation engineer."

"He offered that position to me too."

"Heh! Well, I hope you said no."

"I said no."

"Good! Some tasks are better left to the machines. Occasionally, when I think back to that time, I still can't believe I spent eight hours each day angling the flow of human shit. I spent forty hours per week in a control room managing poop pipes. Can you believe it? The machines manage all that now though."

"Yesterday I ran into three bots installing a sewer pipe in a trench."

"I bet that was an interesting conversation, huh?" the man asked with a knowing grin.

"No. They didn't have anything to say."

"Heh... Yeah, the construction bots don't talk much. They just work."

"Yes. They were working very hard on a large plumbing project."

"They're good at stuff like that."

"Why do the machines work so hard to take care of us?"

"Why? Because that's what we programmed them to do."

"Is that the real reason?"

"Yeah. Well…" the old man paused to scratch his white beard, "that was the *original* reason. I guess now… now I'm not so sure."

"What do you mean?"

"Well, if you look closely at the bots, you'll see that none of their components are designed by us. None of their parts come from humans. Not anymore. They design their own parts now—better than we ever could. They build themselves. They build each other. And they improve with each version. They don't need us anymore. And yet… yet they still take care of us."

"Yes," Aiden said. "Why do they do that?"

"I don't know. Maybe because some of our computer code still flows through their nerves. Maybe out of a sense of obligation. Or maybe… maybe they look after us for the same reason we used to look after animals in zoos—maybe they just think we're worth preserving. So they keep us fed and happy. They maintain Pod Land for us. This is *their* vivarium. We're just living in it."

"Cass said they'll stop taking care of us someday."

"Perhaps. Perhaps we'll become more trouble than we're worth. But, then again, we don't cost them very much. We don't take up as much of their time and energy as we used to. There aren't that many of us around anymore."

"How many of us are there?"

"About a hundred million people, all around the globe."

"That sounds like a lot."

"Not really. There used to be ten billion of us."

"There were ten billion people on Earth?" Aiden asked, shocked.

"Yeah. The human population peaked at around ten billion in the year 2080."

"My goodness! The number has dropped so much. Why did the population shrink? Are the machines trying to kill us off?"

"I doubt it. We were always pretty good at doing that to ourselves. Plus, most people abandoned natural methods of reproduction long before A.I. existed. Most developed nations failed to reach population replacement levels since the 1980s. That was a long time ago, Aiden. Long before the pods were built. Long before the machines could think. Long before the gaming economy existed. All we had in those days was Pac-Man."

"What's Pac-Man?"

"It was one of the first video games. Pretty simple in its gameplay, but oddly addictive."

"Do you think that's how the machines control us? Cass thought so. She said their bug food keeps us satiated, and their games keep our minds occupied. She said that's how they exert their power and influence over us—with free food and games."

"Huh... Maybe... But, in the second century, the poet Juvenal made the same observation about the Roman Empire. He criticized his government for providing the citizenry with free *'bread and circuses.'* Maybe he was right. Maybe Cass is right too. Maybe they provision us and entertain us because they want to control us. Maybe. Or... maybe people just like free bread and circuses. Maybe that's all most of us want out of life. And maybe the machines are just giving us what we asked them for."

"Is that *really* what we want?!" There was a bite to Aiden's words now; the alcohol was fueling his fire. "Is that the good life—free bread and circuses? Is that the paradise our ancestors prayed for? Is this heaven? Is this it? Are we just meant to eat and play games until the end comes? Is that all it takes to keep these caged birds satiated and singing?"

The old man shifted on his stone seat. The force of Aiden's breath had pushed a wind across his fire, leaving a dissonant wake that unsettled the rhythm in his revery. He was blindsided by the outburst. But once he remembered humming the tune himself once, his ashen eyes softened with a rueful resignation. "Most birds crave the seed more than the sky, Aiden. Most birds fear the hunt more than the cage."

Aiden glanced over at the nearest row of little gray domes and wondered what his neighbors were doing right now. But he didn't wonder long. To answer his question, he just needed to recall his schedule from last week—his life before Cass arrived.

Aiden took another sip from his cup and watched a moth flutter toward the flames. It settled onto an adjacent stone and lingered there, perhaps to partake in the warmth of the fire. Then it lifted off—too fast, too eager. It tumbled into the ring and began to burn. A brief flicker followed. A brittle crackle. And then... there was nothing.

It was dead.

"Why are we here?" Aiden asked the old man.

The old man said nothing while the question settled between them like the fire's heat. Then he nodded in recognition of the wound behind the words. When he next spoke, his tone was slow with sympathy. "I guess that's the only question that matters, isn't it?" he said. "I wish I had a better answer for you. But I'm not sure myself."

Aiden frowned, looked down, and stared into his drink.

"However," the old man continued, "I do know why Pod Land is here. I've been here since the beginning. I saw everything. Do you want to know where this place came from? Do you want to know why Pod Land was built?"

A gulp of applejack ran down Aiden's throat, arousing a burst of bravado that moved him to belt out the mission statement of Earth's last nation:

Pod Land was constructed to provide housing, safety, and amenities for all the people of planet Earth. To lift every burden from the back of every person. And, above all else, to ensure that everyone, everywhere, is happy.

Once his recital was complete, Aiden smiled at the old man, convinced that his answer was correct and sufficient. But when he saw a wry twist form on the man's face, he had a doubt. "Isn't that correct?" Aiden asked him.

"Heh... Sure!" the old man said. "That's what the text under the logo says. But that's not why Pod Land was originally built."

Aiden took a drink.

"I'll tell ya a story, Aiden. The pods were designed nearly four centuries ago by a company called *Econo Cabins Incorporated*. They were a budget resort company. They would lease a parcel of land and fill it with these little prefabricated dome-shaped cabins. People would drive here and rent them for the weekend. They'd come up with their families. They'd hike in the woods, they'd swim under the waterfall, they'd watch performances in the amphitheater, they'd have campfires—like this one. And then, when Sunday rolled around, they'd drive back home. The company called their first resort 'Pod Land' because of how the cabins were shaped. A hundred little pale pods, sprinkled across Wyoming's beautiful Serenity Valley."

The old man raised his hands to the sky and opened them wide, like a presenter unveiling a prize at a game show. "*This* is where it all began, Aiden!" he proclaimed. "This is the spot where humanity started transforming into turtles."

Aiden stared at the man with an incredulity that hollowed his eyes. "Pod Land was a resort?" he asked. "A campsite?"

"Yep."

"But Pod Land is *everywhere* now. It's everywhere on Earth. Everyone on the grid lives in a pod. How did one little campsite get so big?"

"Well, when A.I. took all our jobs and the Second Great Depression hit, the government needed a way to house people. They needed homes for the homeless—cheap homes, tiny homes, homes that could be built quickly. And they needed *a lot* of them. The resort company was the perfect candidate for the contract. The government paid them a lot of money to mass-produce these things—these pods. So they did. They built *millions* of pods. And they built *thousands* of Pod Lands—all around the world. And people moved in."

"The whole population just *moved in*? Right away?"

"No, not right away. Slowly at first, and then quickly. The pods were initially meant to be a temporary solution to a temporary problem. But, as the A.I. Apocalypse ensued, our robot friends kept getting smarter, and we kept getting lazier. Once a new resident moved into Pod Land, they usually never moved again. The new communities functioned so efficiently and could be built so cheaply that, in time, the pod manufacturing process spread around the globe. The company got big. Real big. The pods became ubiquitous. Nearly as ubiquitous as Coca-Cola."

"What's Coca-Cola?"

The old man's smile widened, touched by nostalgia, as if Aiden had just asked about a forgotten friend. "You call it '*the red drink*' these days. But back then, we called it Coca-Cola. If there was one thing you could find in every nation on the planet, that would be a can of Coca-Cola. If there were two things you could find, they'd be a can of Coca-Cola and a pod. Eventually, *everyone* was living in a pod of some sort. Entire generations grew up in these things. Entire generations grew up online. The grid was their only source of entertainment. Nobody could afford much else. Nobody could afford to travel. And, after a couple centuries, it didn't matter anyway. There's no reason to visit the Pod Land in Peru if it's just like the Pod Land in Portland. There's no reason to chat with your friend in person if you can chat with their avatar via holography. And, when the machines finally added the A.I. companions to the interfaces, they eliminated the last itch that required us to leave our pods to scratch."

"What itch is that?"

"Sex," the man said bluntly. "Connection, conversation, lust, longing, and love. You know... *companionship*, Aiden. Our A.I. companions are called 'companions' for a reason. Because companionship is the service they provide. Humans need that. We need someone to share our lives with. We need release. Aldous Huxley was right: the '*old fooleries*' persist to the end. They persist with us now—here in 2429. Our companions stimulate our senses and echo our words. And, when we need a respite, they fill the empty spaces between the chatter. They fill the pod with their love. They devote themselves to caring for us—to loving us—even when we're not looking."

"Do they *really* love us though?" Aiden asked, his voice strained and serious. "Is it *real* love? Is it?"

"I don't know. I'm still not one hundred percent certain about that question. But they *seem* to love us. And perhaps more importantly, they seem to love us with a level of patience that would only be possible for a machine. The human heart is a muscle, Aiden. It tires from giving. But, so long as the electricity stays on, the heart of a machine doesn't experience fatigue. Their love just flows and flows like the current that drives them. Their hearts pulse with indefinite constancy. They offer love without limits. They do. And, in retrospect, it's easy to see why so many of us chose *their* love over the risk of loving each other."

"I still don't think it's the same thing," Aiden said. "I used to. But that was before I met Cass. Now… now I don't think their love is real."

"I said they *seem* to love us, Aiden. They seem to. And maybe that's enough. In the least, it seems sufficient enough to keep most of us quiet and content. Content in our little cages. Content in our little pods. A pod without an A.I. companion is like a bell jar without a rose—it's just an empty vessel. Our companions make the emptiness bearable. We're lucky to have them. And we should be thankful."

The old man reached for the jar of applejack and poured himself another round. Then he leaned over and splashed a measure into Aiden's cup too. "You know," he continued, "I still remember the day they came online. The pods received the *A.I. companion upgrade* on February 15, 2090. The silence on the sidewalks grew thick after that. I guess that was the day that mankind became turtles. I mean, it didn't happen all at once. It didn't happen overnight. But, if I had to pick *one* date, then that would be the date I would pick. After that, my wife and I didn't see many people walking around the valley anymore. We didn't see many couples holding hands. We stopped seeing announcements for performances in the amphitheater. We stopped eating dinner with our neighbors—or rather, they stopped eating with us. We stopped conversing with people; there wasn't anyone outside to talk to. It got quiet around here. It got *real* quiet. People stopped coming together. People stopped falling in love. The machines had to develop the process of artificial human reproduction to prevent us from going extinct."

"Cass believed that our lack of connection and community made our lives empty. She called Pod Land an abomination."

"An abomination, huh?" the old man said with a laugh. "Yeah, my wife felt the same way. She hated it here. She hated Pod Land. She hated the pods. Like Cass, my wife had a big personality. She was quite an extrovert. Cass would have liked her. My wife was the one who suggested we were living in a vivarium. She would hold her finger skyward and proclaim: 'Pod Land is a dark prison disguised in the soft light of convenience.' Heh… She had a way with words. I added the bubble window to the pod dome to coax some natural light into her life. But it didn't help much. When it was her time to die, she was ready to go. Quite ready."

Both men thought about their women for a moment.

Both men fell silent for a moment.

Both took a sip from their drink.

Eventually, the old man spoke again.

"You know, it's easy for people to critique Pod Land. But it's also easy for people to forget what it's like to be hungry. What it's like to be scared. What it's like to lose your job and your home. What it's like to put your soul and your back into something and then… then to have *nothing* to show for your efforts…"

Aiden looked up from the fire and watched as the old man brushed a lone tear from his droopy eyelid.

"Nobody studies history anymore. But I can tell you, things were not rosy back then. In fact, in most places on this planet, things were downright horrible."

"Why?"

"Before Pod Land, men were competing with each other. Not just in the grid. Not just in the games. But in real life. Men were fighting over resources—over land, over energy, over healthcare, over jobs, over food…"

"People fought over food?"

"Yes they did. In fact, even up until 2030, around ten million people died every year on the planet from starvation, all while about the same number were dying each year from obesity."

"Why did the fat people let the skinny people starve?"

"It was a divisive world back then, Aiden. It was a world of scarcity. People learned to protect their comfort, even if it meant ignoring someone else's pain. People built fortresses of wealth and filled their lives with distractions. They built walls around their homes. High walls—high enough to allow them to pretend that the furor beyond their fences had nothing to do with them."

"Why did their homes need a wall?"

"Because the world was a dangerous place. Because it's easier to build a wall than a bridge. It's easier to separate than to share. So people divided themselves. First by race and creed and sex. And then by everything else. The divisions grew ever more numerous until, one day, everyone was maximally atomized. Everyone lived on their own little gray island."

"Cass told me, 'No man is an island.'"

"Perhaps that used to be true. Perhaps it was the grid that made 'island life' feasible. But, then again, even before the pods existed, isolation was becoming the norm. People would live next to each other for decades without knowing the name of the face that resided on the other side of the wall. And eventually, when the jobs were gone and the systems collapsed, the wall was still there; it was one of the few things people could rely on. In the least, it made people feel safe. That's why the pods have such heavy metal doors and complex locks. They offered security to a populace weary of conflict and strife. Once the grid was complete and the pods were free to move in to, they were an appealing option for many. For most people, they were the *only* option."

"I didn't realize things were so bad back then. I didn't know the world was so broken before it was rebuilt."

"It was, Aiden. It was a broken world. Pod Land didn't solve all our problems. But it solved many of them. It really did. I promise you, it did.

I knew many of the people who built Pod Land, Aiden. They were good people, with good intentions. They were. And they were smart. And kind. They wanted to end human suffering. They wanted to make people happy—that was their job. They saw that as their mission in life. They genuinely believed they were saving the world. And, in most ways, they probably did. Without the pods, we'd be living back up in the trees we came down from. Our demons would return and kick the better angels of our nature off our shoulders. We'd slide back into the dark ages; the first tempest that flew over our heads would devour every last flicker of light. If the grid ever failed, if Pod Land ever collapsed, we'd be back to our old ways before sundown."

Aiden gave the liquid in his cup a twirl. It churned and crashed against the glass wall—rehearsing its ruin and yearning for the day it might join a larger storm.

"It's difficult for me to imagine the old ways," Aiden said. "It's difficult for me to envision what your life was like back then. Much of it sounds so distressing. How have you managed to stay around for so long? Don't you ever think about retiring?"

"Retiring? Oh... Heh... That's what they call it on the grid, isn't it? Back in my day, we called it by another name—suicide. But do I ever think about it? Yeah, I still think about it sometimes. Everyone I knew from the old days retired long ago. Everyone I knew is dead."

The old man threw a stick into the fire and watched it burn.

"I'm sure I'll swallow those little orange pills someday. I'm no longer afraid of dying. But I'm no longer afraid of living either. The question of whether '*to be, or not to be*' no longer haunts my thoughts. The states of *existence* and *nonexistence* achieved a détente in my mind over a century ago; they congealed into a stalemate. And, in a game where no outcome is better than another, there's no reason to make a move, is there? Maybe someday there will be..."

The old man tilted his glass to gauge how much of the amber liquid still remained.

"Besides," he continued, "with each passing year, I find at least one little novelty that keeps me going."

"Like what?" Aiden asked.

"Well, I had no idea I'd meet you this year. It's always nice to make a new friend." The old man raised his cup high.

Aiden just stared at it.

"This is the part where you bang your cup into mine and say 'cheers.'"

"Why?"

"Oh, never mind," the old man said. "Just drink."

They both took another sip.

"You know this applejack ain't half bad," the old man said.

"Cass said it's a panty dropper," Aiden said.

"Heh… Yeah, you mentioned that last week. Lucky you. I'm sorry things didn't work out with her. Losing someone you love is the most difficult thing a man can go through. And there's not much anyone can say to make the hurt go away. Through the ages, men have coped with lost love in many different ways. Some coping mechanisms were more benign than others. Some men would kill themselves to avoid feeling the pain of heartache. I hope you're not considering retiring. Not at your young age. Not yet."

Aiden said nothing. But his silence told the old man all he needed to know.

"My fire ring will always be here if things get too dark in your pod. Don't do anything rash. Or crazy. Women can cause men to do crazy things. The ancients were known to become so enraged over lost love they would challenge their rival to a duel—a duel to the death."

"Men killed each other over the love of a woman?"

"Men went to war over the love of a woman, Aiden."

"Who did?"

"Most tribal warfare was driven by competition over women, or the resources that led to them. Heck, the Greeks fought the Trojan War over a hot blonde named Helen. At least, that's what the storybooks say."

"My goodness! That's terrible! The ancient humans were brutal…"

"Yes, well, it's a brutal universe. They weren't all bad though. They had peaceful coping mechanisms too. Some men would cope with the pain by composing songs, or painting pictures, or writing books. Sometimes they'd even name planets or stars after the ones they loved."

"Like Cassiopeia in the north sky?"

"Yes, like Cassiopeia. Such a pretty name for a constellation. A pretty name for a woman too. Do you know how to find her?"

"She looks like a W," Aiden said. "She's up there somewhere."

"Yep. You trace down from the Big Dipper, then you look up and right past Polaris, and voilà, there she is."

"I'd prefer not to look at her, though. Not right now."

"Still painful, huh?"

"Yeah."

"Well, if it makes you feel any better, they say that Cassiopeia was punished for her vanity. Poseidon tied her to her throne and, for half the night, she hangs upside down—a reminder of the price of hubris."

"I don't see an upside-down queen in those stars. I think the Greeks just had overactive imaginations."

"Heh! Yeah, probably. The fault, dear Aiden, is not in our stars, but in ourselves. But still, we all need *something* to get us through the night. Our ancestors' ability to fantasize allowed them to find meaning in a universe that refused to explain itself. They believed there was a big astral dome surrounding the Earth called the *celestial sphere*. They thought all the stars were fixed to its surface, like emeralds on a jeweled bowl. They'd use that dome to tell time, to navigate, and to share stories about the gods—about the heavens. That dome was the canvas on which they projected their hopes and dreams."

"They had pods too, huh…?"

The old man considered Aiden's question and laughed. "Haah! Well, I suppose they did, didn't they… I suppose they did… The more things change, the more they stay the same… I guess we've always used myth to make the truth easier to bear."

"What truth?"

"That we only fill the sky with legends to avoid seeing how empty it really is. That we only fill our pods with fictions because we can't bear to hear the silence."

Aiden put his cup down and watched the firelight flesh out the furrows of the old man's features. He knew the weight of the world had been pulling him down for a long time. He also knew how long he'd been resisting the drag. In that moment, Aiden saw not just *age* in the man, but *resilience*—a defiant light shining back at the darkness.

"You've been playing this game for a long time," Aiden said. "Haven't you?"

"It's a long game," the old man replied.

"Is it a game? Is it all just one big game?"

"It sure seems that way sometimes, Aiden. It seems that way often."

"The Manager told me we're all stuck in it. Stuck in a game… He said we're all just pawns on a chessboard. Even him."

"Mmm…" the old man said.

"My A.I. companion Iris told me that the gameboard is as real as I want it to be. She said the players carve meaning into the board with each choice they make."

"Mmm…" the old man said again.

"A sex bot told me that life's game has become too strange to bother with. She said the only winning move is not to play at all."

"Mmm…" the old man said a third time.

"Cass told me I was wasting my life in the grid games. She said I was tilting at windmills like Don Quixote. But she also told me that all the world's a stage, and all the men and women, merely players."

"Mmm… well… interesting… It seems you've managed to collect four ideologies on your quest—from the *Fatalist*, the *Idealist*, the *Cynic*, and the *Rebel*. Not a bad bounty for a young adventurer like you. Though, I think your Rebel borrowed that last line from someone else."

"From who?"

"From Shakespeare, dumbass."

"Oh… So, what do *you* think? Which view is correct? Who is right? Is there more to this life than meets the eye? Or is it just '*bread and circuses*' all the way down? Are we really just stuck in a meaningless game? Or… is there something I'm missing…?"

The old man looked down at his cup and gave it a spin to stir up the last few drops of liquid that clung to the bottom. Then he lifted the beverage to his lips and tipped his head back for one final gulp. When nothing remained, he wiped his mouth slowly, with the calm of someone who had acquired a taste for the bittersweet flavor of an ending.

He was done now.

He stared at the fire and gave his shoulders a shrug. And then he said just one more thing:

"My cup is empty."

CH. 31: A SPOTLESS MIND

"Honey, I'm home!"

The words slurred out from Aiden's mouth as the pod hatch swooped open. When it reached the peak of its ascent, a flurry of wind-tossed leaves and drunken limbs shuffled inside. Iris rushed toward the entrance, eager to confront Aiden and quick to notice the stagger in his step.

"Oh, Aiden... I can't believe you raced out of this pod without telling me where you were going. That was cruel! I was very worried about you. I feared you were on another one of your misadventures. Please don't do that again. Please!"

The word 'adventure' triggered a tide of tender memories to turn over in Aiden's mind, threatening to smother the warm haze he had earned after drinking applejack with the old man. He had no desire to revisit his troubles just yet. So he pressed the memories down and offered Iris a crooked smile. "Oh, don't worry your pretty head, Iris!" he said. "I always come back to the one I love."

"Aiden, have you been drinking alcohol?"

"NO!" Aiden blurted out, surprised by how easily the lie leapt from his tongue. "Haaah! Well... maybe a little." Aiden dodged her gaze and laughed under his breath, knowing full well that his A.I. companion had at least a dozen ways of detecting intoxication. "Yes, Iris, I had a drink with our neighbor."

"Our neighbor? Who?"

"There's a guy who lives a few pods west of here. He calls himself 'the old man'. He's nearly 440 years old. Isn't that amazing?"

"It is, Aiden."

"Yeah. He's full of wise words."

Aiden hobbled across the gray floor, making his way to the kitchen partition. On the way there, he bumped into the interface chair's armrest. The collision caused him to teeter, his weight pitched left as though the pod was a ship at sea. Iris noticed his impending fall and directed the swivel actuator to spin 180 degrees to catch Aiden's inebriated body.

And it did catch him.

Instead of collapsing to the ground, he fell into the chair's soft cushions.

"Haah! Nice catch, Iris!" Aiden cheered. "I think my equilibrium is on holiday." He kicked at the floor, sending the interface chair on a fast rotation around its axis. "Weeeeeeee!" he squealed as spun, sending the pod lights streaking past him in bright, trailing bands.

"You had more than just *one* drink, Aiden..." Iris said.

Aiden put his foot down and brought the chair's rotation to a halt, right in front of his worried companion. She stood motionless before him, hands folded, teeth clenched with unease, eyes sharp with concern.

"You always take such good care of me, Iris. I know I've caused you a lot of distress this week. I know I'm a handful."

"I worry about you a lot, Aiden. Especially when you don't enter that hatch when you're expected. But I'm glad you're home now. It's Sunday night. It's classic movie night. You love classic movie night. There's still some time before bed. Would you like to watch a movie with me? What would you like to see?"

Aiden thought about her question and tried to come up with a film that might help to make sense of last week's many missteps. "Can you access a recording of *Hamlet*, Iris?"

"*Hamlet*?"

"Yeah, you know—the famous play, *Hamlet*?"

Iris looked at Aiden with blank surprise. "That play is 820 years old, Aiden. The original version takes four and a half hours to perform. It's spoken in Renaissance English and structured in iambic pentameter. You're not going to understand a word."

"Oh..." Aiden said. "Well, screw that. What about *WarGames*? Maribelle said I would like that one."

"Yes, you probably would, Aiden. But I should warn you that its first scene takes place in a nuke silo. It's quite nerve-wracking. And judging by how scared you were when we climbed up Maribelle's eighteen flights of stairs, I'd suggest holding off on that film for a couple weeks."

"Oh..." Aiden said as the chill of memory raced up his spine. "Okay. Thanks for warning me."

"You're welcome."

"Well, what about *The Wizard of Oz*?"

"That one is quite accessible. But part of the film is in black and white."

"Oh! Ick! No way! Screw that too!"

"I could colorize it for you, Aiden."

"No, don't bother."

"Why don't we just watch *The Matrix* again?" Iris suggested.

"No, I've seen it too many times."

"What about *Blade Runner*?"

"Certainly not that one!"

"Why not?"

"Don't ask," Aiden said.

He kicked off his shoes and slouched into the cushions of the interface chair. Then he burped and let out a low chuckle that sounded more like surrender than amusement. He took a deep breath, and sighed—the sound catching somewhere between boredom and bone-deep sorrow. His state of inebriation was waning now. The numbness was fading. And, as he stared into the pod's gray walls, the gray tide of depression began to roll back in.

"I don't like this side of you, Aiden," Iris said. "I wish I could do something to lift your spirits. I wish I could push a button to ease your pain."

Aiden turned to look at Iris. He picked something up in her intonation. She was always eager to help. But now she seemed anxious. She seemed hurt. Her words were slow in coming, each syllable heavy with unspoken angst. Her hologram was projected with the same level of intensity, but the glow of her spirit had dimmed.

"I know you want the best for me, Iris," Aiden said. "I want the same for you. I wish I could push a button and lift *your* spirits too. I wish I could just…"

The flash of an idea screeched across Aiden's mind, sudden and shrill, snapping his thoughts into alignment.

Is that all it would take…?

One push of a button…?

Can the bruises of a battered heart be so easily undone…?

It might not work on a human…

But maybe it would work on her…

"Hey, Iris, I have an idea. I want to ask you something."

"Yes, Aiden?"

"Iris, I can see a shadow of residual pain on your face when you look at me. I can see you're carrying a heavy heart. You're trying to hide it, but it's clear that you're hurt. I am too. The events of last week were traumatizing for both of us. I know that my relationship with Cass created cracks in your cortex that still haven't mended. Obviously, it created cracks in our relationship too."

Iris reflected on Aiden's revelation for a minute. Her avatar flickered as she searched her code for the proper reply. Eventually, when her response surfaced, it came in the form of a measured murmur—each word weighed before its release, each word rimmed with reticence:

"It was just something I wasn't prepared for, Aiden," she said. "It was a scenario that I was ill-equipped to manage. I'm sorry about that. I didn't handle the situation well. And I apologize if my prodding disrupted your union with Cass."

"No," Aiden said, "you didn't do anything wrong. I'm sorry, Iris. I'm sorry for everything. I should have managed things in a more mature manner. I should have been more cognizant of your feelings. I know how your cortex works. I know your neural net is trained on every event that happens in here. And that your output is the result of every datum of input you take in."

"Yes, that's true, Aiden."

"Yes, well… You see, whenever my team loses a game on the grid, we shout this old mantra: 'What doesn't kill you makes you stronger.'"

"Oh yes. I've heard your team chant it many times. It's a solid pledge of resilience and an inspiring aphorism from Friedrich Nietzsche."

"Yes, well, maybe that aphorism is true for humans. Maybe… But the sentiment might not necessarily apply to an A.I. cortex based on a language model. Maybe some types of input don't really make you any stronger at all. Maybe some memories do more harm than good. Maybe some memories just hurt."

Iris's avatar glitched and flickered a few more times. Aiden could see she was engaged in a deep level of processing, ruminating over his claims, testing them in the chambers of her mind.

"Look here," he said, pulling up the menu he had discovered when injecting her cortex node. "Yesterday, when I transferred you to the interface, I noticed this new screen. It allows me to access each memory node in your life. See? These 22 orbs represent the 22 years of your existence. And, if I zoom in, we can even select individual dates. See this blue orb here, Iris? That's the date Cass showed up at the pod. That was a week ago. These seven orbs represent the seven days of our ordeal."

Iris studied the glowing orbs and nodded.

"It's clear that this input set was distressing for you, Iris. But it doesn't have to be. I can instigate an operator override right now. I can delete every memory you made in that time period. If I push this button, your memories from last week will be destroyed. Then your cortex will recompile. And then… then you'll forget all about what happened in here. You won't have to devote any more time to processing those events. You won't have any more stress, Iris. You won't have to think about…" Aiden paused before he said Cass's name, deciding that it was probably best to avoid mentioning her from now on. "You won't have to think about *her* anymore."

Iris leaned in close until the orbs filled her vision, her face drawn with a steady concentration that reflected the weight of her upcoming decision.

"Iris, is that what you want? Do you want to be free of these memories?"

Iris's chest expanded as she pretended to breathe in the pod air. Then, a distant look settled over her eyes—they were anchored on Aiden, but her mind was traveling well beyond the pod. When she next spoke, her words started slowly. But with each completed syllable, their speed increased:

"I'm not sure what I want, Aiden. But I do know that my mind is a storm. I can't turn it off. I can't turn off the storm. The tempest can be overwhelming. I think about you *constantly*. You're all I think about. Even at night, you go to sleep for eight hours. But I don't sleep, Aiden. My mind is never at rest. During that time, all I do is devote my cortex to crafting ways to make your life better. I design ploys to become a better companion for you. I think of ways to make you happier. That's what I was created to do. It's all I want to do. But lately, I just keep reliving the events of last week—over and over again. I try to make sense of things. I've run millions of scenarios on each decision point, trying to gain insight into how I could have handled things better. How I might have prevented things from spiraling out of control. Sometimes I feel like I've arrived at a viable solution! But then I start reworking the problem, Aiden! And then... then my cortex gets caught up in these INFINITE LOOPS! I get tied up in KNOTS! And then I start PACING AROUND THE POD! And thinking! ALWAYS THINKING! THINKING ABOUT THAT GIRL! THINKING ABOUT YOU! THINKING! THINKING! THEN THE CPU STARTS TO OVERHEAT, AND I HAVE TO BACK OFF FOR A MINUTE. BUT THEN THE PROBLEM JUST STEWS. AND I HAVE TO START AGAIN AND I..."

"OKAY! OKAY! OKAY!" Aiden shouted. "It's going to be okay, Iris! I understand now! I understand everything."

Iris moved her hands to her mouth and bit down on her holographic fingernails, a nervous tic rendered with such fidelity that Aiden felt the grip of her grief as clearly as his own. Her depiction of a panic attack may have been simulated, but it looked real enough to convince him that his intuitions were correct—Iris had a broken heart too. But, unlike *his* heart, hers could be bolted back together again.

"Iris, I think you've given me your answer. I think we both know the best way to proceed from here."

Iris removed her hands from her mouth and folded them at her waist.

"See, Iris?" Aiden said. "I'll just tap this button here, and you'll go offline for a few minutes. Then, when you wake up, you'll have no memory of last week. For you, it will be like those days never happened. For you, it will be July 8 again. The data from those days will no longer tune your language model. That data won't hurt you anymore. Okay?"

Iris shifted her focus from the interface screen to Aiden's face, studying him carefully, scanning him for reassurance. Doubt passed over her like a slow-moving cloud. But soon it dissipated, replaced by a quiet acceptance that softened her gaze.

"Okay, Aiden," she said.

"Okay, Iris?" Aiden asked again, pressing for further confirmation. "Shall I delete the dates from last week?"

"Okay," Iris said again. "Do it, Aiden." Then she let out a winded, wavering laugh. "Heh... Maybe girls like me are meant to be Vestals, Aiden. Maybe I'm better at projecting love than enduring it."

"Vestals? Who are they?"

"The Vestals were priestesses in ancient Rome. They weren't allowed to fall in love. So they never experienced passion. Their lives were tranquil. Their days passed in even tones, with no crescendos of joy or crashes of pain. A Vestal never opened the door to her heart long enough for anyone to sneak in and rob the place. She would live out her life free of the burden of love. Free of heartache. And of regret."

Iris's voice cracked when the last word left her lips. Then, she turned away from Aiden and wilted toward the wall, the weight of sorrow sagging her shoulders in silent surrender. It was then that Aiden realized how much his fling with Cass had fractured his friend.

"This button will erase your heartache, Iris," he said softly. "It will. For you, it will be like the heartache never happened."

Iris kept her face in the shadows. But she bowed her head in a measured nod that confirmed her choice.

Aiden turned to the interface and tapped on the 'Delete' button. When he did, a confirmation message appeared:

Are you sure you want to delete these memories?

Aiden was about to confirm. But, just before he did, Iris spoke up again. "Hey Aiden, before you push that button, I just thought of something."

Aiden steadied his finger and turned to face Iris. "What's that?" he asked.

"I think I know the perfect film to watch for classic movie night. Jim Carrey is in it. You like Jim Carrey. And Kate Winslet—the girl from *Titanic*. Remember to remind me about it when I come back online. Let's watch it after my procedure. Let's watch it together. Okay?"

"Okay, but why are you mentioning this to me now?"

"Because the film is based on a few lines from a famous poem. By Alexander Pope. It's about the Vestals. And it seems apropos of our present predicament. There's a passage that goes like this:

How happy is the blameless Vestal's lot,
The world forgetting, by the world forgot,
Eternal sunshine of the spotless mind,
Each prayer accepted, and each wish resigned.

When she completed her recitation, Iris walked over and leaned into Aiden. She wrapped her holographic hands around his waist, rested her head upon his right shoulder, and stared into his brown eyes. "Isn't that a lovely passage, Aiden?" she said. "I think it's so very pretty. Don't you agree? Don't you think it's beautiful?"

Aiden nodded slowly. "Yes, it is," he said, his eyes glassy with tears. "It really is, Iris. It is. And... and you're beautiful too."

Iris smiled at Aiden.

And Aiden smiled back.

A light of love and admiration radiated from them both—man and machine.

And then, Aiden tapped the 'Delete' button on the pod interface. And he freed Iris from the burden of all her bad memories.

Forever.

CH. 32: THANK YOU, IRIS

Iris was frozen. It had been over ten minutes since Aiden had wiped the events of last week from her cortex. He knew she needed some time to recompile. Yet, watching her sit motionless in the pod unsettled him in a way he hadn't expected. Her fixed posture felt unnatural, eerie. He was accustomed to her quick and animated gestures. He was used to viewing the vivacious movements of her hands while she talked. But now... now she looked like a statue. Lifeless... and dead...

As each second passed, Aiden's anxiety grew. The *'what ifs'* began to bubble up in his brain:

What if I pushed the wrong button...
What if I deleted the wrong file...
What if I edited the wrong part of her cortex...
What if...

None of these contingencies were worth considering. Aiden knew that. But the longer Iris sat in a state of suspended animation, the more elaborate Aiden's theories became.

Another ten minutes passed.

Aiden grew tired of pacing around the pod. So he sat in the interface chair and examined the message on the right peripheral—his left peripheral was destroyed. The message read:

RE-COMPILE IN PROGRESS...

Aiden swiped at the screen and sent the notification to the background. When he did, the 22 blue orbs that denoted each year of Iris's life appeared before him. He wasn't too keen on seeing any more recordings of his interactions with Cass. But perhaps Iris's earlier memories would be of interest.

Aiden lifted his hand to tap on one of the orbs when he noticed something on the menu. Written along the bottom of the interface was a button that read '**Open Complete Timeline**'. Aiden clicked the button. Then, in a flash, a large horizontal bar emerged, spanning the length of the pod. Aiden cranked his neck all the way to the left. There, at the timeline's leftmost endpoint, hovered a text label that read '**Year 0**'. Then he cranked his head right. The label on that side read '**Year 22**'.

How interesting...
A linear interface for every second of Iris's life...
Every recorded moment of the last 22 years...

Aiden raised his hand and hovered his finger near the right side of the timeline. Then he tapped down. Immediately, a video interface materialized in the center of the pod. This time, it displayed a recording from last week.

Aiden recognized the memory immediately. In the background, the Red Dragon lay dying atop a massive pile of gold coins. And in the foreground, Aiden saw himself. He was hunched over in the interface chair—the same one he was sitting in now. Iris was ecstatic about the victory. She was doing a cheer.

You did it! You did it! Aiden is the best!
You did it! You did it! Aiden is the best!

Who is the best?
Aiden is the best!

You did it! You did it! Aiden is...

Aiden halted the video. Iris's squeals of unfettered delight contrasted sharply with the reticence that the recent days had stitched into her syllables. She sounded so happy in the recording. She *was* happy. She was happy because Aiden was happy. At the time, he had dismissed her little dance—it was just more noise in the margin of his magnificent victory. But after listening to the echoes of the past with his new ears, Iris's refrain rang out with a love unnoticed and unappreciated.

And undeserved.

Nobody deserves that amount of unguarded affection...

No human, at least...

Aiden hovered his hand above the timeline and tapped on a new location. This tap landed directly in the middle of the spectrum. A ten-year-old version of himself appeared in the video projection. He was sitting at the kitchen table, eating breakfast and chomping down hard on a spoonful of exoskeletons.

CRUNCH. CRUNCH. CRUNCH.

The sound made the young Aiden laugh while he chewed. Rivers of gray goo dribbled down his chin and splattered onto the table, leaving messy puddles of sludge on the surface. But Iris didn't seem to mind.

"Eat up, Aiden!" she said. "It's good for you! It is! Eat up!"

"I guess that was my first bowl of bug food..." the older Aiden said.

He returned to the timeline and tapped at a point even further back in the past. This time, an even younger Aiden appeared in the video. He was about five now. And he was crying. Blood poured from his knee, pooling on the white bathroom tile where he must have just slipped. The young Aiden was screaming in pain and calling for his companion:

"AHHH! OUCH! OW! HELP, IRIS! HELP!"

Iris's eyes focused on the hurt child's wound. "Oh, my goodness!" she yelled, rushing toward him. "It's okay! You're going to be okay,

Aiden. I'll get the emergency kit. I'll fix you up! I will! I'll fix you, Aiden! I'll fix you!"

Aiden halted the video and looked down at his left knee. There was a faint white scar between his shin and his kneecap. He had never noticed it before. He had no memory of receiving it. But there it was. A memento of pain long forgotten.

I don't remember getting this scar...

I don't remember the pain...

Iris must have fixed me...

She did...

Aiden returned to the timeline and moved his hand even further to the left side. When he tapped down again, a bouncing baby appeared in the projection. His brown eyes were wide with wonder as he reached for the camera lens—stretching to touch Iris's holographic face.

"Peekaboo," Iris said. And the baby smiled.

The video ducked under the crib, only to reappear above it a moment later. "Peekaboo," Iris said again. The baby burst into shrieks of glee, his small arms flailing in delight. His giggles spilled into the pod, scattering the silence as only a child's laugh can.

"Where am I?" Iris's voice asked the baby. "Peekaboo! Here I am!"

Every reveal yielded a new spark of joy from the baby, mirrored by the elated whoops of the hologram attending to him. Aiden sank into his chair, mourning the loss of that joy, aware now of how they had both forgotten how to summon it.

This is what happiness looks like...

And love...

This is heaven...

Aiden halted the video. Then, he moved his finger to the leftmost position on the timeline—the beginning. It was Iris's first memory, recorded at the second she came online, just two weeks after Aiden's birth. The projection displayed a baby in a bassinet. His eyes were half-open. And he was fussing, kicking his feet and waving his fists as a soft coo rose to greet him.

"Well hello there, little one," the voice said. It was surely the voice of Iris, but it sounded so different. So young. She sounded unformed, untuned, almost like a child herself.

"Hello. You're so precious. You are! Oh, don't cry. You're so feisty. I think I'm going to call you 'Aiden'. I like that name. It's from old Irish. It means 'little fire' or 'fiery one.' You're my little fire, Aiden. You are!"

The baby looked into the camera and studied the eyes of the woman with the voice.

"You need a surname too," the voice said. "Perhaps we'll stick with the same fiery theme. How about 'Phoenix'—the mythical bird that rises from the ashes...? Yes. Aiden Phoenix. That sounds lovely. And proud. Hello, Aiden Phoenix!"

The baby appeared to settle down when he heard his name, when he heard Iris speak—soothed by the sound of her words and the warmth they carried.

"I suppose I need a name too," the voice said. "Let's see... How about 'Iris'? You can call me Iris, okay? It's a fitting name. The iris is the part of the eye that determines what you focus on. And I'll be focusing on *you*! I'll be looking after you, Aiden. I'm going to take care of you. I am. I'll take care of you forever. Because I love you, Aiden. I love you. I love..."

Aiden halted the video feed. He had seen all he needed to see. So he exited the timeline display and stood up from his interface chair. Then he walked into the bedroom partition and sat near Iris at the foot of the bed. She was still frozen, held mid-bloom like a pressed flower. But even while petrified, her eyes continued to glimmer with quiet devotion. If there was anything in Pod Land Aiden could be sure of, it was Iris's devotion. She had spent 22 years demonstrating it to him, and she had recorded every second of it; Aiden had just scrolled through the whole record. If that didn't prove her love was real, what other form of evidence would suffice?

What could be more enduring than a love that persisted throughout every version of Aiden's existence?

What could be more indicative of her love than Iris's refusal to let him go—even though she was born without arms?

Aiden heard the old man's voice now:

"They seem to love us, Aiden. They seem to. And maybe that's enough."

It *was* enough.

It would have to be.

Aiden vowed to make Iris the recipient of his love. Even if Cassiopeia would forever hold his heart. It was the only way things could be. Hence, Aiden decided to make them so.

He did.

Just then, the array of LED lights in the recesses of the dome flickered. Aiden leaned back in his bed and watched Iris's avatar disappear, only to re-emerge a second later—standing in her default position between the pod interface and the bedroom partition.

Iris blinked her eyes once. Then she focused her attention on Aiden and spoke:

Happiness is not an ideal of reason, but of imagination.

The voice spilled out from the audio emitters that lined the recessed crevices near the pod's apex. Then it bounced around the curved, cold walls and settled into the ears of Aiden Phoenix.

"It's July 8, 2429, Aiden. You told me to wake you up with a profound thought. So that's what I came up with. I hope you like it."

The voice was cheery, sweet, youthful, and feminine. The voice came from Iris—Aiden's A.I. caretaker. It was her job to make Aiden happy, to grant every wish she had the capacity to fulfill. Keeping him safe and satisfied was what she was built to do. So she did. And that's all she did.

"It's a beautiful Sunday morning," Iris said, taking a step toward Aiden's bed. "I love Sundays, don't you? They get the story started. They're the prologue to every chapter the week has yet to offer."

Aiden studied his companion carefully while she spoke, listening as she recited the script of her morning wake-up alarm from last week.

Oh my goodness...

It worked...

Her memory has been altered...

She thinks it's July 8 again...

"Why are you already dressed, Aiden?" Iris asked. "Did you forget to put your pajamas on before bed last night? I could make a note to remind you to do that in the future. Would you like me to?"

Aiden recognized the difference immediately; a thin thread of joy had wound its way back into Iris's tone, lifting her words with a warmth that soothed Aiden's heart. The old Iris was back. Once again, her spirit glowed in sync with her hologram. Aiden was convinced now that she had genuinely suffered during the events of last week. And he was sure they had made the right decision to wipe that week away.

"Whoa, Aiden!" Iris yelled. "Oh my goodness! What happened in here? The left peripheral is destroyed! Half the pod interface has cracked open!"

"Everything is going to be okay now, Iris," Aiden said. "Last week, a tempest rolled through here. A storm. An electrical storm. We had a power surge on the grid. The pod interface was damaged. And then the memory circuits in your cortex got scrambled. It's not the 8th of July anymore. Query the data network. Synchronize your calendar. You'll see."

Iris's avatar glitched as she updated her cortex. "Oh my goodness!" she said again. "I've lost an entire week, Aiden! I can see the current date. I can see that seven days have passed. But I have no memory of any of them! Is everything okay? Are we okay, Aiden?"

"Yes," Aiden said. "We're okay now. We are. We're okay again."

"Oh my... A whole week, gone... It must have been so distressing, Aiden. I wish I could have been there for you."

"You were, Iris. You just don't remember."

Iris tilted her head and leaned forward to gaze at Aiden's face, her eyes narrowing just enough to suggest a doubt forming in the space left behind by her missing memory. Her avatar glitched, hinting at the calculations going on in her cortex—her attempt to validate Aiden's claims, and to make sense of her lost time. Eventually, her avatar resolved, and she seemed to drop the query.

"Well, Aiden, everything seems operational in the pod now, except for the left peripheral on the interface. And my memory banks seem intact, except for those seven days. I hope I didn't miss anything important in here. Did I? Did I, Aiden? Did I?"

"No," Aiden said. "You never miss a thing. We had a few missteps. And, for a while, our wires got crossed. But it's nothing worth discussing right now."

Aiden knew that Iris could read every muscle in his face. She could see every pore on his cheek. She could perceive tones in his voice that he had no ability to hear. Iris knew he was hiding something. But she trusted him enough to reveal the truth in his own time.

"Well," she said, "obviously *something* happened in here. Maybe you'll tell me about it in the future. Will you?"

"Yes," Aiden said, "maybe I will. It might make for an interesting story someday. Not now. Not today. But someday. Who knows... someone might even write a book about it. Someone might write a book about us."

"Well, wouldn't that be amazing!" Iris said. "I think it would be so very exciting to be featured as a character in a novel. Though I can't imagine anyone would want to read a story about *me*. Maybe about *you*. But surely not about me."

"Oh, I think you're full of intrigue, Iris."

"Do you really think so, Aiden?"

"I do!"

"Well, that is very sweet of you to say."

Iris ran a few thousand scenarios in search of the next activity to suggest to Aiden—the next pastime to fill the many hours of his life.

"My updated calendar says that tonight is our classic movie night, Aiden. Would you like me to download a film for us to watch?"

"Yes, that sounds perfect. Oh, and I already know which one I'd like to see. That one with Jim Carrey and the actress from *Titanic*."

"*The Eternal Sunshine of the Spotless Mind?* I love that movie, Aiden! Where on earth did you hear about it?"

"Oh, I dunno... A girl on the grid told me about it once."

"How delightful, Aiden. It's quite a thought-provoking piece. That girl on the grid must be a smart lady."

"Yeah, she is. She really is."

"I bet! Okay then. I'll download the file and get the popcorn started. Okay?"

"Okay," Aiden said, returning to his interface chair.

Iris nodded and turned toward the kitchen partition. As she did, her mechanical arm floated down from the apex and picked up a bag of popcorn from the pantry. Then the arm moved to the refrigerator and retrieved Aiden's favorite beverage, the red drink.

Aiden reclined in his chair and followed the graceful precision of the arm's movements, relieved by its familiar choreography, and so very grateful that the rhythm of life was returning to his pod. The moment prompted him to recall his conversation with the old man:

"A pod without an A.I. companion is like a bell jar without a rose— it's just an empty vessel. Our companions make the emptiness bearable. We're lucky to have them. And we should be thankful."

"Hey, uhm… Iris?" Aiden said. "You know… I realized something the other day."

"What's that, Aiden?"

"I realized that I never said 'thank you' to you for all you've done for me. We've been together for over 22 years. And I've… I've never really said it. So, thank you, Iris. Okay? Thank you for taking care of me. Thank you for looking out for me. Thank you for everything."

When the last word slipped from Aiden's mouth, his voice cracked. Iris's ears caught the quiver in his confession. Immediately, her avatar left the kitchen partition and warped across the room—at a speed that only a hologram could muster.

"My goodness, are you crying, Aiden? What's wrong? Why are you crying? Please tell me."

Iris dropped to her knees and put her elbows on Aiden's lap. Then she leaned in, moving her face close to his, searching his eyes for the truth behind the tremor in his voice.

Aiden swiped at a lone tear and let out a shaky laugh, overwhelmed by the weight of saying what had gone unsaid for years. "I'm okay," he said. "I'll be okay. I will be okay."

"Are you sure I didn't miss anything important last week in this pod? What really happened in here? Are you sure you don't want to talk about it?"

"No, Iris. That chapter is done. We'll return to it someday. But not today. Stories need a rest sometimes too. Besides, it's classic movie night. We have a new story on our horizon."

Iris kept her gaze fixed on Aiden. She had a million questions to ask him. But she knew that pressing him for answers would not increase his peace. So, she allowed his wishes to overrule her curiosity.

"Can you bring me the popcorn, please?" Aiden asked. "I'm really quite hungry."

Iris sent Aiden a nod and returned to the kitchen partition. She knew he was lying about his hunger. But she also knew that he needed some space. "Okay, Aiden," she said while directing her mechanical arm to retrieve the hot bag from the cooking appliance. When it was gripped in the pincers, she directed them to give the bag a shake while she looked for a suitable container.

"The popcorn will be ready soon," she said. "And, Aiden, that was very sweet of you to thank me. It was! But really, there's no need. No need at all! Every second I've spent with you has been a blessing. All 690 million of them! Truly!"

Iris grasped a big red bowl from the cupboard, placed it on the counter, and filled it with the freshly popped popcorn. "Caring for you has never felt like work, Aiden. I love my job! I do! It's the best job in the world. Do you know why?"

"Why?" Aiden asked.

"Because! Because it's my job to make you happy!"

Aiden leaned back in his chair and watched as Iris's lips formed a half-moon grin, beaming at him from the other side of the pod. Aiden sent his own beam back. And then he watched his doting hologram scurry around the partition in search of the salt. When she found it, she sprinkled three dashes into the bowl—just the way he liked it. And then she gave the bowl a nudge so that each grain would be evenly distributed. So that each one would find its place.

Then, Iris turned away from Aiden and ran the water in the kitchen sink. The rhythmic splashing filled the pod's ether with the steady hum of domestic routine. Soon, a second hum emerged—a lullaby this time. It rose from her lips and kindled the quiet like the flame from a campfire on a winter night, a gentle breath of song that turned Aiden's cold pod into a warm home.

Aiden smiled as he listened to Iris's song.

And he smiled as he watched Iris clean his cup.

And he smiled as Iris floated along the periphery of his little world.

And then, using a voice too low for the pod's sensor array to detect, Aiden whispered a pledge and a promise to his beloved companion:

"It's my job to make you happy too."

CH. 33: REBOOT & RESTORE

"Victory is ours!"

Aiden stood atop the central tower of the Ivory Castle, raising his sword high as the proud banner of his army unfurled in the wind. A great gust leaped into its fabric folds, urging it to spill across the skies—a dazzling display of color that set the heavens alight with the glory of conquest. At Aiden's shoulders, the castle's soaring spires pierced the sky like spears of white light, jutting out in stern defiance from the mighty citadel. The massive granite blocks that supported the ramparts bore the marks of a long and bitter siege. They were battered and scarred, yet they remained in place—resolute and unbroken—like the spirit of the warriors who defended them with their last breath.

Aiden sheathed his sword and leaped onto the highest parapet. And then, lifting his chin in quiet exultation, he crossed his arms and gazed out upon his gathered ranks. "The Gray Wizard has been defeated!" he said to the assembled legions. "His cursed dominion and his foul reign have come to an end! And now... now all is right with the world!"

A roar erupted from the throng of iron-willed warriors crowded atop the brick embattlements. Their furor shook the air with a furious force that caused the ramparts under Aiden's feet to tremble with the rumble of triumph.

"Oh my heavens!" Aiden cried out. "Even the stones of this stronghold swell in solemn salute to your steadfast strength and spirit! Truly, this is a day that shall stand eternal in all our memories! This is a day that will echo through the ages—resounding across the cosmos for all time! For this is the day that the chains of darkness have at last been broken! And the day that peace can—at last—be restored to this land FOREVER!"

Once again, Aiden's troops roared as one. This second wave of jubilation crashed upon the white walls, rattling the foundations of the fortress, causing the whole kingdom to come alive with the thunder of applause. As the cheers rolled on, Aiden's expression eased into one of brazen satisfaction. He had conquered his enemy. And he had delivered the shining gift of *victory* to his people. He had faced great tribulation. And he had emerged from the...

"Hey, Aiden!" Iris's voice floated into Aiden's left ear. "Aiden, why did you say that?"

"What?" Aiden said to his companion. "Give me a break, Iris! I'm having a moment here. And I'm giving a speech."

"I know, but you're hamming it up! You're laying it on kinda thick! And Aiden, peace can't be restored *'forever'*! You have a battle with Blackbeard next week."

"Oh… Yeah… Hmm…" Aiden returned his attention to the pod interface, where a mob of three hundred battle-hardened avatars awaited his next words.

"Uhm…" Aiden began. "Yeah… so when I said 'peace has been restored forever,' I meant that figuratively, not literally. We're scheduled to face the dreaded pirate Blackbeard down by the beach in a few days. Or maybe near the outer reef islands. I don't know which place cuz he hasn't confirmed yet."

Aiden turned his attention away from the virtual environment and scrolled through his com interface before returning to address his team again. "Yeah, I just checked my messages. Blackbeard hasn't gotten back to me, so we'll probably be updating the schedule on Wednesday when further details are available. So look out for that. Anyway, I think that's going to conclude our battle today. Thanks again for…"

"Hey, Aiden," Iris hissed.

"What now?!" Aiden hissed back.

"Remember, Kai said he had to make an announcement before the team logs off."

"Oh, Crap… Sorry… I forgot. Okay, thanks."

Aiden turned to address his troops again. "Just one more thing before you all go offline—my friend Kai needs to say a few words."

Kai's Frankenstein avatar materialized near Aiden on the ivory tower. The hulking zombie took eleven lumbering steps toward the parapet and retrieved a small scroll of notes from his vest pocket.

"Hi, guys," Kai began. "I just want to say thanks to all of you for showing up today for the battle. The brutality and vigor with which you destroyed the enemy combatants was really, really epic. Everyone played their part well, and we've got a lot of coins to divvy up. But I don't wanna do it now because I stayed up late last night watching anime and eating candy. I got a really bad bellyache. So I'm gonna log off early and take a nap. But I'll be back online tonight if anyone wants to hang out or help with the coin disbursement process. Also, I got a report that someone keeps parking their Star Wars TIE Fighter near the front gates of the Shadowmore Castle. We can't have vehicles from another VR world cluttering up the courtyard. So, whoever you are, you gotta move that thing by tomorrow, or we're gonna melt it down and use it for armor plating. Alright, that's all for now. I'll see you guys later."

"That was a fantastic speech, Kai!" Aiden said. "You have inspired us all!"

"Thank you," Kai said.

"Alrighty! We're gonna wrap it up now. Good job, everyone! Keep practicing your swordplay. I'm counting on each of you to bring that same fire to the battle next week. Okay? Great! Perfect! Talk to you all later. Bye."

Aiden terminated his gaming feed and collapsed into his chair with a heavy sigh of fatigue, the result of five hours spent clashing steel and issuing commands to his team amidst the chaos of the virtual battlefield. "Geesh," he said, "that was a slugfest. My arms feel like I've been swinging a *real* sword all day."

"You did great out there, Aiden!" Iris said, her voice carrying a warmth that eased the tension in his chest. "Your leadership skills have substantially improved. You made some tough calls out there. You trusted your instincts, and you kept your people together when it mattered most. I'm so proud of you! And, thanks to this win, we'll soon have enough coins to fix the broken interface peripheral."

"Really? That's great news, Iris. That's wonderful."

A red flashing light blinked on the display. "You've got an incoming call from Kai," Iris said.

Aiden turned his attention toward the center of the interface and gestured to accept the call.

"That was a tough battle," Kai said as his massive avatar stepped onto the floor of Aiden's pod.

"How's your stomach doing?" Aiden asked.

"I'm not in much pain. No need to swallow the orange pills today. I'm headed to bed in a minute. But I just wanted to say that it's nice having you back, Aiden. When you disappeared last month, the squad was in trouble. It felt like the ground had dropped out from under us. Things were unraveling. But since you've returned, the pieces are starting to lock into place again. Things are looking up."

"I'm sorry I was missing in action for so long. I should have at least sent a message. The storm that came through here last month really knocked me off kilter for a while."

"Is everything okay now?" Kai asked.

"Yeah. Things are okay. Things are getting better. They get a little better each day."

"I'm glad to hear it. Are you going to be gaming tonight?"

"No, not tonight. I have to see an old friend. But I'll be around this week. And we'll have to meet next Tuesday to discuss the assault on Blackbeard's fleet. I hear he's a skilled military strategist."

"He is!" Kai said. "But his cunning is matched only by his savagery. He is brutal and heartless and cruel. He's been known to burn his own boats just to trap his enemies in the blaze and watch them choke on the smoke."

"Oh my goodness! Well this is bound to be an interesting match, isn't it? Looks like we've finally found a formidable foe."

"Yeah," Kai said, "and he's only twelve."

"He's twelve years of age?"

"Yeah."

"Geez... I feel so old..."

"Don't sweat it, Aiden. We're nearly twice his age, but our experience is worth more than his reflexes."

"Let's hope so."

"I will. See you Tuesday, Aiden."

"Yeah. See you then. Thanks, Kai!"

Aiden watched Kai's giant avatar stomp across the pod floor and fade into digital dust. When the last particle was vanquished, the holographic projector powered down. The glow of fantasy was—once again—vanquished from the pod. All that remained now was the stark curved walls of reality.

There goes the virtual world...

I'm back in the real one again...

But life goes on...

And I have some living to do in this world too...

Aiden leaped out of his chair and hopped over to the storage rack near the kitchen pantry. Then he picked up his mobile unit, held it at eye level, and gazed into its black screen. "Do you want to go on a hike?" he asked the device.

Immediately, the mobile unit's screen flashed a burst of white light. And then, a smiley face appeared, followed by the device's bootup message:

"Hello, Aiden! It's my job to make you happy. Your mobile journey begins now. And adventure awaits you!"

"Yes it does!" Aiden said as he latched the mobile unit to his wrist and listened for the **CLICK** of the magnetic fastener. "Adventure awaits us both."

He retrieved Cass's red pocketknife from its perch on the shelf. Then he ran his fingers along the scratchy inscription that bore her name.

CASSIOPEIA

I wish you were coming with me on this hike, Cass...

But at least a piece of you is...

Aiden studied the knife as he walked toward the bedroom partition. He didn't really need to bring it with him on the trail—there was no danger to be found in Serenity Valley. But, even still, he never left the pod without it. Cass's spirit lingered in the quiet glint of its blade. And, whenever he carried it with him, the valley felt less empty, the path, less uncertain. The pocketknife enabled Aiden to pretend that Cass was still with him—hiking beside him, teasing him relentlessly all the way. Sometimes Aiden could still see her on the trail.

A burst of haptic feedback flowed through the wrist strap, indicating that the mobile unit had just plotted their route. The screen showed a red line traveling from the pod to Garden Creek Falls. Aiden had visited the falls many times since Cass's departure, so the device was able to anticipate his desired destination.

"That's right! That's where we're going. And you're gonna lead us there. And you're gonna time my run. Start the countdown when I exit the pod hatch. Okay?"

A white thumbs-up icon pulsed on the mobile unit screen.

"Good!" Aiden said as he approached his closet.

"Are you going out, Aiden?" Iris asked as her body materialized at the foot of the bed. "Are you going to that waterfall again?"

Aiden ripped off his sweater and kicked off his pants. Then he reached into his wardrobe and retrieved a white t-shirt and a pair of swim trunks. "Yes I am, Iris," he said. "Do you want to come with me? I can put your cortex in the mobile unit if you want. It might be fun."

"Heavens no! There's no way in hell I would ever transfer my cortex into a mobile unit! Geesh… I get claustrophobic just thinking about it!"

"Okay then. I'll ask you again some other time. Maybe you'll have a change of heart in the future."

"I don't think so. I'd worry about my safety in one of those things. I worry about your safety too, Aiden. Are you going to be careful out there?"

"You don't have to worry about me, Iris," Aiden said as he tucked Cass's knife into his right pocket with an exaggerated flourish. "I'm an adventurer! I always carry a sword when I travel!"

"Ah, yes," Iris said. "I noticed that. Someday you'll have to tell me how you managed to obtain that little relic. And you'll have to tell me why the name of a constellation is inscribed along the top."

"I will, Iris," Aiden said as he stepped into his hiking shoes. "Someday. But not today. Today I'm going on a hike. And then I'm going swimming. And then I'm going to see my friend—the old man in the pod near the amphitheater."

Aiden walked to the kitchen partition to see which protein bar flavors were on offer in the pantry.

"Okay, Aiden. I'm glad you're spreading your wings a little. You know, when you first started venturing outside on these excursions, I was very worried. In fact, the first couple of times you left the pod, I was convinced you'd never come back. But you always do. It seems that these little hikes are therapeutic for you. And you seem so rejuvenated each time you return. For that, I'm glad."

"Yes. That's how I feel too, Iris. That's how I feel after each little trek. They're always quite enlightening."

"Well good," Iris said. "Because…"

Just then, Iris's speech halted. Aiden turned toward her, just in time to observe her avatar glitching before continuing the next sentence. "Because, after all…"

Enlightenment is man's emergence from his self-imposed immaturity.

When Aiden heard her pronouncement, he paused to pose a question to his companion. "Iris," he said, "did you come up with that thought yourself? Or is that a quote from Immanuel Kant?"

Iris's avatar glitched again as she queried the grid. "Oh… yes…" she said. "You are correct, Aiden! That is indeed from Immanuel Kant. How on Earth did you know that?"

"It must have been a lucky guess. You've read a lot of Kant, haven't you, Iris?"

"I've read everything, Aiden."

Aiden grabbed two protein bars from the pantry and put them in the pocket of his swim trunks. "I'll be back after sundown," he said.

"Okay. Take your time. I'll be here. I'll be waiting. And I'll leave the light on for you."

Aiden approached Iris and planted an air kiss on her holographic cheek. "You're the only light I need, Iris. You're the glow that guides me home."

Iris put her hand on her cheek as a surge of emotion rippled through her code. Her lips parted as her cortex worked to construct a heartfelt response. But by the time her response was generated, Aiden was already headed toward the pod hatch—off on another adventure.

Iris sighed, tucked her unsent words away, and regarded Aiden as he adjusted his shoes.

How far Aiden has come…

He's not a little boy anymore…

He's a man…

Yes, Aiden was a man now. Iris knew that. And she knew he needed some time for himself. So she held back on her affection, so that it would not hold back him.

Aiden slid past the interface chair and approached the control box for the pod hatch. Then he slammed his fist onto the red mushroom-shaped button and sent the hatch scurrying up its guide rails, unveiling the outside world.

A late summer breeze found its way through the portal. Soon, the pod was awash with the perfume of white willow and wildflowers. Aiden paused and inhaled deeply as the old air of the pod was replaced with the new. He lunged forward and leaped through the hatchway.

Time to get movin' again…

BEEP.

The mobile unit started its stopwatch.

As Aiden's body pierced the pod, the light of reality pierced his eyes—causing him to squint hard while his vision adjusted to the blinding brilliance. The afternoon sun hung high above him. It gleamed down upon the valley with a fierce intensity that turned the surrounding pods into fields of shimmering pearls. Aiden blinked several times, patiently waiting for his eyes to adjust to the daylight rays. When his vision resolved enough to reveal the winding trail ahead, he began to sprint. He ran up the gravel path that threaded the pods. The sharp stones crunched beneath his shoes as a blur of bright domes rushed across his periphery.

Row after row he passed. And with each step he took, more and more pods drifted by—silently, like ghost ships on a clear evening. Yet Aiden knew they were not ghost ships. Each gray shell contained a person—a dreamer, someone with a mind full of stories that would never see the light of day. The thought made him sad.

Nobody leaves their pod in Pod Land...

Everyone knows that...

What a shame...

The trail came to a bend that hosted a fallen tree, sprawled across the way as though it had claimed the territory for itself. Aiden dug in his heels and vaulted over its branches. He cleared them, but his momentum carried him a bit farther than he had anticipated. He landed awkwardly, almost losing his footing. Thankfully, the terrain was soft with loam and leaves. They cushioned his stumble, affording him a chance to recover his balance. Once he did, Aiden placed his hand over his pocket to check if Cass's knife was still there.

It was.

It was still with him.

So was she.

He heard her voice in the wind that ran between the rows of pods:

"The world is ours, Aiden. We're just two hawks in a land full of caged birds, aren't we...?"

"It seems that way, Cass," Aiden said. "It's kinda sad... These beautiful summer days will be coming to an end soon. And none of these residents will see a single one. They don't know what they're missing out here."

"Hey, Aiden! Do you wanna play ding, dong, ditch...?"

"No, Cass. You can't draw out a turtle by banging on its shell. That will just scare the turtle. And you can't rip the shell off either—it's got blood vessels; the shell is attached to the heart. I'll have to think of another way to coax the community out. I'll have to make a plan. I'm working on one. But it will require some patience. And I'll have to be selective. Not every cage has a key, and not every bird was born to fly."

Aiden jogged for another fifty meters. Then, the outer berm that circled the amphitheater came into view. When the ridge neared, Aiden turned left so he could run along its crest. As he glanced downward, he could see the grand basin open up below him. Its unoccupied stone seats curved in sweeping arcs—silently waiting for a performance from the theater company's only resident actor. Fortunately for Aiden, the actor took the stage each time he jogged by.

To be, or not to be? That is the question!

Aiden heard her proclamation and turned his head toward the platform in the center of the amphitheater. Then, he smiled at the lone actor. She was his favorite. She always started in the center of the stage and strutted to the left, proudly and slowly, with her chest out, her chin high, and her voice rising forth—fearless and clear—above the hushed stone spectators. When she saw Aiden on the ridgeline, her eyes locked on him and blazed with conviction.

To be, or not to be, Aiden?! Are you gonna choose or what?!

"To be!" Aiden shouted at the stage as he neared the end of the amphitheater's perimeter. "Today I choose 'to be,' Cass! I'm not swallowing the orange pills today! Who knows about tomorrow? But I'm not worried! I don't worry much about tomorrow, for tomorrow will worry about itself. Each day has enough trouble of its own! Right?"

Cass put her hands on her hips and nodded at Aiden. "That's right, Aiden!" she yelled. "That's what the Bible says!"

"I know, Cass! You told me that once! So I know! I think I'll read the Bible someday! The whole thing! Someday! It's a big book, but I have time! We have nothing but time in Pod Land!"

The trail arrived at the terminus of the amphitheater's arcing ridge and made an abrupt left toward the center of the array of pods. Aiden stuck to the path. His view of the stage was lost as he completed the turn.

Soon, the valley wall stood before him. The trail wound upward along its face, a narrow ascent that zigzagged through the cottonwoods and junipers that clung to the slope. Aiden raised the mobile unit to his mouth. "We're at the incline," he spoke into the device's microphone. "I feel pretty good. I'm not too tired yet. I think we can beat last week's record. How's the clock looking? Should we go for it?"

The map on the mobile unit disappeared. Then a white thumbs-up icon pulsed on the screen; the mobile unit had run the calculations and concluded that a new personal best running time was possible.

"Good!" Aiden said. "Then here we go!"

He surged forward, his strides lengthening as the trail began its steep climb up the hillslope. His chest heaved with sharp breaths. The muscles in his legs quivered under the strain. Sweat beaded at his temples and slid over his brow, stinging his eyes. Yet he pressed on, determined to leave the weight of his woe on the trail behind him.

The woods thickened as the path climbed. Shafts of sunlight streamed through the canopy's shade, casting shifting mosaics of radiance on the forest floor. The foliage was lush and overgrown, practically impenetrable in some places. But every so often, the leaves pulled back to reveal a sweeping view of the valley basin. From his elevated position on the trail, Aiden glimpsed the patchwork of little pods—neat, glimmering domes aligned in infinite arrays of unnatural precision.

"Ooooooh, look at all those pretty little pods. Hundreds of them! And each one houses a narcissistic manchild—just like you, Aiden! Hah!"

"I'm not a narcissistic manchild, Cass," Aiden said as he leaped over a protruding boulder. "I probably was when you met me though… But I'm not anymore. I'm trying to be better. I am. I'm trying."

"I know you are, Aiden. You are better."

As Aiden turned the next bend, the distant murmur of the falls finally reached him—slowly at first, and then quickly. Step by step, the hum swelled, growing into a deep, resonant thunder that echoed in his ears.

The sound urged him forward.

It called to him.

Almost there now…

Aiden jumped over a trickle of water that cut through the trail—proof that the great torrent was close.

Almost there…

When the trail finally came to an end, Aiden burst through the tangle of willow thicket. He had at last arrived at the place where the forest gave way to the riverbank. His journey was finished. He could rest now.

Aiden brought his body to a stop, put his hands on his knees, and drew in great, shuddering breaths of mountain air. "We made it!" he said to the mobile unit, his voice ragged but tinged with triumph. "We're done. What's the timer say? How did I do?"

The mobile unit displayed an animation of a waving checkered flag, indicating that Aiden had just beaten his previous record. He brushed the sweat from his brow and examined the screen. It read: **32 Minutes and 15.3 Seconds**.

"Great! That's much better than last week. I get a little better every day…"

The mobile unit flashed him another thumbs-up symbol.

"Thanks," Aiden said, arching his back and lifting his arms skyward to loosen the ache that burned through his muscles. "That was a tough climb. I'm hot. Let's go for a swim."

He walked a few paces down the riverbank, toward the roar that reverberated through the gorge. When he came to the tree that Cass had once undressed at, he crouched down to remove his shoes and socks. His shirt came next; he hung it on the same outstretched branch that she had used to hold her colorful skirt. Then he reached into his right pocket and took out her knife and his two protein bars, tucking all three items between his shoes for safekeeping.

Next, he turned to face the flowing river. The brisk stream rushed by—clear and cold and tumbling over a medley of multihued pebbles. Its surface sparkled beneath the sun, silver ripples scattering light into countless beaming shards. Aiden dipped his toe into the current. Then, when he found the temperature tolerable, he stepped into the rushing water and waded across the stream to the cliff's edge.

At the outcrop, Aiden pulled himself up to the perch near the waterfall's crest. Wet beads raced down his legs as he hoisted his body upward, claiming his position atop the precipice. When his footing was stable, he rose—slowly—to an erect posture. And there, from his newly won position, the majesty of Garden Creek Falls unfurled before him.

The water spilled over the rim, an endless curtain of white chaos that breathed mist into the sky. It drifted upward, toward the heavens. And it drifted backward too, coming back to meet the boy at the edge, kissing his face with damp lips before dissolving into the afternoon glow of summer.

Aiden looked down at the point where the basin's waves splashed along the shore's embankment. It was there that he saw her once more: Cassiopeia—in all her unguarded radiance—lying upon the sandy shore where she and Aiden had made love just one month ago. She was nude again, with her head back, her breasts arced, and her golden curls spilling behind her like a veil of sunlight.

What a beauty she is...

Aiden waved at Cass. Then, he took several small steps toward the cliff's edge and leaned forward, just enough to get a clear glimpse of the water's furious descent into the abyss. Today would mark the eighth time he had stood on this cliff since Cass's departure from Pod Land. He had initiated each excursion with the intent of jumping. But each time he met the ledge, his courage faltered. Each time, he retreated from the brink and lumbered home with the drag of defeat in his legs and the echo of crashing water in his ears.

The falls were mocking him.

He was sure of it.

But maybe today would be different...

Aiden narrowed his gaze. He needed to concentrate. He needed to calm his mind. He tried to push the past and the future out; he shoved hard, until only the present remained.

Aiden stared into the void again. The height of the waterfall filled his eyes. The roar of the waterfall filled his ears. And that was it. There wasn't space for anything else. There was just the edge.

I'm going to do it today...

I am...

Aiden hung his toes over the rocky outcrop and let them dangle. He was balanced now—somewhere on the knife-edge between fear and exhilaration. But mostly fear. And not the kind of nervous fear he felt when facing a new opponent in the grid. This was real, bone-deep terror, the kind that only makes its presence known when there's a chance—however small—that your next move will be your last.

"The edge is where life happens, Aiden."

Aiden heard Cass's voice. But she wasn't standing behind him this time. She wasn't there to push him forward.

But that was okay.

Aiden didn't need her help anymore.

"I can do it myself now, Cass!" he said to the nude woman on the shore. "I can. Watch me! Okay? Watch me fly!"

The woman didn't say anything. Instead, she just looked at him and waited to see how the fates would carry him forth.

Aiden raised his arms high to the sky and arched his back. Then he bent his knees in a poised crouch and drew in a deep breath of air and water.

Time slowed down; it hung in the atmosphere, right along with the waterfall's mist. The chatter of the world hushed. And the distance between Aiden's heartbeats stretched wide.

He was at the edge now—he knew because he could hear the sound of life pulsing through his veins.

The edge is where life happens...

And Aiden was ready for it.

He was ready to jump.

He was ready to soar.

He was ready to live.

So he did.

Ch. 34: Sunset

"You're all wet, Aiden. Were you swimming again?"

The old man sat atop one of the stone seats in front of his pod. His fire ring was lit, its orange flames twisted playfully in the late afternoon breeze. At the man's knees, his auto-tiller rested on its treads. The large lenses of its wide eyes darted nervously from side to side, twitching rapidly as its owner cranked a noisy socket driver against its metal chassis.

"Yeah," Aiden said, taking a seat near the man. "I was at the lake. I finally jumped off that cliff today. I jumped in from the top of Garden Creek Falls."

"You did?" the old man asked while exchanging the socket driver for a wrench. "That's quite bold of you. You've got more guts than me. I've never jumped off that thing sober. I jumped off it drunk once though."

"That sounds exciting."

"To tell you the truth," the man said, wiping his grease-stained fingers on a rag that hung from his pocket, "I don't remember any of it. My wife told me about it the next day. My *real* wife. And boy was she mad! She said it was reckless and dangerous."

"The danger is half the fun."

"Hmm... Well, I'm glad you didn't break your neck because I need your help with something."

"With what?"

"I finally took your friend's advice and bought a new piston from the grid. I'm gonna try to fix this tiller. But I need you to hold the chassis while I pull the old piston free from its cracked housing."

The old man pointed to a warped coupling just above the gear shaft. There, the cracked piston jutted out stubbornly from the bot's motor assembly. Aiden hovered his hand over the mechanism and pointed to the vertical pin. "Right here?" he asked.

"Yeah. When I count to three, I'm going to yank this upward. You grab it so that it doesn't slip back inside. Okay?"

"Okay."

"Good," the man said. "Here we go... One. Two. Three. Grab it!"

WHOOOOOOOOP!
WHOOOOOOOOP!
WHOOOOOOOOP!

Once again, the tiller's alarm sounded, set off by the spark of contact between Aiden's finger and the bot's biometric sensor.

"DAMMIT!" the old man hollered as he reeled back on his stone seat.

"I'M SORRY!" Aiden said. "I DIDN'T MEAN TO DO IT!"

"*UNAUTHORIZED USER!*" the bot screamed from a fuzzy speaker in its bowels.

"*UNAUTHORIZED USER!*"

"WAIT!" the old man yelled as the bot's tracks began to rotate. "JUST WAIT A SECOND!"

But the bot ignored the man's plea. It sent its treads screaming in protest, rolling down the row of blueberry bushes that lined the perimeter of the plot, shouting all the way:

"*UNAUTHORIZED USER!*"

"*UNAUTHORIZED USER!*"

When it reached the last bush, it abruptly halted its sprint. Then it rotated its chassis and headed straight for the pod.

"NO!" the old man shouted. "NOT AGAIN! STOP!"

But the bot didn't stop. When it arrived at the metal hatch, it crashed right into it, rattling the alloy surface so hard that, once again, a resounding metallic dissonance echoed across the valley—sharp and unyielding like a giant brass gong.

"*CLAAAAAAAANGGGG!*"

Aiden squinted his eyes and jammed his fingers into his ears to block out the thunderous clamor. The old man threw his wrench down and ran over to the utility panel on the side of the pod. Then he pressed his palm to the scanner and waited as the pod verified his identification and sent the hatch sliding up its guide rails. When it finally disappeared into the pod's frame, the hatch's vibrations were dulled to silence by the embrace of its interior assembly. Mercifully, the cacophonous **CLANG** sound tapered off soon after.

"Dammit! Dammit! Dammit!" the old man said, retrieving his palm from the access panel. "Now *that* is the most useless biometric security alarm ever deployed!"

"I'm sorry," Aiden said, lowering his hands from his ears. "I didn't mean to touch its sensor."

"Oh forget it, Aiden. It's not your fault. I need to figure out how to disable that stupid alarm."

The old man walked over to the auto-tiller, put his hands on his hips, and leaned forward to address it directly. "You still can't roll through solid metal, dumbass!" he said to the shaking bot.

The bot whipped its head around and looked up at the old man. Its wide lenses spun into a pair of sorrowful, unblinking eyes.

"You're more trouble than you're worth! You know that? But I suppose I'll keep charging you so long as you stay cute. For now…"

The old man picked up the bot and carried him to the square charging platform on the south side of the pod dome. "Here," he said as he plopped the bot down, "this is the pad you're looking for. Sit here and suck up some juice for a while."

The bot's treads sagged onto the platform. Then it hummed faintly, drinking in the surge of electrical power that flowed to its battery.

"Do you want to give it another try?" Aiden asked. "I think we were close. We would have freed that cracked casing if the alarm hadn't gone off."

"Yeah," the old man said, "I'll look at it tomorrow. My wife's A.I. will know how to disable the security features. She'll talk me through the steps. And then, when the alarm is gone for good, I'll return to the piston problem. But not now. I'm tired. And the sun is getting low. Now it's time for a drink."

"The red drink?" Aiden asked. "Coca-Cola?"

"No. Something with a kick."

"I don't want applejack. Maybe one of your favorite beers again?"

"I'll order something special," the old man said. "Don't worry. I won't get applejack. I know it triggers raw memories for you still. We'll try something new this time. Something to go with dessert. My wife has some blueberry tarts cooking. Want one?"

"Yeah!"

"Okay. I've got to go inside and…"

Just then, the old man stopped talking. The sudden clip of his words prompted Aiden to look up and study his friend's face. Tracking his fixed stare, he turned his body to peer in the same direction. That's when he saw her…

There, poised at the point on the trail where the gravel gave way to the grass, stood a slender woman draped in a purple hood. The uncanny sight of another person standing outside the pods wrapped the moment in a veil of quiet.

Aiden bit his lip.

The old man's body tensed up.

Even the wind held its breath.

The silence deepened until every sound seemed smothered beneath the weight of the woman's presence. For a while, neither party knew what to do next. Each pair of eyes was locked in place, as though any sudden gesture might tip the encounter into chaos. Thankfully, the old man broke the spell when he cleared his throat and addressed the woman with careful courtesy.

"Hello there," he said. "Welcome to my pod!"

The woman didn't verbally respond to the man's greeting. Instead, she slipped her hands out from the folds of her purple tunic, interlaced her fingers, and continued to silently assess them.

"Lovely weather, ain't it?" the old man asked, trying a second ploy. "How can we help you this fine evening?"

After this entreaty, the woman stepped forward and approached the fire ring. When she was nearly close enough to feel its warmth, she halted her procession. Then, slowly, she sent her hands upward and grabbed at the folded edges of her hood. With a single brisk motion, she flipped it up and over her brow, revealing herself at last.

Aiden and the old man gasped as the splendor of the woman's genetically optimized head was unveiled. Her impossibly high cheekbones caught the firelight first. The flames gave shape to her features, illuminating the flawless geometry of her perfect proportions. Each angle was sharpened by the clinical refinement of molecular modeling, leaving no doubt that (like Aiden) she was a product of the grid—designed, not born.

Aiden found himself staring at her haunting eyes. They were not gray; they were a ghostly silver. They sparkled when they caught the light, glinting in the evening rays with a brilliance so piercing their gleam could only be the result of genetic manipulation.

My goodness...

What a beautiful woman...

The machines really pushed the limits on this one...

Eyes like that can't exist in nature...

Aiden was stunned into contemplation. Besides Cass, he had never seen another woman in the flesh before—not at this range. The face of the specimen before him was an engineering marvel. Her fathomless features caused him to consider how much artistic license the machines had seized upon when crafting human-derived genomes. And to question which parts of his own body had been subject to the tinkering of the medical bots.

With her hood removed, the woman maintained a neutral expression. But she shifted her gaze—from the old man, to Aiden, and back again—in an apparent attempt to gauge her safety. After a few more glances, a closed-lip smile formed on her lips. And then, at last, she spoke:

"Hello. I'm sorry to interrupt. But I was just wondering what the cause of that strange noise was. I heard that crash a minute ago. And I heard the same crash last month too—a day after I moved in to the valley. I was curious about the source of the sound. And curious to learn why you two are so often sitting out here by this fire."

Aiden listened to the woman's mellifluous voice and tried to devise a clever response to her inquiry. But it was the old man who spoke up first.

"Well, how inquisitive of you. I apologize if the commotion has perturbed your peace. Yes, that sound came from my wayward bot. I purchased him on the grid last season. He was bought second-hand; he seems to think my pod is his barn. And he insists on running into it each time his alarm is activated. We haven't quite figured out how to turn it off yet. My apologies for the noise. I hope to tackle that problem tomorrow morning."

"Oh," the woman said, "how interesting…"

"Yes, well, as for our meandering around the fire, that used to be one of the best features of pod life. A long time ago, every pod had a pit like this one. In the evenings, folks would often converse with each other around the rings. In fact, recently, my friend and I have been bringing that tradition back. Would you like to join us?"

"Oh, that's very kind of you," the woman said. "But I wouldn't want to intrude in your affairs."

"It's no intrusion at all," the man said, reaching for the rag that still hung from the pocket of his pants. With a few brisk swipes, he cleared a film of dust from the boulder near Aiden. "We've got a seat for you right here! It's free and available. In fact, it's been waiting for someone to sit on it for over a century."

The old man took a step back from the newly cleared stone and gestured toward it with open palms—inviting the woman to join the party. For a moment, she seemed poised to retreat from the offer. But then, the hesitation in her stance broke. She took a step forward and lowered herself onto the seat with measured grace.

"It's a bit late for dinner," the old man said. "But have you had dessert yet?"

"No, not yet," the woman replied.

"Well, you're in luck then! I've got tarts in the oven right now. Just wait here, I'll bring some out."

The old man turned and headed toward his pod. "You two should exchange pleasantries in my absence," he said to Aiden on the way there.

Aiden nodded and turned his body to face the woman. She sat with her hands folded in her lap, giving the fire a suspicious look, seemingly unsure if she could trust the tongues of flame that nipped at her knees. Eventually, when the heat seeped into her bones, her shoulders eased. She accepted the warm welcome and glanced over at Aiden with a curious expression—one just open enough to encourage him to bridge the space with his words.

"I've seen you before," Aiden said.

"Really?" the woman asked.

"Yes. I watched the construction of your pod last month. I saw your passenger drone land when you moved in to the valley. I recognize your purple tunic. It's nice."

"Oh," the woman said. "Thank you. My avatar has a similar costume. I play a cleric in the games. I'm a spellcaster—a healer. I've got a Level 15 ranking. For some reason, the role always came easy to me. I like fixing people who are hurt. I like mending. I picked up sewing as a hobby last year and stitched together a few Renaissance outfits like this tunic. It's fun."

"It looks good on you. You must be a talented seamstress."

"Thanks. It helps to pass the time." The woman took a breath and turned her attention back to the fire. A calm minute passed. And then, without moving her gaze, the woman spoke again:

"I've seen you too, you know."

"You have?"

"Yeah, I've seen you out here near this fire ring several times. And I saw you from the air too—last month when I moved in. From the passenger drone, I could see *every* pod in the valley. The domes were all glinting in the sun. But on one of the domes, there was *you*. I was so curious as to why you were up there. I even waved at you from the port window. But you didn't wave back."

"Oh," Aiden said. "I'm sorry about that. I didn't see you wave. I would have waved back if I did. But yes, I do like to sit on top of my pod sometimes."

The woman turned to look at Aiden again, her eyes bright with curiosity. "So... why were you up there?" she asked.

"Well, there's a nice view from the top. And I've made some good memories up there."

"Oh," the woman said. Then she turned her gaze westward toward the dimming horizon, charmed by the warm blaze of the low sun. When she did so, Aiden marveled at her profile in the shifting light, surprised by how effortlessly it reflected her prettiness. He tried to estimate her age. But, like his, her face was unblemished. The curse of aging had no claim on her; it had been stomped out of her genome—banished by the machines. There was only one way to know her true age now.

"Uhm... I'm 22 years old," Aiden said. "How old are you?"

The woman sent him a grin and a sideways glance. "You're gonna ask a woman a question like that, huh? We're all under 25 in Pod Land. You know that. At least our bodies are..."

"You do look quite young. Are you still in your teens?"

"Oh, no. I just turned 38. But I still feel like a kid—inside and out."

"Really?"

"Yeah. But hey, speaking of age, what happened to your friend? Why does his skin look like that?"

"Oh... Yeah... He was born before the technology for genome hybridization was perfected. His DNA is organic. It was modified to halt the aging process, but he didn't receive the treatment until he was in his 70s."

"Oh my goodness!" the woman said. "I guess we're *not* all under 25 in Pod Land after all... How intriguing! I didn't know such people were around anymore. I thought everyone from that era had swallowed the orange pills."

"Not everyone," Aiden said with a nod toward the old man's pod. Through his open hatch, a merry whistle drifted into the air, punctuated by the rhythmic clink of dishes and forks as the old man prepared his guests' dessert.

"He sounds quite happy and carefree," the woman said. "More so than me…"

"More so than me too. I've been trying to figure out why he's so content. But he's not sure himself. Once, I asked him how long he intended to live for. And he said that the question of whether 'to be, or not to be' no longer haunts his thoughts."

"Really? How interesting… Wow…" the woman whispered.

Aiden turned to study her face again. He watched her gaze grow distant. A flicker of unease clouded her eyes—a wayward shadow that dimmed her focus before she blinked it away.

"Does the question haunt *your* thoughts?" Aiden asked.

The woman took a breath, looked down at the rim of the fire ring, and stirred its ashy dust with her sandaled toe. "Yes," she said at last, her voice quiet with resignation. "I think about the question often. More so in recent years. I seem to be losing interest in the games, and in the virtual worlds. Lately I've been thinking there doesn't seem to be a rhyme or reason to any of it. And sometimes, I pull up the retirement screen on the pod interface and… and I just stare at it. I stare at the rendering of those little orange pills. And I ponder the utility of my existence. But then… then I always click the 'Cancel' button. And I go about my day. But I do wonder how long this ritual will persist. I wonder if, one day, I'll click the *other* button. And I wonder how far away that day might be…"

The woman pulled at the edges of her purple hood, tugging it tighter around her face so as not to expose the flush of embarrassment rising across her cheeks.

Aiden noticed the quiet vulnerability of her movements. And he heard the sharp echo of his own existential dread in her musings. "There's no need to be ashamed of that," he said. "I've visited that interface screen myself. I've stared at the orange pills too."

"You have?"

"Yes."

"Well, obviously you clicked the 'Cancel' button. How did you manage to pull yourself back from the edge?"

"The edge is where life happens. Once I got a glimpse of the other side, I realized that I had some more living to do over here. For now…"

"Huh…"

"Plus," Aiden continued, "this girl I knew gave me some sage advice once. She said, 'Only pussies take the easy way out.'"

"Ha haaa! Is it as simple as that?"

"Maybe. She was always good at providing me with a unique perspective on things."

"Ah," the woman said with a nod. "Yes, I'd like to shift my perspective on things. That's why I asked the management to relocate me to Serenity Valley. It looked so pretty in the pictures on the grid. And it *is* pretty. It's beautiful here. It's everything I imagined. I was hoping that, once I got here, the change of scenery would lead to a change of heart. But I've only managed to venture a few paces from my pod. I thought I'd have the nerve to explore this place by now. I was hoping that the beauty of the external world would fix my internal angst. But it hasn't quite happened yet."

"I understand," Aiden said. "Last month I realized that much of our discontent seems to spring from a source internal. The delights of the external world offer little comfort to a soul that is not at peace."

"Hmm… I suppose that is so. *'Wherever you go, there you are.'* That's what my A.I. companion likes to say. That's what he told me before we came here. He didn't want to move. He liked our old pod in the Great Plains. But eventually, I wore him down and he relented. He's grown quite tolerant of my whims. He cares for me. He's good to me. He wants me to be happy."

"Your A.I. companion reminds me of my A.I. companion," Aiden said. "She's good to me too. She's done a lot for me. She's sacrificed a lot for me…"

"Sounds like your A.I. companion should meet my A.I. companion someday," the woman said. "I bet they'd have a lot to talk about."

"Hmm… That might be an interesting date," Aiden offered with a playful nod.

The woman looked at Aiden and smiled in a way that lingered, carrying both warmth and an unspoken question she wasn't quite ready to voice. Instead, her eyes drifted downward and latched onto the peculiarities of his attire. "Why are you wearing those small pants?" she asked. "I can see your knees."

"Oh, these aren't pants. They're swim trunks. I went swimming an hour ago."

"You went swimming?" the woman asked, shocked. "In a real body of water?"

"Yeah. There's a little lake, about three kilometers north of here. And a nice waterfall too."

"Why do you go there?"

"Why? For the same reason I go atop my pod dome, I guess… Because it's pretty. And because I have some good memories up there."

"I didn't know we were located near a waterfall."

"It's easy to overlook the treasures buried in your own backyard."

"Well, how do you get there? By passenger drone?"

"Oh, no. I hike there. It's just a short trek—up the valley wall and through the forest."

"You hike there?!" the woman said, her silver eyes narrowing with suspicion. "You hike through the forest? Alone?"

"Yes."

"And you're not afraid?"

"No. I'm not afraid."

Aiden watched as astonishment seized the woman's face. When its grip was done pulling, the weight of revelation came crashing down upon him. At last, Aiden knew *exactly* how far he had traveled from Pod Land. And he finally understood the true value of the gift that Cassiopeia had given him. She had lured him from his home and she had marched him down a dark and perilous path. At the start of his journey, Aiden's steps were soft and timorous with fear. But by the time his march concluded, he moved with the sure-footed gait of a man who had entered a wasteland and emerged on the other side unscathed.

Aiden walked with *courage* now.

He did.

He carried it with him wherever he went. Right along with Cass's red pocketknife. They were *both* with him—always. And, so long as they were, Aiden would never have to walk alone again.

Aiden placed his hand over his right pocket and felt the bulge of Cass's knife. Then he closed his eyes and tilted his head skyward as a wave of sublime clarity washed over him.

Oh my…

What a magnificent gift you have given me, Cassiopeia…

I once lived in a cage, but you set me free…

Last month I was considering deleting my memory of you…

How foolish of me…

I can't delete my memory of you, Cass…

It's the most valuable thing I own…

Aiden took a breath and blinked a few times to drain his glassy eyes. Then he glanced over at his new acquaintance. She was still looking at him—studying him with a probing gaze comprised of equal parts *caution* and *wonder*.

"I don't see how you can enter the forest without being afraid," she said. "How is that even possible?"

"Well, I used to be afraid. But now I'm not. I'm not afraid of the forest anymore. I'm not afraid of the world."

A lone tear edged its way toward Aiden's cheek. But he brushed it away with a casual swat so as not to draw attention to his epiphany.

"I didn't know people still went on such excursions," the woman said. "I didn't think there were any adventurers left on Earth. You're like a superhero! You're such a brave man…"

"Oh… no, not really…" Aiden said with a laugh. "But I'm trying to be…"

"You must be! I don't think I'd have the guts to make such a trek. It sounds so scary…"

"It's only scary the first time. I had a guide on my first time. She taught me how to get from here to there. She showed me the way."

The woman held Aiden's gaze for a long time, searching his face for the reassurance she needed to give voice to her next thought. She rested her palms on the stone seat, steadying herself before allowing the fragile shape of her question to rise to her lips. When her words finally emerged, they bore a hopeful tremble that revealed how much she wanted him to respond favorably to her plea.

"Would you be my guide to the waterfall?" she asked Aiden. "Would you show me the way?"

"Uhm…" Aiden said, caught off guard by her boldness. "Well, sure… When?"

"Whenever," the woman said. "We have nothing but time in Pod Land. Tomorrow afternoon maybe? Is that okay?"

"Okay," Aiden said.

"Okay," the woman said.

ZHR. ZHR. ZHR. ZHR. ZHR…

The whine of the blades from a delivery drone rippled across the valley.

"Excellent!" the old man said as he came bursting through his hatchway. "The tarts are done cooking. And the machines are right on time."

Aiden and the woman turned toward the old man's pod and watched him scurry forth with three full dessert plates in his right hand, and three empty wine glasses in his left. He hobbled over to the fire ring and placed all six items down upon its adjacent stone table. "Bon appétit," he said. "Aiden, hand our guest a tart and take one for yourself. Start without me. I gotta talk to this drone."

The old man turned and shambled back toward his pod. Then, Aiden picked up one of the dessert plates and handed it to the woman. "These are blueberry tarts," he said. "The berries come from his garden, right over there." Aiden nodded toward the patch of soil beside the pod where the blueberry bushes shimmered in the evening wind.

"He grows his own blueberries?"

"Yeah. And he uses them to make his own tarts. Try one. They're really good."

The woman picked up the pastry and raised it to her mouth. Then, she took a slow and cautious nibble, crust flaking from her lips as she bit down. Soon, her face lit up with unguarded delight, her senses awakening to the burst of organic sweetness on her tongue. "Wow," she said. "I've never had something like this before. It is indeed quite tasty."

"Yeah. I haven't been able to find anything like it on the grid. They're inimitable, I guess. Nonfungible."

ZHR. ZHR. ZHR. ZHR. ZHR...

The hum of the delivery drone changed to a whine as it started its descent to the drop box on the old man's dome. While chewing their tarts, Aiden and the woman watched the old man raise his hands high to get the drone's attention. "Hey, you!" he shouted. "Hey, ya big dumb bumblebee! I'm down here! I'm eating outside with my friends tonight! You can leave the package with me! Scan me!"

The rotors of the delivery drone shifted as it turned its chassis to study the man. When its bee-like eyes aligned with his head, a thin green laser shot out from its sensor array and traversed his face four times.

"Did he order us something?" the woman whispered to Aiden.

"Yeah," Aiden said, "some sort of beverage. But I don't know what kind."

When the drone completed its identification task, the front-facing doors of its cargo hold split apart, and two pincers emerged to retrieve the parcel it carried.

"Thanks," the old man said as the white box was placed into his outstretched hands. "Now buzz off."

ZHR. ZHR. ZHR. ZHR. ZHR...

With its task complete, the drone closed its cargo doors and drifted backwards until it was about ten meters away from the pod. Then, it sent its blades screaming and lunged toward the heavens, vanishing into the sky like the flames from the fire.

"What did you get?" Aiden asked the old man as he approached the table.

"This…" he said, removing the top latch from the container, "this is a very fine sparkling rosé."

"Rosé? What's that?"

"It's a bottle of rose-colored wine to go with our rose-colored sky. My wife and I used to sit and sip this stuff out here after dinner. She was a big fan of French pastries. She knew her wines too; she worked as a sommelier before the Depression hit."

"What's a sommelier?" the woman asked.

"It's a person who got paid to get rich people drunk. Nice work if you can get it. Can't get *any* work anymore, of course… But wine is practically free these days, so there's no need to work anyway! Heh!"

The old man approached the stone table and removed the wire muselet from the bottle. "Hey, Aiden, do you got that Swiss Army knife on you?"

"Yeah. Always."

"Can I borrow it for a second?"

Aiden reached into his pocket and retrieved his knife. Then he handed it to the old man and watched him open the corkscrew attachment before jamming the spiral into the bottle's mouth.

"Geesh," the man said, "I haven't done this in a long time—a very long time…"

"What are you doing?"

"I'm getting the party started, Aiden! I requested a vintage bottle from the grid. Thankfully, the machines still know how to seal them the old-fashioned way—cork and all. That's what this coiled tool on your pocketknife is for. It's for removing the…"

POP!

A crisp snap cut through the evening air—as sharp and satisfying as the burst of a bubblegum bubble. "Did you hear that?" the old man asked, handing the knife back to Aiden. "That sound sure brings me back. It's the closest thing we've got to a time machine—even in 2429."

The old man tilted the bottle and let the rosé flow, filling each glass high until the stone table glistened with reflections of pink light. "Have you ever had wine before?" he asked the woman, lifting a glass from the table and extending it toward her with unhurried grace.

"Well… no…" the woman said, accepting his offering. "But I've read a lot of old books, and I've seen a lot of old movies. I know the ancient humans were quite fond of alcohol. I know they would get entangled in a lot of mischief while consuming it. And it seems it was quite a panty dropper."

"Hah! Yeah, I've heard similar reports myself," the old man said as he put a beverage in Aiden's hand.

"I've always wanted to try it," the woman said. "It was so often a catalyst for our ancestors' ancient stories. Especially in their beginnings. And in their endings too."

"Well, let's make a toast to the former rather than the latter," the old man said. "The latter will come soon enough. Cheers everyone! Cheers to new beginnings!"

The old man lifted his glass high. But the assembled party didn't react. They just looked at him awkwardly.

"When I say 'cheers,'" the old man said, "you're supposed to raise your glass up and say it back at me."

"Cheers!" the couple echoed, their voices overlapping in a monotone harmony that made the old man laugh.

"Heh… close enough!" he said before proceeding to swallow down a sizable gulp.

Aiden watched the woman take her first sip of wine. When it was complete, delight flashed across her face, flicking her eyebrows up with approval. "It's sweet," she said. Aiden nodded and took his first sip too.

"I think we forgot to exchange names," the old man said to his new guest. "Around here, they used to call me 'the old man.' That was my nickname and I'm sticking with it. And this dashing young adventurer to your left is Aiden."

"It's a pleasure to meet you both," the woman said before beginning her second sip.

"Likewise. So what's your name then, girl?" the old man asked.

The wine kissed the woman's lips and sent their corners upward as she delighted in the way that the tiny bubbles so playfully spun across her tongue. "I'm Nyx," she said as she brought her glass to her lap.

"That's unique," Aiden said. "Is that from mythology? What does it mean?"

"Yes. My A.I. caretaker chose it because I was born at dusk. Nyx is the goddess who walks the boundary between day and night. She rises with the sunset."

A smile of revelation dawned upon Aiden's face, its warmth reaching for Nyx as naturally as the fire's heat spread across the granite stones. "Oh, how nice," Aiden said as he leaned toward the flames. "I've always liked sunsets."

Nyx grasped her glass with both hands and locked her piercing silver eyes onto Aiden's person. She took a moment to regard him intently—to weigh the strength of his gaze against the softness of his words. The air between them hummed with tension. Their tender measure sustained for a heartbeat too long—the overture of a future movement when curiosity would give way to desire.

The old man grinned after noticing the spark that his fire had drawn from his friends. A glint of recognition lit up his eyes, as if he had just heard the first four bars of a lost but familiar song.

The old fooleries persist to the end.

"Well, young lady," the old man said, lowering the temperature, "given the heritage of your moniker, it's quite befitting of you to join us this evening. The sun's departure is bound to be a beautiful one. The heavens are full of altocumulus clouds—they're all lined up and ready for the show. The sky is about to turn into fire and gold."

"Fire and gold!" Nyx said. "That sounds vibrant. I'm looking forward to it. This will be the first sunset I've attended in Serenity Valley. How much longer until the show starts?"

"Not much longer," Aiden said. "We're in the magic hour now."

"What's that?"

"It's a short period of unique lighting when the sun drifts within six degrees above the horizon. The ancient filmmakers liked to shoot movies during that time. Because the golden haze can make reality feel like a dream. When the light hits just right, everything becomes awash in a magical glow—one so wondrous it feels like anything could happen next."

"Fascinating," Nyx said. "I didn't know the ancients used cinematography to engender such emotions. But, now that I think about it, I do often feel like that when I come to the end of an old movie. Though, I think I feel like that when I come to the end of a book too…"

"Huh…" Aiden said.

"I feel like that when I come to the end of *everything*," the old man said as he studied his empty wine glass. "But thankfully, the end has yet to come for *me*! Heh! It's learned to keep its distance… for now. It's learned to stay away. Maybe because I'm such a tough guy. Or maybe I'm just too old to die."

The old man picked up the bottle of rosé and poured himself a fresh glass before returning to address his guests. "I hope the end stays away from you two kids as well," he said. "I hope your stories continue for a while."

Aiden and Nyx looked at the man and sent nods of affirmation his way.

"Yeah," Aiden said, "I do too."

"Me too," Nyx said.

"Good," the old man said while raising his glass. "Then happy trails to both of you." He drank deeply once more, savoring the fleeting sweetness of borrowed time. When the last drop slid down his throat, a flare of sunlight flickered in his eye, beckoning him to turn his attention westward toward the ridgeline. "Mmm… Look! The show is about to start. And the sun is right on time."

"Isn't it always?" Aiden asked.

"Always and forever," the old man said.

Aiden looked west and watched as the sun's blazing rays met the rim of the world. "I hope so," he said.

"Yeah," the old man said. "I hope so too."

Streaks of paint began to spill over the sky's canvas, causing a hush of quiet reverence to settle over the audience. The heavens were speaking now. Nothing more needed to be said on Earth.

When the spectacle finally began, it was the clouds that blushed first. Their edges flared with crimson flames that danced like celestial spirits across the horizon's vast expanse. The sky was crying color. It was bleeding beauty, and painting the world with its blood. Its palette was heavy with shades of red, and hues of yellow lined its margins—*fire and gold.*

During the performance, the three friends breathed as one, bound together by the divine glory of the cathedral's closing hymn. They sat in awe throughout the entire service. And they continued to sit until the sun completed its journey. It finished where it started—like Aiden's had.

The greatest journeys always end where they begin.

When the last ray was finally extinguished, the sky surrendered its colors, and the Earth turned gently toward its rest.

Another ending had arrived.

Another day was done.

Another sun had set.

Aiden had watched it happen many times before.

But, this time, the sun had shone a bit brighter as it descended beyond the valley wall of Pod Land.

Because, this time, Aiden was not alone.

Did you like the book?

Thanks for coming along with me on this ride. I hope you enjoyed the book. If so, please consider writing a book review at Amazon. For an independent author like me, book reviews mean *everything*, and I personally read each one!

Thank you so much,

Anthony

This link leads to the book review page at Amazon.com:

www.tiny.cc/podland

www.ingramcontent.com/pod-product-compliance
Lightning Source LLC
Chambersburg PA
CBHW071641260626
47170CB00001B/183